Loves Me, Loves Me Not

Edited by

Katie Fforde

and Sue Moorcroft

Loves Me, Loves Me Not

Joanna Trollope

Nicola Cornick

Judy Astley

Benita Brown

Jane Gordon-Cumming

Sue Moorcroft

Victoria Connelly

Amanda Grange

Jean Buchanan

Anna Jacobs

Nell Dixon

Liz Fielding

Anita Burgh

Joanna Maitland

Adele Parks

Rita Bradshaw

Elizabeth Bailey

Annie Murray

Jane Wenham-Jones

Rosie Harris

Trisha Ashley

Carole Matthews

Louise Allen

Sue Gedge

Rosemary Laurey

Charlotte Betts

Elizabeth Chadwick

Katie Fforde

Sophie King

Jan Jones

Janet Gover

Maureen Lee

Linda Mitchelmore

Christina Jones

Geoffrey Harfield

Margaret Kaine

Theresa Howes

Gill Sanderson

Debby Holt

Sophie Weston

Katie Flynn

Margaret James

Eileen Ramsay

Diane Pearson

MIRA

MIRA is a registered trademark of Harlequin Enterprises Limited, used under licence.

First published in Great Britain 2009.
MIRA Books, Eton House, 18-24 Paradise Road,
Richmond, Surrey, TW9 1SR

HB ISBN 978 0 7783 0311 4
PB ISBN 978 0 7783 0321 3

60-1009

MIRA's policy is to use papers that are natural, renewable and recyclable products and made from wood grown in sustainable forests. The logging and manufacturing processes conform to the legal environmental regulations of the country of origin.

Printed in Great Britain
by Clays Ltd, St Ives plc

Choose your indulgence...

To the wonderful, talented members of the
Romantic Novelists' Association

ACKNOWLEDGEMENTS

The Romantic Novelists' Association would like to thank all of its members who contributed to this fabulous anthology. And also, Caroline Sheldon, for her help and support.

FOREWORD by Katie Fforde

I have been a member of the Romantic Novelists' Association since before the dawn of time or before I can remember, anyway. It's hard to say if I would have become a published novelist without them but I suspect not. Like reading romantic fiction, which has always been what got me through the tough times and still does, the RNA is a constant support. Without them I might well have given up, without them I would never have known the many writers who are now my friends. The joy of my first meeting when I realised I was not the only mad woman in the attic, typing away when I should have been ironing, cooking or generally being a wife and mother, was immense.

Thus, it is a complete pleasure to be asked to be involved with this fabulous anthology. It really is a box-of-chocolates of a book. There is everything in here, whatever your taste. There's sophisticated chic lit, tender romance—funny stories, scary stories and even fairy stories—and every other sort of story you can think of, including a vampire story.

One of the things I particularly like is it represents the vast range of writers and writing that the RNA embraces and shows the sparkling talent that our organisation represents.

Romantic fiction is a very popular, and demonstrably broad, genre and in here you don't just get a lot of wonderfully good reads, you get real value for money.

Enjoy—you can dive into this without putting on an ounce!

Joanna Trollope

Joanna Trollope has been writing for over thirty years. Her enormously successful contemporary works of fiction, several of which have been televised, include *The Choir, A Village Affair, A Passionate Man* and *The Rector's Wife,* which was her first number one bestseller and made her into a household name. Since then she has written *The Men and the Girls, A Spanish Lover, The Best of Friends, Next of Kin, Other People's Children, Marrying the Mistress, Girl from the South, Brother and Sister* and *Second Honeymoon.* Her latest novel is *Friday Nights.* Joanna also wrote *Britannia's Daughters*—a non-fiction study of women in the British Empire, as well as a number of historical novels now published under Caroline Harvey. Joanna was awarded the OBE in 1996 for services to literature.

Find out more at www.joannatrollope.com

Rembrandt at Twenty-Two

I promise you, I saw him from the stage. I couldn't miss him, not the way he was looking at me. I was up there, front row, final chorus, stockings and suspenders, and he was out there, in the stalls, centre, only two rows back. Our eyes met. Well, not just *met*. Our gazes kind of *fused*. I'd never known anything like it, and there isn't a name for it, that kind of attraction, and perhaps there shouldn't be, because it's different every time, different for everyone.

Well, of course, he was waiting at the stage door.

He said, 'Hello, gorgeous.'

I said, 'You foreign?'

He smiled. He had a fantastic smile. He said, 'I'm Dutch.'

I said, rudely, because I was so wildly excited, 'You can't be. Dutch boys aren't tall, dark and handsome. Dutch boys are blond and look like potatoes.'

He laughed. Then he kissed me. Can you imagine being kissed by a total stranger and wanting him never to stop? And then we went for drinks, somewhere hot and dark and noisy, and then he said he'd got to go.

'Go?'

'To catch a plane.'

'Where?'

'Home. Back to Amsterdam.'

'You can't, you can't—'

'Come, too.'

'I can't. I've got a show to do—'

'Come tomorrow.'

'I can't—'

'Come.'

I looked at him. He looked back, like he was looking right into me, like he knew me. Then he picked up a paper serviette and wrote something on it.

'Meet me there. Sunday. Three p.m.'

I peered at his scribble. 'Can't read it—'

'Meet me,' he said, 'in front of my favourite painting. In the Rijksmuseum. Three o'clock Sunday.'

'I've never been to Amsterdam—'

'It's easy,' he said. 'Everyone speaks English.' He leaned forward and kissed me. 'See you there, gorgeous.'

I said, 'Can I have your number?'

He took my hands. He said, 'No need. This is special. This is something else. This is a beginning.'

Of course, I went. I danced myself to a standstill in the Saturday matinee and the evening show, and when I came off stage, Sam, the stage manager, who could do praise as well as he could fly, said, 'Nice work,' looking straight at me. And then I went out of the theatre without a word to anyone and got a night bus to Stansted Airport and the first flight out to Amsterdam. I was so high on the thought of seeing him that you could have powered a city off me. Two, maybe.

That energy carried me through the night, through the next morning. It was like surfing a big wave that never quite got to shore. I bought coffee, I bought apple cake, I went brazenly into a big hotel and used the ladies' room to wash and do my make-up and my hair. I talked to people and he was right, they spoke English, and they smiled, and they talked back to me. And at a quarter to three I was where he told me to be, in this huge old museum, crammed with visitors, standing in front of a painting of a boy with a big mop of frizzy hair and a face like a potato. *Zelfportret ca.1628,* it said underneath. *Rembrandt Harmensz van Rijn at twenty-two.* I stared at him. He looked back out of his painting, over my shoulder as if he was waiting for someone.

He had a long wait. No one came. I waited two hours, and my Dutchman never came. I went out and drank gin, which there seems to be a lot of in Amsterdam, and got myself a weird hotel room near the station, and drank and cried and drank and cried until I fell asleep.

I went back the next day, in case he'd said Monday, not Sunday. And then I went back on Tuesday and Wednesday and Thursday. And, on Friday, something clicked in my brain, and I actually registered the messages on my phone, and a different sick fear slid down into my stomach. The fear of being let down was added to by the fear of losing my job.

'Where the hell *are* you?' Sam kept saying. He sounded furious. And then, 'There are plenty more where you came from. *Plenty.*'

I don't really want to talk about that journey home. You can imagine how I felt—we've all been there. We haven't all been as stupid as to go all the way to Amsterdam to get there but we've all done the dumped, humiliated, disappointed, how-do-I-go-on thing. I looked at myself in my compact mirror as I sat on the bus from Stansted to London and I thought that nobody would ever fancy me again, and that if I were them I wouldn't fancy me, either.

I got to the theatre early, about four-thirty, three hours to curtain up and nobody much in yet but the technicians. I went into the big dressing room that all us girls in the chorus shared and to my relief there was no one in there except Monica, who'd been cleaning up and calming down in that dressing room for about a hundred years. We called her Mon and sometimes, when we were tired or upset because we'd fluffed a move or got kicked on stage, we called her Mum by mistake and she never minded.

She was sweeping the floor. Clots of cotton wool and chocolate wrappers and hairballs. She stopped sweeping when I came in.

'Where've you been?'

I slumped in a chair and looked at myself in a mirror with all those light bulbs round it. I said, 'Amsterdam.'

She leaned her broom against the wall. 'What for?'

I fished around in my bag and pulled out a postcard. I put it down in front of me. 'To look at him.'

She came over. She smelled, as she always did, of fags and carnation soap. 'And?'

'It's Rembrandt. When he was twenty-two.'

Monica said, 'I know about Rembrandt.'

I said, 'I've screwed up. I haven't got a love life and I've lost my job.'

Monica looked at the postcard. 'Twenty-two. How old are you?'

'Twenty-three.'

She sucked her teeth.

I put my head down on my arms, on Rembrandt. I said, 'What am I going to do?'

'When he painted that painting,' Monica said, 'he didn't know his future. Did he? He didn't know he was going to be the greatest. He just knew he could paint. That he'd got to paint.'

'I can't paint,' I said, into my arms.

'You can dance,' Monica said. 'You can dance better than most of them. You can sing.'

'Sam won't let me. Not any more.'

'You know,' Monica said, 'about Samuel Beckett?'

I lifted my head. My eyes and nose were red. 'I've heard of him.'

'He said, "You try, you fail, you try again, you fail better." You've got to try. You've got a future to make. You've got to *try*.'

I sniffed.

'Get up,' she said. 'Get up and get moving. Wash your face. Find Sam.'

Sam was on stage, with the techies. They were fixing something to do with the steps we had to come down, high kicking and singing. There were places where they didn't feel too solid, those steps, and we used to shove each other about to avoid those places. I went and stood beside Sam. He had a clipboard. He didn't look at me.

'Push off,' Sam said.

I didn't say anything. I didn't move.

'You heard me,' Sam said.

'I'm sorry—'

'Too late,' Sam said. 'I've replaced you.'

I said, 'I'm back.'

'Without your Dutchman.'

I said, 'They look like potatoes.'

He wrote something on his clipboard. Then he said, 'At least I don't look like a potato.'

I looked at him. He didn't. He looked fine.

Sam shouted something at the techies. Then he said, 'Go and get me a coffee.'

I went on looking at him. I said, 'How d'you know about the Dutchman?'

'I make it my business to know.'

'About all of us?'

There was a beat.

'No,' Sam said.

'I brought one back,' I said. 'A Dutchman. On a postcard. Rembrandt, when he was twenty-two. I don't think I've ever looked at a man so long. I thought he looked like a potato but he doesn't. He looks great.'

Sam shouted something else. He glanced at me. 'I think I can cope with a postcard.'

I waited.

'Go and get me a coffee,' Sam said again.

'Please.'

'Please. Get two coffees.'

'Two?'

He looked at me, red eyes, red nose, dirty hair. He said, very clearly, 'Two coffees. One for you. One for me. Scoot.'

I felt my arms moving at my sides, like wings rising. Maybe I was going to hug him. He took a step away.

'Scoot,' he said.

'But Sam—'

'Scoot!' he shouted, so all the techies could hear, and then he dropped his voice. 'Don't be long,' he said. He smiled at me. He actually smiled. He had beautiful teeth. 'Don't be long.'

Nicola Cornick

Nicola Cornick studied history at London University and Ruskin College, Oxford, earning a distinction in her Masters degree with a dissertation on heroes and hero myths. She has a 'dual life' as a writer of historical romance for Harlequin Mills & Boon and a historian working for the National Trust. A double nominee for both the Romantic Novelists' Association Romance Prize and the Romance Writers of America RITA award, Nicola has been described by *Publishers Weekly* as 'a rising star of the Regency genre'. Her most recent book, *Kidnapped,* is available now from M&B Books. Her website is www.nicolacornick.com

The Elopement

It was a fact universally acknowledged in the village of Marston Priors that Amanda, Lady Marston, although young, was the un-challenged arbiter of good manners.

'For,' as Mrs Duke said to Mrs Davy, 'if Lady Marston feels it is inappropriate to travel even the shortest distance in a carriage without one's personal maid, I am sure that you will never see me defying convention by going out alone.' Mrs Davy, who could not afford to employ a lady's maid, agreed glumly.

Amanda Marston woke slowly and luxuriously that morning. She knew that the day was well advanced because Benson had drawn back the curtains and the spring sunshine was drawing out the rich and vivid colours from the beautiful new Axminster carpet. She knew she had an eye for design. It was one of her greatest accomplishments.

The scent of the hot chocolate lured her and she reached out a languid hand for the cup. Her fingers brushed the crisp parchment of a letter and she picked it up, still mulling over whether the bed drapes required refurbishment and whether pale green gauze might look dangerously like a harlot's boudoir... Not that she knew anything of such things...

She read the first line of the letter with vague attention, the second with concentration and the third with outrage.

> *My dear Amanda*
> *It is with great pleasure that I can inform you that I have eloped with Mr Sampson. I have always hankered after participating in an elopement so you may imagine my pleasure. I believe that the usual form of words on these occasions is: 'Pray do not come after us.' I am of age several times over and know my own mind, so there is no point in either you or Hugo trying to fetch me back. Indeed, I hope you will both wish me happy.*
> *Your loving grandmother-in-law, Eleanor Pevensey*

Amanda shrieked, an action that startled her as much as it did the footman on the landing outside. Amanda never screamed, not even in a ladylike manner over a dead mouse or small spider. She had always considered having the vapours to be a vulgar way of attracting attention. Now, however, she shrieked again.

Lady Pevensey had eloped.

Lady Pevensey was entrusting herself and all her lovely fortune into the hands of a penniless curate.

Of all the outrages perpetrated by her husband's seventy-seven-year-old grandmother, this was by far the most shocking. Lady Pevensey had been living at Marston Hall for six months and Amanda had found her a serious trial. Lady Pevensey rode to hounds, swore like a trooper and forgot all about visiting hours.

But none of these offences against propriety was as dreadfully scandalous as an elopement.

Amanda actually spilt drops of chocolate on the beautiful linen of her bedclothes. Never had she felt so overset, not even when the silk for her new evening gown had been quite the wrong shade of rose-pink.

She shoved the chocolate cup aside and tumbled from the bed, grabbing her swansdown-trimmed wrap and hurrying to the door that connected her room to that of her husband.

She turned the knob. The door was locked. She remembered that it had not been used in the past six months and only at very irregular intervals in the three years of her marriage. For some reason this state of affairs suddenly made her feel more than a little troubled.

She ran barefoot to the door onto the landing, only to be confronted by the footman, whose Adam's apple bobbed with shock at the sight of her ladyship *en déshabillée*. Normally Lady Marston would not emerge from her room until she was immaculately attired. This was unprecedented.

'Where is Lord Marston?' Amanda demanded, waving the letter agitatedly in the footman's face. 'I require to speak with him immediately!'

The footman boggled. Lady Marston never required to know where her husband was, treating his whereabouts as a matter of utmost indifference. Red to the tips of his ears, he managed to stammer that Lord Marston had breakfasted several hours earlier and, he believed, was out on the estate.

'Then pray send to find him,' Amanda snapped, 'and send for Crockett. At once!'

Choosing her morning outfit was usually one of Amanda's favourite occupations but this morning she found that the merits of her cherry-red promenade dress or her pale yellow muslin did not interest her. She had grabbed a lilac gown when her maid arrived and dressed with a lack of care that startled the poor woman severely. When Crockett enquired how she would like her hair arranged, Amanda said, 'I do not have the time!' scooped up the letter and positively ran down the stairs.

Lord Marston had not yet been found but Amanda remembered vaguely that he had said something about his sheep at dinner the previous night and so she set off towards where she imagined the pastures might be. Following a mixture of bleating and hammering, she located Lord Marston a good mile away, by which time her dainty slippers were ruined and the hem of her lilac gown three inches deep in mud.

Amanda did not notice, however, for as she drew near she realised that it was Hugo himself who was hammering in fence posts. His jacket discarded, his rolled up shirtsleeves revealed strong, bronzed forearms. The muscles moved beneath his skin as he worked with grace and precision. Amanda, who had been about to exclaim over the inappropriateness of her husband undertaking manual work, discovered that her mouth was suddenly dry.

Hugo caught sight of her and straightened. In the spring sunshine his eyes gleamed vivid blue in his tanned face. He rubbed his brow and Amanda saw a drop of sweat run down the strong brown column of his neck. She should feel disgusted but suddenly there was a curl of something quite other than disgust in the pit of her stomach. Why had she never noticed before that Hugo was so attractive?

'Amanda?' Hugo came up to her and caught her elbow. The warmth of his hand seemed to burn through the silk of her gown. 'What the devil are you doing here?'

His gaze, normally so inscrutable, slid from the tips of her muddy slippers to her flushed cheeks and lingered on the hair loose about her face. Suddenly there was something speculative and heated in his eyes that made Amanda feel even more light-headed. It was not the sort of look a man should give his wife of three years. She could not remember Hugo *ever* looking at her like that. It was not respectable. Nor was his bad language. But it seemed incredibly hard to drag her gaze away from his, let alone to correct him.

'I…um…' Amanda made a huge effort to remember why she had needed to talk to him. *Lady Pevensey.* She held out the letter. 'Your grandmother, Hugo! The most disastrous thing! She has eloped with Mr Sampson! We simply have to stop her.'

Hugo dipped his head over the note, affording her a most enjoyable view of his broad shoulders under the damp linen of his white shirt. He wore an old pair of breeches that Amanda would normally have scorned. But how well they fitted his muscular thighs and what a fine figure he had. She blinked. What on earth was wrong with her? Lady Pevensey's elopement had overset her nerves, of course, and running around in the sunshine without a bonnet was very bad for her. She needed to lie down in a darkened room.

With Hugo.

The thought slipped into her mind and she was so shocked that she blushed. She saw that Hugo was watching her, a quizzical smile in his eyes. Another curl of excitement lit her blood, only stronger than before. To cover her embarrassment she snapped, 'Well? What are you going to do, Hugo? Your grandmother has run off with a man half her age!'

The smile did not fade from Hugo's eyes. 'I do not think you are quite correct there, my dear. Mr Sampson came late to ordination and I believe he is now in his sixties—'

'He is still young enough to be her son,' Amanda said. 'And that is not the point, Hugo. The point is—'

'That she is rich and we wanted her money and now there is a danger she will leave it to her new husband instead,' Hugo finished.

Amanda gaped. 'How very vulgar you sound!'

Hugo shrugged his broad shoulders. 'Is that not what you meant, Amanda?'

Amanda struggled. 'Well, I suppose… But I would not have put it so bluntly.'

'Why not?' Hugo's smooth tones seemed to hold the very slightest hint of mockery. 'We both know that Grandmama's twenty thousand pounds would be most welcome.'

'Yes,' Amanda said, still struggling, 'but I wish to save her from a terrible mistake.'

'Rot,' Hugo said cheerfully. 'The only mistake you wish to save her from is leaving her money away from us!'

Amanda wondered whether too much fresh air had gone to Hugo's head. He never normally spoke to her like this. Usually he was courteous to the point of indifference. She felt an unexpected pang at the thought.

'You are mistaken,' she said carefully. 'I do not think it right for Lady Pevensey to marry a man even twenty years her junior.'

'Because of the scandal.'

'For her personal happiness!' Amanda burst out, though admitting to herself that her husband was absolutely right.

'Oh, I should not worry about that. Sampson is a fit and vigorous gentleman for his years. I imagine he will make her very happy.'

'Hugo!' Amanda was appalled, her mind awash with most inappropriate images of Lady Pevensey and her new husband disporting themselves in the bedroom.

'I mean that they have a shared interest in hunting and the outdoors,' Hugo said, 'as well as a lively interest in more academic matters. That is more than many couples can boast. Whatever did you think I meant, Amanda?'

'Nothing!' Amanda shook her head slightly, trying to dispel the images and at the same time trying not to take too personally Hugo's comment about couples who had nothing in common.

'Well,' she said, 'since it seems I cannot persuade you to try to prevent this elopement, Hugo, I shall set out for Gretna Green immediately.'

Hugo gave a crack of laughter. 'You? You do not even know where Gretna Green is!'

'The coachman will know,' Amanda said, finding a temper she did not even know she possessed. 'Really, Hugo, you are in a strange mood today! I shall travel with Crockett and if we make good time I am sure we may overtake them.'

'And then what? On whose authority will you send them home?' Hugo looked highly entertained. 'You are not dealing with a recalcitrant schoolroom chit, Amanda!'

Amanda, thoroughly annoyed, made to stalk away. By now she was miserably aware of the state of her hem and the soaked material of her slippers. The wind had teased her hair to a haystack and she was cold.

But Hugo caught her hand. It felt warm and comforting but also intimate and exciting. Hugo never normally held her hand.

'Wait,' he said. 'I cannot permit my wife to travel to Gretna unprotected. I will come with you. If we are fortunate we may even reach Oxford by tonight.'

Amanda was so surprised that she stepped into a puddle. Hugo swung her up in his arms. 'Hugo!' Amanda gasped, clutching his forearms, which felt remarkably hard and lean. 'What on *earth* are you doing?'

'Merely helping you over this muddy ground, my dear.' His breath tickled her ear, sending goose bumps along her neck. Amanda could smell his scent—fresh air and sweat and the faint hint of sandalwood cologne. What could be the matter with her? She had thought that an unwashed male body would repel her rather than making her head spin. It was perhaps fortunate that Hugo's shoulder was so close. She leaned her head against it and lay quiet all the way back to the house.

Once Amanda had recovered from being carried home she banished her husband to wash and change his clothes and hurried to do the same. There really was no time to waste, no matter how indulgent Hugo felt of his grandmama's misdemeanours. Hugo was famously—infuriatingly—easy-going, but Amanda knew that Lady Pevensey's elopement would be the talk of the county. Everyone would whisper and gossip and titter and commiserate and it would be intolerable. Lady Pevensey's lack of decorum would reflect on her. Her position in Marston Priors might well be under threat. It was not to be borne.

It therefore took her a mere hour and a half to don her travelling gown, instruct Crockett on the packing of her portmanteaux and descend the stairs to find her husband waiting, immaculately dressed in jacket, pantaloons and Hessians. On seeing her, he checked his pocket watch.

'Less than two hours. And only three cases! You are to be congratulated, my dear.' His gaze fell on Crockett, attired in a plain cloak and grasping a small bag. 'Alas, I fear we cannot accommodate your maid, my love. I have had the small carriage prepared for the sake of speed and there is room only for us— and your luggage, of course.'

Amanda halted. 'But I cannot travel without Crockett! Hugo, it simply isn't done. She must come!'

'Nonsense,' her husband said bracingly, steering her out of the door. 'What could be more decorous than that you be escorted by your husband? I may act as lady's maid.' He gave her a look that Amanda could only think was provocative. 'I am not inexperienced.'

'Indeed?' Amanda's travelling gown suddenly felt a trifle too hot.

She was still wrestling with her unfamiliar and rather disconcerting awareness of Hugo as the carriage clattered through Marston Priors and onto the toll road as the Wiltshire Downs unrolled around them. She had been in a closed carriage with Hugo many times and had never suffered this affliction. Indeed, she realised, she had taken him for granted.

Brought up from an early age to see the acquisition of a husband as a desirable sign of standing, she had gained her married status at the age of one-and-twenty, a little late because she was particular. Hugo had been easy to reel in and she had thought they were well suited. He was handsome, titled, well connected and wealthy without being extravagantly rich. More importantly, he had an equable humour, he was generous and did not interfere in her running of the household. She had thought, until that moment in the hall ten minutes before, that he would always permit her to have her own way. As for intimate matters—Amanda blushed inwardly but forced herself to think about it—she had been pleased that after their honeymoon Hugo seemed not to want to trouble her with his attentions more than twice a month and latterly not at all. Her mama had explained that a lady must be decorous at all times, particularly in the marriage bed, and Amanda had tried to follow that advice. She had been aware of a disappointing result but had put it from her mind.

Now, though, regarding her husband as he lounged with elegant grace against the cushions, she felt a stab of anger. It seemed quite wrong that he should thwart her in the matter of the maid and, more importantly, that he should be so relaxed when she was in a state of advanced fluster. She had not been herself since seeing him in his shirt and breeches but that could not account for this uncomfortable awareness. After all, she had even seen him with no clothes on at all. But she had looked away, as a lady should. Heat and agitation made her shift on the seat and Hugo looked politely concerned.

'Are you quite well?'

'I feel a little strange,' Amanda admitted. 'I think I am anxious because we set off in such a rush.'

'Of course,' Hugo murmured, his bright blue gaze fixed on her in a manner that made the breath catch in her throat.

'Tell me about your sheep.' Amanda searched desperately for a distraction from her curious feelings. 'Last night at dinner you said that you wished to buy a flock of a different breed.'

Hugo looked surprised. 'I thought you were not attending. I was not aware that you had an interest.'

Amanda had, in fact, very little curiosity about sheep but she was prepared to express an interest in just about anything if it helped lessen the strangely intense atmosphere between them. And, after a while, she forgot she was indifferent to her husband's interests. They chatted about everything from Hugo's improvements to the estate to the literature preferred by Amanda as first Wantage and then Abingdon were passed, with a change of horses and some refreshment in both towns. There was no sign of Lady Pevensey and her beau, although an elderly lady eloping with a curate would surely seem noteworthy, and although they asked at every post house they reached Oxford with no news. Between Oxford and Banbury Amanda fell asleep and woke to discover that she was resting her head on Hugo's shoulder and his arm was about her. She raised her face to see him smiling down at her as he smoothed the tumbled hair away from her face.

'I do not recall you ever venturing out without your hair in some sort of complicated arrangement,' he commented, toying with the end of the ribbon that held her curls. 'This is vastly more becoming and I am less likely to be stabbed by some ornament when I am close.'

The carriage lurched to a stop and he kissed her lightly before releasing her and moving to open the door.

'Where are we?' Amanda stammered, disconcerted to feel her lips tingle from the imprint of his.

'At the King's Head in Banbury. I will bespeak a room for the night.'

It was only when the groom was helping her down that Amanda realised he had said one room rather than two and prickles of excitement and apprehension raced through her. But when the landlady had shown them up the stairs to the spotlessly clean bedchamber, she found her husband as adamant on the subject of the room as he had been on the subject of the maid.

'Two rooms?' A dangerous light lurked in his eyes. 'Out of the question, my love. Although this is a most respectable inn, I could not endanger either your life or your virtue by leaving you alone. You must sleep with me and then you will be quite safe.'

'You must sleep in the chair,' Amanda argued, panic building in her throat as Hugo slipped off his coat and loosened his neck cloth. He seemed so at ease, so confident, so thoroughly in control. It was making her nervous.

He laughed. 'Have a heart, my sweet! I have lurched over bad roads all day on a wild goose chase. The least you can do is let me share your bed. I am your husband and it is perfectly respectable.'

It felt quite improper to Amanda, unaccustomed to such close proximity with her husband, but he pressed a glass into her hands and she did not argue. The wine had been warmed and it tasted strong and sweet. Amanda felt the colour bloom in her cheeks and delicious warmth spread through her. The knot of tension inside her started slowly to unravel.

The landlady brought a rich beef stew into their private parlour. Amanda was surprised to discover it tasty. She was yawning, which was unforgivably rude, but when she tried to apologise Hugo only laughed and filled her glass again. By the time the meal was over she was almost asleep and her elbow kept sliding off the table. Eventually Hugo scooped her up and carried her through to the bedchamber.

'You seem to have been sweeping me off my feet all day,' Amanda whispered, aware that she was now extremely cast away and that the room was spinning slowly. She looked up into his face and could see the shadow of every individual eyelash cast against the hard line of his cheek. She raised a hand and ran her fingers over his cheek, fascinated by the roughness of his stubble. His eyes closed and she saw a muscle tighten beneath her caress, but then he set her down and started to unfasten her gown with brisk, impersonal movements. She felt his fingers against the nape of her neck, then lower, down her back. The gown eased and she stepped out of it, feeling abruptly and overwhelmingly shy. Gently, he sat her on the bed and knelt to remove her shoes and to roll down her stockings. The candlelight was in his blue eyes, his expression intent and serious and Amanda's stomach dropped with longing and a feeling she identified, with absolute amazement, as lust.

She must have made a small sound, for he looked up and their eyes locked for a long moment. There was a hard, bright light in his that made her feel quite faint and then—she was never sure how it happened and afterwards she did not care—he rolled her on the bed and his hands were in her hair and she was reaching for him with a fever that equalled his own. He kissed her as though he was starving and she kissed him back and her ribbons and laces were wrenched apart and his clothes were thrown on the floor and they came together exultantly, desperately, with love and lust and no thought for propriety until they lay panting and astonished in each other's arms.

Afterwards, when she had slept for a little and they had made love again more slowly, Amanda smiled to see her three portmanteaux, packed with respectable night clothes, sitting superfluously in the corner of the room.

'You promised that it would be perfectly proper for you to share my bed,' she said, 'but that was decidedly improper.'

She felt Hugo's chest move as he laughed. 'I cannot dispute that. Did you like it?'

'Yes!' There was a great deal to be said for bursting out of the restraints of propriety. 'I cannot think why I did not do that before. It was so much more fun when I join in.'

Hugo laughed again. 'For me, too.' He shifted so that he could look at her. 'I am sorry, Manda.' His affectionate use of her pet name made her smile. 'I knew that you had been brought up to believe that physical intimacy was to be tolerated rather than enjoyed and I did not make sufficient effort to persuade you to a different point of view.' He ran a hand over her bare shoulder and she shivered. 'I was disappointed that you did not seem to want me and so I withdrew from you when I should have talked.'

Amanda snuggled closer. 'I am sorry, too, Hugo. I was young and foolish and I thought that to catch a husband was the end of the process rather than the beginning.'

Hugo smiled. 'We have wasted a lot of time.'

'Yes, but we can make up for it.' She kissed him. 'How far is it to Gretna Green?'

'Too far,' Hugo said. 'Rather than trying to prevent my grandmother from marrying again, I would rather return home and invest the time in getting to know my own wife properly.'

Amanda smiled. 'I would like that extremely.' She rubbed her fingers gently over his chest. 'I love you, Hugo. In that respect I am happy to follow my mama's advice that it is quite appropriate to have an affectionate regard for one's husband.'

'I love you, too.' Hugo rolled over to kiss her properly.

'Manda,' Hugo said, as the carriage rolled back through the gates of Marston Hall next day, 'I have something to confess.' He took a deep breath. 'Grandmama has not gone to Gretna. She is marrying Mr Sampson at Bath Abbey on the twenty-third of this month. She would very much like us to be there. She left me a note yesterday, too.'

Amanda stared. 'But if you knew that, why on earth did you let us set out for Gretna...?' She stopped.

'I am sorry,' Hugo said, smiling so charmingly that Amanda's indignation started to melt like ice in the sun. 'If you re-read the

note that Grandmama left you, you will see that she never mentioned Gretna at all. When you made that assumption—and
when you appeared not indifferent to me—I was determined to
take the opportunity to try to mend matters between us.' He
smiled. 'I would have gone all the way to Scotland if I needed
to, Manda. You are that important to me.'

Amanda started to laugh until the tears rolled down her face
and her stomach ached with great gales of mirth that her mother
would surely have thought most unbecoming. When the coach
drew up on the gravel she grabbed Hugo's hand and dragged him
into the hall.

'You owe me something for that deception,' she whispered,
standing on tiptoe to kiss him. His arms went about her.

'Anything, my love.'

Then both of them became aware, somewhat belatedly, of the
presence of Mrs Duke and Mrs Davy, who had evidently called
only a few moments before and were studying their amorous
embrace with horrified expressions.

'Mrs Davy, Mrs Duke!' Hugo said. 'I do apologise. Is it visiting
time? Alas, Amanda is exhausted from our travels and needs to
lie down immediately. As do I.'

And he carried his wife up the sweep of the stair and closed
the bedroom door very firmly behind them.

Judy Astley

Judy Astley started writing in 1990, following several years of working as a dressmaker, illustrator, painter and parent. Her sixteen novels, the most recent of which are *Laying the Ghost* and *Other People's Husbands,* are all published by Transworld/Black Swan. Judy's specialist areas, based on many years of hectic personal experience, are domestic disharmony and family chaos with a good mix of love-and-passion and plenty of humour thrown in.

Judy has been a regular columnist on magazines and enjoys writing journalism pieces on just about any subject, usually from a fun viewpoint. She lives in London and Cornwall, loves plants, books, hot sunshine and rock music—all at once, preferably—and would happily claim that listening in to other people's conversations is both a top hobby and an absolute career-necessity. Visit Judy's website at www.judyastley.com

Speed Limit

X. Ex. At risk of getting a frostbitten bum, I sit on the low wall outside the town hall and look up at the brilliant blue winter sky where the vapour trails from a pair of aircraft have left a big white cross. It looks like a huge celestial kiss—a pair of in-love angels, perhaps? No, too fanciful, get real, Claire, I tell myself. It's just a couple of distant planes criss-crossing the globe above us. I think—briefly—of the bliss of a kissed X contrasted with the pain implicit in the term 'Ex'. Sad that these two sound so alike and yet…and yet. But it's all right. I'm now safely over my own Ex—cheating rat—though maybe not quite ready to hurtle full-on into another relationship. So silly, so hasty, I gave that one a go way too soon, pretty much straight after the break-up. Lovely Max, set up for me by well-meaning friends who embraced the 'get back on the horse' philosophy, was a delight—we got on so well and it was obvious there was real romance-potential there… but, oh, please, not yet, I thought at the time, running scared. That suddenness of being 'with' someone again so quickly after the drawn-out end to a five-year marriage gave me an out-of-control rushed feeling, a certainty that I'd whizzed from the hurt of loss directly to risking it all happening again without pausing for breath. Good grief, I'd barely got used to losing custody of the wedding present toaster.

Several dates in, I didn't at all like turning down Max's out-of-the-blue offer of a weekend in Barcelona but I heard my newly discovered cautious side suggesting to him that we slow down, take some time out and just be friends for a while. Trouble is, everyone assumes there is an underlying message in that particular line, and it's not a positive one. I liked Max a lot and he liked me—so he gave me what I'd asked for: space, solitude and time to think. Under other circs Max-and-me could have been…well, who knows? I certainly won't know, not now, not with him—the 'space' drifted into weeks, now months. I suppose it was too much to hope, after I'd effectively dumped him—and, oh, how teenage that sounds!—that he'd be OK with the occasional no-strings drink and a bag of nuts at the pub when we could have been strolling down Las Ramblas in the Catalan sunshine and getting cosy over tapas and Rioja.

It's a shame you can't put potential lovers in a cupboard for a few months, then get them out when the previous livid emotional scars have thoroughly healed. He must have thought I was a completely hopeless case, wittering on about wanting to try being alone, needing to Get To Know Myself. All rubbish really. A few months on from that moment of Being Sensible and I can tell you that existing determinedly on your own is highly overrated. What's so great about being in sole charge of the TV remote? Who needs *quite* that much spreading-out space in bed? And, as the song doesn't actually go: if I don't know myself by now…

'Hurtling', by the way, is the reason why I'm here, a bit early, waiting to join a half-day Speed Awareness class and learn how

Not To Drive Too Fast. As an alternative to points on my licence it's likely to be a few hours well-spent. I had no excuse: being caught on a speed camera doing thirty-five m.p.h. in a thirty limit was bang-to-rights, even if it was a deserted dual carriageway, late at night, running my fox-bitten cat to the emergency vet. Sorry—did I say no excuses? We've all got our stories.

It's time to go in and I check in with the jolly-looking organiser in an anteroom full of sheepish-looking fellow law-breakers. Slightly nervously, we smile at each other; someone makes a quip about us being in detention like naughty schoolchildren, and our 'teacher' grimaces and mutters, 'There's always one…' I sense he's got a running bet with himself about how many minutes into the proceedings some wag would come up with that one.

But it *is* like being in class, and we all sit in rows at desks with a computer each. Apart from a scurrying latecomer who whooshes unseen into a seat at the back, we're all quiet and con-centrating. The first part of the session is all mouse-clicking—on the computer screen there is a video in which we're 'driving' a car; we have to click when we feel too close to the car in front. Appropriately enough, I'm pretty sure I'm being too cautious here—I want to keep a good safe distance. Same with the speed test: I want to slow the virtual car right down. I smile to myself, thinking how like my life this is, these days. Having raced into a young marriage, the first of my group of mates to go for the full-scale meringue frock and multi-layered cake event, now look at me: avoiding a new closeness the moment it comes my way. Oh, well, no point brooding—right here, if I'm not careful, I'll score *nul* points for being easily distracted.

We do hazard perception next. The video has me driving in a variety of scenarios, inner city through to country lanes. I clock the cyclist, the horse-rider, the schoolchildren, the skateboarder, an ambulance, some elderly ladies. Click, click,

click goes my mouse but there doesn't seem to be an option for 'possible love interest' lurking in those on-screen streets. Perhaps they aren't such a hazard after all. Too late now anyway, I tell myself. I mean, I *could* call Max, obviously, or send him a cheery email, but what's he going to assume this time? That I'm fickle and flighty? That I'm ditsy and dithering? And of course he won't be free anyway—you don't get many delightful, attractive, entertaining, *unattached* men like him to the pound—it would be his turn to back right off. Who wants to line themselves up for a definite *ouch?* If we're talking risks and hazards here today, I think I'll pass on that particular one.

We've had our talk on speed limits and been reminded about Highway Code points that a lot of us had forgotten about since our driving test days. I pick up my bag and coat and say goodbye and thanks to the class tutor.

'Claire—I thought it was you!' And there he is—the class late-comer was, oh, heavens…Max, almost as if I'd 'thought' him into existence. 'I'm surprised to see *you* here, Ms Careful!' he teases as we walk together towards the street door.

'Oh, well, you know, I just took it a bit fast on a vet run one night. Emergency, but no excuse, I know!' I explain, heart pounding, words tumbling madly. 'What about you?'

'Ah, it was by the roadworks up near the airport. I was on my way back from…'

'Barcelona?' I interrupt, too fast. I can't understand this heart-sink feeling inside. Did he go there with someone else? I'm shocked at how much the very idea hurts. We only went out together for a few months—what proprietary rights do I have over one flippant weekend suggestion? None at all, I tell myself firmly, trying not to picture him with a stunning blonde and a guidebook, discussing the finer points of Gaudi's architecture.

'Dropping my sister off at Terminal Five, actually!' He laughs.

'And if you feel like risking it with a criminal driver, could I offer you a lift home?'

I feel embarrassed, flustered—he's laughing at me now, for the Barcelona comment. What a giveaway, what an idiot I am! Which part of careful/slow/risk-free was that particular little gaffe?

We collect his scarlet Toyota from the car park and he pulls out onto the main road.

'Bearing in mind the class we just did, I'll take it very, very slowly,' Max assures me.

'Good,' I say. 'Well within the speed limit, then.'

Are we talking about driving? Something tells me we're not, entirely. I sense it's not just me who's trying not to laugh.

'Absolutely,' he replies. 'And, if you've got time, I don't suppose you fancy a spot of lunch?'

'That,' I tell him, 'would be lovely. Where do you suggest?'

'I know a lovely little *bodega*.' He's teasing me, smiling wickedly. 'Perfect tapas, a delicate little Rioja…'

'Sounds perfect—where is it? Is it local? It's not…'

He laughs properly now, reading my daft, crazy thoughts.

I glance up through the windscreen—the X hasn't quite faded from the sky. Or maybe it's a new one—hard to tell. I could say that all across the planet the sky must be full of kisses, or I could go with superstition and decide it's a Sign.

'No, Claire, it's not Barcelona! Just off the High Street is a bit more down-to-earth, I'm afraid. But who knows? One day.'

'Yes, who knows?' I say as his hand brushes against mine. 'Maybe some day…'

Benita Brown

Benita Brown trained as an actress but after marriage and four children she switched to a writing career. At first she wrote for radio, then girls' and teenage story papers such as *Mandy, Judy, Jackie* and *Blue Jeans.* She wrote her first contemporary romantic novel as Clare Benedict when the youngest of her children was poised to go to university. There were six more Clare Benedict novels before she changed genre and began to write under her own name. The Benita Brown novels are regional sagas and the first nine are set in Tyneside in the Victorian and Edwardian eras. One of these, *Fortune's Daughter,* was long listed for the RNA Major Award. Her latest novel, *The Starlet,* moves forward in time to 1946. It is the story of Carol Marshall, a small town girl who wins a talent competition and begins a career in films. For more information about Benita and her novels visit www.benitabrown.com

Save the Last Dance for Me

When Laura and Raymond took to the floor other couples would stop dancing to watch. The girls' expressions were wistful as they imagined themselves in Raymond's arms. But the men had eyes only for Laura. They were totally enraptured.

She was lovely. Dark hair, blue eyes and as slim-waisted as Vivien Leigh in *Gone With the Wind*. I was the perfect foil for her— tall, with mousy hair, and pretty enough without being beautiful.

Laura and I had been friends ever since our first week at school when she had lost the shilling her mother had given her for the Penny Bank and I had given her sixpence of my own. I can't remember if she ever repaid me but I wouldn't have cared because I was thrilled to be the chosen friend of the most popular girl in the class.

Raymond and Bill had struck up a friendship when they had been posted to the RAF station to the north of the town near the lighthouse. Bill was from a farming family in Yorkshire but, the youngest of five sons, he wasn't needed for the war effort.

No one knew what Raymond's job had been but it had got around that if it wasn't for the war he'd have been in films. He was certainly good-looking enough; in his flying officer's uniform he looked sensational.

That first night Laura had pretended not to notice them. She went on talking as if she wasn't perfectly aware that they were coming towards us across the empty floor. Just as the music started Raymond coughed gently to attract Laura's attention. She turned and looked up at him with those dark-fringed blue eyes. He didn't speak. He simply held out his hand. When she took it he pulled her gently onto the dance floor.

Bill had been standing behind and he turned to watch them go. After a moment he looked at me and grinned. He asked me to dance and I accepted. I might have realised, even then, that I would not have been his first choice.

From that moment we were a foursome. Bill, tall, rangy and nice-enough looking with hair as mousy as my own, but nowhere near as handsome as Raymond with his dark hair and laughing grey eyes. The four of us went to the pictures together or for walks along the promenade, but most of all we went to the Roxy.

I was hurt that Laura didn't tell me first. Surely she could have trusted me not to let the cat out of the bag? She and Raymond took to the floor that night with her left hand resting gracefully on his shoulder. But there was something different about it. First one, then another, and soon every one of the girls swirling by noticed the engagement ring. The band kept on playing but the dancing stopped and the girls gathered round to admire the sparkling diamond while the young men slapped Raymond on the back and called him a lucky devil.

There was already an air of exhilaration. The allies were advancing on Berlin and everyone was convinced that the war in Europe would soon be won. Down at the Roxy, the music seemed more upbeat, the dancers more animated, and all the talk was about what we would do when the war was over.

Laura didn't want to wait. Her parents owned Seacrest, a small hotel on the seafront. Her father, Ted, said he was sure he could manage a respectable reception and her mother, Thelma, made a wedding dress from one of her old evening gowns. She also found something for me because, of course, I was going to be Laura's bridesmaid.

But a couple of weeks before the wedding Bill came to see Laura. We were in the lounge of the Seacrest, where we often met before going to the Roxy. Bill bought the drinks and we sat with Laura between us on the banquette behind one of the tables.

'Where's Raymond?' she said.

I saw Bill's knuckles whiten as he clasped his glass. 'Laura, I'm sorry…'

'What is it?' She sounded frightened.

'Raymond didn't make it home from the mission last night. I saw him go down somewhere over Holland.'

A shocked silence—and then Laura started to cry. It was Bill who held her until the storm of weeping subsided.

Raymond was posted missing, presumed dead. And over the next few weeks Laura's grief turned to anger and her anger into a feverish urge to live life to the full.

'Take my advice, Jeannie, eat, drink and be merry for tomorrow we die. And that's from the Bible,' she said when I tried to persuade her to live less hectically.

There were any number of young airmen who lived by the same principle, and who could blame them? They were risking their lives almost daily. They were good-natured, high-spirited and brave. And something about their uniforms made them positively glamorous. Many queued to dance with Laura, although none could match Raymond.

But Laura had forgotten what it was like to be without a man of her own. It was inevitable that she would eventually settle for one of them. And the lucky man just happened to be Bill.

I never found out what Laura did with Raymond's ring, but the next time she got engaged I was the first to be told. She said that she knew I was fond of Bill and she'd thought it best to tell me herself so that I could be prepared before the announcement.

'Kind of her!' my mother said that night when I wept at the kitchen table. Dad shook his head and quietly retreated.

'And she actually asked you to be her bridesmaid!' my mother exclaimed. And then she surprised me. 'Well, listen, our Jeannie, I hope you said that you'd be delighted.'

I stopped crying and looked up in astonishment.

'You think I should?'

'It might stop the tongues wagging.'

I knew what she meant. Everyone was wondering whether I would be heartbroken, angry, never speak to Laura again. My mother, wise as usual, thought the best way to prevent all specu-lation, whether spiteful or sympathetic, was for me to act as though I was pleased for Laura and I hadn't really cared that much for Bill.

Tongues did wag, but about Laura, not me. There were many who thought she was marrying in indecent haste and that maybe she should have mourned a little longer for Raymond. But that sort of thing happened in those days. Blame the war.

Bill did the gentlemanly thing, by the way. I found him waiting for me outside work one day and he walked me home. He said, 'I hope you understand. After all, we haven't been more than good friends, have we? I'll always be fond of you but, with Laura, it's entirely different.'

So Laura and I wore the dresses her mother had made after all. When the bride and groom opened the dance everyone applauded, but then fell silent, remembering. Was it fanciful to imagine Raymond's ghost following the bride and groom round the floor?

The war in Europe ended in May. VE Day was celebrated with street parties, a civic bonfire on the links and a gala night at the Roxy. There were tears of joy for those who had returned and sorrow for those who never would. And of course there were families who had to wait another three months before the war in the Far East ended.

Bill was one of the lucky ones who was demobbed quite soon and he took Laura to Australia where an uncle had a sheep farm. Bill didn't think that raising sheep in the Antipodes could be very much different from raising sheep in the Yorkshire Dales.

Ever since she had left school Laura had helped her parents in the hotel. Ted and Thelma were upset, not only because their daughter was leaving to live at the other side of the world but because they had imagined that Bill and Laura would stay and take over the running of the hotel one day. But they wished them well.

Nothing much changed for me. I continued working in the shoe department of the Co-op, trying to make my window displays exciting with the never changing supplies of clogs—no coupons needed—and wedge-soled shoes.

The lads stationed at the air base began to leave and the town's own servicemen started coming home. There were some tearful farewells and some worried reunions but nights at the Roxy went on pretty much as before, except there were fewer people in uniform.

The King, in his Christmas broadcast, spoke of the dark days we had lived through and of the joys of being together at last to share the things we found most precious. But also of those who would never return and how we would remember them with pride; how we must pray that these brave men and women had found everlasting peace. I found myself wondering what kind of peace Raymond had found.

It was spooky, really, how it happened. One night in January the band at the Roxy was playing the Dick Haymes hit *Laura,* a slow and smoochy number. My partner was Ron, the gangling lad from the bacon counter. The glitter ball was spilling its usual magic that softened faces and hinted at unspoken dreams.

Carried away, I found myself thinking of Laura, my beautiful friend, who had waltzed off with my beau, and yet she still had a place in my heart. For a moment I forgot my partner's two left feet and his nervous grin. I was back in the days when Laura and Raymond had held us all spellbound with their dancing.

Then I became aware that some of the dancers had stopped and that they were all looking in the same direction, shocked.

Forgetting that I was supposed to let my partner lead, I steered him through the crowd until I could see. And then I gripped the poor lad's arms so fiercely that he yelped with pain. Raymond was there.

Perfectly still, he stared into the crowd. As his gaze roamed over the couples he grew more and more agitated. The band had become aware that no one was dancing and had stopped playing. I pushed poor Ron rudely aside.

In the silence Raymond noticed me. 'Where is she?'

I took his hand and I led him away from the dance floor and into the foyer.

When I collected my coat from Hilda, the cloakroom attendant I saw a battered suitcase resting on the counter.

'It's his,' Hilda said, nodding towards Raymond, her eyes round with wonder. 'Still a smashing-looking lad, isn't he? Even in that awful-looking demob suit.'

I put on my coat, picked up Raymond's suitcase and took his arm. I wasn't sure what I was going to say and he must have sensed my confusion.

'It's all right,' he said. 'I knew she wasn't here. I suppose I just didn't want to believe it.'

'Where are you staying?' I asked.

He shrugged. 'I thought maybe Ted and Thelma would put me up at the Seacrest but they couldn't show me the door quick enough.' He smiled dejectedly. 'I expect I'd better find somewhere for the night.'

'That's all right,' I told him. 'You're coming home with me.'

My mother was in the kitchen, concentrating on the pan of milk heating for cocoa. She didn't lift her eyes when she heard the back door open. 'My, you're home early.'

The silence must have alerted her for at last she turned. 'Good God. Raymond.'

In that split second of inattention the milk rose in the pan and would have boiled over if I hadn't rushed forward and lifted it from the heat.

'Well, shut the door, then,' my mother said. 'You'll want some supper.'

Raymond looked bemused but he sat at the kitchen table while my mother warmed up what was left of the soup we'd had earlier. Her eye fell on his suitcase.

'You'd best go and make up the bed in the spare room,' she told me. 'Although I'd better warn you, lad,' she said to Raymond, 'it's cold in there.'

This brought the first smile to Raymond's face. 'I think I can cope with that.'

I hurried upstairs to get clean sheets from the airing cupboard, all the while thinking of everything other than a cold bedroom that Raymond might have had to endure since I'd last seen him.

Down again, I found my father in the kitchen drinking his cocoa. We sat together, a comfortable gathering, although Raymond was quiet.

'Well, then,' my mother said when we had finished. 'I'll leave you to wash the dishes, our Jeannie. Don't stay up too long, will you?'

Despite my mother's instruction, we talked well into the early hours.

I think it was something to do with my mother's matter-of-fact way of greeting him, but by now Raymond had thawed a little. 'No one else survived the crash. By some fantastic fluke I was flung clear with hardly a scratch on me. I felt so guilty.'

'Why?'

'Well, I was the pilot, wasn't I? And they couldn't even trust me to get them home safely.' He stared down at the table. 'A Dutch family found me. By then the plane was burning. They dragged me away. Took me in. I couldn't speak, not even to thank them.'

'Shock?'

'Maybe. They hid me until the war ended, then they handed me over to the British army. I was sent to a military hospital near Cologne. I still couldn't speak. They thought I'd lost my mind. Maybe I had. I had difficulty in remembering my own name. I think I was trying to escape from who I was.'

He looked up suddenly. 'Do you think that's crazy?'

'No.'

'Then the nurses arranged a dance. They dragged along anyone who could walk and some who couldn't. The band began to play. And I remembered Laura.'

Now it seemed as if he couldn't stop talking. All his memories of that time rushed out. I knew I wasn't going to get much sleep.

The next day, Sunday, my mother said we should let Raymond have a lie-in. I helped Mum prepare the vegetables and then I went down to the Seacrest.

Thelma was serving breakfasts but the only guests were a middle-aged couple and their airman son who had just been demobbed. So I sat at one of the empty tables with a cup of coffee. Every now and then Laura's mother gave me a nervous glance. When the guests left the dining room she joined me. 'I can guess why you're here.'

'What did you do with his letters?'

She wasn't prepared for that. 'Letters?' She tried to sound surprised.

'Raymond wrote to Laura, he never got an answer.' I stared at her and she couldn't meet my gaze.

'Well,' she said, 'I mean, some letters did come but it was too late. We didn't want to upset her.'

I leaned back and studied her, obviously wanting to escape but not knowing how to do it with any semblance of dignity.

The night before, Raymond had told me that as soon as his troubled mind had gained some equilibrium he had written both to his mother and Laura. Very soon he'd had an answer from his family solicitor regretting to inform him that his mother had passed away not long after receiving the news of his plane being shot down.

'My mother was all alone,' Raymond said. 'My father died some years ago.'

'How dreadful.' I reached across the table and took his hands.

'But Laura never replied to my letters. I was frantic. I thought she might have died in an air raid. I tried to persuade the powers that be to release me—compassionate grounds and all that—but they said I was mentally unstable. In the end a wise nursing sister pointed out to them that it was not knowing what had happened to my fiancée that was making me unstable. Grudgingly they agreed. So I came here and they told me that she had gone—had married someone else. She hadn't waited.'

'But you were—'

'Posted missing, presumed dead. *Presumed* dead. She didn't wait very long to find out if I'd really kicked the bucket, did she?'

There was a silence as we stared at each other. 'Did Thelma tell you who Laura married?'

He returned the pressure of my hands and smiled at me sadly. 'She married Bill. I'm sorry, Jeannie.'

I couldn't speak; I just held on to his hands. He seemed equally reluctant to let mine go.

'Thelma told me that my letters had never arrived but I'm not sure whether I believe her.'

And that was why I was sitting in the dining room of the Seacrest the next morning. My silence must have prompted Thelma to try and justify herself.

'Listen, Jeannie,' she said, 'I couldn't put Laura through all that again. I mean, she'd found a good man in Bill and to call the wedding off at that stage would have been too much for her.'

'How can you say that?' I shook with anger. 'To find out that her fiancé, the man she loved, was still alive, how could that be too much to bear?'

'Because by then she'd given her heart to Bill.'

'Given her heart? Do you believe that?'

'Why else would she marry him?'

There was nothing I could say. I could hardly tell her that some folk thought Laura was so determined to be married that almost anyone would do. I believed that Laura had been genuinely heartbroken and that Bill had been kind and understanding and that it had been entirely understandable for her to clutch at his support.

But as Thelma and I faced each other over the table I remembered what Raymond had said the night before. *She didn't wait very long to find out if I'd really kicked the bucket, did she?*

I got up to go. Thelma hurried after me.

'Jeannie, you're not going to do anything, are you?'

'What do you mean?'

'Well, you're not going to write to Laura and tell her that Raymond has turned up, are you?'

'No, I won't write.' She needn't have worried. After one or

two letters, Laura had stopped writing to me. I'd had enough pride not to pursue the matter.

'Good girl.'

Thelma tried to embrace me but I pulled away and hurried out of the hotel and along the seafront to the cries of the gulls and the waves crashing on the shore.

I expected that Raymond would go home—wherever home was—but he didn't.

'What is there to go back for?' he said. 'My mother's dead, I have no brothers or sisters, my father's business was sold some time ago. There's still some money owing to me and I'll tell the solicitor to sell the house. But I'll have to find a job.'

It was my lunch hour and we were sitting in Vicky's Tea Rooms having poached eggs on toast.

'Will you go back to acting?'

Raymond looked astonished. 'I beg your pardon?'

'Acting. I mean you were on the stage, weren't you, and about to go into films?'

'I was a photographer. I worked for my father's small studio but when he died I became a sort of freelance. I wasn't much good with the sort of posed family portraits my father did. I suppose I wanted more action.'

'But we all believed that when the war began you had been on the point of becoming a film star.'

Raymond smiled. 'Blame Laura. I was vexed when I discovered that's what she was telling people but I didn't want to embarrass her by putting things straight.'

'But how could she have got that idea?'

'I'd been commissioned by an agency to do some head and shoulder portraits of young hopefuls that were to be sent round the casting directors. The agent told me that I looked like film star material myself and offered to sign me up. So the story she put about wasn't exactly a lie.'

'Would you like to be a film star?'

'I'd hate it. I'm much happier behind the camera.'

'So what will you do?'

'I might try my luck over there.' He nodded towards the window.

I turned my head and saw he was looking at the local newspaper office.

I wished him luck and hurried back to work. Clouds were gathering and I could smell rain. But despite the dark clouds my spirits soared. I couldn't understand why I was so happy until I realised that it was because Raymond, who could have gone anywhere he pleased, had decided to stay here.

My mother said Raymond could lodge with us until he was 'on his feet' and we all tried to get back to a normal existence. The first time Raymond came with me to the Roxy I could see that everyone felt awkward. But gradually the mood relaxed and we were treated as part of the crowd.

Raymond made a quick trip back to his old home in Elstree. He cleared the house and then handed the keys over to the solicitor. He didn't bring much back; only his clothes, a couple of cameras and several boxfuls of photographs.

The local paper didn't take him on straight away. They gave him some unpaid assignments as a trial. One or two of his photographs appeared in the paper, then he was told to try and write words to go with them. They called it 'copy'.

Eventually they gave him the verdict. That evening after tea he was very quiet. It was my mother who was brave enough to ask him what had happened. Raymond looked grave.

'Well, they said my photographs were all right.'

'Only all right?' Dad asked.

Raymond nodded, looking down at his plate so we couldn't see his expression. Then he suddenly looked up and grinned. 'But they said my writing was first class.'

We all looked at each other, completely baffled.

'So?' Mum said. 'Are they giving you a job or not?'

'They are, but not the job I applied for. They've offered me a job as a reporter. I start next week.'

Well, Mum got her bottle of sweet sherry from the sideboard and we all drank to his success. But the smiles faded when Raymond said that he wouldn't be taking advantage of our kindness for much longer. He intended to find a flat. Mum told him there was no need for that and Dad said he was welcome to stay, but Raymond said that he might be working awkward hours and he didn't want to inconvenience us. We could see that he'd made up his mind to go and I was completely unprepared for how desolate that made me feel.

I cleared the table and hurried into the kitchen. I was surprised when Raymond followed me and shut the door.

'I don't need your help,' I said waspishly.

'I haven't come to help. Or, rather, I have, but there's also something I want to say to you.'

'What?'

Raymond laughed. 'Jeannie, if only you could see yourself. Please don't scowl like that. I'm nervous enough.'

'Why should you be nervous?'

'Because I have no idea what your answer will be when I ask you to marry me.'

I don't know how long we stared at each other. Me with my eyes wide with shock and Raymond looking as nervous as he claimed he was. And then, without anything being said, we were in each other's arms.

When my mother came into the kitchen to see what was keeping us, the dirty dishes were still in the sink. We moved apart, smiling foolishly, and all Mum said was, 'About time. I couldn't be more pleased, lad.'

Raymond was to wear one of his pre-war suits for the wedding. I was resigned to wearing my best skirt and jacket. It was a serviceable navy-blue serge, not exactly a bride's first choice, but Pamela in the haberdashery department found a posy of silk anemones that had been behind the counter since before the war, enough to make a spray for my lapel and also to decorate my extremely unglamorous felt hat.

Then Dad came home with some parachute silk. It was perfectly legal. A pal had told him that they were selling it off at the air base and that, as it was coupon free, women were snapping it up to make underwear and curtains, as well as wedding gowns.

My mother and Pamela made my dress and when I tried it on for the final fitting the three of us cried.

'You look beautiful, our Jeannie.' My mother sounded surprised.

'Of course she's beautiful,' Pamela said loyally. 'That's what being in love does!'

'No, it's more than that,' Mum said. 'She's like the ugly duckling.'

'Mum!' I spluttered.

'No, I mean it. You were just an ordinary lass and, of course, everyone compared you with Laura, but you've become a truly beautiful woman.'

So we all cried again and when Dad came home from The Fat Ox he shook his head, lit his pipe and retreated behind the evening paper.

I was a June bride. Pamela was my bridesmaid and Dennis, one of Raymond's new pals from the paper, was best man. After the service we walked across to The Fat Ox for the reception in the room upstairs. While everybody was eating and drinking Mum quietly packed a hamper of sandwiches, sausage rolls and angel cakes for us to take away with us.

We couldn't afford a honeymoon so we spent the first night of our married life in our little flat above Ida's Hat Shop in Park View. Raymond had moved in weeks before and had completely redecorated every room.

Mum had also put a bottle of sherry in the hamper and we picnicked on the hearthrug by the glowing bars of the electric fire, like children who weren't quite sure if it was all right for them to be alone with no one to tell them what to eat or what time to go to bed.

I couldn't remember ever being so happy. For weeks after the wedding I lived in a kind of blissful glow. But one night when I came home from work my happy little world received a jolt.

Raymond had got home before me and he was sitting at the table looking at photographs. At first I thought he was looking at his own old photographs but then I noticed that it was the shoe box of my own snaps that Mum had brought a few days before; I hadn't got round to finding a home for it.

There was no reason why Raymond shouldn't look at the photographs. Over his shoulder I saw myself as a baby, as a schoolgirl enjoying picnics on the beach with my parents, and a later one of me grinning and wearing Dad's air raid warden's tin hat. As my eyes roamed over my past I saw Raymond slide one photograph under the others.

But he looked up as if nothing had happened. 'You should put these in an album.'

'I might, but now let's put these away so I can set the table.'

I gathered them up quickly and put the box back on the sideboard. Next day was half day closing and I got home early. I lifted the lid and took out the top few photographs. I knew exactly which one I would find at the bottom of the pile I'd picked up from the table.

There were just three of us. Laura, Bill and me. Their wedding day. She was holding her bouquet and clasping his arm. I stood a little apart, clutching my own bouquet. We were all smiling, just as the photographer had told us. I put the photograph back and shoved the shoe box into the bottom of the wardrobe. Out of sight, out of mind. Except I couldn't forget the way Raymond had hidden the photograph beneath the others, as if he didn't want me to know which one he had been staring at.

But Raymond seemed happy enough and I was content. As Christmas drew near I began to make plans to have Mum and Dad at our place. I started putting things away and spent my spare time going through recipes in magazines.

It was during a tea break at work that Pamela came looking for me. 'I thought I'd better tell you.'

'Tell me what?' I said without looking up from the recipe for an economy Christmas pudding.

'Laura's home.'

I raised my eyes slowly. 'What?'

'Laura, she's come home. She's left Bill.'

There it was, everything that would take my wonderful world and shake it up—maybe smash it to smithereens.

'Why has she left him?' I asked. I wondered if someone had written and told her that Raymond had survived the war.

'She hated it. The life out there. Miles away from the nearest town—all those sheep—and nowhere to go for a night out. Anyway, she's home. And…well…' Pamela paused uneasily.

'What?'

'She must have found out by now about Raymond.'

'Yes.' Suddenly I felt cold. 'Yes, I suppose she has.'

That night Raymond and I had planned to go to the Roxy. I looked at him over the table as we ate our Welsh rarebit and wondered if I should tell him. I didn't think he knew because he acted pretty much as usual, telling me about his day and asking me about mine.

I could have told him then. *Oh, today,* I could have said, *nothing much happened except that Pamela told me that Laura has come home.*

But I didn't. I washed the dishes and got ready and hoped that at least she wouldn't be coming along to the Roxy. I mean in those days a woman who had left her husband simply because she was bored attracted scandal. Surely Laura wouldn't want to draw attention to herself?

I was wrong. The dancing hadn't even started when she walked in. Raymond and I were sitting at a table under the balcony and he had his back to the dance floor. He heard the shocked gasps and the murmurs of surprise and he looked at me. 'What's happened?'

All I could do was stare.

Raymond frowned and turned his head slowly. I couldn't see his face, but I didn't need to. A wave of nausea hit me as I sensed his shock.

'I'm sorry,' I whispered. The words caught in my throat.

He turned to look at me. 'Why?'

'She's left Bill. I should have told you.'

'Why didn't you?'

I didn't have time to answer him even if I could have. Laura had seen us and she came straight across the floor. People drew back and I don't think it would be exaggerating to say that some held their breath.

Just as if nothing had happened, just as if there had been no years in between, she smiled at Raymond and held out her hand, as he had done the first time he had asked her to dance. She didn't even look at me.

The music began and they started to dance. People watched, just as they had before. There was no denying that together they were the most glamorous couple anyone had ever seen.

Gradually the other couples surrounded them and soon I saw only glimpses of my friend and my husband as they moved around the floor. And then I lost sight of them altogether. I stood up and searched keenly as the couples danced by, but soon there was no denying it. Raymond and Laura were no longer there.

Cold. I felt so cold. I made my way to the foyer and collected my coat from Hilda.

'They're up there,' she said, nodding towards the stairs that led to the little snack bar.

I was mortified that anyone should think I was looking for them. I didn't say anything. I put my coat on and walked out.

It was bitterly cold on the promenade. The wind gusted viciously, snatching my breath and knifing cruelly through my body. But, instead of making for home, I headed north towards the lighthouse and watched its wide beam sweep across the turbulent waters. Tears made cold tracks down my face and every now and then I tried to rub them away with my gloved hands.

I stopped when I reached the cemetery. The dead end of town, as we used to joke when we were children, and turned round to go home. There was nothing else to do.

The front door seemed to open of its own volition the moment I put my key in the lock. My mother was standing there. She must have been waiting in the tiny hallway, listening for every footstep.

'Where the hell have you been?' she asked, and I knew she was angry because I hardly ever heard her swear.

'Walking,' I said.

'Honestly, Jeannie, if I wasn't so pleased to see you I would smack you! Now, come upstairs and take your coat off. Sit down by the fire and I'll make you a cup of cocoa.'

Cocoa. My mother's remedy for all ills and upsets.

'Your father and Raymond are out looking for you,' she said when she came back into the room. 'Your father's sick with worry and Raymond's near demented.'

'Raymond?'

'Yes, Raymond, your husband. Remember him? He told us you'd simply walked out on him at the Roxy and, when he realised you'd gone, he came straight home. When he found you weren't here he thought you might have come to us.'

'Did he tell you why he thought that?'

'Yes, he did. Laura's back and he…'

Before she could say any more we heard the front door open and worried voices on the stairs as Raymond and my father ascended.

'She's here,' my mother said even before they had opened the door of the living room.

'Thank God,' Raymond said.

My father just stared. I could see his distress and it would have broken my heart if there had been anything left to break.

'We'll go now,' my mother said. 'You two need to talk.'

I watched them go. Raymond just stood and stared. He's going to tell me now, I thought—tell me that he still loves Laura.

So his next words took me by surprise. 'Why did you run away?'

Did he really need me to tell him?

'Because you went with Laura,' I said. 'I saw the way you danced with her. I realised that you still love her. You lost her once and now she's come back.'

'Do you really believe that?' he asked.

I nodded mutely.

'Well, you were wrong!' I don't think I had ever seen him look so angry. 'Completely and utterly wrong.'

'But you left the floor together—you went up to the snack bar.'

'And what did you imagine we were doing? Did you think we had fallen into each other's arms?' His face was white.

'I...it crossed my mind.'

'For God's sake, Jeannie. I had to talk to her. I knew from the moment she pulled me on to the dance floor that she hoped we might get together again and I had to tell her as soon as possible that it wasn't going to happen.'

'Why not?' I whispered. 'Don't you love her any more?'

Raymond sank down on the sofa beside me and pushed a lock of hair back wearily.

'Of course I don't. Don't you know that by now? Don't you

know how much I love you? How grateful I am for every day we've had together?'

I turned to look into his face and saw the truth. I couldn't help it, I began to sob.

Raymond put his arm around me and drew me close.

'Don't cry, my Jeannie,' he said and those were probably the most romantic words I've ever heard.

Neither of us spoke after that. We lay in each other's arms on the sofa. The clock on the mantelpiece ticked, the bars on the electric fire glowed comfortingly and we fell asleep.

In my dreams I heard the music playing but there was no one in the ballroom except Raymond and me. He walked towards me across the dance floor and held out his hand. Then he pulled me into his arms and we began to dance.

Jane Gordon-Cumming

Jane Gordon-Cumming began writing when she was about seven and used to make up stories about the teachers at school to entertain her friends. Making people laugh has been her main object in life ever since. She has had many short stories in magazines and on the radio, as well as in the OxPens anthologies of stories set in Oxford. Her first novel, _A Proper Family Christmas,_ was published in 2005, and she is working on _A Proper Family Holiday,_ set in a Gothic dower house in Gloucestershire. Jane is Deputy Treasurer of the Romantic Novelists' Association and Secretary of the Oxford Writers' Group. She lives in Oxford and is married to Edwin Osborn. When not writing, she enjoys trips on _Worcester,_ their diesel-electric narrowboat, works as a volunteer in archaeology and sings in two choirs. You can read more about her on her website www.janegordoncumming.co.uk

Taking Life Seriously

It all started when I was sacked from the naughty food company—for being silly. You wouldn't think it was possible, would you? It was the most amazingly silly job anyone could have, making marzipan penises and sugar boobs for party novelties and adult stocking-fillers all over the world. They're particularly big in Japan, I gather—the market, that is, not the penises and boobs. The only reason anyone would have for taking a job like that would be for a laugh. And so that you could tell people what you did when they asked at parties. It made a real change from the usual run of primary school teachers and computer operators, I can tell you.

So how did I manage to get myself sacked from Edible Erotica? It's a long story, involving a visiting dignitary from a chain of sex shops in Kiev and a packet of Durex. For such a silly company, they took themselves far too seriously. I should have stayed at the building society.

'The trouble with you, Gina,' said my friend Leonora, 'is that you're just not serious-minded enough. That's why you can't hold down a proper job, or why you never seem to have a boy-friend.'

Leonora is very serious. She's a social worker for a start—or was till she decided to stay at home to look after Jacyntha and Tyrone. She has really serious hair, dark and floppy, held back by a Sloany hairband, and wears knee-length skirts and brown tights and Edinburgh Woollen Mill cardigans.

'You were just the same at school. Yes, I know it was funny when you put a fig leaf over that nude statue in the art room, and the red dye in the showers when we were doing Macbeth. But…well…one grows out of that sort of thing, doesn't one?'

It wasn't exactly a question.

'You're pushing thirty now. Middle age isn't so far away. And that's when a young girl with a wacky sense of humour starts to become an eccentric old maid! You don't *want* to end up alone, do you?'

'No, I suppose not.' On the other hand, did I want to end up like Leonora?

'Well, if you're ever going to find someone suitable to settle down with, you'll simply have to get men to take you more seri-ously.'

Men were a bit of a sore point. As Leonora pointed out, I'd never had anything approaching a long-term partner. My relationships, assuming they survived the first few dates, tended to degenerate, as she would put it, into friendship. I have a lot of really good friends who are men. They like the way I make them laugh and that they can talk to me as an impartial member of the female sex without feeling there's any danger of things getting heavy between us.

'And do you have someone in mind?'

'I have, as a matter of fact. He's called Patrick.' There was an unexpected gleam in Leonora's brown eyes which, in anyone else, might have been taken for lust. 'He's absolutely *gorgeous*, Gina! As soon as I saw him, I thought how perfect he'd be for you. I met him at Mike's Christmas party.'

'Oh. A lawyer, then.'

'There's nothing wrong with having a serious job.' She frowned at my expression. 'Mike says he's very highly thought of by the firm. He's well-spoken and intelligent, and *really* good-looking…'

'And still unattached? He must be gay or have some weird personal habits.'

'Of course he's not gay!' Leonora flushed at the idea of anything so unconventional. 'As a matter of fact, he's just come out of a relationship with a *woman*. Oh, well—' she sighed, relieving me of my empty mug with a resigned air '—I had thought of inviting you both to dinner with some of Mike's other colleagues but I suppose it wouldn't work. You're not serious-minded enough to attract someone like Patrick.'

'Huh!' Why should I be deprived of this paragon of manhood, just because I had a naturally light-hearted attitude to life? 'I could be serious if I wanted.'

'I don't think so, Gina.' Leonora considered me sadly. 'You're just not that sort of girl.'

I tried looking like that sort of girl. It meant screwing one's mouth up into a line and sitting up straight in the chair with one's feet neatly together.

'Well, if you're going to make silly faces…'

'No, honestly! It just needs a bit of practice. Why don't you ask Patrick round in, say, a month's time? I'm sure I could become serious in a month.'

It turned out I had a week. After that the firm were sending Patrick to deal with a complicated case in York. Maybe it was the doubtful look she gave me that led me to assure Leonora that this wasn't a problem.

It couldn't be that difficult, surely? I had an expert coach and, under her strict supervision, I embarked on a regime of intensive training.

'For heaven's sake, don't tell him where you used to work,' she advised. 'If anyone asks, you're still with the building society. And you won't mention that awful newspaper you take, will you?'

'I only read it for the problem page,' I protested. 'That three-in-a-bed picture story last week raised a serious dilemma.'

Leonora's derisive snort suggested she didn't think so. 'Make a note of some of the articles in this.' She passed me their copy of the *Guardian*. 'And try to remember your favourite pro-gramme is *Panorama*, not *Celebrity Wife Swap*.'

'Patrick had better be damn well worth it,' I muttered under my breath.

'He is, believe me.'

I turned up early, as instructed, on the Saturday evening, feeling like a boxer fully prepared for the big fight. Or perhaps I should say a racehorse ready for the National, because I fell at the first hurdle.

'Good Lord, Gina, you're not wearing that, are you?' My trainer greeted me with a scowl.

'They're my best jeans.'

'You can't possibly wear jeans to a dinner party! Come upstairs. I'll see if I can find you something of mine.'

My heart sank as I followed her. Keen though I was to look as serious and grown-up as Leonora, I simply could not see myself in her clothes. She opened the wardrobe and began to fling things on the bed.

'Try this one.'

Unwillingly I took off my jeans and pulled on a long dark skirt. She handed me a long dark jumper to match.

To my surprise, it made me look slim and rather cultured. I turned this way and that to let the skirt swish and admired myself in the mirror.

'And we must decide what to do about your hair.'

'What's wrong with my hair?' I said defensively.

No one ever thinks they have a perfect body, do they? Even

if I could have an inch or two miraculously removed from my hips and added to my bust, I'd probably still moan that my nose was too big. But I do like my hair. It's a sort of dark gold, thick and wiry, and springs out of my head in a cheerful, unruly manner that used to drive the teachers mad at school.

'It's so… *young*-looking. You need to have it back from your face.'

'Let me try one of your hairbands.' This surely would be the transforming touch, the insignia that would turn me into Leonora.

It looked gross—a freaky Alice in Wonderland, high on something. I whipped it off again, deeply disappointed.

'Let me have a go.' Leonora started pulling my hair back, twisting it round her fingers and sticking grips in. She was doing it into a bun.

'I hate it like that…' But the words froze in my mouth. A complete stranger was beginning to face me. Ethereal, mysterious and very, very serious.

'Take your make-up off,' said Leonora.

With surprising skill she applied a touch of bronze to the outside of my lids and a hint of kohl underneath.

'Pearls!' I breathed. 'I must have pearls.'

Leonora had pearls.

The effect was stunning. I opened my mouth and shut it again.

'The kids want to kiss you goodnight… Bloody hell!' Mike halted in the doorway, a child in each hand.

Jacyntha was the first to recover. 'Gina looks like a mummy,' she said uncertainly.

Tyrone's face began to crumble. 'I don't *like* her!' he wailed.

'It's her new serious image. Doesn't she look lovely?' Leonora glared at her husband and children. I stuck out my tongue at them as I glided through the door.

Patrick was the last guest to arrive and, although my heart beat faster when the bell rang, it was more the feeling of embarking on a driving test than the prospect of meeting someone Leonora described as *gorgeous*. Mike is a dear, but you wouldn't exactly call him good-looking, and I'd no reason to think our tastes coincided in that any more than in everything else.

So I was absolutely floored when Leonora brought him into the room. 'You all know Patrick, don't you? Except Gina, I believe.' And he turned out to be—well, gorgeous! He had dark curly hair, a curvy kissable mouth and what I might have sworn was a twinkle in those deep blue eyes, if I hadn't known him to be a serious-minded lawyer.

He took my hand in a warm, enclosing grasp. 'Pleased to meet you, Gina.' And for one mad moment I wanted to make it the *real* me that Patrick was meeting. But then I remembered how a man like this was never going to be attracted to someone who greeted him with a silly joke about solicitors. He'd want an earnest, solemn sort of girl who took an interest in the important matters of the day.

'How do you do, Patrick?' I responded politely. 'Global warming is a terrible problem, don't you agree?'

'Er…yes.' He looked a little startled.

'Childhood obesity, too. And it's so sad that people still hunt elephants for their tusks.' I frowned in a concerned manner.

Leonora was frowning in just the same way, so I must have got it right. She shook her head, obviously astounded that I was doing so well, and took Patrick off to find a drink.

It's amazing how you can play a role once you've got the costume. Dressed up as Leonora, I *was* that serious girl. During the starter I regaled them with my views on the Health Service. As we ate our terrine of duck, I canvassed opinions on the Middle East. Pudding was enlivened by a discussion on Chinese orphanages. Leonora was staring at me open-mouthed. I knew she hadn't thought I could do it. Patrick was clearly stunned. He hardly said a word all through dinner, presumably mulling over the serious issues I had raised.

Soon after Leonora had served coffee, Patrick excused himself, saying he didn't like to leave his elderly mother at home alone. The others seemed to find that they had to leave, too, and very shortly we had the place to ourselves.

'That's funny,' said Mike, as we helped Leonora pack the dishwasher. 'I thought Patrick's mother lived in Brighton.'

Leonora sighed. 'I suppose it was silly to think a sophisticated man like Patrick would ever go for someone who just can't help playing the fool.'

It was a relief to change back into my own clothes and brush my hair into its wild and woolly self. I'd shown that I could do Serious, but it was nice to see Gina again in the mirror. It was still only about ten o'clock when I set off on the short walk home. For some reason, I felt a bit depressed. As I passed the pub on the corner, it occurred to me I could do with a drink. I'd held back on the rather serious wine that Mike had provided, wanting to keep a clear head for the task in hand, but there was no need to stay sober now.

I'd bought myself a rum and blackcurrant and was just looking round for a seat when... No, it couldn't be! Elderly mother, indeed!

I was about to hide and then thought, why should I be the one to be embarrassed? Instead, I went over and greeted him with a bright, 'Hello there!'

Patrick looked up from his pint and I saw puzzled panic cross his face as he desperately tried to work out where he'd met me before. Oh, this was going to be good!

'You look pretty miserable,' I observed, sitting down beside him in a friendly manner.

'Do I?' He edged away nervously.

'Yes. Anyone would think you'd just been to a dreadful dinner party and had come in here to cheer yourself up.'

'Ah!' One could hear pennies dropping. He eyed my lurid drink. 'I could say the same about you.'

'Well, there's a coincidence.'

'I don't know what yours was like, but there was this terrifying girl at mine,' Patrick confided. 'She seemed to have spent her life reading miserable newspaper articles and watching gloomy documentaries.'

I smirked, as one who'd got full marks in the exam. 'A *serious* sort of girl, you mean?'

'Yes, very.' He pulled a face.

'Oh!' I was rather taken aback. 'Don't you like being serious, then?'

'Not in the least.' Patrick sighed. 'Just because I'm a lawyer, everyone expects me to be solemn and stuffy but I get quite enough of that in my job. I'd much rather be with someone who can see the fun side of life. Someone who'd drink strange purple concoctions instead of dry wine, for example. Now, I can tell that *you're* not serious at all.'

'I can be, if I try.'

'Yes, I know you can.' That was definitely a twinkle. 'But maybe it's a talent you should save for when you're with serious people.'

'Unlike you?'

'Unlike me. I really prefer being quite silly.'

So Leonora had got Patrick all wrong. But she had been right about one thing. And he was even more gorgeous when he smiled. I could see that my new challenge would be to make him do that as often as possible.

'Speaking of jobs, you should hear about the place I used to work. You'll never believe what they made…'

Hardly a challenge at all. He was laughing already.

Sue Moorcroft

Sue Moorcroft has managed to wriggle out of all 'proper jobs' and works full-time as a writer and a creative writing tutor. As well as her novels, *Uphill All the Way* and *Family Matters,* she has sold over one hundred and thirty short stories to magazines in the UK, Norway, Australia, South Africa, Ireland and Sweden, three serials, the occasional article and has written courses for the London School of Journalism. She won the Katie Fforde Bursary Award in 2002. She likes reading, yoga and Pilates and scuba-dives in a bimbly kind of way. She's an armchair formula one addict and hates anyone trying to talk to her when she's watching a race. Her latest book, *Love Writing—How to Make Money Writing Romantic or Erotic Fiction* is available in January. For more information about Sue and her writing, visit www.suemoorcroft.com

The Malta Option

'I want to talk!'

Alicia angled her white lacy hat against the glare of the sun. 'We're talking.'

'Only because I followed you to Malta!' Grant, unwisely for one who disliked hot countries, wasn't wearing a hat. His dark hair lay damp against his forehead.

'We *could* have talked when I was in England,' she observed reasonably. She fixed her eyes on a bright orange bus chugging through lots of other orange buses and past the horse-drawn carriages called *karozzini*. Hordes of people milled around the Triton Fountain in the centre of the terminus and the air rang with voices.

The sun was a demon in Malta in July and no one with any sense stood out in it like this. She fanned herself with the big soft-cover book about the history of the Malta Railway. She'd bought it to read this afternoon in the gardens. She kept herself afloat financially at the moment by writing articles about Malta: travel, historical, profiles of Maltese opera singers and snooker players. Her father had been Maltese; she was fascinated by the rocky island, so it was a labour of love.

'But you were having a hideous time,' she allowed, softening.

He gazed down into the Great Ditch over the metal railings that edged the bridge to the city gate. Here and there shrubs had seeded themselves into crevices in the mighty ramparts of Valletta, the honey-coloured citadel. 'What's going on, Alicia? You've abandoned your life, your family, your friends. You've been here for weeks—how long before you come home?'

'Months, probably. But I hope for even a year or two.'

The shadow of stubble hollowed his cheeks and his eyes were very blue. He clenched his fist. '*A year?* I've been wrapped up in myself, I know, but I thought you'd understand why. That you'd wait.'

Between them hung the memory of that ghastly day when everything had changed, when he'd arrived at her door, red-eyed and desperate. 'The doctors say Robbie hasn't got long. It's just a matter of time.'

Even now, she wanted to stroke his face, to kiss the sad lines from his mouth. Place her cheek against the hardness of his chest and hear his heart beat. 'I *did* understand! I do. Having to watch Rob—you must've been out of your mind with grief when the diagnosis was leukaemia. I realise it became impossible for you to leave as you'd promised. I waited as long as I could.'

Grant touched the hot skin of her arm. 'When Rob died I was in hell. In a black place inside myself. Michelle and me didn't even pretend that the marriage was worth saving once he'd gone.' His voice shook. 'But I wasn't ready to let myself be happy with you. I needed time.'

'Of course!' Alicia sighed. But time could be so elusive.

She wished desperately that she was alone in the air-conditioned apartment she rented in Sliema, across Marsamxett Harbour. If she began to cry here, with him, she'd never stop.

Her arms would wind around him; she'd press herself against the warmth of his body and plead with him to stay with her for the rest of her life. Time! It seemed so simple to him, to let time heal.

But she mustn't cry! Instead, she shoved her book under his nose. 'Did you know a railway used to run right here? Under the city? Under our feet? It came out in Freedom Square, by The Opera House.'

He flinched. 'A *railway?*'

She scrabbled through the pages of old photographs. 'Right here! Look, below us, on the floor of the ditch, you see that platform and the railings—that was the station! Amazing, isn't it? It ran underground from here and came out in Floriana by another big gateway, the Portes des Bombes, about a kilometre away. Look at this photo, look at the city gate. You can see it's the same place, can't you? Even if it's eighty years since the railway shut down.' Her voice was shrill. She sounded like a phoney. But at least she wasn't crying.

Slowly, he glanced from the photograph to the ditch, to the gate and back to the page. 'Yes. I suppose you're right. It's the same place.'

'Isn't it *fascinating?* Steam trains beneath the rock. There must've been ventilation shafts everywhere. I think it's extraordinary.'

He wiped sweat from his forehead. 'I suppose it looks romantic in the black and white photos, all those upright old guys in suits and hats and women in the black costume—'

'The *faldetta*. Also called the *ghonella*. It was the traditional costume—'

He shoved the book into her bag. 'Alicia! Really, it's *not* extraordinary. Few things are! The railway was part of everyday life then, and the remains are part of the scenery now. That tunnel down there has been turned into a garage. The platform is just an empty block of stone.'

She wriggled her hands free. '*I* think it's extraordinary, the way the remnants have survived. I'm going down to look at it.'

He called after her. 'It's just a piece of rock! The island's made of the stuff!'

She halted suddenly, seeing it through his eyes. An abandoned platform and a couple of blocked off tunnels. Anger rose inside her like a swarm of bees. 'Well, I'll show you something that *is* extraordinary, then!'

She marched away through the teeming bus station, threading through queues at the kiosks for fig rolls with their fragrance of oil and honey, following the foot of another level of fortifications.

He came up behind her. 'This is madness in this heat, Alicia. Let's go somewhere cool. We *must* talk. I need to make you understand what I went through.'

But she did! Her heart had broken for him and once she'd thought she would wait forever. Funny how forever had changed.

She led him down a zigzag path with a battered signpost to the Lascaris War Rooms. 'It will be cool in here. This little tunnel is cut right from the rock, look, and it goes down and down.' Their footfalls echoed down the hewn steps as they descended through the tunnels, emerging here and there into the fresh air, only to turn and enter another level. At the entrance to the war rooms she paid for them both in euros and they were given small cassette players to provide a commentary. 'It's a complex of rocky cells that housed the military operations command for naval movement in the Mediterranean during the Second World War.'

Every time Grant tried to speak, Alicia jumped in with a fascinating fact. 'This was actually Montgomery's office.' She showed him a tiny chamber with a tin desk and filing cabinet. 'And the next was Eisenhower's. They could look over into the operations room below and see where their ships were on that enormous map.' Mannequins garbed in dated woollen uniforms representing the service personnel of more than sixty years before stared glassily at the chart.

'I see.' He remained one pace behind, his cassette player clutched, unused, in his hands as she drifted from room to room, up and down stairs.

They reached the end of the tour and handed back the hardware. 'So, wasn't that an extraordinary place?' she demanded.

He shrugged.

They climbed back up through the network of tunnels and, finally, the zigzag path. Alicia rushed them along like tourists from a cruise ship, trying to devour the city in an afternoon. 'We're really close to the Upper Barracca Gardens, here—you'll never have seen a view like it.'

He'd stopped trying to talk and she was glad. His hurt was so much easier to deal with when he wasn't wringing her heart with his words. They sweated their way up to the gardens and he strode beside her, surly as a bear, fidgeting while she bought bottles of ice-cold water. She took him to the viewing rail at which other tourists hung, oohing and aahing at the beauty and magnificence of Grand Harbour below them with its five creeks of clear blue sea dancing blindingly in the sunshine, the wakes of every vessel, from tiny motorboats to cruise liners, criss-crossing the waves. 'There,' she breathed. 'How about that? The extraordinary only takes a little looking for.'

Even Grant in a black mood couldn't quite ignore the majesty of Grand Harbour. He watched the boats and gazed at the cities on the other shore and let the breeze ruffle his hair, sipping from the bottle of cold water. She settled beside him at the railings.

Without warning, he dipped his head and kissed her with cold, watery lips.

'No!' She jumped back. And then, seeing his hurt, 'Grant, I'm sorry—'

'It's OK. I get it. I shouldn't have just turned up here.' He was already walking away, defeat in the slope of his shoulders.

She turned back to the view, the sea and the boats and the buildings melting together as her eyes filled. Better to let him go. Better in the long run. Fishing tissues from her bag with shaking hands, she blew her nose, hard.

And, because her heart was breaking, she murmured, 'Grant, darling, it's only because I'm ill!' But she was careful to say it only under her breath.

Then, suddenly, his hand was on her arm. *'What?'* He spun her to face him. 'What do you mean, ill?'

Heart pounding, she shook her head, unable to speak through a throat rigid with sobs. She hadn't meant him to hear. Had she?

'How ill?' He uncapped her bottle of water and lifted it to her mouth.

'Pretty ill,' she managed. She brushed his hair out of his eyes tenderly. 'Too ill.'

Despite the heat of the day, he was white, not red like so many of the laughing, smiling tourists clicking away at the panorama and each other. 'I can't play guessing games. Not about illness. Please tell me.'

She sighed. 'It started with a lump.' She indicated her breast, the time bomb she carried under her T-shirt, the nightmare in her bra, the enemy. 'Breast cancer. Like Mum. Like Ginny.'

They took the ferry back to Sliema and trailed up the hill in silence. Dust gathered itchily between her bare toes. Once, he put his arm around her to prevent her from being bustled from the narrow pavement, but mainly they walked through the streets without touching.

Her apartment was small but comfortable with a shower room, a lounge with a kitchen at one end and a bedroom. She didn't have much with her: summer clothes, some books, her laptop and MP3 player. She didn't need much. She spent a lot of her time reading books about the history or rattling off on a bus to visit catacombs, the hypogeum, the cliffs, the churches, to drink Marsovin wine or eat pastizzi. She hadn't told any of her Maltese relatives that she was here. She needed time alone.

She brought iced water to him on the blue leather sofa.

He put it down untouched. 'You've seen doctors?'

'Doctors. Consultants. I've had the scans and the biopsy.'

With a groan he pulled her down against his body. 'God, Alicia! Why you? Why now? I can't believe it.'

Despite her intentions, she allowed herself to remain in his arms. A few precious minutes! To sag against him, take comfort from his sweet familiarity. 'You know that so much is hereditary. My mother died of breast cancer and my sister—' She swallowed. 'Ginny is dying.'

His arms tightened and she enjoyed the sensation of captivity, the weight, the heat, even though it burned to have her breast flattened against his ribcage. He curled himself around her and kissed her hair, her temples. His hands smoothed her back. She closed her eyes and breathed him in, even his faint smell of fresh sweat. Grant. Her lover. Her love.

'You've had so much to go through alone. But after Robbie—'

She pressed still closer. 'I knew I couldn't drop anything else on you after Robbie. I saw the way you shied away from any detail about Ginny's cancer. But I'd gone through every scan and therapy and operation with her so there was a certain comfort in there being no nasty surprises. I coped. I'll continue to cope.'

'My poor darling.' He made a little space so that he could study her chest. 'Which…?'

'The right.'

Tentatively, he touched it through her white T-shirt. Then slid his fingers gently through the scoop neck to run his fingertips across her flesh, making her shiver.

Relief took ten years from his face. 'No mastectomy?'

She smiled, although her heart wrenched. 'No, darling.'

'Did radiotherapy do the trick? I guess you haven't had chemo.' He stroked her hair, plaited back from her face and little curls frizzing around her face from the heat.

She took his hand and kissed it. She could lie to him. He wouldn't realise straight away.

They could have time together. A little oasis of pleasure and love. A week. Two weeks. She might even return with him to England for a while and keep up the pretence for precious months.

But she loved him too much for that. 'I've had no treatment.'

His movements stilled. Panic flashed into his eyes. 'I thought it was the sooner the better? Isn't that what they said to Ginny? She had radiotherapy to shrink the tumour and—'

'And then a double mastectomy,' she finished for him. 'And more radio. And chemo. And she went on Tamoxifen to keep the cancer at bay. But up it popped in her neck and they dug it out there. And now it's on her lung and she's having more chemo. She's lost her hair again. But—' she took a deep breath '—I don't have the same kind of cancer as her. I have IBC. Inflammatory Breast Cancer.'

He was shaking. She could feel him thrumming as if he were an idling car. Sweat oozed into the creases of his fingers. In his eyes she saw the same despair as when he'd known there was no hope for Robbie. 'Is that an OK form of breast cancer?'

She shook her head.

He cleared his throat. Sweat popped up across his cheeks. 'So why aren't you having treatment?'

She kissed him again. It might be the last time.

She couldn't look him in the eyes. 'Because there's no point.'

His hands clenched around hers until she thought her fingers would splinter. *'No point?'*

Tears left prickly little trails on her cheeks as they plopped in quick succession onto her chest. The words hurt her throat as she forced them out. 'IBC is rare. It's all the bad things, Grant! Aggressive, fast-growing, invasive! So I've refused treatment.'

'But chemo—'

'Chemotherapy's oversold. It'll slow things down a bit but at what cost? You've seen Ginny! Losing her hair, can't keep anything down, exhausted, sleeping twenty hours a day!'

Suddenly he was shouting, right in her face, lips drawn up like an animal's. 'You *can't* refuse treatment! You don't know how much time they can give you unless you let them try!'

And she was shouting back. 'I *am* refusing treatment, I *have* refused treatment! Because I've watched my sister die by degrees over the last three years while they cut things off her and out of her. Yes, she's had three years but how much of that has she spent being miserable? It was the same for Mum! At least, this way, I'll enjoy some of what I've got left!'

His eyes blazed with pain. 'I can't let you die.'

'You can't do anything else.' She lifted his hands and kissed them rapidly, desperately. 'I'm not alone, others choose this. It's a gentler way, Grant. They call it the South of France Option. I just made it the Malta Option because I'm happy here.'

He lurched to his feet. 'So you're going to do nothing?'

Her heart was hammering. 'Not quite nothing. I've got an exercise plan to keep me strong. I swim and walk every day, I eat loads of fruit and avoid dairy. I bought some drinks through the Internet that have had amazing results in a few cases.'

His voice dropped. 'You're not telling me you're fighting aggressive breast cancer with herbal tea?'

Exhausted, she let her head drop back. 'It's about as much use as anything else.'

Slowly, he backed away.

'So I'm supposed to just watch you die?'

Fresh tears squeezed out from beneath her lids. 'I came here so no one has to watch.'

Then he'd backed right across the room and was at the door to the apartment. The door opened and he stepped through it.

She didn't even watch him leave. He'd watched his child die and he wouldn't be able to see her go, too. She understood. She *understood!*

Her tears dried and she watched the sunlight fade from the day, listening to the rumbles and hoots of the traffic on Tower Road and voices on the stairs as other, happier people came and went.

It was midnight. And a tapping at the door.

'It's me.' His voice was low.

She'd been reading in bed in a white nightshirt, too tired to sleep. She let him in. He was a good man and it would rip at his conscience if she made him leave without saying goodbye.

He took her delicately in his arms, stroking her rippled hair back from her face.

'Is there pain?'

She nodded. 'Some.'

His fingers moved to her top button and flicked it open. 'I'll rearrange my work so that I can stay with you.' Two more buttons. His hands were unsteady.

Her heart leapt but still she tested him with a protest. 'You had so much time off last year for Robbie!'

A fourth button and a fifth. He pushed the shirt from her shoulders. It slid, slowly, down her arms. Baring her to his gaze. 'You're beautiful. I love you. I'll do whatever it takes. Just let me stay.'

Hope soared. 'We could go home to England; you don't like Malta! The heat—'

'—is not important. If the Malta Option is what you want and all I've got left of you, then that's what I'll take.' He stooped and touched a kiss like a butterfly to her breast. The one that was red and swollen and ridged.

The tears began again. But she was not entirely sad. They'd have to talk about the sensible stuff and the bad stuff. But not yet. First they were going to enjoy what they had.

'You're a wonderful man.' She put her cheek against his collar-bone and let herself enjoy the thud of his heart where their bodies touched. 'Truly. I always find something extraordinary in Malta.'

Victoria Connelly

Victoria Connelly grew up in Norfolk and now lives in London with her artist husband. She has written all her life and has had great success with her magical romances in Germany. The first—about a group of tiny guardian angels—has been made into a film. Her first novel published in the UK, *Molly's Millions,* is a romantic comedy about a lottery winner who gives it all away in true Robin Hood style. She also writes for children. Find out more at www.victoriaconnelly.com

Mummies and Daddies

The Egyptian rooms of The British Museum are my favourite place to sketch.

I usually start in the galleries where the colossal statues stare down at the hordes of tourists, their stone eyes seeming to see everybody at once.

Ever since I can remember, I've been obsessed with all things Egyptian. There was something about the shapes of the hiero-glyphs and the graceful figures from their ancient tombs that fired my imagination at school. That's when I started drawing my own pharaohs and mummies and writing stories about them. Ever since I discovered the collection at the British Museum, I've visited at every opportunity. It's a constant source of inspiration for the books I now write and illustrate.

And here I am again, collecting last minute notes and sketches for a children's book, climbing the west stairs towards my fa-vourite haunt. I remember how much Matt used to hate me coming here.

'You spend more time with those mummies than you do with me!' he'd shout. I never tried explaining my fascination with the mummies to him because he'd never understand. As far as Matt could see, my books were just a nice little hobby. He didn't even bother to look at them when they were published. I'm glad I never dedicated one to him.

Walking through Early Mesopotamia, I remember the last time Matt shouted and me—calmly and quietly—telling him, 'Please be out of my flat by the time the British Museum closes. That's eight-thirty on a Thursday,' I'd added, ducking to avoid the football he'd thrown. I wouldn't miss those lying around the flat, I'd thought as I left, seeking sanctuary in the Egyptian galleries for the hours until my home was my own again.

That was three months ago and I still can't believe that I fell for him. How ridiculously optimistic love can be sometimes. We were so different and yet I'd always thought it would work out somehow. But I was Egypt and he was Everton.

As I enter the Egyptian rooms, I breathe a sigh of relief. It's always such a welcome sight and it's busy today, which is fun for me because I'm a great people-watcher. I get my sketchbook out and make a start. At first, I focus on the cabinets filled with mummies but I inevitably find myself drawn to the tourists. There's a young couple with their arms around each other's waists, moving as one through the room; a young mother with a toddler and her pale face and red eyes tell me she hasn't had a good night's sleep for some time; and then there's a father with his young son—and I can't help noticing how handsome the father is. And he has the cutest smile I've seen in a long time.

I watch them. The father's taking time to explain things to his son. He points out the colours, the materials—the blazing golds and rich lapis lazulis and, like most of the other tourists I've watched over the years, they're taking great pleasure in spotting the familiar figures: there's Horus the falcon-headed god, and Anubis with his jackal head.

I continue watching the father as he calmly answers each of his son's questions, quickly scanning the cards in front of the objects and hastily gaining the information his son wants.

'What's that?' the son asks, pointing into one of the cabinets.

'Er—' the father falters '—that's a shabti.'

'What's a shabby?'

'Well—' his eyes quickly dart for information '—it's a little model in the shape of a mummy that was thought to come to life after death. They were used as servants. The more you had buried with you, the better.'

The son looks absolutely fascinated and I look across at the brilliant blue shabti, turquoise like a summer sky, and wish I had a team at home to help me with the chores, which always get left in favour of my drawing.

The father and son move to another exhibit—the cabinet with the fabulous golden mummies. They stand in front of the largest, with its long ebony hair and huge almond-shaped eyes rimmed with black. Her passive face stares into eternity and she is almost smiling, but not quite. She reminds me of the Mona Lisa—there's that sort of peace about her. She's one of my favourites.

'Look at the gold!' the father says.

I smile. It's obvious to me that this is their first visit and they're both as captivated by the mummy as I was when I first saw her. The boy's mouth has dropped open into a wide 'o' and the father's eyes have gone quite round with wonder. And I suddenly realise that I'm drawing them both. My pencil is flying across the page: the father's kind, open face and his wavy, slightly wild hair, and the boy's sparkling eyes and his inability to stand still for longer than three seconds.

Once my sketch is more or less complete, I move through to

the next room, where I know there's a bench near the mummy known as Ginger. I sit down, glad to have the weight off my feet for a while. This room's much bigger and lighter, less oppressive than its neighbours but no less crowded. My eyes travel—inevitably—towards Ginger—the body of an ancient man who's been naturally mummified in the desert sands. He always pulls in the crowds.

Today, he attracts the father and his son I've been sketching.

'Hello,' the father says as he spies a seat next to me. 'Mind if I sit here?'

I look up from my sketchbook, disarmed by his cute smile. 'Not at all.'

We look around the room together as his son stands, fascinated, by Ginger.

'You know, I could come here every day,' the father says suddenly and I smile. 'Couldn't you?'

I bite my lip, not daring to tell him that I almost do. 'It's one of my favourite places,' I say instead.

He then notices the sketchbook on my lap. 'Can I see?'

I find that I'm blushing as I show him my scribbles.

'They're really good,' he says. 'Is this what you do for a living?'

I smile shyly. 'I've had a few books published.'

'Really?' He looks surprised and I'm wondering if that's a good thing.

'Just for children.'

'*Just?* They're the toughest audience.'

I nod. 'I guess they are.'

'You like children, then?' he asks.

'Oh, yes! I love them. I'd like some of my own one day.' And then I blush. How awful did that sound? He smiles at me and I'm heartily relieved that I haven't sent him running for the nearest exit. 'How old's your son?' I ask quickly.

'Billy's eight tomorrow. This is our big day out today. Can you believe, I offered him the whole of London and he chose to come here? Wanted to see the mummies.'

For a moment I want to ask about Billy's *real life* mummy but it would look much too forward, wouldn't it?

'And what will you be doing to celebrate tomorrow?'

'He'll be at his mum's,' he says.

My eyes widen a fraction.

'We're divorced,' he explains.

'Oh.' I fish around for something slightly less inane to say but nothing comes to mind.

'He's having a party over there. Cake, friends, entertainer—the works!'

'Sounds fun.'

'Don't you believe it! Fifteen eight-year-old boys and girls crammed into a thirties terrace is anything but fun!' He laughs and tiny crinkles spread around his eyes like little rays from sunshine. 'I got off lightly with our day out, I think.'

I glance over at Billy, who's still examining the mummified body of Ginger.

'You can see his fingers and *everything!*' he shouts across to us. 'Cool!'

'So, might I have heard of some of your books?' the father asks me.

'*Night of the Mummies,*' I say, choosing my most popular title.

'You're kidding! That's Billy's favourite book.'

'No!' I gasp.

'That's why we're here today. He won't stop talking about mummies. *Please* tell me there's a sequel.'

I nod proudly. 'Out in time for Christmas. *Dawn of the Mummies.*'

'Excellent!' he says. 'Wow! I can't believe I'm sitting next to the writer. Billy!' he calls. 'Billy—come here.'

Billy runs over.

'Billy, you're never going to guess who this is,' his father says. 'The writer of *Night of the Mummies!*'

'No way!' Billy exclaims. 'Really?'

I nod. 'I'm very pleased to meet you,' I say, smiling at him.

'Wow! That's—like—my favourite book in the whole world! Is there going to be another one?'

'In time for Christmas.' His father's delighted to pass on his insider information.

'And will it have Sethmosis in it?'

'Newly wrapped and ready to rise from the dead again,' I tell him.

'Excellent!' he says. 'That's him in the next room, isn't it?'

'The one lying flat, yes.'

'*Told* you, Dad!' Billy says.

His dad shakes his head. 'He knows your book inside out. He's been spotting all your characters next door.'

I turn to smile at Billy again but something's caught his eye on the other side of the room and he's on the move once more.

'I actually came here today because of the new mummy book,' I say. 'Just putting together a few finishing touches.'

'Can I see?'

For a moment I hold back. I'm nervous, which is silly really because I spend most of my time sketching in public and it's usual for people to peer over my shoulder and pass comment on what I'm doing. But here's a real-life reader of mine and, as I hold out my sketchbook, I suddenly worry that he won't like what I've drawn.

He takes the sketchbook and looks over the last page of drawings I did of the mummies. 'Oh, this is good,' he says. 'Look at this guy! Looks like he'll be trouble in the new book.'

'That's what I was thinking,' I say.

And then he flips the page and sees the sketch of him and his son.

'I'm sorry,' I say hastily. 'I didn't mean to.'

His eyebrows are raised and he looks momentarily stunned. 'It's really good,' he says. 'I don't think I've ever been drawn before. And Billy. You've really caught him. All that energy he has—you can really see it.'

'Thanks!' Relief fills me.

'Oh, I'm Oliver,' he says.

'I'm Sarah.'

'I know. Sarah Galani. My favourite writer.'

I beam at the unexpected praise.

Suddenly, Billy is upon us, grabbing his father's hands and doing his best to drag him up. 'Come *on,* Dad!' he says. 'Let's see the rest.'

Oliver looks at me and shrugs. 'I think it's time to go,' he says, as if apologising.

'Here,' I say, tearing the page out of my sketchbook spontaneously. 'I'd like you to have it.'

He looks surprised for a moment but then asks, 'Will you sign it for me?'

I smile and nod, signing my name at the bottom right-hand corner of the page before scribbling something else there, too. I hand it to him. He takes it from me and, seeing what I've written, smiles, and it's one of those smiles you can feel in your very bones.

I watch as Billy drags him into the next room and they slowly merge and disappear into the crowds.

I sit perfectly still, just thinking. I've never, ever thought that I'd meet anyone in The British Museum, which strikes me as odd considering how much time I spend here. But it all seems perfectly logical now—like people who sign up for evening classes hoping to meet their soulmates over a pottery wheel or computer keyboard.

I watch the tourists come and go and realise that I probably won't get any more sketching done today. As I walk through the familiar rooms, I wonder if Oliver will call the number I scribbled down for him.

But then I remember the way his face lit up as he saw it and, as I descend the west stairs, I have a feeling that I might be seeing that smile again soon.

Amanda Grange

Amanda Grange was born in Yorkshire and spent her teenage years reading Jane Austen and Georgette Heyer whilst also finding time to study music at Nottingham University. She has had sixteen novels published, including five Jane Austen re-tellings, which look at events from the heroes' points of view. *Woman* said of *Mr Darcy's Diary:* 'Lots of fun, this is the tale behind the alpha male,' whilst the *Washington Post* called *Mr Knightley's Diary* 'affectionate'. *The Historical Novels Review* made *Captain Wentworth's Diary* an Editors' Choice, remarking, 'Amanda Grange has hit upon a winning formula.' *Austenblog* declared that *Colonel Brandon's Diary* was 'the best book yet in her series of heroes' diaries.' Amanda Grange now lives in Cheshire. Visit her website at www.amandagrange.com

Just Deserts

The night was wild. The wind howled and the hail battered the windows of the inn. The parlour was empty, save for a gentleman who sat quietly in the corner of the room with a glass of port, the single candle on the table in front of him casting a flickering light but leaving his face in shadow.

The door opened and a second gentleman entered. Young and handsome, he was dressed in a red coat, but when he approached the fire it could be seen that his cuffs were frayed.

The landlord followed him in and took his order for wine, as the sound of a shrill voice floated through the door.

'I will not have you looking at other women, John. You must learn to behave yourself in public, even if you cannot behave in private. I will be stopping your allowance until you have learnt your lesson.'

'Damn you, Sophia! You knew what kind of marriage we had when we made it; it is too late to regret your bargain now.'

'Nevertheless, I will not have you embarrassing me in public.'

'I will not dance to your tune! I am a man, not a puppet. Keep your damned allowance. You seem to have forgotten that I have money of my own.'

'I am forgetting nothing. Your fortune will not keep you in coats and hunters. It will certainly not allow you to gamble and keep the more expensive kind of mistress. You look surprised. Did you think I did not know? But no matter. As long as you are discreet, you may keep as many mistresses as you choose, but when we are in public you will pay attention to me and make every woman in the room jealous.'

'I wonder at you wanting that kind of attention,' came the sneering reply.

'I cannot live without any compensation for my disappointments and if my tastes run to jealousy instead of affairs, then what is it to you? I am going to bed. I suggest you do the same, with a clear head, so that in the morning you will have come to your senses.'

The stairs creaked and a light woman's footstep could be heard going upstairs. Immediately afterwards, the landlord left the parlour and an ill-humoured gentleman in a many-caped greatcoat entered. He removed his coat and threw it over a chair, droplets of water flying everywhere. He threw himself down beside the fire. 'Women are the very devil.'

'There is nothing wrong with women,' said the man in the red coat sourly. 'It is wives that are the curse.'

'Ah, there speaks a married man,' said the newcomer with a wry smile.

'George Wickham,' said the man in the red coat.

'John Willoughby,' returned the other.

'At least your wife is rich,' said Wickham.

'An heiress,' said Willoughby, putting one leg over the arm of the chair. 'Miss Grey, as she was. A great catch. Everyone told me at the time that I was the luckiest of men.'

'And so you were!' said Wickham, impressed. 'I saw her myself, and I would have been glad to marry her. She had fifty thousand pounds, had she not?'

'Aye, and she has it still, for she will not part with a penny.'

'No?' asked Wickham, looking at Willoughby's expertly tailored new coat and his shining boots.

'Maybe a little, then,' admitted Willoughby grudgingly. 'But only so that I will look well in public and make her friends jealous. When I think of the woman I could have married…' He sighed. 'Her name was Marianne. She was a beautiful young girl, good-humoured, passionate, romantic…you should have seen her, Wickham, as I saw her, on that first day, running down the hill with the wind in her hair, as free as a bird, until, by some lucky chance she fell and sprained her ankle and I had the good fortune to be able to carry her home. The feel of her in my arms! And the sight of her, blushing profusely, whilst her heart beat a tattoo against my chest. I tell you, Wickham, if I had married *her* instead of this shrew I would be a happy man.'

'Then why did you not do so? Let me guess. She had no money.'

'No. She was poor. But it did not signify, for I was due to inherit a fortune.'

'Ah. Then your tale is like mine, for I should have inherited a fortune, too, or at least a living, and a rich one; and if I had, then I would have been able to marry a woman of my choice.'

Willoughby looked at him and laughed. 'You do not have the look of a clergyman. Do not tell me you meant to take holy orders, for I will not believe you!'

The landlord entered with a bottle of wine and a glass.

'Another bottle, and another glass, landlord,' said Willoughby. 'The best you have in your cellar.'

The landlord bowed and left the room, whilst Wickham poured his wine and drank, then pulled a face.

'Sour?' asked Willoughby.

'Abominable,' Wickham admitted.

'Never mind, you will join me tonight. We will drown our sorrows together—unless you still have plans to join the clergy?' he asked.

Wickham laughed. 'Not I. But I would have taken the living anyway. And then I would have sold it, and a good price I would have got for it as well, for it was one of the best in England.'

'What happened?' asked Willoughby.

'The old man who left it to me had a son. The son decided I was not fit to hold the living and bribed me not to take it, giving me a paltry sum in exchange. I should have held out for more, but my debts were heavy,' he said with a sigh.

The landlord entered. Willoughby poured himself a glass of wine and savoured it, then poured a glass for Wickham.

'Another bottle,' he said to the overjoyed landlord, then changed his mind and said, 'Another two.'

As the landlord left, Willoughby turned again to Wickham.

'We have both suffered through the interference of relatives,' he said. 'In my case, it was not a son but a great-aunt, a wealthy woman with no children. She was not expected to live for more than a few months. I was her heir, until certain rumours reached her of a girl I had taken up with. She told me that unless I married the girl she would disinherit me. I ask you, Wickham, what man would marry a sixteen-year-old girl he had taken to London for a few weeks, a girl with neither money nor useful connections, just because he had got her with child?'

'Only a fool,' said Wickham.

'Though in one way at least it was my own fault,' said Willoughby, 'for I should have made sure she had no one to come after her. I thought I had done so. I knew her to be an orphan, but I neglected to ask her if she had a guardian.'

'And had she?'

'She had. The worst kind, for he was a colonel, no less, by the name of Brandon.' He drank deeply. 'He had the effrontery to tell me to marry her and, when I refused, he called me out.' He blanched and drained his glass. 'I thought I was done for. But the fool deloped.' He poured himself another glass of wine and added bitterly, 'Not that it did me any good, for once my aunt had disinherited me I had to marry money and so I could not marry Marianne anyway.'

'A sad tale,' said Wickham. He was full of sympathy, for he was drinking Willoughby's excellent wine. 'You have suffered at the hands of an aunt and a guardian, though you, at least, escaped marriage to the girl who threw herself at your head. I have suffered at the hands of a son and a guardian and, worse still, they were one and the same man: Fitzwilliam Darcy.'

'Darcy?' exclaimed Willoughby. 'I know the name. Indeed, I know the estate, one of the finest in the country. He is a powerful man to have against you.'

'Indeed. He not only deprived me of my living but he robbed me of an heiress: having spent the paltry sum he gave me for the living, I soon found myself short of funds again and I looked about me for a means of alleviating my difficulties, to find salvation in the form of Georgiana Darcy. She was fond of me, and a little effort on my part secured her affections. I must admit that the idea of being revenged on Darcy added to her appeal. He had deprived me of one living, it was only right that he should provide me with another.'

'And marrying an heiress was a living you knew you would find congenial, I suppose?'

'Far more congenial than making sermons! So once I had wooed her I persuaded her into an elopement.'

'And Darcy found out?'

'It was the merest chance. He paid her a surprise visit and she, foolish girl, told him everything, so the elopement came to naught. I left the neighbourhood and went into Hertfordshire, only to find that Darcy was staying there. Damn the man! I am sure he came between me and an heiress I was pursuing there, a Miss King; in any case, she was sent away to Liverpool and so that, too, came to nothing. I left the neighbourhood and went down to Brighton, where I came across Lydia Bennet, a girl I had known in Hertfordshire.'

'Let me guess. She was sixteen, eager for a trip to London…a few weeks of fun, and then…'

'And then Darcy came after me. He was, by the unluckiest chance, enamoured of Lydia's sister and, not wanting a scandal in the family, he told me I must marry her. Marry Lydia Bennet! A girl with no money and no sense.'

'But with connections.'

'Connections to Darcy, who has never done anything for me but the meanest things and who has used me ill from beginning to end. But once again my debts were pressing and I had no choice but to settle for a paltry sum. I was a fool. I should have held out for more money, or run. I could have married an heiress. I know how to make myself agreeable to women. If only I had done so, I could be as you are now,' he said bitterly.

'Married to a shrew,' Willoughby told him.

'But a shrew with money.'

Willoughby acknowledged the point.

'But there is one advantage to having a poor wife,' Willoughby said. 'At least you can do as you please. She has no hold over you, and you do not have to listen to her nagging.'

'Indeed, no,' said Wickham with a wry smile. 'I never listen to a word she says. But I walk around in an old coat, I have nothing to ride, save an old nag, and I drink—when I am not fortunate enough to fall in with a friend—' he said, raising his glass and draining it '—the most damnable wine.'

Willoughby shook his head and sighed. 'Marriage is the very devil.'

'Amen,' said Wickham, pouring himself another glass.

There was a slight stirring in the corner and the gentleman sitting there stood up.

'And what of you, friend?' asked Willoughby. 'What is your tale? Come, pull up a chair and join us.'

'I am sorry, gentlemen—' said he, coming into the light.

'Darcy!' said Wickham.

Darcy made him a bow. '—but I am fortunate enough to love my wife.'

He went upstairs, where he found Elizabeth sitting in front of her dressing table in her nightgown, brushing her hair. As the candlelight fell on her dearly loved features he thought how lucky he had been to meet her, to come to know her, and then to love her—and even luckier that she had loved him in return.

'What are you thinking?' she said, looking at him in the mirror.

He walked over to her and took the brush out of her hands, then began to brush her hair, smoothing her hair after each brush stroke with his other hand. Every touch of her hair and her scalp sent powerful surges of emotion through him.

'I was just thinking how lucky I was to find you, and to win you. If not for you, I would never have known what it was like to love and be loved, and nothing can compare with that feeling.' His hands stilled and he met her eyes in the looking glass. 'When I think of how many people are forced to go through their lives with those they dislike or despise, through vanity or avarice or bad luck, I realise how fortunate I have been to find you, dearest, loveliest Elizabeth,' he said softly.

'And I you,' she said, putting her hand up to touch his. 'I always knew that I could never marry unless I met a man I loved and esteemed, a man I could not live without, and I often thought that I would end up an old maid. I pitied Charlotte when she took Mr Collins. I would have pitied her even if he had not been so ridiculous, for she did not love him. But, having met you, I even pity Jane, for although I know she loves Bingley dearly, I am sure she cannot love him half as much as I love you,' she said with a smile.

'Do you think our difficulties made us love each other more?' He rested his hands on her shoulders.

'Perhaps, yes, I do, for without them we would not have changed. You would have remained proud and resentful and I would have remained blindly prejudiced, caring more about exercising my wit than discovering what lay beneath the coldest, proudest exterior, and finding something wonderful beneath.'

'You are right, we have both changed. If not for you, I would have been deeply angry with Wickham when I saw him downstairs just now—'

'You saw Wickham? He is here?'

'Yes, he is drinking with John Willoughby and they are bemoaning their fates. We met the Willoughbys in London, if you recall.'

'Yes, I remember. He was a handsome young man, but he seemed very unhappy; he had been paying attention to Marianne Dashwood, if the gossips were to be believed, but then he abandoned her and married an heiress. I recall his wife. She was very cold.'

'Very cold and very rich.'

Elizabeth shivered. 'I think I will get into bed,' she said.

Darcy smiled, and she smiled back at him, and then he lifted her up in his arms and carried her over to the bed.

As he did so, his eyes never left hers, and their deep connection reminded him of all the pleasures that love had brought them and all the pleasures they had to come.

And before he lost all rational thought he knew himself to be the happiest of men.

Jean Buchanan

Jean Buchanan, a Scot brought up in Wales, read English at Oxford, then went into publishing. Marriage, motherhood and writing took over in the 1980s, though she still freelances for Oxford Dictionaries of Quotations—her favourite project so far is *Love Quotations* (1999). Her husband is a theoretical physicist, their son is grown up and she is currently writing a rom-com. Her writing career started with short stories for *Woman's Weekly* and *Bella,* then a TV script for *Jackanory Playhouse* (BBC 1). She moved into sitcom with her TV series *The Wild House* (shortlisted for a British Comedy Award) and *Welcome to Orty-Fou,* and she has also written for puppets. Her employment CV includes a brush with the civil service, selling gents' ties in the poshest department store in Wales and organising international conferences. She can make fingermice and gets truculent about the quality of ice cream. Her interests include early music, France, Scottish country dancing and ornithology. Her hobbies are croquet, Scrabble, and planning holidays in the South of France but ending up in Barnstaple.

The World's a Stage

Never marry an actor.

This is the most vital piece of advice ever given to an actress. At least according to actresses who *have* been married to actors or, in some cases, to a succession of actors. I heard it on my first and last days at drama school, on most of the days in between. And afterwards.

Actors are regarded as feckless, touchy, always banging on about 'craft', liable to upstage you, hopeless at vehicle maintenance and home repairs and frequently skint. As several of my friends have already discovered. And the actors who caused such large amounts of human misery were also—of course—devastatingly good-looking. A girl has to hang onto her self-possession and also, particularly in the case of handsome actors, her chequebook.

So when I left drama school, proudly clutching my diploma and eye-wateringly convinced that the world was my oyster, I was on my guard about handsome actors. From the moment I started my first paid acting job, small non-speaking parts in a provincial

Christmas panto—village girl, maid in castle kitchen, dancing lady at ball—and also ice-cream-seller during the interval—I remembered the advice.

All the more homely actors were married or firmly attached so I concentrated on furthering my career and establishing unromantic professional friendships with the handsome actors. Part of me thought this was an awful waste, even though all around me I could see them breaking other girls' hearts like glass.

Then I got work in television drama. Girl in bus queue. Waitress in bistro. Girl on hospital trolley. Girl in bed at end of ward. I was a background artiste, the lowest of the low, but it added to my CV and paid a few bills.

Then I was offered voice-over work for television commercials. It was better paid and I got to sit down. Voice-over work isn't at all glamorous—it takes place mostly in high-tech underground sheds and it's more tiring than you'd think but it pays bills faster than standing around in the background—or even lying around in the background.

I became the voice of a seal point Siamese wanting its MoggyBrex—superior, drawly, self-indulgent—the voice of a new range of deodorants—mild, soothing, confidential—and I extolled the virtues of a particularly repellent-looking mushroom pie—earthy, rural, dependable.

Although Hollywood wasn't exactly beating a path to my door I was getting a reasonable amount of work. But on the romance front things could hardly have been less promising…

My friend Kate, who lived round the corner, was in the same boat. She had a highly paid fourteen-hours-a-day job in the City. We met up when we could, which wasn't that often, given the capacity of our work to send us all over the place—hers involved first-class travel and five-star hotels; mine didn't.

We met in coffee shops or in Kate's palatial flat or in my teeny studio flat and over lattes or wine we sympathised about the lack of eligible men in our lives. These conversations usually ended with one of us saying that it was pathetic. On this occasion, it was Kate's turn. 'Let's face it,' she said, refilling my glass. 'It's pathetic, isn't it?'

And then, suddenly, everything changed for Kate. I had just got the occasional hurried text message when out of the blue came the announcement of her engagement. *Hope for us all,* I thought, on the why-not principle. A few days later I got an invitation to the engagement party. *Fancy Dress,* it said firmly in the corner.

Well, I knew about fancy dress. I visited the nearest theatrical costumier's, about ten minutes' walk away from my flat, and put down a deposit to hire a lovely floor-sweeping vaguely mediaeval number in crimson velvet that reminded me of Sleeping Beauty. Just right. I arranged to collect it the afternoon before the party.

I chose an engagement present, a salad bowl glazed green and white. I packed it up with plenty of padding, wrapped the box in bright pink paper and tied a big silver bow around it. Perfect.

On the day of the engagement party I did an emergency voice-over in the morning and by three o'clock was back in my flat, finishing lunch and thinking about strolling down to the theatrical costumier's to collect my costume. After that I should have time to slip into a bubble bath. But then my phone rang. It was someone at the costumier's to say that they'd just discovered a mistake with the booking. I couldn't have my lovely crimson Sleeping Beauty dress as it was still out on hire. They could offer another dress of comparable quality but it belonged to a different period and I'd have to go and collect it from their other branch, which was miles and miles away.

The sky faded by three shades of blue. The sparrows on my bird-feeder sounded grumpy.

I wallowed briefly in a ten-minute bath, threw on some clothes, grabbed my bag and picked up the pink parcel containing the engagement present. Time was tight, so I'd have to go straight to the party once I'd collected my costume. I trekked across several postal districts and an hour later I reached the other branch of the theatrical costumiers, when they were on the point of closing.

They let me have a discount for inconvenience, which I accepted with as much grace as I could muster. I paid up and the elderly assistant was just putting the costume into a box when she suddenly said, 'You'll have someone to help you get into this, dear, won't you?'

'No,' I said. 'I'm going to change when I get there.'

The assistant sighed heavily and opened the box again. 'You'll never manage it by yourself,' she said. 'Too complicated. Come into the fitting room.'

You'd think I'd have realised, with my training. The dress and the corset underneath it laced up at the back—in the era my costume belonged to they had maids, lots of them. And then there was the wig.

'You don't look bad in that,' the assistant said grudgingly, once she'd shoehorned me into the dress. The corset underneath helped, of course, and the dress material, heavy blue silk, was really pretty. There were even large concealed pockets where I could stow essential items—keys, money, mobile phone, lipstick and a mini *A to Z*.

The assistant let me leave my bag and clothes there. 'By the way, dear,' she said. 'Should I recognise your voice?'

I said no. It saved time. I thanked her, picked up my parcel, left the shop and headed for the nearest bus stop.

It's difficult to walk down the street unobtrusively when you're dressed as Marie Antoinette. *And* carrying a large pink parcel.

Several old ladies laughed behind their hands. Two men tried unashamedly to look down my cleavage. Small children's mouths dropped open.

'I bet she's advertisin' something,' said a spotty teenager to his spottier friend. He managed to speak and leer at the same time. 'What you advertisin', darlin'?'

'Cake,' I said, and strode on.

The bus driver thought it was hilarious. I had to stand sideways in the aisle because of my skirt, which was very wide and held rigidly in shape from the waist downwards by panniers, ludicrous framework-like structures where the pockets were hidden.

I got off the bus, put the parcel under one arm, fished out my *A to Z* and turned down a side street. A little lad in a baseball cap asked me if I was a time-traveller. 'Yes,' I said. 'But if you see the Doctor, promise that you won't tell him you've seen me.'

He looked impressed. 'What's your Tardis like, then?'

'Sedan chair,' I said. One should try to keep in period.

'What's in the parcel?'

'Anti-gravity,' I said. 'Urgently required on Gallifrey.'

'Why have you got an *A to Z*, then?' he called after me. Obviously a bright child.

I stopped briefly. 'It only *looks* like an *A to Z*,' I said mysteriously.

And then at least four people asked whether I was going in for a fancy dress competition as a spare toilet roll cover. I attempted to smile charmingly and tell them that actually I was going as a tea cosy.

'Just a minute, love,' the last one said. 'Don't I know your voice?'

'Do you have a cat?' I asked.

'Sure,' he replied, mystified.

'In that case, you probably have heard me before.' I took a deep breath, drew myself up to my full height and said, 'I am the voice of MoggyBrex.'

'Wow!' he said. 'Can I have your autograph?'

'My cat hates the stuff,' said an interested onlooker.

'So would I, if I was a cat,' I said recklessly and moved on, hoping that the terms of my contract didn't include not dissing MoggyBrex.

A few moments later a taxi slowed down at the kerb beside me and a man about my age, with brown curly hair, eyes that crinkled at the corners and a nice smile, put his head out of the window. At another time, in another place, I would have found him wildly attractive. He had the looks that normally make me go weak at the knees.

'Excuse me.'

I ignored him.

'Excuse me,' he said again. 'Where are you heading?'

I walked rapidly.

'1785,' I said. 'Rift in the time/space continuum over Versailles.'

The taxi moved with me. Just what I needed, a kerb-crawler who wouldn't take *no* for an answer.

'Stop!' he called to the cabbie, then opened the door and leapt out. He was wearing an early nineteenth-century naval uniform with a swallow-tail coat, white breeches and buckled shoes and there was a cocked hat under his arm—think Lord Nelson, but about a foot taller and with the full complement of arms and eyes. 'I suspect we're both going to the same place.'

It took at least five minutes to get me and the parcel into the taxi and he ended up squashed against me because of the panniers. 'I don't mind if you don't mind,' he said gallantly. 'Remind me to straighten your wig when we get out.' I had no option but to lean against him. I could feel his heart beating, smell his aftershave and gauge the size of his shoulders. I remembered how long it was since there had been anyone like him in my life.

All too soon we arrived at the venue, an impressive private house, and tumbled out of the taxi, for which the early nineteenth-century naval officer insisted on paying. Then we were directed around the house to a stunning garden and a large marquee. A three-piece band had been put under the willow tree and were working their way through favourites from Gilbert and Sullivan.

'Let me get you a drink,' said the naval officer. 'Oh, hang on, I haven't introduced myself. I'm Oliver Kitteridge.'

'Sally Grant.'

'I suppose I should stay in period and bow,' he said, and then bowed quite beautifully. 'And your costume makes you far too early to be shaking hands.'

I curtsied, which was what they did circa 1785. Normally I'm quite good at curtseys—one has to be. But it felt very peculiar with the panniers. And the parcel.

'I'll get that drink,' said Oliver. I parked my parcel beside a flower arrangement and took a glass of champagne gratefully. My estimation of Oliver, which was pretty high already, went up a few more notches. He said he'd left his hat behind the bar. 'And I'm sorry about the costumes,' he added. 'I mean, about guests having to wear costumes. Kate's always been crazy about fancy dress, ever since she was given a fairy princess outfit at the age of three. And last year some fool gave her the DVD of *To Catch A Thief* and she's practically worn it out watching the costume ball scene. Talked about nothing else for a fortnight.'

He seemed to know an awful lot about Kate. Pennies started dropping in a way I didn't want them to drop. 'Just a minute,' I said as my mind went blank on names and an unwelcome thought struck me. 'You're not Kate's fiancé, are you?'

'Good God, no,' he said. 'I'm her cousin. Let me get that glass refilled for you. And I'm not anybody's fiancé, by the way. Or anybody's anything.'

We were on our third glass of champagne when I said to him, 'I suppose you've got a job in the City, as well?'

'Sort of,' he said. 'Members of our family tend to end up studying maths at university. And then they go into the City.'

'Like Kate,' I said.

'Exactly,' he said.

'And now she's marrying someone else in the City?'

'Yup. Hugo. Plays the banjo, speaks three languages and cheats at Monopoly. I suppose we should go and greet the happy couple.'

I picked up the parcel and we went to find them. Kate, looking happier than I'd ever seen her, was dressed as a fairy princess— surprise, surprise—and Hugo was wearing knee-breeches and a frock coat. 'People keep asking me if I'm Ken,' he said. 'Who's Ken?'

'He's had a very sheltered upbringing,' said Kate to me. 'He's only got brothers.'

'Kate's told me a lot about you,' said Hugo charmingly, after they had fought their way into the parcel and admired the salad bowl.

'She's the voice of Florabunda deodorant,' said Kate. 'And Mrs Morrell's Country Mushroom Pies. *And* MoggyBrex.'

'Really?' said Oliver. 'That's so much more interesting than what I do. Shall we go and get some food? It's in the marquee. They might even have some of Mrs Morrell's Country Mushroom Pies.'

Mercifully, Mrs Morrell would have been way out of her league. There were platters of blinis, beautifully decorated canapés and a carvery buffet with huge bowls of glistening multi-coloured salads, then profiteroles and syllabub and shortcake and mounds of fresh strawberries and raspberries. And the cham-pagne never stopped coming.

As we ate, Oliver asked me about my work, even the hanging-about-in-the-background jobs and the ice cream selling. I supposed that if he worked in an office surrounded by computer screens and financial data he would find what I did fascinating. I asked about his work but he said that he couldn't say much for reasons of confidentiality.

'Do you think you can dance in that thing?' He eyed my dress doubtfully.

'One way to find out,' I said.

The band had relocated to the fringe of the dance floor and was now playing a selection of classic French numbers. 'Oh, lovely,' I said. '*La Mer*. My favourite.'

'Very appropriate,' he said, 'given your costume. And, come to that, mine: France and the sea.' He took my hand and led me on to the dance floor. Then he took me in his arms and we started to dance. I felt a delicious anticipation of the electricity of physical attraction. Our bodies touched lightly. Crunch.

'Dear God,' said Oliver. 'What on earth have you got on under that dress?'

'You don't want to know,' I said.

'Don't be so sure,' he murmured.

We went on dancing until the band pleaded desperate thirst and announced a break and then we walked around the garden. There were lanterns strung in the trees and the scents of jasmine and lavender drifted lazily. The evening was getting impossibly romantic, which I suppose was appropriate, given that it was an engagement party. Oliver took my hand. 'We could go and look at the pond,' he said. 'They were going to light it.'

I said, 'You know this garden?'

'Of course I do,' he said. 'It's Kate's parents' house. I spent some of my formative years here—catching tadpoles, watching dragon-flies, getting covered in mud.'

Coloured lights glowed from the trees around the pond and, of course, there was a bench.

'This isn't as romantic as I'd hoped,' said Oliver. 'I can't get closer to you than about two feet.'

'Sorry, it's the panniers. The most fashionable ladies at Versailles had to go through doors sideways.'

The party ended some time after midnight when the champagne ran out and the band got to the end of their repertoire and said they'd have to start on Gilbert and Sullivan again. 'Let me take you home,' said Oliver. 'I'll just go and get my hat.'

We found a taxi and Oliver helped me in. 'At least no one's going to ask to share the cab,' he said, settling on the opposite side of the seat from me. 'And I think I'm learning how to cope with your costume. D'you need some help with that seat belt?'

When we arrived at my rather humble apartment building, Oliver paid off the taxi. 'I'll see you to the door,' he said.

'What about getting home?' I said. He waved a set of keys at me.

'Kate's flat,' he said. 'Just round the corner. She's staying with her parents. So I can crash at her place. I borrowed her keys when I went to get my hat. I thought perhaps I could take you out to lunch tomorrow.'

'Dressed like that?' I couldn't resist asking.

'If necessary,' he said. 'But I thought I'd go out and buy some clothes. Unless some of Kate's will fit me... No, not really.'

'Clothes...' I felt my face drop. 'I can't get out of this dress by myself,' I said. 'It's all done up at the back with laces and things.'

'Can I help?' he asked.

'Er—' I wondered momentarily about the advisability of this.

'I could do it with my hat over my eyes,' he suggested.

There was nothing for it. He came up to the flat. Getting in and out of the lift was quite an experience, and once we'd got my front door closed he put his hat down and undid the laces on the dress for me. 'You'll have to loosen them as well,' I said. 'Or else I won't be able to get out of it. And then the same with the corset.'

'It's amazing what they did before Lycra,' he said. 'Will that do?' he asked about five minutes later.

'Fine. Thank you.' I had to hold up the front of the dress to stop it sliding downwards. Then he kissed my back between my shoulder blades. It was wonderful. Electric. A concentration of all the sensations that had been trying to get through that wretched corset.

'You've got a lovely back,' he said as I turned round.

He kissed me on the lips.

'I ought to go,' he said. He kissed me again. 'I really ought to go,' he said.

'Yes,' I heard myself say, then I kissed him back.

He did go. The lock clicked softly behind him.

Always leave them wanting more, I thought. I wasn't sure whether it referred to him or me.

The next morning he turned up at about half past eleven in chinos and a pale blue shirt, with an enormous bunch of flowers. We went for brunch, then to an art gallery and dinner.

From then on we spent all the time we could together, as much of it as possible with our arms wrapped round each other. The days passed in a haze of happiness. Oliver's work was punctuated by early starts and working late into the evening. My diary showed a more haphazard work pattern, the norm in my profession. When Oliver was working and I wasn't, I filled in odd hours with exercise classes or went to the cinema.

One afternoon, when I was sitting in a small studio cinema waiting for a recently released rom-com to begin, I saw something that made my heart lurch. It was Oliver, looking completely different and in the sort of company it didn't occur to me that he would keep.

I'd have to confront him, I realised as I slunk out of the cinema after the film finished. Mentally, I rehearsed what to say.

Oliver turned up at my flat that evening with an armful of cornflowers. 'The colour reminded me of your eyes.' He bent to kiss me, but I moved out of the way.

'You've been deceiving me,' I said.

'Oh, God,' he groaned. 'You've found out. I can explain everything.'

'That new rom-com,' I said. 'I went to see it. I also saw you. Before the film even started. Man in commercial for Henley aftershave.'

'They only picked me and the other guys for that ad because we could row.'

'Not just that,' I said. 'In the film. Hero's old school friend with six lines in wine bar.'

He looked sheepish.

'Admit it,' I said. 'You're an actor. No wonder you always change the subject when I ask about your job.'

'It's a fair cop,' he said. 'It's like this—Kate told me about all the stuff about not getting involved with an actor. The actual wording, if I remember correctly, was *would not touch with a bargepole.* Then I fell in love with you the moment we met and I didn't want to muck up my chances...'

'And what about working in the City?' I asked sternly.

'It's true. I've taken part in performances of readings there for charity.' I could believe that—he had a fantastic voice. 'And I temp there quite a bit. It pays well. And I really have got a degree in maths. I just did a lot of acting at university. And then I went to drama school.'

There was a pause. 'Can you forgive me?' he asked.

'You lied to me,' I said.

'No, I didn't. I misled you. That's different. It all depended on the interpretation.'

He was looking at me with the most serious expression I'd ever seen on his face. 'Are you going to forgive me?'

I looked at the cornflowers and his brown eyes and curly hair and thought about the way he'd kissed my back. And all the subsequent kisses and the hours we'd spent together and the wine we'd drunk and the jokes we'd laughed at and the smell of his aftershave—even though it was probably Henley aftershave.

I took a deep breath. Was I going to have to rethink my attitude to the most consistent advice ever handed down from one actress to another?

'Well?' he said.

'I'll have to think about it,' I said.
I held the pause for about twenty seconds.
And then I kissed him.

Anna Jacobs

The author of forty-five published novels, Anna Jacobs freely confesses to an addiction to story-telling. Fortunately, she is not very domesticated, so has plenty of time to produce two to three novels a year, writing sagas for one publisher, modern women's fiction for another. She is fascinated by women's history and by the challenges women face in today's changing world. Her books have been nominated several times for Australian Romantic Book of the Year, which she won in 2006, and she is among the top few most borrowed authors of adult fiction in English libraries. She's still in love with her own personal hero, and she and he live half the year in Australia, half in England. Discover more about Anna's writing at www.annajacobs.com

Will You Dance?

Western Australia, January 1921

When the ship docked at Fremantle, Gracie Bell was on deck with the other passengers. She stared round with a sinking heart. The West Australian port looked so scruffy, like a large village with an untidy collection of tin roofs. The summer heat made sweat trickle down her face. It was like standing in front of a hot oven.

Never mind that, she told herself. In Australia she'd find a more interesting job and make a better life for herself. She wasn't working as a maid ever again, hated being shut up in a house all day. During the war she'd worked as a conductress on a motor omnibus, but once the war ended she'd lost her lovely job to a soldier returning to England.

She hadn't emigrated to look for a fellow, though. All her married friends worked like slaves and were always short of money, not to mention having one baby after the other. She didn't fancy that. Maybe one or two children would be OK, not eight, like her mother.

When she came out of Customs she found her sister, Jane, waiting for her on the dock, looking pregnant, hot and weary, with her husband Tommy beside her. Her brother-in-law had grown fat in Australia, reminding Gracie of an overstuffed cushion. *He* didn't look at all tired.

He eyed her up and down, nodded in approval and loaded the luggage on the motor car.

'Is this your car?' she asked, trying to make conversation.

'No. I've borrowed it from my friend Bert. He and I work together.'

'Since we live in Perth, not Fremantle,' Jane said brightly, 'this is easier than taking a train into the city. It was very kind of Bert, don't you think?'

'Yes.' She saw that more was required and added, 'Very kind indeed.'

'Tommy's doing ever so well at work. We're buying our own house now.'

Tommy smirked and, as soon as they set off, dominated the conversation. Talk about bossy! Gracie tried to maintain a polite expression but what she really wanted was to talk to her sister.

Jane, who seemed to have lost all her old spirit, gave her a warning look and shook her head slightly when Gracie mentioned her hopes for the future.

What was going on?

The next day being Sunday, they went to church, then Tommy worked in the garden. Gracie couldn't believe how many tomatoes there were, just growing in the sun, not needing a greenhouse. She'd never eaten them newly picked before, or peaches, either. They were much nicer than tinned ones.

Bert, Tommy's best friend, always came to tea on Sundays, and

Jane spent her sister's first day in Australia baking a cake and some scones, red-faced, rubbing her back from time to time. Gracie had hoped to go out sightseeing and said as much.

Jane looked over her shoulder and whispered, 'We'll go out during the week. There are some lovely shops in the city. But Tommy likes things to be just so on Sundays, so if you don't mind helping…?'

They were to eat out on the veranda, so Gracie swept outside and dusted all the furniture there. She tidied up indoors as well, which consisted mainly of picking up after Tommy. Didn't that man ever carry his own empty teacups back into the kitchen, or put away his daily newspaper?

She was very disappointed in his friend Bert, who was nearly as fat as Tommy and just as fond of his own voice.

During the tea party, conversation was mainly between the two men. As he talked, Bert stared at Gracie in the same assessing way Tommy had, and it made her feel uncomfortable. She didn't know where to turn her eyes.

The hosts insisted on clearing the table and making another pot of tea, which left Bert and Gracie alone.

'You're even prettier than your photo.' He leaned across and, taking her by surprise, planted a big, moist kiss on her lips.

She tried to pull away, but he dragged her to her feet, pressing his body against hers. She wasn't having that. Stamping on his foot, she scraped her shoe down his shin, causing him to yelp, then she retreated to the other side of the table.

'What do you think you're doing?'

'Protecting myself. And I'll do worse than that if you ever grab me again. How dare you take liberties with me? What sort of person do you think I am?'

'Aw, come on, Gracie. Don't be stand-offish. Jane and Tommy have told me so much about you, I've been dying to meet you. You can't blame a fellow for getting carried away.'

Dying to meet her? Alarm bells rang in her head. Just wait till she got her sister alone. She'd find out what was going on.

'Isn't Bert a nice fellow?' Jane said brightly next morning after Tommy had left for work.

'No.'

Jane looked so horrified, Gracie knew her suspicions were correct. 'Did you invite me to Australia to pair me off with him? *Jane?* Answer me.'

'My goodness, it's going to be hot again today. I'd better go and water those tomatoes.'

Gracie barred the doorway. 'You did, didn't you?'

'I thought it'd be nice if you lived nearby. And Mum's been worried about you not marrying, with your young man being killed during the war. There are a lot of spare women now and Bert's a really good catch. He'll be foreman after Mr Minchin leaves, you know.'

'I don't care how much money he earns. He can only talk about himself and I never did like men with yellow hair and bright pink skin.'

'Don't say that to Tommy, *please*. Why don't you just…you know…give Bert a chance?'

Gracie pretended to read the newspaper. She found an advert for an employment bureau and tore it out secretly.

The following day, ignoring her sister's protests and pleas to wait another week or two, she put on her smartest clothes and her best hat. It had an upturned brim decorated by a fabric flower and was worn pulled down to the eyebrows. It showed off her eyes and she had loved it so much that she'd paid thirty shillings for it, a huge extravagance.

She found the employment bureau without difficulty and marched inside, refusing to give in to the butterflies in her stomach. They questioned her about her experience, then offered her a job.

She stared at the woman in dismay. 'But I told you: I *don't* want to work as a maid. I want something more interesting.'

'There aren't many other jobs for young women without clerical skills, so it's either work as a maid or in a shop.'

Gracie had a quick think. If she worked in a shop, she'd have to pay for lodgings and she'd never save any money. Of course, she could stay at her sister's, but that'd mean putting up with Tommy's bossiness, not to mention facing Bert's leers and fumbling hands.

With a sigh, she agreed to consider a live-in maid's job. But, she vowed to herself, it'd only be for six months. She'd save and look around for something more interesting once she got used to Australia.

'I have a vacancy on a country homestead in the south-west, working for Mrs Gilsworth. She's an excellent employer, pays top wages and even provides the uniform.'

Gracie fanned herself. 'Is it cooler there?'

'It's always cooler in the south.'

'And is there a town nearby? I'll take it, then.'

'When can you start? Mrs Gilsworth is rather desperate for help.'

'Would tomorrow be too soon?'

'I'll telephone the local post office and they'll send her a message. I can find out within two hours, but I'm sure she'll engage you.'

When Gracie got home, her sister took one look at her and burst into tears. 'You found a job, didn't you?'

'Yes.' She tried to ask Jane if she knew anything about the south-west but all her sister could do was worry about what Tommy would say.

Tommy said a great deal that evening, like 'ungrateful' and 'taking advantage', as he chomped his way through an overloaded plate.

Gracie only had to think of Bert to know she was doing the right thing. In the end, she went to bed early to escape the chilly atmosphere.

But she found it hard to sleep, tossing and turning in the narrow, creaking bed. She was more than a bit nervous about going to live over a hundred miles away from the only people she knew in Western Australia.

The next morning Gracie followed the porter into Perth railway station and watched her trunk and suitcase loaded onto the train. Jane had insisted on coming with her and, even at this late stage, tried to persuade her to change her mind.

'For goodness' sake, stop nagging! I'm taking this job and that's that!'

'But you came all the way to Australia to be with me and—'

'To make a new life *near* you! Not for you to marry me off to one of your husband's friends. I lost one man to the war and if I ever meet another I like enough to marry he'll be *my* choice, not yours. And he won't have yellow hair.'

Gracie was relieved when the train chugged out of Perth station in a cloud of steam. She felt very alone as she stared at the grass, burned beige like straw by the hot Australian sun south of the city, so different from England. She missed the greenery, missed her other brothers and sisters, too.

It was so hot, she took off her gloves and fanned herself with her hat. There wasn't much to see and she was alone with only her thoughts and worries for company.

She arrived at Bunbury, a hundred miles south, in the early afternoon. She got out of the train smiling determinedly. The other passengers hurried away, but she waited to be met.

A tall man dressed as a chauffeur strode across to her. 'Miss Bell?'

'Yes.'

'I'm Finn. Mrs Gilsworth is waiting over there.'

'I've got a trunk to pick up, a blue one.'

'I'll see to that.'

His eyes were admiring and Gracie felt flustered. He was nice-looking, with dark hair, twinkling grey-blue eyes and an upright way of holding himself, like many ex-soldiers.

Mrs Gilsworth was plump and expensively dressed. Her eyes narrowed as she looked Gracie up and down. 'I see Finn found you, Bell. The car is this way.'

Gracie sat in the front next to Finn, who barely said a word, while Mrs Gilsworth never stopped talking about what she had bought at the shops in Bunbury and the dinner party she was giving next week. To hear her talk, Bunbury was a big town. It seemed very small to Gracie.

They drove along country roads, which seemed to get narrower and dustier by the mile. Occasionally, they passed through small clusters of houses. Talk about the ends of the earth! Then at last they turned off on to a long drive to a sprawl-ing wooden house surrounded by verandas and a cluster of farm buildings. Gum trees shaded the house, the leathery leaves a faded green.

It looked very different from the English countryside. Gracie swatted a fly. The scenery wasn't nearly as pretty here.

Finn drew up at the front door of the homestead and opened the car door for Mrs Gilsworth, then got back in and drove round to the back of the house. He removed his chauffeur's cap and tossed it on the front seat, rubbing the mark it had made on his forehead. 'Welcome to Fairgums, Gracie.'

'The agency didn't tell me what a long way from town this place was.' She studied her surroundings.

Finn shrugged. 'You can save more money in a place like this. Nothing to spend it on.' He grinned. 'I like that hat. Makes your eyes look big and mysterious.'

This compliment was so unexpected, she could feel herself flush slightly.

He led the way inside, where he introduced her to Cook, a large motherly woman whose hands never stopped working.

'I'm very pleased to meet you, Gracie. You look a cheerful lass. The last housemaid was a sourpuss, but she still got herself a husband. They're real short of women in the country.'

'I'm not looking for a husband, thank you very much!'

Cook laughed. 'They'll come looking for you.' She wiped her hands. 'I'd better show you your bedroom, then you can come and help me.'

The room was large, with a single bed and a mosquito net. A black and white uniform was laid out on a chair and several maid's caps on the chest of drawers.

Cook pointed towards the uniform. 'That should fit you nicely. *She* likes the servants to dress up all fancy when we have guests. Just a print dress and apron will do the rest of the time, but she does like her maids to wear a cap.'

Gracie sighed.

Cook smiled sympathetically. 'I know. Young women don't like caps, but she's a bit old-fashioned. She's all right otherwise, not stingy with the servants' food.'

Once alone, Gracie stared out of the window. Only cows and fields to be seen. She'd expected there to be other farms nearby, at least. She had a little cry, then scolded herself and changed into a print dress, sighing as she pinned on the starched white cap provided. She hated the dratted things. But at least Mrs Gilsworth paid good wages, far better than they did in England.

Later in the afternoon Cook told Gracie to ring the bell on the back veranda, then take the weight off her feet for a few minutes.

An elderly man who joined them was introduced as the gardener. Finn followed, shirt sleeves rolled up, collar open, looking very manly and energetic. He took a piece of cake and winked at Gracie.

She sipped her tea, grateful for its familiar warmth. 'How far away is the nearest town?'

'We drove through it—Beeniup, five miles back.'

She stared at him. 'That's not a town. It's not even a village. What am I going to do on my days off? Is there a cinema anywhere near?'

'No, but there's a church social one Saturday a month for the young folk. The missus lets me have the car to drive us into town.'

'Who's "us"?'

'Just me and you at the moment. The other servants are too old for dancing.'

Cook pretended to slap him for saying that and he pretended to be afraid.

He turned back to Gracie. 'Do you like dancing? You look like you'd be good at it.'

She loved dancing, knew all the latest dance tunes. But she wasn't sure she wanted to go to a social event with Finn. He was more than a bit cheeky, if you asked her.

Trouble was, he was really good company and as the days passed he made her laugh, cheering her up when she was feeling homesick, which he seemed to sense even though she tried to hide it. He had a little dimple at one corner of his mouth and she kept watching for it. But he was a thinking man, too, asking her about England, where he'd been stationed for a time during the war.

Without his company, she'd have gone mad.

But, occasionally, he stood too close and, for some reason, that set her pulse racing. She always moved away quickly, trying not to let him see how he'd affected her. She didn't intend to marry another servant, so it was no use starting anything—however attracted you were to a fellow.

Three weeks later, fed up with the isolation, she agreed to go to the church social.

Anything to get away from the homestead. And maybe she'd make some friends in Beeniup.

Her sister had been right: Gracie had made a mistake taking a job out in the country. But six months would soon pass and at least she'd save money. She kept reminding herself of that.

On the day of the church social, Gracie wore her best summer dress, calf-length in soft voile trimmed with lace. It was the same blue as her eyes.

Finn waited for her in the kitchen, looking very spruce in a dark suit and white shirt, his skin rosy and newly washed. He smelled of shaving soap and fresh air.

He let out a long, low whistle at the sight of her. 'We're in trouble,' he told Cook.

Gracie looked down at herself in puzzlement. 'What do you mean?'

'Mrs Gilsworth will have a fit when she sees you in that outfit.'

She studied herself in the mirror. 'What's wrong with it?'

'Nothing! But you look so pretty, she'll start worrying about you getting married. She's lost three maids that way in the past eighteen months.'

Flustered, Gracie picked up the small iced cakes Cook had prepared, because women had to take something for supper, it seemed. 'Well, are we going?'

'Your carriage awaits, madam.' He flourished a bow and opened the door.

Their eyes met and her heart skipped a beat. He was a *very* attractive fellow. But she wasn't getting tangled up with a servant. She wanted to escape from that.

At the doorway of the church hall she hesitated, suddenly nervous.

Finn smiled at her. 'Come on! I'll introduce you to a few people.' He led the way, nodding and smiling, seeming to know everyone.

He left her with two young women and she enjoyed chatting to them.

'You are lucky, working with Finn,' one said, sighing.

Before Gracie could ask why, the music started and fellows crowded round. There seemed to be twice as many young men as there were young women. She danced with three different fellows, enjoying the fuss and attention, even though none of them was a good dancer.

Finn elbowed another man aside as she came off the dance floor the third time. 'Fancy cooling down outside, Gracie?'

'That'd be lovely.'

As they walked out together she could see heads turn their way. 'Why is everyone staring?'

'Oh, they always watch newcomers.'

A few couples were strolling up and down the scruffy sunburned square of grass behind the hall. The night air was cool and the moonlight bright. Finn made her laugh and they stayed out there for two whole dances.

As they went back inside, he put one hand on his heart. 'May I ask you for a dance, Miss Bell?'

'Why certainly, kind sir.'

It was a waltz, her favourite, but being held closely by Finn made her feel breathless again. He was so tall, his teeth white in his suntanned face, his smile seemingly for her alone. He was a good dancer and she relaxed, letting him lead her round the small dance floor.

'Our steps match well, don't they?' he murmured as the waltz ended. 'Another dance?'

'That'd be lovely.'

Just before the supper break she went out to the lean-to at the back of the hall to powder her nose.

'You certainly didn't waste any time,' another girl said. 'Getting Finn for your fellow! I'd give a week's wages to have him smile at me like that.'

'*What?* He's not my fellow. We just work together.'

'But he took you walking outside. Round here, that's a sign you're courting.'

Fury sizzled through Gracie. The sneaky rat! She wasn't letting him get away with tricking her like that. If he wanted to court her, he had to ask her first. But surely—no, he couldn't really be trying to court her! Not so quickly.

She went back inside the hall, marched across to him and said loudly, 'I'm finished with you, Finn O'Connor! I never want to speak to you again.' Then she stormed off. She didn't look at him as she forced down a piece of cake that tasted like sawdust and chatted brightly to another young woman.

'What did Finn do to upset you?' the other whispered as Gracie discarded the empty plate.

'Never you mind. How can I get back to Fairgums without him? Does anyone else go that way?'

'No, and it's five miles!'

Gracie scowled across the hall at Finn, who grinned and winked at her. What a nerve! She elevated her nose and looked away.

When the dancing began again, she saw him start towards her and slipped outside. Grimly determined not to drive back with him, still furious at him for tricking her, she stood in the shadows, trying to think what to do. Five miles wasn't all that far, she decided. She'd walked five miles many a time. She didn't have a coat to retrieve, not in this heat, and was carrying her handbag. She'd pay for the empty plate out of her wages, if necessary.

Anger carried her along the one and only street of Beeniup at a cracking pace. Apart from the church and its adjacent hall, the town consisted of one general store, a place advertising stock feed and farm supplies, and seven houses. Most people lived out of town on farms, apparently, though she didn't call this a town, whatever the locals said!

She walked quickly along the road that led to the homestead.

A few minutes later she heard the sound of a car engine behind her and her heart began to pound. She looked round for somewhere to hide. But there were only open fields with wire fences, so she kept on walking, head held high.

Finn stopped the car. 'Get in, you idiot! There's no need for you to walk.'

She glared, arms akimbo. 'I'm not going anywhere with you from now on. How dare you make people think we're courting?'

He looked at her pleadingly. 'Because I knew if I didn't do something, the other blokes would be all over you. I could see the way they were looking at you and…well, I wanted you for myself.'

All the air seemed to vanish from the world. Gracie tried in vain to stay angry. Couldn't.

He stopped the engine and jumped down.

She couldn't move, not a step. In the moonlight, Finn looked rather like Douglas Fairbanks, her favourite film star. He was just as handsome. For a moment she wavered, swaying towards him, then she forced herself to turn and start walking again, afraid now of what she might do if he came too close.

He took her by surprise, scooping her up into his arms, laughing softly as she gasped.

'Let go of me!' She tried to sound angry, but couldn't. Of their own volition, her arms slid round his neck. It felt so romantic, so right.

'I'll never let you go,' he said as he set her down gently by the car, helped her inside and closed the door on her side. He got in but didn't start the engine, just stared ahead, fiddling with the steering wheel.

He surprised her again, asking very quietly, 'Am I so bad?'

'I…don't know what you mean.'

'If you say you don't fancy me, I'll stop pestering you, Gracie. Only…I thought we were getting on well. You're so pretty and lively, and…I can't stop thinking about you. All day you're in my thoughts. I walk past the kitchen a dozen times a day, just to catch sight of you.'

It was her turn to stare into the distance. No use denying it; they did get on well. And she did like him. But it was too soon. Far too soon. She hadn't known him a month.

He took her hand.

She should have pulled hers away but heat flooded through her body. He had such warm, capable hands, always busy, always fixing things. She loved to watch him working.

'Gracie?'

The way he said her name sent shivers through her body.

'You should have *asked* me before telling folk we were going steady, Finn.' She couldn't stop her voice wobbling.

'Yes, I should. I'm real sorry. Will you forgive me?'

She felt her anger fade. 'Perhaps.'

The silence was charged with tension. She didn't dare look at him.

'Can I kiss you?'

He didn't wait for an answer, but pulled her close and kissed her long and hard. No other man's kisses had sent such longings running through her. 'We Aussie blokes don't waste time when we want something. Soon as I saw you, Gracie, I knew.'

'Knew what?'

'That I wanted to marry you.'

'Oh. Oh, my goodness!' They took things more slowly where she'd grown up. A fellow courted a girl for months or even years before proposing. But…she'd not met a man like Finn in England. He was…special. And she wanted him to kiss her again, very much, could still taste him on her lips.

He raised her hand to his lips and kissed it gently. Even that made it hard for her to breathe properly. 'I've got plans for the future, you know, Gracie. I'm not staying a chauffeur for long.

Only I haven't said anything to the others because I don't want Mrs Gilsworth to know yet.'

Hope flared up in her. 'What are you planning to do?'

'Start my own garage. Not in Beeniup, in a bigger town. I'd do car and bicycle repairs, sell and repair tractors, sell a few cars and the petrol for them, too. Cars are the coming thing. One day every family will own one, not just rich people. Years I've been saving for my garage, all through the war. I'm nearly ready to get going now.'

She looked at him, thinking hard. Should she be as pushy as him? Yes, she had to be or she'd have to give up all her dreams.

'What about me?' she asked.

He frowned. 'What do you mean?'

'I don't want to be shut up in the house all day. Would there be a place for me to work in that garage of yours? I could...I could keep the accounts and sell the petrol, maybe sell other things, too. I worked on a motor omnibus during the war. I know quite a bit about motor vehicles already.'

'Most women wouldn't want to get their hands dirty. Most women would want the man to provide for them after they're married.'

'I'm not most women.'

A little line furrowed the middle of his forehead, then one of his wonderful smiles lit his face. 'No, you're not like anyone I've ever met. And yes, you can work with me. Until the children come along, anyway.'

'I don't want a lot of children, though I do want a family. But two or three would be plenty. It's no fun having babies, you know.'

Another of those considering looks, another nod. 'You're on.'

She gaped at him. Could it be that easy?

'Well? You haven't said yes yet, Gracie Bell.'

It was such an enormous step to take, she still hesitated. Could she just dive into marriage with a man she'd known less than a month? People would say she was mad. But it felt so right. And if you couldn't be mad on a moonlit night with the most handsome fellow you'd ever kissed proposing to you, when could you?

Excitement ran through her and something else, some elemental response to Finn the man, Finn who intended to make his fortune, Finn who wouldn't lock her away inside the house. She looked at him and took the biggest chance of her life. 'Yes.'

'You mean—you will marry me?'

'I just said yes, didn't I?'

That dimple appeared again. 'I didn't think it'd be so easy. It's the first time I've ever proposed to anyone, you see. I've been practising what to say out in the paddock, asking the cows what they thought.' He pulled her closer. 'I'll do my best to make you happy, Gracie, and—'

Something occurred to her suddenly and she couldn't help chuckling.

He broke off, staring at her in surprise. 'What are you laughing at?'

She put up one hand to caress his cheek. 'Not you, Finn. Never you.' She could feel him relax, see his smile return. 'I was thinking of poor Mrs Gilsworth.'

His grin showed his instant understanding and they spoke in a chorus.

'She'll have to find herself another maid.'

As he bent his head to kiss her again, she strained towards him eagerly, sure that the moonlight was brighter than it had ever been before, the night breeze softer and more richly perfumed—and her days as a housemaid numbered. What more could a young woman ask?

Nell Dixon

Nell Dixon lives in the Black Country with her husband, three daughters, a tank of tropical fish, a cactus called Spike and the remains of her sanity. She writes warm-hearted contemporary romance for Little Black Dress and Samhain Publishing. Her recent titles include *Things to Do, Blue Remembered Heels* and *Animal Instincts.* She was the 2007 winner of the RNA Romance Prize with *Marrying Max*. You can find out more by visiting her website at www.nelldixon.com

Wishing For George

'You're a *what?*' I tried to remember if I'd put the veg knife back in the block or if it was still on the counter behind me. Everything I'd ever seen in the movies had taught me that lunatics and knives weren't a good combo.

The woman scowled. 'I'm a fairy.'

'Oh-kay.' I thought it best to humour her. After all, she'd appeared in my kitchen unannounced while my back was turned and there were a lot of sharp implements lying around. I didn't want to star in a home movie slasher flick. 'Um, you don't look much like a fairy.'

She sniffed and adjusted the shopping bag that dangled from her chubby forearm. 'And you would be an expert on the appearance of fairies, would you?'

'Well…'

'I suppose you were thinking I'd look like bloody Tinkerbell? We're not all nine inches high.' She smoothed her orange rain mac over a substantial tummy. 'Anyway, let's get on with it, shall we?'

'Get on with what?' I watched with some alarm as she delved into her bag.

She rolled her eyes as if I was stupid. 'Your wish. Ah, here it is.' She fished out a twig.

'Wish?' I was going mad; I had to be hallucinating. A plump middle-aged woman was in my kitchen waving a bit of tree and claiming to be a fairy. If I was going to be mad, why couldn't I have hallucinated George Clooney?

I have a bit of a thing for George.

The woman gave a heavy sigh. 'Your wish. The one you made on the first day of spring at the municipal well on the seafront.'

I gaped at her.

'Well?' She sounded a touch exasperated.

'But, how did you know? This is a joke, isn't it?' I'd been set up. I looked around the kitchen, trying to spot the hidden camera. 'It's not a real wishing well.'

'Oh, and you're an expert on that, too, are you?' The woman pushed back her sleeves.

'I'm going mad. This is a dream.' A few weeks ago when I'd been dawdling along the seafront with nothing better to do, I'd lobbed fifty pence into the well and made some stupid wish about finding my true love. Now I'd been divorced for a couple of years, I'd been feeling a bit lonely. It would be nice to have a bit of company about the place again.

'Do I look like a dream? It's always the same with you humans.'

I couldn't help it—it must have been nerves or something—but I sniggered. It probably wasn't the best idea when I had a mad woman claiming to be a fairy and armed with a stick in my kitchen.

'When you've quite finished.' Her tone was icy.

'Sorry, what did you say your name was? It just sounds so incredible.'

The woman looked a little mollified by my apology. 'My name is Muriel.'

I bit my lip.

'We're not all called Blossom or Snowflake.'

'No, I suppose not.' I wasn't really in a position to comment, my mother having christened me Sylvia after a Dr Hook song. Thank heaven I wasn't born ten years later—I might have been lumbered with Madonna.

'Right, we'd better get started. Now, about your require-ments.' She tilted her head to one side and peered at me through her spectacles.

I decided I might as well play along. 'The usual, I suppose— tall, dark, handsome. I don't suppose you could get George Clooney?'

Well, if you don't ask, you don't get—or so my mother had always said.

'Not for fifty pence.' Muriel waved her stick and everything went a bit whooshy. Pinpricks of coloured light danced in front of my eyes and my ears gave a loud pop. The next thing I knew, we were in the middle of Tesco.

'How about him?' She pointed her twig at a dark-haired man pushing a trolley. I was impressed—he certainly looked the part. But then I realised his trolley was full of organic meat-free produce.

'I don't think I can be doing with all that soya and Quorn. I like a bacon buttie.'

Muriel sighed and waved her stick and we were off again. This time we arrived in PC World.

'What about that one?' Muriel indicated a tall man in a navy suit studying the label on a digital camera.

'Not bad,' I said, but then he moved. 'Oh, no, he's wearing white socks.'

Another wave of the twig and we disappeared somewhere else again. It went on all afternoon until I started to feel quite sick.

After I'd rejected number fifteen—on the grounds that he still lived with his mother and had an involuntary twitch—I sensed that Muriel had become a bit edgy.

'I can see why you're still single,' she muttered on our return to my kitchen.

I didn't like her tone. 'Well, you're the fairy. You're supposed to find my true love, not whoever happens to be wandering past.'

Muriel glared at me through her glasses. 'I'm doing my best.'

'You *have* done this before, haven't you?'

The embarrassing silence told its own tale.

'Normally my sister, Ethel, does this kind of thing, but she's in bed with flu so Queen Gertrude took me off my normal job to cover for her.'

That explained a lot. 'What is your normal job?'

'I'm a car park fairy,' Muriel announced proudly.

My blank expression must have been a giveaway.

'Hadn't you ever wondered how a space suddenly appears in a full car park, just when you need one?'

I couldn't say that I had, really.

'Well, that's me. It's a hard job—lots of pressure,' Muriel said.

'Look, I don't think this is going to work. Why don't you go back to Queen Gertrude and say I couldn't be suited? Then you can go and play with the traffic and I can go and lie down. All that whooshing about hasn't done me a bit of good.'

She didn't look impressed by my suggestion. 'Oh, I can't do that. It's against the rules. No fairy can leave a wish unfulfilled. Have you got a guest bed? Maybe we could try again tomorrow.'

I needed a drink and a lie down. 'What if I accept anyone? Would that work?'

Muriel tapped her stick thoughtfully against her palm. 'No. You asked for your true love so I have to get the right one. It's the rules, you see.'

I could see I was stuck with her. 'I'll make up a bed, then.'

★ ★ ★

I woke the next morning convinced I'd dreamt the whole thing, but when I got downstairs Muriel, the failed fairy cupid, was eating my cereal and watching breakfast TV.

'Perhaps we should try further afield today,' she said brightly as I slouched past her to make a cup of tea.

'How much further? I'm not good at languages.'

Muriel sighed and looked me up and down.

'What?' I'd showered and dressed before coming downstairs and my tracksuit and T-shirt looked perfectly clean and re-spectable. I mean, Muriel was hardly in a position to comment—she wore an orange mac, for heaven's sake.

'You don't think you may have your sights set a bit high?' She scooped the last of the Honey Nut Cheerios from her bowl.

'Listen, I made a wish to find my true love and you said you would find him.' She needn't get all hoity-toity with me. If she hadn't turned up yesterday I'd have been perfectly happy making a sponge cake and hoovering the fluff from between the cushions on my sofa. I wondered if Queen Gertrude had a com-plaints department.

Muriel had a strange look in her eyes. 'Your true love?'

'Yes!'

'Dark soulful eyes and gleaming dark hair?' She warmed to her theme.

Finally, she seemed to be getting what I wanted. 'Yes, that's it.'

'Who'd be devoted to you? Adore you?'

I nodded eagerly. Maybe George Clooney was a goer, after all. I allowed myself a little daydream, me lying recumbent on a couch in his Italian villa while he fed me grapes and hung on my every word. 'Perfect.'

Muriel set down her bowl. 'I know just where we need to go.'

I waited for the by now familiar whoosh and pop. Italy, here I come.

Someone nuzzled my cheek. I could barely open my eyes, I was so excited. A pair of dark brown eyes looked adoringly into mine.

A sweet little King Charles spaniel gave my face another loving lick.

'Meet George. Your true love,' said Muriel, and vanished.

Liz Fielding

Award-winning author Liz Fielding was born with itchy feet. She took herself off to Africa at the age of twenty, met her husband in Zambia, gave birth to her children on different continents and finally came to earth in a tiny village in West Wales. With more than fifty books in print she has been nominated for numerous awards, including the RITA, which she has won twice, and the Romantic Novelists' Association Romance Prize, which she won in 2005 with *A Family of Her Own*. In 2008 she received a Lifetime Achievement Award from *Romantic Times*. Recent titles include *Secret Baby, Surprise Parents* and *Christmas Angel for the Billionaire*. For more details visit her webpage at www.lizfielding.com

The Partnership Deal

Annie Latimer took the baby vest from the washing machine, held it for a moment to her cheek. Soft, sweet and dangerous. Just the kind of thing that made even the most sensible woman go wobbly at the knees. Rang the alarm on her biological clock. Made her stumble as she stepped up to the top rung of the professional ladder.

Fortunately, her twin sister had grabbed all the domesticity genes before the egg split; making it in a male-dominated corporate world where the words 'maternity leave' were professional suicide required a single-mindedness that left no time for biology.

She dropped the vest into the laundry basket. While Sarah had married the boy next door and set about populating the world single-handedly, Annie was a whisker away from the boardroom. Was the possessor of a designer wardrobe that was not permanently covered with baby spit. Owned a minimalist loft apartment overlooking the river with a full complement of electrical appliances—including the essential drier.

How Sarah, with three children under the age of six, managed without one was a mystery but she'd refused one, even as a gift.

There was being 'green' and then again, Annie thought, there was being an idiot, but while she and her sister were identical in appearance, they had always been chalk and cheese when it came to life choices.

Fortunately the sun was shining so she picked up the clothes basket and headed for the environmentally sound washing line in the back garden. Playing 'mummy' while her sister was having a well-deserved holiday in the sun, courtesy of the company whose organic baby cereal adorned her clothes on a regular basis, having *completed the following sentence in ten words or less...*

Not that it had been easy to shoehorn her sister out of her domestic rut. 'Who,' Sarah had asked, her big blue eyes twin pools of innocence, 'can I possibly entrust with my three precious children for eight whole days?'

Annie knew she'd walked right into that one and took it on the chin like the sucker she was, waving her sister and brother-in-law off for a much needed holiday—one they were no doubt even now using to create yet another little replica of themselves.

Fortunately, modern technology meant that she was as good as in her office even when up to her elbows in laundry.

Right now baby George was asleep under a net in the shade. Molly, three years old, copper curls and a smile as sweet as sugar, was eager to help with the pegs and Jack, just turned five, was kicking a football into his mini goal net.

Her cellphone was in her pocket.

Her wireless laptop connected permanently to the internet.

All was well with the world.

'Blue peggie,' Molly said, holding up a pink peg.

'*Pink,* sweetie. It's a *pink* peggie...peg,' she corrected herself hurriedly. She cringed when her sister used baby talk. It had never occurred to her that it was contagious.

'Blue peggie,' Molly said again, this time holding up another pink peg.

'*Pink,* Molly.' She bent down, took another peg from the basket. 'This one is blue.' She jerked around as a screech of tyres from the far side of her sister's dense hedge shattered the peace of the morning, heart in mouth as she waited for the crash.

But there was no crash, no rending of metal, no cry for help and after a moment she let out her breath and smiled reassuringly at Molly. She hated loud noises. 'Just some dumb man driving too fast,' she said.

Molly gave her a wobbly smile. 'Pink peggie.'

'That's right!' Annie pegged up a tiny pair of dungarees. 'Pink peggie, blue dungarees.'

Realising that she hadn't heard Jack's repeated cry of 'Goal!' for a minute or two, she half turned to check what he was doing but was distracted by the sound of a car door slamming, a man's raised voice from the far side of the hedge. A very angry man, if the words 'stupid', 'idiot' and 'fool' were anything to go by. Maybe he'd scratched his precious car.

Serve him right for speeding...

Remembering her nephew, she looked around. He'd already given her several bad moments with his disappearing acts before popping up out of nowhere. She couldn't see him.

Calm, she thought. Calm. Nothing could have happened. The side gate was safely shut.

'Jack!' she called again, louder, as she picked up Molly, heart thudding.

She hadn't taken more than a step before the gate was flung open by one of those tall, dark and impossibly handsome men you read about in romances but never seem to encounter in real life. Or if you do they're married and, truthfully, if they weren't you'd have to wonder why.

Tall, dark but, in this instance, scowling.

He was holding Jack under one arm and Jack's football under the other. The football was flat and Jack was trying very hard not to cry.

'Jack!' Then, 'What do you think you're doing?' she demanded, flying across the lawn in full protective mode. Matching TDH's scowl and raising him a glare.

'What am *I* doing?' he demanded, countering her outrage with downright fury. 'What were *you* doing, allowing a child to run out into a busy road? It's a miracle he wasn't killed!'

'It's not busy!' At least it hadn't been until they'd used it as a diversion around the roadworks.

His lip curled with disapproval and he was right. There was no excuse.

Molly began to whimper into her shoulder. 'Shh, precious,' she cooed into her curls. 'No one's angry with you.' Then, reasonably, quietly as if she were talking to a dangerous animal, she held out her hand and said, 'Please, just put him down.'

The man looked at her for what seemed like forever before lowering him, gently, to the ground. Jack instantly scuttled behind her, where she could feel his little body trembling against her leg. Or maybe it was her leg that was trembling.

'What did you do to him?' she demanded, but didn't wait for his answer. She knew. She'd heard him. 'You shouted at him, didn't you?'

'Of course I shouted. Anyone would have shouted—'

'He's just a little boy!'

'He shot out in front of my car. I thought I'd killed him!'

'You hit him!' she exclaimed, her hand flying to her mouth.

'No, I damn well didn't hit him, but it was no thanks to him. Or you!'

'Mind your language,' she said, by now glaring for England, even while she checked Jack over for damage. There were no obvious injuries, apart from a scraped knee, but you couldn't be too careful. Maybe she should run him up to Casualty to be on the safe side...

'I didn't hit him,' the man repeated, this time minus the expletive, but through firmly gritted teeth. 'I think he might have tripped over the kerb.'

'So?' she demanded, noticing what very good teeth they were. Handsome was an optional extra in men, a bonus, but good teeth were non-negotiable. Not that it mattered... 'You decided to make up for your omission by shouting at him?'

'I hit this,' he said. He offered her the flattened football and Annie let slip a word that was far worse than the one he'd used.

Annie knew exactly why he'd shouted. Why, fear-fuelled, she was shouting back. It was just a flattened football but it could so easily have been Jack's head...

Jack's head crushed beyond repair.

And she'd be the one to blame. Responsible. Have to face her sister. Have to live with it for the rest of her life. As would he...

'But I wasn't yelling at the boy. I was yelling at whoever was stupid enough to allow a child this young to play in the road. With a ball,' he added, derision battling with anger and coming out about even.

A wave of faintness swept over her and she put out a hand to steady herself on the gate but it swung away from her and it was TDH who caught her, his broad chest stopping her from falling on her face and taking Molly with her.

'It's okay,' he said, rather more gently.

'No... No, it's not. You don't understand—'

'I understand that you've had a shock. You should sit down.'

'Y-yes,' she said, shivering against him, actually grateful for a pair of strong arms. 'I'm so s-sorry...' Then making a determined effort to pull herself together. If her male colleagues could see her now they'd never take her seriously again. 'Truly,' she said more firmly, easing away. 'It must have been a shock for you...' Her apology faltered as she spotted the beige smear that had appeared on his immaculate shirt front. Baby cereal. It got everywhere, including her hair. She should own up, offer to sponge it off. In the circumstances, it was the least she could do. 'I'm sorry...' she began again, then stopped, horrified.

After a mere twenty-four hours of playing mummy, Annie Latimer, the ice-cool corporate lawyer with boardroom ambitions, was morphing into her mother. Her brain softened by an excess of domesticity. Falling headlong into the tender trap.

She needed to get back to her laptop. Check on the progress of the takeover bid, launched at start of business today. Find out what the City was making of it.

Pulling herself firmly together, she offered her hand. 'I'm Annie Latimer.'

'James Carpenter,' he replied, taking it. Nice name. Solid, dependable. Good handshake. Cool, capable hand.

'Thank you, James Carpenter.'

'You're welcome, Annie Latimer.'

For a moment they stood there, hand in hand. He was the first to let go.

'I don't understand how Jack could have got out,' she said quickly, to cover the unexpected hollowness of her empty hand.

He shook his head impatiently, clearly unimpressed by her understanding on every level. 'Is there anyone here? Someone to make you a cup of tea? You've had a shock.'

She resisted the temptation to throw another little wobbly. 'No... No, I'll be fine, really.' Then, having declined the 'pathetic little woman' role, said, 'But you've had a shock, too. I should be offering you the traditional hot sweet tea.'

First aid was a duty, she told herself.

For a moment she thought he was going to accept, but then he took a step back, as if deliberately distancing himself.

'All I want is a promise that you'll keep your child under control and your gate shut.'

Her child? 'No…' Then, furiously, 'Do you think I'm totally irresponsible? The gate was shut!' Actually, the hot sweet tea might not be such a bad idea after all, but in the meantime she took a steadying breath and repeated, 'The gate was shut and Jack can't reach the catch. Show him, Jack,' she urged, because for some reason it was desperately important that she convince him she wasn't some irresponsible female who'd let a child run into the street.

Or maybe she just needed to convince herself.

Jack knew he was in trouble and didn't argue. Instead, he sidled towards the shoulder-high gate, keeping as far from James Carpenter as possible. Even on tiptoe his small hand was a good ten centimetres short of the catch.

James Carpenter was not convinced. 'Maybe he doesn't need to reach the catch,' he said. 'Maybe the catch is as useless as you are because, whether you want to believe it or not, he chased this ball into the road.'

'I bought it for his birthday,' she said, staring at the remains of the football he was still holding. As if it were important.

Stupid…

That was what he'd said and he was right because, protest as she might, Jack had got into the road. Right beneath her nose. All that had saved him was this man's attention to the road, and his sharp reflexes.

Before she could thank him again, he handed her the remains of the football and said, none too gently, 'If he's going to see another birthday, I suggest you get your husband to fit a child-proof lock on to this gate and check out the fences when he gets home. Jack got out somehow.'

'Good plan. If I had a husband,' she said as he snapped the gate firmly shut behind him so that only his head and shoulders were visible.

On the point of turning away, he paused, staring at her for the longest moment and Annie suddenly became intensely aware of the baby drool and sticky fingermarks on her T-shirt. None of which had seemed to matter much five minutes ago.

'You're on your own?' he asked finally.

Before she could answer, the baby began to wail from his shady corner and she managed a wry smile. 'Not exactly,' she said.

Since he seemed, finally, to be lost for words it was probably just as well that the cellphone in her pocket began to ring. She didn't answer it, even though she was waiting for a call from the office, but, taking it as his cue to leave, he nodded curtly and walked away.

Still she didn't answer her phone, for once leaving the message service to pick up the call, and a second or two later she heard the soft clunk of a car door, the murmur of an expensive engine and, unable to help herself, she peered over the gate just in time to catch the tail end of something very desirable in silver disappearing around the corner. Driven by something equally desirable in Italian tailoring, the beige smear on his snowy shirt lending a touch of humanity that made him more, rather than less, attractive.

She couldn't have sworn that her wobbly knees were entirely due to her nephew's close call.

How shallow was that?

Pulling herself together, she cleaned up the graze on Jack's knee and stuck on a giant-sized dressing, then checked him over for any other damage. Once she was happy that he'd come to no real harm, she changed the baby, a task which, God bless her environmentally responsible sister, involved terry towelling, pins and a degree in origami.

Then, and only then, when she'd made herself a very necessary cup of hot sweet tea, did she check her voicemail. The call was not from the office, but from her sister, putting in a dawn call from the Caribbean to check on her precious chicks.

'Sarah, sorry,' she said. 'I was wrestling with a nappy when you rang.'

'You didn't rush out and stock up on disposables the moment I left the country, then?'

'Would I dare? So what are you doing phoning home when you should be making the most of the sun?'

'I just wanted to check that you were coping.'

'You just wanted to check that your children survived the night. Here, talk to them yourself. It's Mummy, Jack. Say hello,' she said, passing over the phone as if it were red-hot.

'Hello, Mummy…' He listened for a moment, then said, 'I've got a plaster on my knee and Aunt Annie yelled at a man because he said "damn" and then she said a really bad word and then…'

Annie quickly grabbed the phone and passed it to Molly. 'Say hello to Mummy, Moll.'

'Hello, Mummy. I helped Aunt Annie peg out the washing today with pink peggies, then the man shouted and I cried.' She listened for a moment, then held up the phone. 'You now,' she said.

Annie groaned, but her sister was laughing. 'Tell me about the man who said "damn".'

'He was a double glazing salesman,' she said—the first thing that came into her head. 'I got baby cereal on his nice clean shirt.' It wasn't a lie, exactly. For all she knew, he *was* a double glazing salesman. A very successful one if his chosen method of transport was anything to go by.

'You got *that* close to a double glazing salesman?' Sarah asked. 'Tell me more.'

'It was nothing. Jack hasn't got more than a scratch on his knee, by the way,' she went on quickly. 'I did the whole Florence Nightingale bit. You'd have been proud.'

James Carpenter was having a very bad day. That child on the road…

His blood ran cold; he just kept seeing it over and over. It had felt like years until the brakes bit. Had he been jet-lagged? Distracted by a diversion that had taken him through an unfamiliar area? Or by the sudden launch of a takeover bid that had come out of nowhere? Like that boy.

He'd just dived beneath his wheels…and when he'd gone over that ball… Not that there was any excuse for shouting at the boy the way he had. He was too young to know better. Unlike his mother.

He didn't know whether to be angry with her, feel sorry for her or…

'Mr Carpenter?'

He looked up to discover his new PA standing in front of him, as if waiting for an answer to a question that he hadn't heard.

'Sorry, Emma, I was miles away.'

In a garden with a tigress defending her cubs. A vulnerable tigress with large blue eyes, dark red hair. A slightly dishevelled, very lovely, very domesticated tigress.

With three young children.

'I'm going out for coffee. Can I bring you something? A sandwich? Doughnut? Coffee?' She paused. 'A new shirt?'

'What?'

He glanced down, saw the smear on his shirt pocket, rubbed at it.

'It looks like baby cereal,' Emma said thoughtfully.

His hand stilled over the mark, over his pounding heart. Remembering how she'd felt against him as he'd caught her, held her, when she'd stumbled forward as her legs had given way. How she'd clung to him.

Until that moment he'd been almost blind with rage at her, at himself, but then he'd been holding her, breathing in the scent of clean laundry, fresh air and everything else had gone out of his head.

Or maybe he'd lost his head the moment he saw her.

Then she'd made an effort to pull herself together, stepped back and he'd seen the tiny miniature of her lying against her shoulder. The same blue eyes, copper curls a brighter version of her mother's sleek cinnamon hair. And he'd crashed back to earth, desperate only to get away.

And then she'd said that thing about not having a husband.

Was she a widow? Separated? With three small children. It must be a fairly recent split because the baby he'd heard crying couldn't have been very old...

He caught the questioning lift of Emma's brow.

'If it's baby cereal it won't come off without the full laundry experience,' she assured him. 'Believe me. I've been there. And you do have a board meeting in less than an hour.'

'Yes.' Not the day to look less than one hundred per cent in control. 'White. Collar size sixteen. Thanks.'

'What's going to happen?' she asked.

'About the takeover?' No doubt she was worried about her job. 'They couldn't have timed it better, could they?' he said. He'd only returned from the US twenty-four hours ago. Hadn't planned to be in the office until next week. 'I need information. Everything you can find. Send someone else out for the coffee.' Then, 'Emma...' She waited. 'I need a football, too.'

'A football,' she repeated without expression.

'For a small boy. About this big,' he said, holding out his hand to indicate Jack's height. 'And a childproof bolt. For a gate.'

'A football and a bolt. Right. And coffee?'

'Make it tea,' he said. 'With plenty of sugar.'

James Carpenter. The name lingered, but Annie didn't have to Google his name to find out more. She'd logged on to the financial pages to follow the news on the takeover and right at the top was a link that made her mouth go dry.

She clicked on it, hoping, praying... But God clearly had more pressing matters to attend to, because there he was, on her screen. James Francis Carpenter had flown in from the United States to step into his uncle's shoes. Take over as CEO.

If she'd had any doubts it was the same man, there was a photograph of him. For the second time that day she let slip a really bad word.

It had been perfect. A company with a great record, talented staff, but weakened by the ill health of its founder, a man who'd been too stubborn to quit, too well respected to be forced out. It had been a perfect match for her own company, which had raced ahead of itself and was long on contracts, short on high quality software engineers. She'd put together the plan, taken it to the board and, if the takeover went well, her own career would soar.

If not...

Nothing was going to go wrong.

This made no difference, she told herself. James Carpenter might be the cavalry, but he was too late. When they next met it would be across the boardroom table. And, instead of wanting to hold her hand a moment too long, he wouldn't want to know her.

It had been a long, hard day. James had spent most of it chasing down information and, in the meantime, putting his own coun-termoves into action. Now he wanted nothing more than a hot shower and something to eat, he thought, as he pulled up outside the tidy suburban house. It was late and there were already lights on inside, but there was enough light to do what he'd come for.

Annie had finally settled the children. Who knew it would take so long to put three small children to bed? Read stories. Clear up the bathroom. She was exhausted. And, despite a 'high-five' update from the office, where they'd been shovelling up shares as fast as they came on the market, a niggling little voice in the back of her head kept telling her she was in trouble.

That James Carpenter was going to be a very different kettle of fish to his uncle. She kept remembering the fleeting impression of strength, capability. Gorgeousness.

Forget gorgeous. This was business. She gathered up dirty clothes and towels, promising herself a relaxing bath the minute she'd set the washing machine going.

She'd just made it to the bottom of the stairs when the front doorbell rang and, tucking the washing beneath one arm, she opened it and found herself face to face with the man who'd dominated her thoughts all day.

James Francis Carpenter.

Her mouth opened, but nothing came out and he held up the bag he was carrying. 'I brought Jack a replacement for his football. And a lock for the gate.'

'You did?' Her voice was little more than a squeak. Guilt would do that to you. Not that she had anything to feel guilty about. 'That's…um…really kind.'

'If you've got a drill, I'll fix it now.'

Annie swallowed, tucked a damp strand of hair behind her ear and said, 'Actually, Jack confessed that there's a gap in the hedge. Apparently it's not the first time he's kicked his ball into the road.'

'It's going to be a chicken-wire job, then?'

'It's covered,' she said.

'You've got someone who does these jobs for you?'

'My brother-in-law is king of the DIYers.' Then, although her head was telling her to say thank-you-and-goodnight, her heart wasn't listening, she said, 'Can I offer you that cup of tea now?'

'I was really hoping you'd say that.' He smiled and Annie's knees went down for the second time that day.

'I'll…um…just get rid of this.' Indicating the armful of washing, she led the way through to the kitchen, flinching as she saw it through his eyes. Not that it was awful. Just…lived-in.

Unlike the pristine slate and stainless steel of her own kitchen. Preparing ready-meals for one didn't make a place looked lived-in. A home.

Maybe she hadn't entirely escaped the domesticity genes after all. Or maybe the alarm on her biological clock had just woken her up to the fact that a top of the range drier couldn't love you back.

Tough, she thought. You can't have it all. Then caught her breath as James crossed to the kettle.

'What are you doing?' she demanded.

He glanced at her, then at the kettle, then back at her. 'Making a cup of tea?'

'But you can't… I didn't…'

'Actually, I can. My mother had a demanding job and taught us to be self-sufficient. And you've got your hands full with the washing.'

'Us? How many of you are there?'

'I've three sisters and a brother.'

'And your mother had time for a career, too? What did— does she do?'

'She's an investment banker.'

'Good grief.'

'You're surprised?'

'Not that she's an investment banker. That she managed to hold down a full-time job and produce five children.'

'According to her, it was simply a question of good organisation. Where do you keep your teabags?'

'Oh, there aren't any teabags. My sister…'

Oh, help!

'Your sister?' he prompted.

'My sister composts for England,' she said. 'Any particular kind? Of tea?'

'Something strong, I think. It's been that kind of day. Assam?'

'No problem.' Then, 'About this morning. I never thanked you properly—'

'It wasn't just Jack's adventure. It's been a rough first day in my new job.'

'Rough?'

Her fault on all counts.

He shook his head. 'It's nothing I can't handle. What about you, Annie? You have a sister. Is that all?'

Relief that he'd changed the subject warred with a desperation to know what he was thinking. What he was planning. Relief won. She wanted to forget business while she could. Just be herself.

Except that being herself meant being his enemy.

'Just one sister,' she said. 'Sarah.' Then, 'Tell me about your new job.' Unable to look him in the eye, she busied herself with the milk.

'I've just taken over an IT company. It's a family business,' he said. 'My uncle started it back in the sixties.' And suddenly he was talking. How his uncle had started a software company in his father's garage back in the early days of the IT revolution.

How the company had grown, become a world leader in its field, writing programs for communications satellites, expanding into security software that wasn't available on a disk at the local computer supermarket.

She knew all this, but not the way he told it. With passion. Pride.

'My own field is finance and I've been in the States, the Far East, Japan for the last few years but when Uncle William had a heart attack last year he asked me to take over.' He shrugged. 'He recognised it was a different world. That software engineers don't make the best CEOs.' He shook his head, staring into the empty cup he was holding. 'It took me a while to wind up my own affairs and now the sharks are circling, scenting blood. Today another company launched a takeover bid—'

'James… Please.' She couldn't bear it. 'Please. Don't say any more.'

He stopped. Looked up.

'I'm the shark,' she said.

He didn't exclaim with horror. Didn't do anything. Just waited.

'You said it, James. Your uncle's company—your company had lost its edge. You have a terrific R&D team, a great client list, but something was missing. It was rudderless.'

Until today.

'And your company needs to expand,' he said. 'You've got the financial backing, the international contacts, a severe lack of a quality product.'

She nodded, relieved that he understood. 'I saw the possibilities, took it to my board. If I succeeded I would be a director by the time I was thirty…'

She broke off.

He knew.

His visit tonight had nothing to do with locks or footballs—

'How did you find out it was me, James?'

'I did what you'd have done in my shoes, Annie. I spent the day getting to know my enemy and found myself looking at a photograph of Anne Latimer. A talented and ambitious young corporate lawyer with red hair, blue eyes and a twin sister called Sarah. A sister who has three children. Jack, Molly and George.'

'How on earth—'

'There was a feature on you in the women's pages of one of the broadsheets.'

'Oh…yes. So why did you come here? Clearly it wasn't to fix my sister's gate.'

'On the contrary. I'd already bought the football and the lock and I didn't have any other use for them.'

'Really?' She discovered she was smiling. He'd known and he'd come anyway.

'And then, well, I saw what you saw. You're right, Annie, we're a perfect match, and my first thought was to make a counter-bid. Go after you. Make you sorry you'd messed with me.'

She swallowed.

'But then I had a better idea. Why waste time and money fighting each other?' He tucked a loose strand of damp hair behind her ear. 'It's a perfect partnership, Annie Latimer. We are a perfect fit. So I was wondering whether you'd consider a merger?'

'A merger?' The words were like cotton wool in her throat.

'Your company, my company?'

Of course. What else could he possibly mean?

Then, while her heart was unaccountably plummeting to her boots, he leaned in to her and said, 'You and me.' He didn't wait for her answer, but closed the connection, kissing her slowly, thoroughly, taking all the time in the world to demonstrate his commitment.

She had to admit he made a convincing case...

After what seemed like an age, he drew back an inch and asked, 'Do we have a deal?'

She smiled. 'I think we need to negotiate some more,' she said, and—because she believed in equal partnerships—she put her arms around his neck and kissed him back.

Anita Burgh

Anita Burgh was born in Kent. She began to write in her late forties and was first published at the age of fifty. She has subsequently had twenty-three novels published, numerous articles and short stories. Her themes are those of class, rejection and wealth. She writes books set in the modern world but also historical novels set in Victorian and Edwardian times—her latest being *The Cresswell Inheritance* trilogy. She has been a member of the RNA for many years, was a committee member and has been short-listed for the RNA Romantic Novel of the Year award. Now in her seventies, she enjoys teaching and mentoring others who are, as yet, unpublished. She continues to write novels, proving that authors never retire. For more information about Anita and her writing visit www.anitaburgh.com

Rose Cottage

Rosie Milner, like most expatriates, had long held the dream of the thatched English cottage she would one day own. It would, of course, have overgrown roses round the door, lattice windows and a garden packed with flowers. A chocolate box of a cottage…

Dreams were one thing, reality another. Such cottages existed but, it appeared, were rarely for sale. And then one day the details of Rose Cottage arrived at her London flat. It was in the right part of the country, the right period, it had an inglenook and its name boded well.

Upon viewing it, Rosie found it was far from idyllic.

The thatch of the roof had been replaced by corrugated iron. The roses which climbed over the front had been neglected. The windows were nineteen-fifties metal and the garden was obviously the fly tip for the rest of the village.

It would be difficult to say who was the more surprised, she or the agent, when, within five minutes' inspection, she offered the asking price. She simply could not help herself. She wanted it, she felt drawn to it and she felt she knew it, she was truly home—it was as simple as that.

The agent was apologetic; her offer would not be accepted for it was to be sold by sealed bids and the competition was keen. He suggested she get some estimates for the work needed and introduced her to a builder he knew, Keith Johnston. She had found a gem since he understood exactly what she wanted to do and was in total accord with her plans.

The wait was agonising. But it was her bid which was accepted—no doubt helped by the fact that she eventually offered thousands over the starting price…

'You realise you're certifiable?' Andrew, her fiancé, pronounced.

'It's got potential.'

'There's no bathroom.'

'There will be.'

'And what's that odd smell?'

'It's not odd. It reminds me of sandalwood. My father's after-shave smelt like that.'

'The kitchen looks a health hazard.'

'I'm having it gutted.'

'There's not one room I can stand up in, the ceilings are too low.' It was true, at over six feet he had to stoop. 'If you ask me, you're wasting your money.'

'But I'm not asking you, am I?' He looked surprised at her tone. But she felt fiercely protective towards the cottage.

'Well, don't expect me to come and stay.'

Surely she should not be feeling such a sense of relief at his words? She kissed him to reassure herself.

Builders, she decided, lived in a parallel universe with a different timescale to her own. The delays were many. Frustrated with the hold-ups, Rosie, much to Andrew's disapproval, decided to camp at the cottage to get things moving. That was what she had hoped—it did not transpire. Keith, she soon realised, was not tardy, he was a perfectionist.

'If you're lucky enough to own a gem like this then you owe it to restore it flawlessly.'

'I couldn't agree more. I just wish perfection didn't take so long.'

Keith chose to ignore her dig and continued to fit the new wooden window frames she'd had made at great expense.

The villagers were like all others she had met—curious. Having lived in the countryside before, she knew not to mistake this curiosity for friendship; she was fully aware that it would take time to develop—if ever. They were not forthcoming about her cottage. In fact, if mentioned, they abruptly changed the subject. Philly Potts, another newcomer who had lived here a mere fifteen years, was more open. Apparently the cottage had been empty for thirty years. 'Do you know why?' Rosie asked.

'It was all very strange. It belonged to an old lady, a Mrs Johnston—her son had lived here but, when he died, she shut it up and refused to sell. When she passed on, her family needed money—or so I've heard. They are a strange lot, that Johnston family…' Philly imparted this information with relish but refused to be pressed further.

'Keith, I was told today that a Johnston lived here. That's the same name as you.'

'It's common in these parts,' was his cryptic reply, and why he should look shifty was puzzling.

Surprises were coming thick and fast. Rosie discovered from an indiscretion by the estate agent that, rather than paying over the odds, her bid had been second to lowest. 'Then why did they accept my offer?' she asked the flustered agent.

'Perhaps they took a shine to you.'

'But I never met anyone who owned it…'

Andrew was equally unhelpful. 'There's one born every minute,' was his only comment on her good fortune.

Why her? It began to bother her. And there was more. If she asked in the village, no one knew anything significant about the building. She didn't believe them; they knew something.

'Why not go to the local paper? See what the archive says,' Andrew finally suggested.

Once there, she wished she hadn't searched. It was a sad history she uncovered. Thirty years ago, the year of her birth, the owner of Rose Cottage, a Jason Johnston, was about to be wed when, two days before the ceremony, his fiancée was drowned when the local river broke its banks. Crazed with grief, he had hanged himself here at the cottage. It made a shiver go down her spine.

'Not that I've felt anything creepy,' she told Keith. 'No ghosts.'

'Then no harm's done.' Keith was concentrating on pointing the inglenook.

'He must have loved her deeply, don't you think? No one would top themselves over me.'

'I'm sure they would. If they loved you enough,' Keith replied.

Keith's remark made her think. Should anything happen to either Andrew or herself, would their lives be blighted? She came to the sorry conclusion that they wouldn't, let alone be so sad as to commit suicide.

Andrew was true to his word and still refused to visit. 'I'm not the bucolic type,' he'd explained. So every other weekend she went to London to see him. It did not take her long to realise he was angry with her for *'wasting'* her money on such a *'hovel'*.

'I'm sorry you don't understand, Andrew. I love it. There's something about the place. I feel so at home there. And some-times of an evening when I'm quiet and reading, I feel a calmness and happiness which is new to me.' She was not about to tell him that at times like that the smell of sandalwood was at its stron-gest—he'd think her loopy. Nor would she confess that she looked forward to it and was disappointed those evenings when the scent did not materialise.

'Sentimental rubbish.'

'Why do you always put me down?'

'I don't think I do. You're becoming obsessed with the place, that's the problem. It's as if it has a hold over you.'

'Now who's talking rubbish?'

On the drive home she fretted over the evening's events. She reached the conclusion that they were becoming incompatible. She also realised that she felt a deep sense of relief.

In the evening, when Keith had left, she found she could not get the thought of the hanged man out of her mind. She would wonder where he had *done* it; although it was probably better she did not know. Strangely, she felt no fear. She wanted to find out more; she wanted to see what he'd looked like.

The editor of the local newspaper was a friendly soul and, she found, interested in the case.

'I was a cub reporter at the time; I remember it well. A fine couple they made.'

'You knew him?'

'Not well. But our paths sometimes crossed.' And he began to burrow amongst the piles of yellowed newspapers—the fiche, just her luck, was broken.

With the report of Jason's suicide was a photograph. He was shorter than Andrew, so the ceiling would not have mattered. He was better-looking than him, fine-featured—it was a sensitive face. He'd been a poet. The editor had a copy of his work.

They were not very good poems, but touching, most of them about Rosemary and their love—what a coincidence that she had the same name even though she never used it…

She became curious about Rosemary.

The editor delved back into the piles of yellowing newspapers. 'Here we are. I knew we published one at the time of her inquest. Dreadful floods that year.'

The face that looked back at her was pretty. She was dark-haired and it looked as if her eyes were grey, but from the newsprint it was difficult to see for sure. Kindly, the editor had copies made for her.

'She died on my birthday—isn't that creepy?' she told Keith the next day as she showed him the photo.

'Well, she had to die on somebody's birthday,' he said with unimpeachable logic. He peered at the photo. 'Pretty little thing—she's got grey eyes, just like you.'

'I wouldn't mind looking like her. Weird fashions, aren't they? Just look at those platform shoes!'

The worst thing, she decided, was that from this tragedy she was learning how impoverished her own relationship was. She broke off the engagement.

Andrew was beside himself. For a very short moment she hoped it was with heartache but she soon realised it was with hurt pride.

Should she have felt guilt? She didn't. If she was honest, this was the happiest she had ever been. Alone in her cottage, with just Jason for company.

'What, you mean it's haunted? I thought you said it wasn't,' Keith responded when she told him.

'No, silly. I don't believe in ghosts. No, I've decided to write a book with Jason as the hero—it is so romantic.'

'Novels should have happy endings, not miserable ones.'

'Maybe I'll change it, then.'

Thoughts of Jason filled her days. As the novel progressed, she felt she was beginning to know him more each day. She liked him. In fact, she would go so far as to say she was falling in love with him—she wondered if other authors felt like this or was she odd? Strange things were beginning to happen—she could write whole pages and sometimes she could not remember writing them; it was as if someone was writing for her. She liked to think it was Jason.

Then he began to appear in her dreams. At first it was just fleeting, but then he took a stronger and stronger role. The best night of all was when he kissed her. And in her dreams the smell of sandalwood was always present.

The first night they made love it was so real that when she awoke it was to search for him in her bed and when she found he was not there she wept.

Now she rarely went out. She did not need company—she had Jason. She would hold conversations with him, convincing herself she heard his voice. They might be dreams but they were of such intensity that she felt he was alive, that he had just popped out and would return soon. So she could not be away from her cottage for a minute in case he chose this day to come...

She waited with eager anticipation for the scent of sandalwood—it was him, she was convinced. When she smelt it she knew he was there.

'You ought to get out more, you look so pale.' Keith, the work now complete, had popped in to see how she was.

'I don't feel the need.'

'You'll go batty on your own. It's your birthday tomorrow. Let me take you out for a drink.'

'How did you know that?'

'You told me. Remember when you told me Rosemary died on your birthday?'

'Better you come here—I've got some champagne.'

She watched him as he walked down the path. He was rather good-looking, despite being fifty if he was a day.

Pity he wasn't Jason.

Keith arrived at seven on her birthday, as arranged. There was no response to his knock. He went round the back and let himself in. 'Anyone home?' he called.

He found her in the newly decorated sitting room. She was sitting in her favourite wing chair, a contented look on her face. Beside her were two glasses and an empty champagne bottle.

'Sorry I'm a few minutes late.'

She did not reply; she couldn't. She was dead.

Scrawled on the surface of the mirror on the wall was the one word. 'Rose.'

'Came to get her, did you, brother? I thought you might,' he said to the room, where the smell of sandalwood swirled about him.

The minute he'd set eyes on her he had known she was the one. He'd never liked to tell her that she was the dead spit of Rosemary, who had died the day she was born, and that Jason had always called her Rose. There'd be no point frightening her.

The doctors would no doubt say it was a heart attack, but Keith knew better.

Joanna Maitland

Joanna Maitland is a Scot living in England, just a few miles from the Welsh border. She loves having access to the history of three countries as background for the Regency historical romances she writes for Harlequin Mills & Boon. There are eleven so far, taking the reader to Regency England and Scotland, and to glittering European cities like Paris and St Petersburg.

The Aikenhead Honours, Joanna's recent trilogy, features the intrigues of the Russian Emperor's visit to London in 1814 *(His Cavalry Lady),* spies at the Congress of Vienna *(His Reluctant Mistress),* and the hazards of the Hundred Days in France, prior to the battle of Waterloo in 1815 *(His Forbidden Liaison).* There's also a follow-up e-book, *His Silken Seduction,* available from www.millsandboon.co.uk

Details of Joanna's books are available on her website at www.joannamaitland.com

This story is dedicated to fellow author and friend, Kate Lace.

The Trophy Hunter's Prize

June 1814

After the searing brilliance of India, London seemed subdued, like a watercolour by a novice artist who had mixed his paints too thin. Andrew Mortimer shivered a little, in spite of the summer sunshine.

He straightened his elegant new coat and strode down Piccadilly towards the park, where there should be open space and fresher air to breathe. Before long, however, the crowds slowed him almost to a standstill. Yet they seemed good-humoured. With a nod here and a word of excuse there, he might make his way through.

''Ere! Wot d'you think y're doing?' cried a large florid woman when he tried to edge past. She looked him up and down, noting the expensive clothes and the unusually brown skin. 'Fur-riners,' she muttered darkly. 'Never did 'ave no manners.'

Still, she had made a little space for him to pass. Andrew managed to reach up to touch his hat and said, in his most affected

English drawl, 'Why, thank you, ma'am. Most kind.' The woman's jaw dropped. Very satisfying.

He had gone only a few yards further when he was forced to stop altogether. The huge crowd seemed to draw breath as one, then it let out an ear-splitting roar and surged forward towards the Pulteney Hotel, carrying Andrew along. He had to put all his efforts into keeping his balance. When he was at last able to look about him, he saw that the Tsar of Russia had appeared on the hotel balcony above them. And, not three yards from where Andrew stood, a small figure in a pale dress was being trampled in the crush.

He yelled a warning. No one seemed to hear. He flung himself at the men who barred his path. He shouted at them. No reaction. There was just too much noise. As he pushed and pushed, his mouth came close enough to yell into one man's ear. The man moved a fraction.

Andrew forced his body through the tiny gap. He could almost touch her now. Just a yard or so more. Her muslin skirt was spread across the filthy roadway. How was it that these men did not realise the harm they were doing?

They were all gazing up at the Tsar, their arms raised, their mouths open to bellow their delighted approval of the hero who had defeated the tyrant Bonaparte. The London mob had made its choice of the young and virile Emperor of Russia over their own fat, frivolous Regent.

Andrew was close enough now to see her. She was dirty, young and frightened. She seemed to be screaming for help. But he could hear nothing. With a huge effort, Andrew shouldered aside two men who were in danger of treading on the girl. He reached down, grabbed the little figure by the arms and heaved.

Nothing. He redoubled his efforts and heaved again.

It was like pulling a difficult cork. One moment her body was stuck fast. The next Andrew was toppling backwards with her. But he did not fall. The wall of people held him upright.

In his arms, the girl was still screaming and now, with her head against his shoulder, he could hear it very well. It hurt. He used his chin to nudge aside her broken straw bonnet and put his lips against her ear. 'Pray hush. You are safe now, I promise you.'

She uttered one final piercing scream. Then, putting her mouth against his ear, she cried, 'Safe? You are like to ruin me, you numbskull. Look at my gown.'

He looked down. Her skirt still lay spread on the ground in a drift of filthy muslin pinioned by enormous boots. Like pressed flower petals edged with footprints. The lady in his arms was dressed in little more than a shift and torn stockings.

It had taken Andrew nearly an hour to bring her home. On foot, for no cab could get through. Miss Kate de Lacey looked rather forlorn now, dirty and dishevelled, standing alone in the front hall of her mother's modest house. She was clutching her ripped skirts with one hand and his coat around her shoulders with the other. Her ruined bonnet had been pulled down around her face, to defend her from prying eyes. Including his.

Andrew looked towards the door. He had no desire to witness the inevitable confrontation between Miss de Lacey and her mother, who had every right to be furious. Miss Kate had confessed that, in her reckless desire to get close to the visiting royals, she had wilfully disobeyed strict orders to remain with her elderly maid. Like half of London, she was trophy-hunting mad. To make matters worse, she had turned out to be the daughter of Andrew's own distant cousin, the late Sir Hubert de Lacey.

Given their kinship, Andrew was duty-bound to present himself to the widow. But now was definitely not the time for introductions.

'Might I trouble you to return my coat, Miss de Lacey?' he

asked formally. He had told her of their relationship, but he was not sure she had been listening.

'What? Oh. Oh, yes, of course.' She managed to remove the coat with one hand and held it out. The fingers holding up her ruined skirts were white with the effort of trying to preserve her decency.

'I shall leave you now, ma'am.' Andrew quickly donned his coat, which was much in need of pressing. 'With your permission, I shall call again tomorrow, to see how you do.' He started for the door.

At that moment a voice, full of anguish and concern, cried out, 'Oh, Kate!' Squinting past the girl, Andrew saw a pair of neat slippers and the hem of a plain grey gown at the top of the staircase.

He did not wait for a glimpse of the lady's face. He bowed vaguely in the direction of the stairs and ran lightly down the steps to the flagway, pulling the door behind him. Through the heavy wood he heard the sound of women's voices, rising in a chorus of question and complaint.

The house seemed to have been restored to normality after the previous day's uproar. Andrew handed his card to the maid who had opened the door. Odd that Lady de Lacey did not keep a manservant, or live at a better address. Sir Hubert had been a very wealthy man.

'If you will wait a moment, sir, I will enquire if Lady Sarah is at home.' The maid bobbed a quick curtsey and hurried upstairs.

Lady Sarah? Sir Hubert, though a mere baronet, must have married the daughter of an earl, at least. It would have been a business arrangement, Andrew supposed; Sir Hubert's wealth in return for a trophy wife to display on his arm. Andrew shrugged his shoulders. Such a trophy was, after all, what he himself had come home to acquire.

But that thought raised the long-buried memory of the trophy he had failed to win all those years ago, and of how much he had suffered. He tried to thrust the image aside, as he had always done. For once, he failed. He saw again the Golden Toast of London. The Incomparable. The woman with a heart of ice.

Andrew, with no fortune and no prospects, had known he was not acceptable as her suitor. He had intended only to enjoy the touch, the scent of that luscious forbidden fruit. But he had been too young to remain aloof. After a few encounters, and even fewer dances, he had lost his heart. The Incomparable had laughed. In his anger and despair, he had cursed all womankind. And he had fled to India, intending never to return.

The hem of a dove-grey gown appeared on the staircase above him. Was the lady herself coming to welcome him, to do him honour for rescuing her child? Most unusual, if so. Slowly, the rest of the gown appeared. Followed by a slim white neck.

He would not have recognised her. Even in such a plain gown, Kate de Lacey was breathtakingly lovely. And she descended the stairs with the poise of a duchess. She seemed to float towards him, holding out her hand. Then she added a dazzling smile that hit him like a punch in the gut. 'Mr Mortimer. Cousin Andrew, I should say. Pray come upstairs. Mama has ordered tea.'

Approaching the threshold of the sitting room, Andrew found himself unable to take his eyes off the young lady by his side. How had he failed to see beyond yesterday's grubby little hoyden in the ruined bonnet? Kate de Lacey was truly an Incomparable. Such amazing beauty would catch at any man's senses.

And the mother?

Lady Sarah stood waiting by the fireplace. She was a mature and still lovely woman, who looked much too young to have a child of Kate's age. He crossed the room to bow over her outstretched hand. She was adjusting her skirts nervously, inadvertently drawing attention to her dowdy grey gown and to several neat darns at the hem. Even to take tea with the man who had rescued her daughter, Lady Sarah had to wear an old mended gown. Andrew felt a stirring of anger at his dead cousin. How could an honourable man fail to provide for his widow and child? The poor lady was clearly purse-pinched.

Andrew raised his head to look at her lovely face. They had not met before; he would not have forgotten a beauty like Lady Sarah. Yet she could not begin to compete with her own child, in spite of the strong resemblance between them. Kate de Lacey, Kate the Incomparable, would be a glorious golden trophy for the man who possessed her.

Perhaps he should be that man?

The notion rippled through him, warming his blood. Now that he was wealthy he had determined to take a trophy bride, for he had learned, long ago, that love led only to pain. Marriage should be a business arrangement. So why not this girl? It would be a fair exchange: the widow's lifelong comfort for the daughter's hand. Miss Kate was very young but she had both beauty and breeding. There would be real satisfaction, too, in marrying the girl who would be the next Golden Toast of London.

His decision was made. This time, the Incomparable would be his.

'Mr Mortimer, I must tell you how grateful I am to you for rescuing Kate yesterday.' Sarah shuddered a little at the memory. 'Without your help, I dare not think what might have happened to her.' With a slightly wobbly smile, she waved him to a seat. 'Is it also true that you are my late husband's cousin?'

'A distant cousin only, ma'am,' he responded quietly.

Sarah warmed to that low, modest response. Not at all like her late husband. Sir Hubert had been squat and bald, prematurely aged by his penchant for good living and loose women. This man was much younger, perhaps in his late thirties. He was tall and loose-limbed. Not handsome, exactly, especially with that dark complexion, but his features were striking, full of strength, yet with an underlying hint of gentleness. She caught her breath on that wayward thought. How on earth could she possibly know that?

Sarah forced herself to attend to making the tea. For several minutes she kept the conversation centred on mundane family matters, and something of Cousin Andrew's history. She learned that he had left for India about a year before her own come-out. No wonder they were strangers. She, in turn, explained that Sir Hubert had been dead for over two years, and that the title had gone to a son by his first marriage. She did not say, in terms, that the new baronet had failed to provide for his stepmother, though it was true. But she could not lie directly to a relation; she had to admit, when asked, that she and Kate were no longer in contact with the man.

Kate had quickly become bored, as usual. 'I must warn you, Cousin Andrew,' she broke in eagerly, 'that Mama has scolded me roundly for my trophy-hunting yesterday. But how else would I ever see the crowned heads of Europe?' She had bowed her head a little, but she was looking up at him flirtatiously through her lashes.

Where had she learned that little trick? The child was a minx!

'Kate!' Sarah did not attempt to conceal her disapproval. 'I must ask you to forgive her, sir. And to accept that she is not the hoyden she would have you believe.' She passed him his teacup with a hand that was not quite steady. What was the matter with her? A woman of nearly five-and-thirty should not be overset by one male visitor, however attractive.

Cousin Andrew smiled. 'Believe me, ma'am, Miss de Lacey's spirited conversation is most welcome. Even single gentlemen become bored with simpering misses and awkward silences.'

Kate giggled, then clapped her hand over her mouth.

Sarah sighed. 'You will have to learn to mind your manners before next year, Kate, or you will be denied vouchers for Almack's.'

The amusement vanished from Kate's face. Yet in a moment she had recovered, straightening her spine as if she were a seasoned hostess. 'Sugar, Cousin Andrew?'

Sarah shook her head, unable to suppress a smile. Looking across at Cousin Andrew, she saw that he was smiling, too. Rather indulgently, Sarah thought. Was he developing a fondness for Kate? Or was he simply dazzled by her beauty?

'Do I collect that Miss de Lacey is to make her come-out next year?' he asked blandly.

Kate audibly drew breath to reply but then paused.

Sarah nodded approvingly, grateful that her daughter seemed to be learning at last. 'Yes. When she is seventeen. That is, we hope so.'

He sat up rather straighter in his chair. 'Lady Sarah, I am fixed in London for some weeks now, while I complete the arrangements for the estate I am about to purchase. In Wiltshire. I intend to make my home there.'

Sarah had been too well-schooled to allow herself to show more than mild interest in his declaration. But she knew, as any mother would, that a single nabob settling in England would soon be in search of a wife. And he wanted Sarah to know it, too.

He set down his cup. 'I was planning to remind myself of the beauties of London.' He glanced swiftly from mother to daughter, and back again. 'I was wondering, ma'am. Would you allow me, as a near relation, to escort Cousin Kate on her trophy-hunting excursions? To the City for the parade tomorrow, for example?'

Kate's sharp intake of breath cut across Sarah's measured reply. 'A gentleman's escort is very welcome in London just at present, Cousin Andrew. Thank you. Perhaps you would call for Kate around two?'

★ ★ ★

It had been enjoyable at first, accompanying Andrew and Kate to all the events. But now, after weeks of Kate's gazing and exclaiming, the Tsar and the King of Prussia and all the other visiting royals were leaving for a review of the fleet and then for home. Sarah was delighted. Kate, predictably, was begging to be allowed to follow them. She had not the first idea of economy.

'No, Kate,' Sarah said firmly, 'we are not going to Portsmouth. You have been indulged enough.'

Andrew smiled but said nothing. For a second he caught Sarah's eye, but then looked away swiftly, as if afraid to share a confidence with her. She was almost sure that he, too, was tired of all their gadding about. Was he also tired of having Sarah as the third in their little party? It was not that she did not trust him to keep the line, even with only Kate's maid as chaperon. It was Kate she did not trust. She looked like a young lady but she still tended to behave like a child. Did she even begin to understand that Andrew was courting her? Sarah doubted it.

Andrew was every inch the honourable gentleman and very attractive indeed, even though he was at least twenty years older than Kate. More suited to mother than daughter.

Dear God! Where had that come from? Sarah felt the blood draining from her face. Her racing pulse told her the truth of her own feelings. In spite of all her resolutions, she had given her heart to Andrew Mortimer. Stupid. Impossible!

She forced herself to confront stark reality. Andrew was a most eligible *parti*—who was courting her own daughter!

It was not to be wondered at. Kate was young and incredibly beautiful. What single man of means would look twice at a poor widow in a darned grey gown? The most Sarah could hope for now was an early declaration, so that Kate could make her come-out as a married lady. Let Andrew pay for it all. In truth, Sarah could not.

'What say you to ices at Gunther's?' Andrew's playful invitation interrupted Sarah's melancholy train of thought.

Kate almost managed to swallow her whoop of joy.

'We should be delighted, Cousin,' Sarah answered more sedately. As usual, she manoeuvred Kate between them as they walked. In all of their outings, Sarah had never once taken Andrew's arm. She did not dare. Particularly now.

'London will be very boring without the royals,' Kate said a little peevishly. 'What on earth are we to do now?'

'You might spend a little more time on your music, my dear. Your performances are spirited but, sadly, far from note-perfect.'

Kate pulled a face. Not for the first time, Andrew intervened to help her. Maybe he was becoming truly fond of her, in spite of her mischievous starts?

'If you permit, ma'am, we might perhaps visit the sights together? In the afternoons, of course, once Cousin Kate has done her music practice.'

Sarah tried not to smile. He might be courting the daughter but it was the mother he was supporting this time.

Kate began to protest but Andrew ignored her, keeping his gaze fixed on Sarah. It was more than a little disconcerting.

'Soon we shall have the celebration for the centenary of the House of Hanover. I hope, ma'am, that you will allow me to escort you both. The spectacle promises to be magnificent.'

Magnificent it certainly was. Hyde Park was full to overflowing to watch the re-enactment of the naval battle on the Serpentine. Kate was in raptures at the prospect. Sarah felt more subdued, remembering young men of her acquaintance who had died in naval battles. It seemed that Andrew, too, had lost friends, for he did not echo Kate's enthusiasm. To Sarah's surprise, he seized and pressed her fingers, murmuring words of sympathy.

Shocked, she snatched her hand from his. She must not let him touch her. 'I think Kate would prefer to watch the balloon ascent in Green Park. We must make haste if we are not to miss it.' Putting an arm round Kate's waist, Sarah hurried for the exit.

He followed them, as Sarah had known he must, for a gentleman could not leave ladies unescorted. He caught up with them just as the balloon was being prepared for release.

The young flier climbed into the basket. Then the tethers were loosed and the balloon rose into the sky, pushed swiftly by the wind towards the east and the river. They watched as it grew ever smaller.

Kate turned to Andrew. 'I wish I could do that,' she said wistfully.

At that moment there was a shout of alarm. The ropes holding the topmost part of the balloon had given way. The balloon itself seemed to be escaping through the hole in the netting. Several women screamed, but Sarah's throat was too tight to make any sound at all. She swallowed hard and reached for Kate's hand. The whole crowd was holding its breath, waiting.

At last it seemed that the flier's efforts had stopped the balloon's escape. 'Look! He has held it. And he is bringing it down.' Andrew's voice was calm and reassuring. As they watched the balloon's increasingly swift descent, he dropped a comforting arm round both their shoulders. 'Do not be concerned. I am sure he will land safely.'

Kate managed a watery smile in response. Sarah could neither move nor speak. She allowed herself to relax into the warmth of his touch. Just for a moment. Just this once.

They spent the evening among the more refined delights of St James's Park, though Sarah had been horrified to discover that the entrance fee was half a guinea. Faced with Kate's enthusiasm, Sarah had had to allow Andrew to pay, for she could not. It reminded her, yet again, that her beautiful daughter would not have the come-out she deserved. Perhaps marriage to Andrew truly was the best solution, in spite of the difference in age. He would make her a kind and considerate husband. Sarah was now quite sure of that.

The park was like Vauxhall on a full night, with thousands of ladies and gentlemen eating and drinking, or taking boat trips on the canal, or strolling about to admire the star and crescent lighting along the waterside and the magnificent illuminated pagoda on the bridge. Kate was enchanted.

But it had been a very long day and Sarah had spent too many hours in Andrew's company. 'It is nearly ten o'clock, Kate. I think we should return home.'

'Oh, no, Mama. Please. We cannot miss the fireworks. Do let us stay. Cousin Andrew will look after us, if you ask him. I know he will.' She turned pleading eyes on Andrew.

He turned to Sarah for guidance.

She hesitated. To look into Andrew's laughing eyes was a mistake. She lowered her gaze quickly and said, 'The decision is yours, Cousin.'

'Then I am at your disposal, ladies,' he said, offering each of them an arm.

Kate took it eagerly. Sarah wavered. But Kate was frowning anxiously. Clearly, she did not like to think that her mother had any reservations about their new-found cousin. And if he was to be Sarah's son-in-law, she must have none. Or none that Kate would ever see. She placed her fingers on his arm.

'Stay close,' Andrew warned them, leaning confidingly towards Kate, then towards Sarah. 'Even Society crowds can be danger-ous. We want no more accidents.'

Kate hugged his arm in response. Sarah did her best not to react at all, though the warmth of his flesh seemed to penetrate all the layers of clothing between them. Her fingers tingled.

Andrew led them through the crowd to a good vantage point

among a stand of trees that provided welcome support for weary backs. He spread Sarah's shawl on the grass for them.

'But how shall we see the fireworks if we are sitting down?'

Kate's boundless energy was beginning to become a little wearing, Sarah decided. But perhaps Andrew saw it as a virtue.

'I promise, Kate, that I shall have you on your feet the moment there is anything to see.' He had to make good on that promise within five minutes. First the bridge was lit up in gold. Then unbelievably rich illuminations began, painting vivid pictures. *Victory over tyranny* was the theme. The Regent was announcing to his people that he, and the House of Hanover, were solely re-sponsible for everything. It was rather easier now that the other royal candidates for the victor's crown had left the country.

Artillery announced the start of fireworks in all the parks.

'Oh, look.' Kate pointed. 'Does not the pagoda look beauti-ful?' Fiery showers were pouring from every tower of the pagoda and flights of rockets from its top lit up the sky. The myriad colours were reflected in the gently flowing water of the canal. Against the dark canopy of trees, the effect was magical.

'We are much indebted to Cousin Andrew for this indulgence. He—' Sarah stopped short with a gasp. 'Is it truly only fireworks? It looks—' In her panic, she grasped him by the arm and used his given name. 'Andrew! It looks to be on fire!'

In the distance, the pagoda was ablaze. As they watched help-lessly, engines began to play water on the fire. Yet it showed no sign of subsiding. Flames were leaping into the air, vying with the fireworks that continued to burn in their rainbow colours, throwing even more sparks into the dry timbers of the pagoda.

'Pray God there is no one inside,' Sarah murmured fervently, her fingers clenched tight together.

'Amen,' Andrew said quietly.

The crowd surged forward, hemming them in. Everyone seemed to be intent on watching the blaze, as if it were just another firework spectacle. Men were climbing into the trees all around, in hopes of getting a better view. Sarah was horrified. How could they be so callous?

She did not see the rocket. One moment she and Kate were standing impotently, watching fire engulf the pagoda, the next Andrew had pushed them to the ground and thrown his own body on top of them for protection.

Their cries of outrage were drowned by a shriek of pain. Above them. A second later, one of the men in the tree fell heavily to the ground with a gaping wound in his calf. Sarah and Kate were spattered with blood.

Kate screamed and rolled away from the wounded man, her hand to her mouth. Her face was turning green. Then the huge branch above them split from the trunk with a crack like gunfire.

Sarah looked up. It was falling. It was going to crush them both.

She saw horror in Andrew's face. His gaze flicked between them. They were too far apart for him to shield them both. Kate was nearer. He must save her!

Sarah offered up a silent prayer and closed her eyes.

The next moment, the full weight of his body landed on top of hers, just as the branch fell on them both. She heard his groan of pain, quickly stifled. And then she heard Kate's screams. She was injured!

'Kate!' Sarah's cry was muffled by Andrew's coat. She pushed against him. 'Andrew, she's hurt. Let me up. We must go to her.'

He rolled off her and she pushed herself to her feet, marvelling that she was totally unhurt. But what of Kate? Kate had not had the shelter of Andrew's strong body.

Sarah flung herself towards her child. Kate was still screaming. But she was clearly unhurt. Merely hysterical. Without further ado, Sarah slapped her sharply across the cheek. The screaming stopped.

She glanced back at Andrew. He was lying on the ground. Ominously still. She must go to him.

But first she had to stop the other man's bleeding. Willing herself not to think about Andrew, she began tearing strips from her petticoats.

Sarah was astonished when Andrew was announced. It was only a few hours since she had seen him carried into his lodgings, apparently gravely hurt. Kate had become so agitated that Sarah had put her to bed, with a few drops of laudanum to make her sleep. Then Sarah had sat alone, wondering and worrying.

She went to welcome him, both hands outstretched. She was not going to shun his touch. Not now. 'Andrew. You are truly unhurt? I cannot believe it. That enormous branch. And you took the full force of it on your back.'

He made a valiant attempt to shrug his shoulders and almost succeeded. Sarah found that she was immensely proud of this man, who would soon be asking for her daughter's hand. And he would make Kate a good husband, if only the child could—

Andrew pressed Sarah's hands. 'What matters, my dear, is that you are safe,' he said, looking down into her eyes.

This time Sarah allowed herself to return his gaze. She owed him this small degree of honesty, even if he were to see things in her eyes that he should not know.

For a long moment he gazed at her. 'Kate, too, of course,' he added at last.

His words brought Sarah back to reality. 'She disgraced herself. Totally unscathed, but screaming like one possessed. I sent her to bed. She is such a child still. Andrew, I…' She swallowed. She had to warn him, no matter how much it might hurt. 'I have to tell you that Kate sees you only as a friend, not a suitor. I'm afraid she is too young for…for marriage. To anyone. Perhaps if you could wait a few—'

He stopped her with a finger to her lips. 'I have been a fool. A complete and utter fool. The lady I desire to marry is a grown woman, strong and beautiful. Not a trophy wife, after all, but a friend, a partner. A lover.' His finger caressed her lower lip with a featherlight touch, then withdrew a fraction.

'Can there ever be any hope for me, Sarah?'

'But you are courting Kate.' It was not what her heart was saying.

'I was. Until I had to choose between you.' He offered Sarah his hand. 'It has to be you, Sarah, my love. It always will be.'

In that moment Sarah knew that there would be both joy and love, after all her years of struggle. Deliberately, she put her fingers into his and lifted her lips for their first kiss.

Adele Parks

Adele Parks was born in Teesside, NE England. She studied English Language and Literature, at Leicester University. She published her first novel, *Playing Away*, in 2000; that year the *Evening Standard* identified Adele as one of London's 'Twenty Faces to Watch'. Indeed, *Playing Away* was the debut bestseller of 2000.

Prolific, Adele has published nine novels in nine years, including *Game Over*, *Tell Me Something* and *Love Lies*—all nine of her novels have been bestsellers. She's sold over a million copies of her work in the UK but also sells throughout the world. Two of her novels (*Husbands* and *Still Thinking of You*) are currently being developed as movie scripts. *Young Wives' Tales* was shortlisted for the Romantic Novelists' Association Award 2008.

Since 2006 Adele has been an official spokeswoman for World Book Day and wrote a Quick Read, *Happy Families*, as part of the celebrations of World Book Day 2008. To find out more about Adele visit www.adeleparks.com

Grating Expectations

It wasn't entirely Sarah's fault that she had such specific—and high—expectations about the trip to Venice. *Everyone* agreed that a marriage proposal was 'more than likely'. Everyone being her mum, her sister and her four closest friends—one married, two single, one gay—a reasonable cross section of society—at least of Sarah's society. After all, David and Sarah had been together for four years, three months and they lived together, admittedly in *his* flat with *his* name on the mortgage and utility bills but Sarah bought the groceries and she'd redecorated the place from top to bottom—that meant something.

They travelled club class. Which was an unnecessary luxury for a short haul flight and therefore, Sarah thought, proof positive that David wanted this to be a 'particularly special' weekend. Her preference was that he'd pop the question right at the beginning of the mini-break. Perhaps tonight? Then they could utilise the rest of the time planning the wedding or, rather more accurately, Sarah could spend the time telling David what she wanted for her big day. She had very clear views and, frankly, little actual discussion would be required—although she'd be sensible enough to disguise that fact when the time came. She'd selected the church, venue, menu, band and bridesmaids. She had a good idea about the style of dress—but all the wedding magazines agreed you didn't really know until you actually tried on a selection. So finalising that detail would have to wait.

David wasn't into big romantic gestures so there was a reasonable chance he'd propose somewhere unsuitable, like on the plane or in a restaurant. Sarah had never liked the idea of restaurant proposals. A few of her friends' boyfriends had gone down that route and the girls always claimed to be happy enough with it, but Sarah knew she'd be put off her food and she didn't like waste. Besides, how do you hug and kiss with a table in between and everyone watching?

Sarah talked non-stop on the plane so that David wouldn't find an opportunity to ask. She chattered about the bread rolls, her ankles swelling on flights, whether it was worth sending postcards to friends and family—anything rather than have him ruin her big moment by proposing somewhere inappropriate.

They emerged from the airport and Sarah was thrilled to see a beautiful mahogany boat waiting to take them to the mainland. Surely this private hire meant the proposal was well within reach? As they slipped through the sea, the sunshine made everything appear glittery, the breeze lifted Sarah's hair and she felt like a Bond girl. Now, the boat limousine would be an *ideal* place to propose, she thought.

'Isn't this just perfect?' she said, staring intently and meaningfully at David.

'Bit blowy,' he replied without taking his eyes off the map.

David had an innate distrust of foreign taxi drivers and made a big deal of following their chosen route from airport to hotel so as to ensure the cabbie took the most direct path. Secretly,

Sarah doubted that he had any idea how to read a map of the sea and waterways but felt it would be rude to point out as much.

It was about four o' clock by the time they dropped off their bags at the hotel; David suggested they went straight out to make the most of the late afternoon sunshine, perhaps buy an ice cream. Sarah agreed but insisted on taking a quick shower and changing her outfit. She didn't want to be proposed to wearing the jeans she'd travelled in. In the end it took about an hour and a half for her to shower, exfoliate, reapply make-up and select the outfit she did want to be wearing when she agreed to become Mrs Johnson.

Unfortunately, by that time the sun had slipped behind a large cloud. David grumbled and commented that stilettos were impractical footwear to forage around the cobbled streets of Venice.

Sarah was in love with Venice. She'd known she would be; she'd decided it *was* the most romantic place in the world the moment David mentioned he'd booked a mini-break. She'd read all about Doge's Palace, she'd imagined them strolling through Piazza San Marco and taking a trip to the Accademia for weeks now.

Venice did not stink; Sarah had never believed it would, despite all the grim warnings she'd had from people—like the lady in the dry cleaners, Mike from next door and the lads in the post room at her office—people who didn't have an ounce of romance in their bodies.

Mooching around the baroque backstreets, they stood outside churches and wandered across umpteen pretty bridges. Despite the lines of washing flapping in the breeze, Sarah thought these streets had a shabby charm and were perfect backdrops for David to pop the big question. Clearly he did not agree. He kept resolutely silent, despite her numerous hints about how *romantic* everything was and how *perfect*. They ambled along the waters of St David's Basin. How was it described in the guidebook? A mirror to reflect the majesty and splendour of the Basilica of San Giorgio Maggiore. True enough. A perfect place for a proposal. Sarah dawdled. She leaned her elbows onto the iron railing of a bridge and gazed out onto the canals. It was a lovely view, although she hadn't expected to be in the shade of the buildings quite so much and wished she'd worn long sleeves. In her imag-inings they were always walking in the sunshine. David leaned his bum against the railings and looked in the opposite direction; Sarah tried not to be disconcerted.

'David, isn't this just so wonderful?'

Sarah gently bit her lower lip. Last week they'd been watching some chat show on TV. They'd ordered a takeaway and opened a bottle of wine. They'd chomped their way through half a box of Milk Tray, not the type of confectionary Sarah would ever take to a friend's dinner party but, in fact, their favourite. The host was interviewing Hollywood's latest hot bit of stuff who kept biting her lower lip whenever she was thinking about a question. David had been mesmerised.

'Do you have a mouth ulcer, love?' David asked.

'No, why?'

'You keep chewing your lip. I thought you were in pain. I've got some Bonjela in my wash bag. I'll dig it out for you when we get back to the hotel.'

'I don't have a mouth ulcer.'

'Maybe you've started to bite your lip as a compensation for giving up biting your nails.'

She'd always been a nail biter; David hated the habit and had often urged her to stop. She'd tried but had never gone longer than two days without caving in and having a nibble; that was until she imagined something sparkly on her third finger, left hand. Stumpy nails would so ruin the effect.

'No,' she mumbled, somewhat exasperated. Clearly, her pro-vocative lower lip nibbling was doing nothing for David. She looked around for something to talk about but, despite the wealth of history, culture and bars, she was stumped. They endured a fifteen minute silence, the first of their relationship.

Eventually David asked, 'Do you fancy something to eat? The local dish of squid pasta is supposed to be worth trying.'

'I'm tired, let's just go to bed,' and, so that he was absolutely clear, she added, 'to sleep.'

Saturday followed the same pattern. Sarah woke up hopefully and dressed in a way that she thought appropriate for accepting a proposal. David woke up bewildered and a bit resentful that a romantic mini-break in Venice hadn't culminated in even a whiff of sex. Despite the top-notch hotel with four-poster bed and everything. His bewilderment and resentment grew as Sarah spent the day acting increasingly weirdly. Normally so relaxed and such a laugh, she'd started to behave in a way that defied belief. Did she think he was a complete moron? He wasn't impervious to the dawdling at Kodak moments and outside jewellery windows. He knew what she wanted—she was being obvious and, frankly, her behaviour was terrifying.

He *had* been going to do it. Of course he had. Why not? The girl was a marvel; he adored her. Or at least he thought he adored her. But her peculiar pushy behaviour was making him... nervous. Suddenly, he didn't like the way she munched her food and her walk was funny, sort of lopsided. This wouldn't have been a deal-breaker under normal circumstances but what was normal about your girlfriend holding a gun to your head, full of emotional bullets that she so clearly wanted to spend?

He'd planned to take her to Santa Maria Gloriosa dei Frari, arguably one of Venice's most sublime religious treasure troves, to see Titian's gloriously uplifting *Assumption* altar painting. He'd wanted to propose to her in front of that painting; *he* was also capable of assuming, planning and plotting. But her needy expectations had ruined everything. He felt she was presuming, second-guessing and, worst of all, waiting. Now he felt that he might return to England with the Princess-cut diamond still in his jacket pocket.

By Sunday they were barely speaking. Sarah insisted that she didn't want to go to a market—unheard of. David said he had no appetite for visiting restaurants—a first. Instead of enjoying the café orchestras, cooing pigeons and constant traffic of waiters serving alfresco diners, Sarah complained that St Mark's Square was too boisterous. She rushed towards a gondola, no longer envisaging romantic opportunities—she'd given up on that; it was Sunday evening and they were leaving early the next day—but she desperately wanted to be away from the crowds, which, as far as she could ascertain, were entirely made up of besotted lovers.

They drifted gently on a gondola, away from the crowds. Sarah stared at the stars glistening in the navy sky and wondered if she could be bothered to comment to David that the scene was perfect. She thought he'd ask, *Perfect for what?* in an impatient voice, as he had every other time she'd helpfully pointed out the perfect moments on their trip. Not that there had been so many today. Of course, everything was still as interesting, steeped in history, culturally amazing as when they'd first arrived—only, somehow, things weren't so perfect now.

David asked the gondolier to stop singing. He whispered to Sarah that he had a headache, although she'd never known him to suffer from one before. He also muttered that the whole experience had been excruciating and a rip-off at sixty quid per person for twenty minutes entertainment. Sarah wondered what to do next. She supposed she'd have to finish the relationship. It was clearly going nowhere fast. She couldn't just sit around and wait for David to finally decide she was the girl for him, or, worse, decide she wasn't. She had ovaries shrivelling by the minute, she didn't have unlimited time.

But she loved him so.

She couldn't imagine life without him. It was all so depressing and wrong. Nothing was turning out as she'd hoped and now she could even detect unsavoury wafts from the sewer and stale sweat from the gondolier's T-shirt.

David felt miserable. Really low. He'd thought the break would be such a laugh. He'd really splashed out—good flights, cool hotel, booked the best restaurants. Not that they'd actually honoured a booking as yet—Sarah had cried off on Friday *and* Saturday. He wondered if the jewellers accepted returns. What a waste. Things couldn't get any worse unless, of course, he lost the ring.

Panic! David self frisked in a frantic attempt to track down the little box.

'What is it?' asked Sarah.

'The ring! I've lost it. On top of you being a freak I've lost the damned ring.'

'What?'

'Sorry, I didn't mean to call you a freak.'

'That's OK. I meant the other bit. What ring?'

'An engagement ring, of course. Christ, it is dark. Can you see a ring? It cost a fortune. I can't believe this! It's in a blue box. Will you?'

'Yes, I will.'

'Look for it!'

'Oh, right. I thought you meant—'

'I'm unlikely to propose at the moment I've lost the ring, am I?' snapped David. Sarah was already on her hands and knees. In that instant she completely forgot that she was wearing high heels and a white skirt. She groped around the damp and dark gondola floor. Her round bottom bobbed up and down and something shifted back into place for David. Sarah no longer seemed overly keen or controlling. She was concerned and well-meaning again. He loved her curvy bum and everything else about her. His gut turned.

'I'll do you a deal: if we do find the ring, I will propose, OK?' David laughed.

'Deal, and if I like the ring I'll accept,' she added with a grin.

Rita Bradshaw

Rita Bradshaw was born in Northamptonshire, where she still lives today. At the age of sixteen she met her husband and they have two daughters, a son and three grandchildren, plus the most recent addition to the family—a gorgeous little puppy who's the latest in a long line of beloved dogs. Twenty years ago, Rita's first attempt at a novel was accepted for publication by Harlequin Mills & Boon under her pseudonym, Helen Brooks, and her fifty-seventh novel, *The Boss's Inexperienced Secretary,* was published in July 2009, with a seasonal-themed story arriving on the shelves in November, in time for Christmas. Rita also writes gritty north-east sagas for Headline Publishing under her own name. Her thirteenth paperback, *Gilding the Lily,* was published in the summer and *Born to Trouble* will be available in January 2010.

The Angel with the Wet Black Nose

Her heart in her mouth, Cassie opened the back door. *Please, please don't let him be there.* A small whine told her her prayers of the last hour or two had gone unanswered, even before her gaze dropped to the small shaggy dog sitting on her snowy doorstep.

'Shoo,' she said hopefully. It didn't work. It hadn't worked at six o'clock when she had first noticed him when she had taken some rubbish to the dustbin. It hadn't worked at seven o'clock when she had checked to make sure he was gone and he'd rolled over to have his tummy tickled, nor at eight when she had opened the kitchen window and yelled at him.

Bending, she felt gingerly for a collar amidst the tangled wet fur. There wasn't one. The little dog stared trustingly up and she wrinkled her face. 'Don't look at me like that; I'm not responsible for you being out in this weather and on Christmas Eve, of all nights. You must have a home to go to.'

But did he? He might be a stray, although he seemed plump enough under all that hair. 'Look, I'm not used to dogs,' she told him firmly. 'Go and bother someone who is.' She glanced up and down the tiny terraced gardens in the row of one-bedroomed Victorian cottages. Her neighbours on either side were away for Christmas and there were only one or two lights showing along the row.

Another plaintive sound brought her attention back to the mutt. Wondering if he'd bite if she tried to pick him up, she slowly inserted her hands under the little belly and carried him the few yards to the end of the garden. She tipped him over the thigh-high picket fence into the narrow lane which ran the length of the terrace. He jumped straight back over and was waiting for her on the doorstep when she retraced her footsteps.

'OK, you've made your point. You're not going quietly.' Glaring at him, she sighed. 'You'll just have to stay out here and freeze, then.'

He lifted one dripping paw entreatingly.

'Oh, boy, you're good.' Aware she was being made a sucker of by yet another male—and this time one with four legs and a tail—she opened the back door and waved her hand for him to go inside. He didn't need to be told twice.

As she followed him in, there was a sudden hissing and a whirl of movement and Milo, her big ginger tom, leapt six feet on to the kitchen shelf, sending Christmas cards and spice jars raining down on to the tiled floor. Oh, hell, she'd left him curled up on her bed but he'd obviously wandered downstairs to see what was what.

The dog ignored Milo completely, wandering across to the cat's food bowl and crunching the dried food he found there with the air of one who wondered what all the fuss was about.

Milo deposited in her tiny sitting room and the door shut, Cassie surveyed her canine guest, who had curled up on the rug in front of the wood-burning stove. He stared back at her, head on paws and big brown eyes liquid-soft. Fetching a towel, she lifted him up and gave him a brisk rub-down, to which he submitted with good grace, licking her hand once or twice with a small pink tongue. Immediately she'd finished he resumed his position on the rug.

He couldn't stay here. But it was gone nine o'clock on Christmas Eve—who could she call? The vets had long since closed. There was the police, she supposed. But if they came and took him he'd spend Christmas in a cage, and hadn't she read somewhere they only kept stray dogs for a short time before they were destroyed? An animal sanctuary might take him but they'd probably be shut for Christmas, too.

'You're a pain.'

The tone of her voice must have disturbed him because he whined but didn't move so much as a paw, obviously fearing he might be thrown back into the cold and dark if he made a nuisance of himself.

'Look, I'm not in the mood for a visitor, OK? This Christmas was supposed to be a case of shutting the door and not seeing a soul until the New Year, apart from Milo.'

He raised shaggy eyebrows and again a noise came from his throat but this time it sounded as if he was encouraging her to tell more. Aware she was having a conversation with a dog and that her family and friends would take this as confirmation that she had finally cracked after the last horrible few months, Cassie plumped down in her rocking chair, the dog at her feet.

'This Christmas I was going to be on my honeymoon in Lapland but my fiancé dumped me three months ago.' It was the first time she had actually brought herself to say it and the words hung in the air. 'It was very public and very messy. He ran off with my best friend, you see. Classic, I suppose. But it's not such old hat when it actually happens to you. I'd known him since we were kids and we'd been engaged forever, which meant our families and friends were all entwined. Everyone took sides.' She shook her head. 'We'd just put a deposit on this place, perhaps that's what panicked him into finally coming clean.'

The dog pawed at her leg. 'You want to sit on my lap? Come on, then.' Once he was settled she went on. 'Anyway, I decided to still buy the house and I'm glad I did. And do you know something? I wouldn't take him back now if he crawled on his hands and knees. I would have done, at first—I'd have done anything. But now I'm finding I can manage by myself. I'm twenty-eight years old, I have a good job at the bank and there is going to be life after Greg.' She sniffed. 'And these tears are not for him but for all the time I wasted. And so this Christmas is a time of taking stock and drawing a line under what's gone and I wanted to do that by myself. Can you understand that?'

A hairy face nuzzled her hand and she began stroking the small shaggy head.

'And I was being smothered by my mum and dad and friends, to be honest. They mean well but they have a certain note in their voices when they talk to me. Poor Cassie. And it makes me feel almost guilty that I've decided I've had a lucky escape. If Greg could have an affair with someone for twelve months—*twelve months,* mind—before we were married and without me knowing, what would he have done after? But it does sort of knock your faith in the male of the species.' The dog whined. 'Present company excepted, of course,' she added hastily.

It was quiet in the kitchen, peaceful.

At ten o'clock Cassie made herself a cup of coffee and the dog polished off a plate of chopped chicken and biscuits. She took Milo a bowl of tinned salmon as an apology but he was at his most regal, hardly deigning to look at her and then stalking upstairs with his tail in the air.

It was just after this that the knock came at her front door. The fat lazy feathery flakes of earlier had turned into a full-scale blizzard; the hooded muffled shape in front of her resembled a snowman. 'I'm terribly sorry to bother you on Christmas Eve, but you haven't by any chance seen a small dog looking lost, have you?'

Instead of the rush of relief she should have felt, Cassie's heart gave a little pang. 'He's in my kitchen; he wouldn't budge off my back doorstep earlier. At least I think it's your dog; I doubt if there are two lost on Christmas Eve. Come in and make sure.

'I can let you in the kitchen if you come round the back. Go to the beginning of the row of cottages and you'll see a lane leading to a car park. There's a gate at the side of it which opens on to a back way and the gardens are off that. I'm number sixteen.'

She opened the door to his knock a couple of minutes later. He'd thrown back his hood and was stamping his boots on the doorstep. It was obvious that the dog was his by the rapturous welcome the animal was giving him.

'I'm sorry about this; I only moved into the village today.' He picked the dog up and fussed him as he spoke. 'One of the removal men dropped a bureau and it scared him half to death and the gate was open…' He shrugged eloquently.

His voice was deep and smoky which, for some reason, made her spine tingle. His features were too rugged to be called good-looking but he had the bluest of blue eyes.

'How long have you been looking for him?'

'Hours and hours.' It was rueful. 'My house backs on to open fields so I scoured them first and then the quarry. I was frantic.'

His house backed on to open fields. Something clicked in her mind. 'You're not the new doctor, are you?' Village gossip had been full of the fact that a young doctor was moving into the rambling old house housing the surgery at the edge of the town some time over Christmas.

He nodded, holding out his hand. 'Jack Carter.'

'Cassie Price.' His handshake was firm, strong. 'Is there anyone at home waiting for news?' she said carefully. 'You can ring from here, if you like.'

'No, it's just me and Murphy.' He ruffled the dog's fur.

Murphy. Nice name. She liked Jack even better. Taking a deep breath, Cassie smiled. 'I've just made some coffee. And I can rustle up a turkey sandwich if you're hungry after all that tramping about?'

'I ought to say I wouldn't dream of imposing further but, to tell you the truth, I haven't eaten since this morning and there's only biscuits waiting for me at home. I was going to introduce myself at the village shop once I'd got the furniture sorted and stock up on essentials but, with this one hightailing it, everything went by the board. I could always open a tin of Murphy's dog food, though.'

He smiled a lazy smile and Cassie's heart flipped over like a pancake on Shrove Tuesday. Silently telling herself to get a grip, she said, 'I think I might be able to do better than dog food. I've got plenty of supplies in, what with the atrocious weather forecast and all.'

'Well, if you're sure…'

Actually—she was. She didn't know if it was the combination of jet-black hair and blue eyes, or the fact that he was tall and lean with satisfyingly broad shoulders, but Jack Carter had that certain something which if it could be bottled and sold would fetch a small fortune.

Several rounds of turkey sandwiches and umpteen cups of coffee later, Cassie knew a lot more about Jack and all of it good. He was single, thirty-six years old, and had spent the last few years since qualifying from medical school working his way round Europe and gaining a shed-load of experience. Now, in his own words, he was ready to put down roots.

When he eventually uncoiled his long frame from the sofa she realised with a little shock of surprise that it was well past two in the morning.

'Surprisingly, in view of the start of the day, this has been a great Christmas Eve,' Jack said softly. 'Happy Christmas, Cassie.'

His kiss was merely a brief stroking of her lips but Cassie felt the impact down to her toes. It took all her control to say steadily, 'Happy Christmas, Jack.'

It had stopped snowing when she opened the back door. The moon was high, its cold brilliance shining on the virgin snow and causing it to sparkle like diamond dust. A deep hush blanketed the night, broken only by Murphy snuffling in the snow and then rolling over and over in doggy ecstasy.

'Crazy mutt.' But Jack wasn't looking at Murphy.

Cassie gazed back into the glittering blue eyes. This night was the start of the rest of her life and she found she wanted this man to be part of it more than anything else in the world. 'I've enough food for Christmas Day lunch for two.' Three, counting Murphy. Four with Milo.

His uneven mouth curved in a smile that made her tingle. 'If that's an invitation, I'd say you're an angel.'

This time when he kissed her it rocked them both. When he raised his head they stared at each other and then laughed, ringing out in the cold air like Christmas bells.

She watched him walk to the gate with Murphy at his heels. The dog's tail had a jaunty wag to it and Cassie realised that if there was an angel about tonight, it was one with a wet black nose.

Elizabeth Bailey

An avid reader from an early age, Elizabeth Bailey grew up in colonial Africa under unconventional parentage and with theatre in her blood. Back in England, she trod the boards until discovering her true métier as a writer, when she fulfilled an early addiction to Georgette Heyer by launching into historical romance. Eight years and eight books later, Elizabeth joined the Harlequin Mills & Boon stable, fuelling her writing with a secondary career teaching and directing drama. With eighteen historical novels published, she is also now widening her scope with modern mainstream novels which, like the story in this anthology, explore the world of the unexplained. Further information at www.elizabethbaileybooks.com

A Matter of Time

It was a trick of the light. It must be. The eye in the portrait could not possibly have winked. Meriel regarded it intently.

The face was vibrant, unusual in the stylized Tudor look. There was the inevitable pointed beard resting on a high lace ruff, a doublet of rich black cloth, matched by the plumed hat, with a single earring nestling in one lobe. The features were intensely masculine, with a strong nose and high aristocratic cheekbones. Dark eyes seemed to follow as Meriel shifted her position. And one of them winked again.

She backed off. Was she going mad? She glanced up and down the long gallery and found it deserted. She had stupidly lagged behind and now the tour guide had moved the others on.

Faint fear rose as she turned back to the portrait. The eyes caught at hers again and she gazed warily back. Nothing happened. Yet they seemed eerily alive, as if they engaged with Meriel on some level.

An involuntary shiver shook her and she strove for calm. Imagination, that was all. A clever artist, whoever painted this, but it was just a portrait. Meriel moved closer and peered at the gold-plated inscription, reading aloud 'Sir Nicolas Presteigne, 1570.'

The Presteigne family had owned the place, she remembered that much. Meriel wished she had listened more closely to the guide. 'All right, Sir Nicolas Presteigne, you can stop looking at me in that unnerving fashion because I'm going.'

In the periphery of her vision, as she turned away, Meriel caught the ghost of a smile. She stopped dead, her gaze flying back to the picture. No smile, no movement. She was dreaming.

'You are not dreaming.'

A chill crept over her. If she was not dreaming, who had said that?

''Twas I, Nicolas. You hear me inside your head.'

A tattoo built in Meriel's chest. It was insane, yet the intensity of the dark eyes dragged at her mind, willing her to believe. She resisted.

'This can't be happening. I don't believe in ghosts.'

'Ah, but I am not a ghost, Meriel.'

'How do you know my name?'

'I can see into your mind, into your heart. I know all there is to know of you.'

Meriel let out a shaky laugh. 'How can you possibly know anything about me? You are a product of my imagination.'

This time she distinctly saw him smile.

'Am I indeed?'

Panic began to set in. 'Oh, my God! I saw your lips move.'

They moved again. ''Tis needed, for you must believe. Else you will not help me, and there is much at stake.'

She began to feel light-headed. If she was neither mad nor dreaming, then it must be a trick. 'If you're so clever, Sir Nicolas Presteigne, why don't you come down off that wall?'

The beard shifted, showing a set of excellent teeth. 'Ha! A challenge? Just as I suspected, you are a woman of strong character.'

'I'm a woman who is about to walk away.'

There was a sound like a shifting breeze and the gallery darkened. Meriel glanced quickly about. Candles set into wall-sconces where light bulbs had been! The thick carpet had disappeared, the doors at either end vanishing into darkness.

'Do you now believe?'

Meriel jumped. The voice was deep, echoing. She dared a look. A gentleman stood beside her, black velvet doublet and hose richly embroidered. And he was wearing the face of the portrait, clearly amused.

'I never refuse a challenge.'

Meriel struggled for breath. She backed away. 'Delighted to meet you, Sir Nicolas, but I must catch up with my party.'

He threw back his head and laughed, harsh in the eerie silence that surrounded them. 'They are no more, my pretty.'

Meriel felt the rising rhythm of her heart. 'Look, I don't know what's happening, but—'

The words were choked off as he caught her hand. 'There's no time, Meriel. Listen! They're upon us already!'

He began to run, dragging her with him. She felt heaviness against her hips and legs but was beyond wondering why. Somewhere behind she could hear footsteps, swift and loud upon the wooden boards.

'This way!'

Her captor pulled her through a doorway and flattened himself against the wall. His voice was hushed. 'They are in pursuit. You hear them?'

She did, closer now. Her pulse quickened. 'Who are they?'

'Enemies.' He grinned. 'But we'll outwit them yet. Onward!'

Down a lengthy corridor they sped, slipping through a doorway into an unknown room and out at a half-seen exit. The candlelight was intermittent and for the most part she stumbled down corridors in darkness. Once she tripped but the firm grip at her hand held fast and a swift arm came about her until she steadied.

At last Nicolas called a halt, pulling her through a narrow entrance and softly shutting the door. He leaned against it, breathing hard.

Meriel clutched at a panelled wall behind, trying to get her breath. In a vague way, she supposed she must soon wake and find it a dream. But at this moment the wood felt solid and the ghost—if it were one—looked all too real.

He shifted into a room, far from spacious, lit by a double candelabrum that stood upon a high dresser. Besides the dresser there was a chest and a single chair by a little table.

Nicolas headed for the latter, throwing off his plumed hat and tossing it aside. Meriel noted the sleek black hair, cut short about his ears. He pulled down a slatted cover on the table. His fingers played with small drawers. A writing table? Intrigued, she moved forward and discovered why her legs dragged. She was in Tudor dress.

Her glance swept down, taking in the tight patterned corset and the full velvet skirts, heavy about her waist and hips. Her arms were covered in long embroidered sleeves, with padding at the shoulder. A restriction at her neck proved to be a stiff ruff of lace propping up her chin. The ensemble felt natural, as if she wore it every day.

'This can't be real.'

Nicolas turned his head. 'You do not yet believe?'

Meriel lifted her skirts. 'These clothes. I don't understand.'

'Do not trouble your head with it, my pretty.'

He turned. Something in his fingers sparkled in the light. 'The Presteigne necklace. It is over a hundred years old.'

It was a collar of gold, threaded through with pearls, and from its base dropped myriad red stones, winking. Meriel touched a fingertip to one and Nicolas caught the finger.

'Rubies. And worth a fortune.'

Over the necklace, Meriel met his dark gaze and its glint caused a sudden flutter in her breast. Her finger burned where he held it.

'Is this why you wanted my help?'

For answer, he bent his head and his lips touched briefly at her fingers. A sliver of heat shot through her.

'Turn round.'

Meriel obeyed. The collar came about her neck and she felt his fingers at the back, below the ruff, tingling warmth against her skin.

'There. Guard it well!'

Meriel raised her hands to the necklace at her throat. Guard it? From what? Or was it from whom? Before she could ask, Nicolas took her hand again and moved to the door. Cautiously he opened it, his ear to the crack. The wait felt like hours, the suspense intolerable.

The door swung softly inward and his grip tightened.

'Where are we going now?'

'Hush!'

Meriel tiptoed behind as he crept through the door. Outside, he stopped again. There was no sound, and no one in sight. They started off down the long corridor, Nicolas lithe and silent, like a cat.

A glimmer of light ahead showed a corner. Nicolas paused and Meriel tensed.

'What is it?' A whisper squeezed through a dry throat.

'It may be a trap.' Just loud enough for her to catch.

'What do we do?'

'Go on. We have no choice. We must get back to the gallery.'

They sneaked onward into the light. A figure sprang into their path, full into the glare. He was garbed much as Nicolas, puffed breeches and a doublet of dark green. In his hand was the hilt of a naked sword, its point aimed at Nicolas.

Meriel's blood went cold. A scraping sounded in the dark

night and a sword was in Nicolas's hand as he dropped into the fencer's pose.

'Damn your eyes, Presteigne!'

Nicolas laughed, an ugly sound, rasping in Meriel's ears. 'Did you think to take it without a fight? On guard!'

A lunge and steel scraped on steel. The swift cut and parry was terrifying, as the vicious blades sliced in and out. It seemed that the two men were even, for Nicolas was driven back as many times as he drove the other man forward.

Yet in a moment he began to gain ground, driving his opponent up the corridor and out of the light. The end was swift.

She saw Nicolas lunge and then he had closed with the enemy. There was a struggle, a sword spun away and his opponent went down to a blow from the hilt of Nicolas's weapon.

'That will hold him for a while. Swiftly now.'

They were running again. But the sound of the fight must have travelled. There were shouts and the echoing of several feet. Nicolas let out an oath.

'Curse the villain! He has brought an army.'

Meriel caught sight of two shadows, moving fast. Nicolas backtracked. He flung open a door and bundled Meriel inside, slamming it as a cry sounded outside.

'They saw us. You must hide. Through there!'

A thrust at her back and she plunged behind a fall of heavy curtain. Losing balance, she fell against the wall. It gave way and she tumbled through a doorway into a well-lit chamber.

Blinking in a sudden glare of candles, Meriel took in a huge four-poster bed hung with curtains of red and gold, drawn back to reveal a female form propped upon one elbow, dark hair loose about her shoulders.

A finger beckoned. 'Have you the necklace safe?' The woman stretched towards the jewelled collar. 'Give it me.'

Meriel drew back. 'Nicolas told me to guard it.'

A pair of pale eyes glittered. 'It is mine. Give it me!'

'Who are you?'

'Avoline Presteigne! And the necklace is mine.'

Meriel put her hands to the back of her neck, feeling for the clasp. From behind her came a furious expletive as a hand grasped her arm. Nicolas was there, his sword drawn and ready.

'Will you betray me, lady? You had as well slit my throat as give the necklace to that trollop!'

The woman reared up, spitting fury. 'I shall have it, Nicolas. It is mine! It was given me.'

Nicolas held her at bay with the point of his sword. 'Yes, on that accursed day that made you a Presteigne. But it is not yours, Avoline. It stays in my family.'

'I curse your family!' returned the woman. 'And this slut around whose thieving neck you choose to place it.'

'She has naught to do with this.'

'She is in this. Up to the neck, it seems.' The pale gaze, fierce now, veered to Meriel's face. 'Mayhap the Queen will be minded to give it a bloodier girdle—and remove that pretty head from off her shoulders!'

Barely had the implication of these chilling words sunk in when the door burst open behind them. It was the man who had attacked Nicolas.

The woman in the bed screamed, 'He has the necklace! See, he has put it on that harlot's throat.'

'You will regret this, Presteigne,' growled the newcomer.

But Nicolas had Meriel by one hand and was backing her towards an inner door, sword poised.

The man came on, lunging fiercely to the attack. Nicolas parried as he retired, ignoring the screams of fury from Avoline in the bed.

In a moment, Meriel was outside the door and Nicolas was slamming it shut. He turned the key and she heard a muffled howl of rage from the other side.

'No time to lose. He has too many men within call. We must run for our lives!'

They flew down a passage and entered another corridor. Nicolas thrust through a doorway and, pulling a key from his pocket, locked the heavy studded door that barred any pursuit.

'With luck, they will not think to look for us here.'

The air struck chill and Meriel shivered. It was dark, but a faint light penetrated from above, showing her a winding stone stair.

'Where are we?'

'The tower. We may gain the upper storey, cross the roof and come upon the gallery from the other side of the house.'

Meriel let out an involuntary sigh.

'You are weary,' came softly from the shadow ahead of her on the stair. ''Tis but a short way, I promise you.' She saw a flash of white teeth in the half-light. 'And we are done with running.'

'I'm glad of that.'

Climbing behind him, Meriel remembered this was not real. Yet her earlier life felt more of a dream at this moment. Was she trapped in an alien world? And all for the sake of a necklace. She touched the collar at her throat and shivered, recalling Avoline Presteigne. What was the woman to Nicolas? A feeling washed over her that she recognised as jealousy. Absurd. Was she in danger of losing her heart as well as her head?

The stairs ended and she felt Nicolas's hand at her elbow, guiding her. Heat coursed through her and Meriel hardly noticed where she trod until she found herself out under the stars, at the mercy of a stiff breeze.

Moonlight flooded the land and Meriel gazed out upon a vast world of shadowed hills, dark with the silhouettes of many trees. It was beautiful. Behind her, she could feel warmth emanating from Nicolas's body.

'If this is a dream,' she uttered helplessly, 'then I don't want it to end.'

His voice was tender. 'Still so uncertain, sweet doubter?'

Meriel's throat ached and she blinked away threatening tears. She faced him, searching the pale gleam of his features.

'Who was she, Nicolas?'

The dark eyes were sombre. 'My wife.'

It came as no surprise. And it should not matter. He was only a ghost.

'And the man who fought you?'

His lips twisted, a bitter look. 'Her lover. Not that I care for that.'

Meriel experienced a surge of hope. 'Why not?'

He met her gaze, his tone soft as silk. 'You know why not, Meriel.'

Her heart pattered unevenly. 'Why does she want the necklace?'

He sighed. 'The fellow is powerful and close to the Queen. Avoline wants the jewels for a gift to the sovereign, in the hope that she will thus be induced to grant a divorce.'

'You don't want a divorce?'

'It is nothing to me. But the necklace is an heirloom.'

'Then why does Avoline not use some other jewel to bribe the Queen?'

'Avoline knows that the Queen has seen the Presteigne necklace often. Elizabeth covets it, as she covets anything of worth.'

'But what have I to do with all this, Nicolas?'

The dark eyes searched hers. 'You, my Meriel, will hide the necklace for me, and make it safe for ever.'

'I don't understand. And I don't know why I am involved.'

His glance locked with hers. 'You know it well, my pearl. Would that time might surrender to the moment and stand still awhile.'

There was a husky quality to his voice. Meriel felt his arms encircle her and his face came near. Weakness almost overcame her and she closed her eyes. A breeze brushed across her lips. So soft, so gentle.

And then a kiss from lips as alive as the heart that beat in her own breast. Warm, they were, and full of passion. In all the dreamings of her youth there had been nothing to compare with this. She came away quivering and dropped her head against his chest. She felt him cradle her.

'Nay, my sweet love, do not tremble so. There is naught to fear now.'

He drew her head up and Meriel smiled. 'It's not fear, Nicolas.'

There was a faint revival of the teasing look that he had worn in those first extraordinary moments. 'Is it not, my heart?'

The look struck Meriel with an abrupt sensation of impending loss. She drew away. 'This is going to end soon, isn't it?'

For answer, Nicolas enclosed her in his embrace, his fingers imprisoning her cheek so that she looked into his eyes. The dark gaze was tender, roving her face as the moonlight played over his.

'I will remember you thus. Your beauteous eyes of green, your silken skin and the light of night's shadows in your hair. I will remember how you fit so snugly in my arms.'

Pain tugged at her heart. 'Why can't I stay?'

'You know it cannot be, dear one.' Nicolas bent his head and kissed her swiftly. 'We must away.'

The gallery appeared deserted. Meriel waited while Nicolas cast a wary glance this way and that, peering into the gloom. Though the candles in the sconces were alight, they provided only a modicum of illumination.

''Tis safe enough, I think.' He looked down at Meriel and squeezed her hand. 'Take heart, my dove. We are at the last hurdle.'

Meriel eyed him uncertainly. 'What do you want me to do?'

'That you shall know soon enough. Are you game for the finish of the race?'

Had she any choice? Her life was no longer her own. It had been turned upside down and inside out, and she had lost all will to fight against fate—or nightmare, if that was what it was. All she knew was that she had found this extraordinary man. And she was going to lose him.

She gathered her courage. 'You know I am with you. Lead on.'

His eyes gleamed against the shadows. For one breathless instant, Meriel dared to hope as he lifted her hand to his lips.

'I chose well, my Meriel.'

Swift but cautious, Nicolas drew her halfway down the long gallery. As he paused, Meriel heard the distant sound of footsteps, moving fast.

Fear caught at her, familiar in the world she now inhabited. Nicolas's attention was concentrated upon the portraits on the wall above his head. She seized his arm.

'They're coming! Don't you hear it?'

He turned, looking off into the gloom. 'We have not much time then. Come, Meriel, get into the frame.'

She stared. 'What do you mean?'

Nicolas gestured at the wall. 'You must enter there, do you see?'

Looking up, Meriel took in a gilded frame where no portrait hung. Only an empty canvas, yellowed with age.

'Swiftly now, my pretty, for I must go.'

Bewildered, Meriel looked at him. 'Nicolas, I don't know how.'

His finger brushed her cheek. 'You have only to step inside. For this brief time, farewell, my heart.'

He was leaving her. Seized with an absurd desire to hold him back, Meriel reached out. Her hands met air. Nicolas was gone.

The how or why of it paled beside the dreadful fact. Emptiness yawned inside her. She was alone. It was over.

Only it was not over, Meriel realised, glancing down to find herself still clad in the Tudor garments that felt so much a part of her. The gallery was as yet lit only by candles, and she became aware that the sound of running feet was nearer than before. The pursuers were almost upon her.

Desperate, Meriel glanced up at the empty frame. *You have only to step inside,* Nicolas had said. A door clattered open against the wall and light burst into life at one end of the gallery. Her heart jumping, Meriel caught sight of the woman Avoline, robed in purple, behind her the same man who had tried to dispose of Nicolas.

She was alone and trapped. With only one way of escape and that impossible.

A shriek came from Avoline Presteigne. ''Tis his harlot! Quick, seize her! She has the necklace.'

Meriel cast frantic eyes up at the picture frame. Fear seemed to freeze her limbs. And then it came. In her head. His voice— urgent, but blessedly welcome.

'Up with you, my bird, for the love of heaven!'

Meriel drew a breath, closed her eyes and walked into the wall.

A commotion of feet thundered in her ears. They blundered to a halt, and were superseded by a howl of rage. Meriel's eyes flew open.

She was high, but she could see faces there below. The contorted features of Nicolas's wife, upturned towards her, and the swarthy anger in those of her lover. The figures were foreshortened, all face and squashed bodies.

As Meriel struggled with the new perspective she saw Avoline's finger lift and point. The voices were indistinct, muffled in timbre, as if they sounded through a veil.

'My necklace. She has stolen my necklace!'

'A pox on that husband of yours! Where is he?'

'What care I for Nicolas when the necklace is gone?'

'And the Queen waits.'

A hoarse laugh came from the woman and Meriel felt her glare.

'She will wait in vain then, for it is forever lost to us now.'

The man moved. 'Come, Avoline. 'Tis useless to stand grieving. If the necklace is gone, it is gone. We must find some other way.'

Grumbling, the woman allowed herself to be led away. The two passed out of the periphery of Meriel's vision. She let go her breath and experienced a sensation of floating.

She was standing in the gallery. Daylight flooded in from a bank of windows behind her, falling on the portrait that stood upon the wall above her. A chill crept into Meriel's chest as she stared up at the painting.

She might have been looking into a mirror!

Those same Tudor clothes that she had worn were upon the figure in the portrait. Below the stiff ruff of lace was a collar of gold, threaded through with pearls and rubies. The Presteigne necklace.

Meriel put a hand to her throat and found the collar of her jacket, alien to her fingers. She was back in modern clothes. There was carpet beneath her feet and unlit bulbs had taken the place of candles in the wall-sconces.

Confused, Meriel backed away from the picture. She would have believed it all a dream, only how could she refute the evidence of her own eyes? It was unmistakably her face—which Nicolas had caressed with aching tenderness.

Nicolas!

Turning, Meriel flew down the gallery, almost skidding to a halt before the portrait where it had all begun. A horrid sensation of numbness dulled her mind.

There were Nicolas's dark eyes, his pointed beard resting on the lace ruff. Only the face was no longer vibrant. The teasing gleam, the glowing fire had gone, and the paint was cracked and old. She was back—if she had ever been elsewhere. She was in the here and now. But Nicolas was long dead.

'Are you lost?'

The voice penetrated Meriel's tense absorption. It had a timbre that struck an odd chord in her memory. She turned.

'Everyone has gone, you know.'

There was a tentative smile on the man's lips, but Meriel could only stare.

It was his face.

'Can I help? You seem a bit bemused.'

Meriel could not utter a word. Nicolas. It was Nicolas to the life. Only without the beard. She took in the casual clothes. Jeans and a sweatshirt. But the black hair was much the same length, waving a little. And in the dark eyes of this stranger there was the same vibrant glow. Meriel found her voice.

'Who are you?'

She did not wait for his response but cast another glance up at the painting, as if to emphasise the similarity. He glanced up at the portrait of Sir Nicolas Presteigne.

'You've seen the resemblance, then. My ancestor. A man of unusual talent, by all accounts. Something of an alchemist.'

Turning miracles in time?

The voice went on, its quality all too familiar. 'This is—or was—the family home. My grandfather opened it to the public. Had to, in those days.'

Meriel could feel the tremor in her limbs. The heir to the Presteigne name turned concerned eyes upon her.

'You look pale. Are you faint? Can I get you anything? Tea, perhaps?'

She had no will to reject him. 'If it's no trouble.'

The flash of white teeth threw a coursing pain into Meriel's chest. 'I'd be glad of the company. I'm the caretaker here, you see.' His lips twitched. 'How are the mighty fallen!'

A faint laugh was surprised out of Meriel and the lightness at her head began to recede. She eyed him, wanting to ask, but afraid to hear the name. Instead, she tried a different question.

'Do you live in the Manor?'

'Lord, no. Just a cottage in the grounds. Probably belonged to one of the tenants in the old days.'

Meriel was almost overwhelmed by sadness. 'Don't you own anything any more? Has it all gone?'

'I own the cottage.'

'Nothing else?'

He shook his head, a rueful look in the dark eyes. 'You can't keep a place like this these days. My father tried. Made a business of it. I grew up here and I love it. Which is why I negotiated for this job when we eventually sold out to the Trust.'

This was real, whatever it was that had happened in that strange interlude between. This she could touch and hold on to. It was solid.

'Shall we get that tea?'

Meriel was about to assent when she remembered. No, there was no leaving here until she had found out.

'Not yet. I want to show you something.'

The portrait had not changed. It was no dream for it was just as she had seen it. She turned to the man wearing Nicolas's face. He looked puzzled. 'She's a bit of a mystery, that one. No one knows just who she was, nor why she should be wearing the Presteigne necklace.'

'You recognise it?'

He glanced briefly at her. 'Of course. It's worth a fortune. It went to a museum long ago.'

'Then it remained in the family?' Meriel asked eagerly. 'It wasn't lost to him?'

'Him?'

'Nicolas. The man in the portrait.'

He shrugged, obviously bewildered. 'Why do you ask? It still belongs to the family but it's on permanent loan.'

'Then you own it?'

There was a half-smile in his eyes, faintly teasing. 'Why the third degree?'

Meriel caught an unbearable echo of Nicolas in both face and voice.

His expression altered. 'Forgive me, but I've just noticed the oddest thing.' His glance flicked up. 'It's uncanny but you resemble the woman in this portrait.'

There was a moment of silence. Meriel prayed he would let it alone. When he spoke again, softly, she felt a rush of tenderness as the timbre in his voice struck ever stronger against the memory.

'What's your name?'

She dared to look at him. 'Meriel.'

The smile reached into her heart and twisted. 'Right then, Meriel, let's get that cup of tea.'

Meriel followed as he led the way, treading briskly along the carpeted gallery. Her life had changed, ended, and now began anew.

The face from the portrait turned as the owner of the Presteigne necklace reached the door. 'By the way, I haven't introduced myself.'

It came out without thought, like a recollection tucked away in the mists of time, waiting its moment.

'You don't need to. I know who you are. You're Sir Nicolas Presteigne.'

'Yes.' And Nicolas winked at her. 'These days, though, it's just Nick.'

He held out his hand. Meriel moved to take it, and his warm grip enclosed her fingers.

Annie Murray

Annie Murray was a 'childhood writer'. Her career was helped a great deal by belonging to Tindal Street Fiction Group in Birmingham and by winning the SHE/Granada TV Short Story Competition in 1991. She has published short stories in a number of anthologies as well as *SHE* magazine. Her first regional saga, *Birmingham Rose* appeared in 1995 and reached *The Times* bestseller list. She has since published more than a dozen others, including the 'Cadbury books', *Chocolate Girls* and *The Bells of Bournville Green, Family of Women* and her latest, *A Hopscotch Summer*. Annie has four children and lives near Reading. You can find more at www.anniemurray.co.uk

On the Stroke of Mid-Life

The river is like green glass this morning, reflecting a pale winter sky as I jog beside it. I try to enjoy every detail—sunlight on leafless trees, the red glow of berries in the hedge—rather than dwelling on my own stupidity.

What's important, I tell myself, is being here now, not hurrying to reach somewhere else. Besides, once you reach your forties you can be grateful for your body agreeing to run anywhere at all. And further besides, I've just come mortifyingly close to making a catastrophic fool of myself as a woman. A *middle-aged* woman, however much my hair makes me look twenty from behind.

I started jogging after Chris. I work mainly from home and it's easy to get flabby and brain-dead stuck at the desk all day. I hope I'll see the back of all that soon, now I'm easing my way out of IT into my own business: reflexology and aromatherapy. I have the house in a lovely spot near the river, three clients so far—all likeable—and here I am: new life, new me. That's what I felt at first, after he left: euphoria, with it all opening up, exciting new start, running my own show, free to come and go as I pleased.

But loneliness creeps up on you slyly, like a virus in the blood: no one there to discuss what to have for dinner, no one to snuggle up to at night.

Chris is five years older than me. 'It's a mid-life thing,' he said. 'I don't seem to know who I am any more. I've lost myself.'

But both of us had been pretending for far too long. Whatever forces had kept us in amiable convergence through our twenties had slewed, until we were altered planets receding from one another.

None of it was the nightmare it might have been. We never had children—it never happened for us. Chris bought me out of the house and we opted not to open hostilities over every CD and Mexican rug. Neither of us is materialistic. I was to keep Dotty, our bouncy brown and white spaniel, because I am the one at home. Walking her keeps me fit-ish, but I began to notice what the polite might call 'extra love handles', and a certain bonniness under my chin. Where would it end? I wondered, in blobby panic.

In the meantime, Chris, after a disastrous fling with someone called Sarah, wants to come back. His calls convince me of the impossibility of this and leave me feeling even lonelier. Hence the endorphin-and-elixir-of-youth-seeking exercise.

I saw the boats on the first day. I eased myself into the first run in my new blue tracksuit and shirt—warm up well if you're over thirty!—along the sward of meadow which edges the water on one side, overlooked from the other by the magnificent houses of overpaid money-shufflers. Sorry, city bankers. I seemed to have plenty of energy at first. Perhaps I wasn't as decrepit as I feared! There weren't many people about, only a dog walker and a middle-aged bloke in a leather hat on a bench, deep in a book. Pretty funny time to be reading at eight in the morning, but then there are plenty of weirdos in this town.

After a short time, just as my legs started to feel as if they were full of wet sand, a voice grew louder along the path.

'*Stroke! Stroke!* OK—pull in! Pep talk!'

The duffel-coated coach on his bike, megaphone in hand, braked by a wooden landing stage and the eight, beautifully controlled, skimmed to a halt and the crew feathered their oars. I could hardly stop now, not with eight super-fit rowers as an audience!

It was hard not to feel self-conscious as I goaded my shrieking muscles, my 'love-handles' juddering and face turning puce in the freezing air. Even my one redeeming feature, hair of coppery, pre-Raphaelite abundance was scraped back in a scraggy ponytail.

It was the stroke who caught my eye. The one at the back of the boat and therefore, from my point of view, at the front. His upturned face showed rock-grey eyes, fantastically sculpted cheekbones like Michelangelo's *David* and a head of thick mahogany hair. Caught my eye is a bit of an understatement. And he was half-smiling, despite the abuse being hurled at them.

'You total *idiots!* You're crap! You're all over the place! I've never seen such a bloody shambles!' The coach looked at his watch. 'We've only got... Oh, for God's sake, the bloody thing has stopped!... 'Scuse me—have you got the time?'

'Yeah—' I said, casually grasping this fantastic excuse to catch my breath. 'It's eight twenty-seven.'

'Thanks—my battery—you wouldn't believe it...' The coach, morphing suddenly into Mr Nice Guy instead of *Obersturmführer* as he had been a moment ago, grinned at me. 'Sorry about the ear-bashing. Hope it hasn't spoiled your run?'

Suddenly I felt as if I'd joined some sort of heaven-born league of the athletic. I could feel 'David' looking at me.

'Oh, no—not at all. How's the training going?'

'Better than you might think!' The Michelangelo masterpiece called out in a voice that resonated through me like the deep C string on a cello. 'Listening to him you'd think we'd never taken a boat out before!'

Scattered laughter from the others.

'Well—' I shifted my weight gently from one foot to the other, like a dedicated runner who really has to get on '—you looked pretty good to me. Good luck—I s'pect I'll see you again.'

'Yeah, sure,' the coach said. 'What's your name?'

'Alex!' I jogged away, feeling I'd rejoined the human race. People say I look young for my age. That's what not having children does for you. I ran off. The bloke with the book looked up as I passed with a flash of blue eyes.

'Morning!' he said.

'Morning!' I cried magnanimously to a mere sedentary being with strange habits. I did like his hat, though. And wondered what he was reading.

It was amazing the way 'David' pitched camp instantly in my thoughts. He colonised them. I saw the boat quite regularly. I thought I'd jog once or twice a week, but most mornings I've found myself pulling on my trainers, apologising to Dotty that I'm leaving her behind and pounding along the river. In case I see them. Which I quite often do.

They started to wave. The coach always called hello. After the first two pep talks at the landing stage that I 'happened' to run into, he yielded up his name, which was Mike. But it was 'David's' wave I waited for. I know a woman of my age should have more sense, but I began to be convinced that he liked me. More than liked. He was the one who spoke, whose eyes would look me up and down. My hair is striking, of course, and now I'm getting fitter...

Gradually I learned all their names. Andrew, Paul, Bernardo. 'David', whose name I almost didn't want to know in case it turned out to be something awful like Wayne or Gordon, was in fact Tobias. *Perfect!* He was very friendly. But nothing like as friendly as I was in my fantasy life. That's another thing that creeps up on you—hunger for the feel of another's body, and Tobias's tanned and toned form and I had plenty of virtual tender exercise. In my dreams he was a most accomplished lover. I started to feel lithe and attractive again and in with a chance of being wanted.

I was becoming a frequent figure on the towpath. The hat and book man and I had begun to exchange regular smiles and waves.

'Hey, Alex!' Mike the coach called to me last Friday when we all showed up on the towpath together, our breath unfurling white on the air. 'We're meeting up at The Grapes for a Christmas drink tomorrow. Fancy coming along?'

'Go on—it'll be a laugh!' Tobias called, making my heart gambol like a little rabbit.

'Sure,' I said, trying to sound as if I regularly drink out with a gang of super-athletic men I'm old enough to have given birth to. But, I convinced myself, Tobias might be as old as thirty, which only made him fifteen years younger than me. If it was the other way round, no one would bat an eyelid, would they?

I dithered over what to wear and went for the casual, sporty look—a decent pair of jeans and figure-hugging top, showing just a hint of cleavage, and I put my hair up so as not to look like Crystal Tips, added mascara and a dab of perfume. I looked good—for my age. I hadn't done this sort of thing for years and I was more nervous than I could admit. I didn't like to ask myself what I really expected.

The pub was incredibly loud. I fought my way through to where the lads were sitting round a big wooden table cluttered with glasses.

'Alex—hi!' It was Mike who got up to greet me. 'Great that you could come. Can I get you a drink?'

There were girls of course—lots of them. My foolish, peri-menopausal dream bubble popped instantly at the sight of the lovely blonde specimen of womanhood perched on the arm of the bench next to Tobias, laughing down into his eyes. She looked all of eighteen. He, I admitted to myself, looked all of twenty-two. I smiled and nodded hello. It was Mike, I realised, who wanted me here. Mike who was closer to my age, with his stocky build and kind face. But I didn't want Mike. He had never crossed my mind.

I took a seat and for a time we all chatted at the top of our voices and I smiled and felt more and more like everyone's mother.

'Anyway,' I said lightly, after draining my glass of lager, 'I'm just on the way to another do. But it was nice to pop in.'

'Oh—' Mike looked downcast. Maybe he felt like everyone's uncle. 'Shame you can't stay.'

It's made a difference to the jogging. I still do it, of course, but I find I'm only keen to get out of bed a couple of times a week. There's been a frost, making the ground ankle-ricking hard, but the sight of the skeleton-white trees is a wonder. I, poor foolish woman, have seen no rowers, as they are on holiday, and have pulled myself together. That was a close one, in folly terms. Chris was right about mid-life—it's as if the map you once knew has been swivelled round.

It's quiet this week and I jog along, enjoying the sensation of my legs moving. People are indoors, getting on with Christmas week, keeping warm. But the leather hat man is here, as he so often is. Two days ago I said good morning and he replied, raising his eyes from the latest book. I can see him now, on that bench close to the lane which runs down from the main road. This time, he looks up and watches as I run towards him.

'D'you like doing that?' he asks as I come close.

Do I say *Yes,* and keeping running? Or stop?

'Mixed,' I say, stopping, but still flexing my legs. 'But, overall, it makes me feel better.'

He watches me, weighing my words. I feel something very deep might come out from under the brim of that interesting hat but in the end all he says is, 'Yes. Well, that's good.'

He has a very direct blue-eyed gaze and a rugged face with the makings of a beard, twiglet coloured. He looks like a forester.

'What are you reading?' I've been wondering this since I first saw him but have been too distracted by the blessed infant Tobias.

He turns the book over. Wilfred Thesiger.

'The great desert wanderer,' he says. 'I suppose I'd've liked to have been an explorer. But there's not much left to explore now. The world seems to have been covered.' His voice is gentle, and he gives off an air of someone who thinks, which is pretty rare.

'Why are you here?' I ask, waiting for him to show signs of mental instability—of the sort that goes with thinking too much.

'Oh, I've just come off shift.' He speaks looking across the river. A grebe flips under the water just in front of us. 'I work nights—staff nurse, medical ward. I can't go straight home to bed; I have to put the night down first. So I've been coming here a while.' After a pause, he adds, 'Only now, there's a bit more to it.'

'Oh?'

He looks at me directly, his gaze sage and boyish at the same time. 'I like to watch you running.'

This is where I'd normally be tempted to make a stalker joke, but I don't. He's too sincere and serious. His voice is a deep, melodious cello, with a touch of melancholy that appeals to my heart. He's about the same age as me, I realise. And real.

'Well,' I say foolishly, 'that's nice.' And I admit to myself that the days he has not been sitting here I have missed his quiet presence.

'Sit down, if you've got time? I suppose there's someone waiting for you at home?'

I sit. 'Just my dog, Dotty. You?'

He shakes his head. 'She left me. Two years ago. With our little boy, Daniel.'

'I'm Alex,' I say, and put out my hand.

'Here—' He has on soft leather gloves, which he pulls off and gives to me. 'You'll get cold. I'm Joel.'

The gloves feel comforting, warm from his big woodcutter's hands.

'We're the arse-uppards age group when it comes to relationships, aren't we?' he says ruefully. 'Get to your forties, and wham!'

'Mid-life… Yes…' I grin. 'Time for all sorts of foolishness. Like taking up running.'

'That's not foolish—you look great.'

'Thanks,' I say, truly grateful for this. Sitting here with him feels comfortable, like the beginning of a journey that I want to make in his company, where I already love the landscape. 'Will you tell me about Wilfred Thesiger?'

Jane Wenham-Jones

Jane Wenham-Jones is the author of three novels and a non-fiction book—*Wannabe a Writer?*—a humorous look at the trials and tribulations of becoming a scribe. She has also contributed to several short story anthologies and two cookery books, the latter being a particular achievement since she barely knows where the kitchen is. As a freelance journalist, she has had numerous short stories and articles published in women's magazines and the national press and is the agony aunt for *Writing Magazine*. Jane has appeared on a variety of TV shows—from *Ready, Steady, Cook* to *The Politics Show*—and many radio programmes and is regularly booked as an after-dinner speaker. Find out more about Jane at www.janewenham-jones.com

Wolf Whistle

I stood in front of the mirror and tried not to cry. It wasn't just because my swimwear seemed to have mysteriously shrunk or even that a scary anniversary was looming. It was the reality I was facing in the glass. These things creep up on you. One day you're happily prancing about in your bikini and the next everything's rather wobbly and best-covered-up. Suddenly you find yourself putting back the T-shirt with the sparkly bits and the risqué slogan, as you're just a bit too old for that sort of thing…

'You are fat and forty,' I told my bare stomach. It quivered.

I should have been feeling great. John had brought me to the most beautiful part of Spain as a birthday treat. He'd really splashed out and I was doing my best to enjoy it. It *was* lovely. Our villa was gorgeous, cool tiled floors, patio doors opening onto the pool, bougainvillaea splashing colour down the white walls. We spent scented evenings sitting on our terrace, the air warm and soft, lunchtimes overlooking the harbour sipping chilled white wine in the hot sun. We'd left the kids at home. It was just the two of us. It should have been perfect but I had this horrible sick feeling in the pit of my stomach because builders didn't whistle from building sites any more.

They were putting up new villas down the road. We had to walk past them to go to the beach, bar or shops. I didn't give them a second glance until I went down there on my own one morning to get some bread. The girl walking ahead of me was in her twenties, long blonde hair swinging, denim-skirted hips swaying, acres of long golden leg. There was a chorus of approval from the scaffolding as she sauntered by. She tossed her head, threw up a hand in a disparaging and decidedly rude gesture and strode on.

And I suddenly realised—that hadn't happened to me for a long time.

Before it was my turn to pass, I sucked in my middle, shook back my short, freshly-coloured-to-banish-the-grey locks, thrust out my chest and adjusted my sarong into a new fetching angle that showed just a bit of thigh. The crew had all gone back to work. Most of them didn't even look up. But I slowed down anyway, gazed boldly at the nearest workman and gave him a big smile.

He gave me a friendly nod and smiled back—like he might at his mum. Come to think of it, I was probably old enough to be his mum.

Back in our bedroom, I stared at my rounded tummy and the interesting network of lines around my eyes—and then at the dress I'd brought to wear out on my big night. The one that had looked so slinky and alluring on the matchstick person in the shop window. I held it against myself and stretched it across my front. It wasn't unlike the dress I'd worn on my twenty-fifth—when I was still slim and glowing. Now I'd look like a celebration dumpling.

'Forties are cool these days, Mum,' my sixteen-year-old daughter

Kelly had said comfortingly before we left. 'Look at Madonna,' she added, as if there might possibly be a comparison to be made. 'She's still sexy.'

'I am clearly not,' I said to John, wounded. 'Not one of them even bothered to whistle.'

'You used to moan when they did,' John reminded me. 'You used to say it was sexist.'

'Hmm.' I did not wish to hear anything rational. 'Then at least I had the choice of being offended. Now I haven't. I am old and decrepit.'

I paused for John to gallantly refute this but I raised my eyes to see him gazing in open-mouthed admiration at the pretty dark-haired waitress in the cropped white T-shirt who was sashaying her way between the tables.

'See!' I said. 'Even you'd rather ogle her!'

John looked at me. 'Actually,' he said mildly, 'I was just hoping Kelly doesn't slide off and get her belly pierced like that while we're away.'

I pulled a face. 'With my mother in charge? I was twenty before she'd let me have my ears done. Twenty,' I added bitterly. 'We don't appreciate youth at the time, do we?'

John laughed. 'You poor old thing! Downright ancient, aren't you?'

'I'm glad you think it's funny!' I said hotly. Stupidly, I felt the tears rise in my eyes.

John frowned. 'Perhaps you...'

I glared, daring him to even think PMT. 'I'm not,' I snapped. 'Or were you going to suggest the menopause?' I sniffed huffily.

'What?' He looked startled. 'I was going to say: have another drink. It's your birthday tomorrow.'

'Don't remind me,' I said crossly, a hand over my glass.

I woke in the morning to find the other half of the bed empty. I sat up in alarm. Had I driven John away with my grouchiness?

The whole evening had been awkward after that and John had eventually lost patience. 'It's only a number,' he'd said irritably. 'We all get older—you'll just have to face it.' We'd got into bed hardly speaking.

Now he'd gone, leaving a note on the bedside table. *Gone to Beach Bar for Breakfast.* No card. No kisses. I looked at it with a fresh lump in my throat as I suddenly felt ridiculous and selfish. John had tried so hard to make this lovely for me and he was right. I might as well accept I was middle-aged and start acting it instead of flouncing about like a petulant adolescent. Or—as Kelly's words rang in my ears again—perhaps I should cut my hair, start going to the gym and get my own navel pierced. I threw on my T-shirt and shorts and ran my fingers through my hair. Whatever I did, who cared about a bunch of Spanish builders? Right now I was going to find my husband…

I was too busy framing my apology speech to be looking at the scaffolding this morning. I was almost running as I hurried down the hill towards the beach but the noise made me jump. I looked round for a local beauty but there was only me. And, high up on a plank, clutching one of the poles and looking a little green around the edges was John. He waved, wobbled, put two fingers back in his mouth and emitted another ear-splitting whistle.

Various heads in safety helmets appeared and followed suit.

I put my hands to my mouth as a rose fell at my feet. Moments later John clambered down a ladder beside it, looking grateful to be on solid ground. 'If I were a builder, I'd always whistle,' he said.

As he kissed me there was a cheer from above and a catcall of things that I presume were Spanish for, 'Get in there, John.'

'You're still pretty gorgeous to me,' John said, wrapping his arms round me. 'However old you are.'

I hugged him back, feeling suddenly light and happy and

Madonna-like after all. I looked at him through lowered lashes and adopted my sexiest tones. 'Even if I get my belly-button pierced?'

John poked a finger into my midriff and ducked as I tried to thump him. But he was holding me tight as he grinned. 'You'd have to find it first…'

Rosie Harris

Rosie Harris was born in Cardiff and for several years worked in the City Hall. Her husband, Ken, was from Wallasey and after they married they lived on Merseyside for many years. In the nineteen-sixties she ran her own agency, Regional Feature Service, writing articles for most of the provincial newspapers. During the seventies she became Editorial Controller for a non-fiction house. In the nineteen-eighties, after publishing a number of non-fiction titles, she turned to fiction and during the eighties and nineties had a number of short stories published as well as five books by Sphere under the name Marion Harris.

Since 2002 she has had some twenty books published by Heinemann/Arrow. She sets her books in the nineteen-twenties because she has a great admiration for the women who were wives and mothers in those days. In 2005 she was one of the judges when Arrow and ASDA collaborated in a major national competition to find the next big saga writer.

Her most recent titles are *Love Changes Everything* and

The Quality of Love. The next, *Whispers of Love,* will be published in March 2010. Find out more about Rosie and her writing at www.rosiebooks.co.uk

Baby Love Rules

Pressed against the rail on the upper deck of the *SS Cathays,* Bronwen Davis scanned the quayside, her eyes screwed up against the early June sunshine. The upturned faces became a blur as she tried to pick out her sister and two brothers from the crowd gathered on the dockside. The ship's hooter, warning that they were about to sail, sent a mixture of apprehension and excitement through her.

Ever since she could remember, Bronwen had envied the seagulls their ability to fly out over the mud banks of Cardiff Bay to where the Bristol Channel met the sea. She'd dreamed of the day when, by some magic, she would do the same.

And now, it seemed, that day had arrived but not for the reasons she had dreamed about. Any moment, the *SS Cathays* would set sail on her long journey across the Atlantic.

Overcome, Bronwen clutched the rail as the expanse of water between the ship and Cardiff Pier Head widened. There was no turning back; as maid to Lily Bonner she was as committed to making a new life for herself in America as the Pilgrim Fathers had been when they'd sailed from Plymouth over three centuries earlier.

Apprehension mounted as the last speck of her homeland disappeared. With a lump in her throat, she wondered if she would ever see Cardiff or her family again…or reach American soil in safety.

Less than two months ago the *Titanic* had set out on just such a voyage and hit an iceberg with a dramatic loss of life. Elwyn, her childhood sweetheart, had been one of the crew and, like so many others, was never seen again. For her, this trip was a pilgrimage as well as the start of a whole new life.

As she descended into the bowels of the ship in search of her employer, the swaying motion made it difficult for her to keep her balance. It was a hundred times worse than the swaying of the trams that ran from the Pier Head up to The Hayes.

Mrs Bonner had warned her it might take a day or so to find her sea legs but she'd never thought that a ship of this size would pitch so much.

'Are you all right?' gasped Bronwen. 'The ship's rocking like a cradle!'

'There's no need to worry about me.' Mrs Bonner laughed. 'I'm a seasoned traveller. I've never been seasick in my life. I'm more concerned about where I'm going to put all my belongings. Everywhere's so small.' Mrs Bonner led the way through her stateroom into the adjoining bedroom.

To Bronwen's eyes it was spacious and magnificently furnished. There was a double bed, a screened off corner containing a washstand and toilet necessities, as well as a writing table and a deep cupboard.

By the time they'd unpacked, the *SS Cathays* had reached the open sea and was being buffeted by enormous waves.

'If you're feeling seasick then you'd better go and lie down,' advised Lily Bonner when Bronwen clutched at her stomach and breathed heavily.

Bronwen found that her own cabin on the deck below was a mere slit of a room, barely large enough to turn round in. The bunk bed was so narrow that Mrs Bonner, who was now eight months pregnant, would never have been able to lie on it. Bronwen was afraid that she might fall out if she turned over in her sleep.

Bronwen still felt ill next morning. The moment she lifted her head everything in the cabin swam. It was the same every day from then on. In fact, they were within sight of the American coastline and the pounding of the ship's engines had dropped to a gentle pulsating throb before she ventured up on deck.

Wan and listless, she leaned against the rail, trying to control her heaving stomach and show enthusiasm as Lily Bonner, waving her hands, pointed out the various waterfront landmarks as they approached the harbour.

Bronwen tried to concentrate but the horizon was lifting and falling rhythmically in time to the pulsating engines.

'I'm desperately sorry,' she apologised. 'You've been looking after me instead of me taking care of you, but I...I've never been ill like this in my life.'

'The moment you put foot on dry land the feeling will go,' advised Lily. 'Some are good sailors and some are not. At least that assures me of one thing... You won't be in any hurry to go rushing back to your little island. The thought of having to cross the Atlantic Ocean will put you off!' she said, laughing.

Bronwen closed her eyes. Countless times she'd asked herself if she had done the right thing in agreeing to accompany Lily Bonner back to America. Yet what alternative did she have? Once her father learned that she was expecting a baby, he would have turned her out and even her sister and brothers would have shunned her for bringing disgrace to the family.

She shuddered, reliving for the thousandth time that terrible night when she'd heard that the *Titanic* had gone down and knew that Elwyn would never come home to marry her.

More than once, when Lily Bonner had sat by her side, stroking her brow and trying to calm her, Bronwen had been tempted to confide in her. Being eight months pregnant herself, perhaps Mrs Bonner would understand her dilemma and not hold it against her?

As the motion of the boat steadied, Bronwen struggled to pull herself together and take an interest in the strange new land that was now to be her home.

New York Harbour was so much bigger than Cardiff Docks. She'd never seen so many ships lying at anchor, or so much bustle. Although everyone seemed to speak English, it was with a gravelly drawl that sounded strange to her ears after the lilting voices of her homeland.

Lily Bonner changed subtly when they sighted New York Harbour, obviously excited to be coming home. Bronwen was surprised to learn after they'd disembarked that New York was not their ultimate destination.

'We'll be staying over until the baby is born and then we'll be going on to Rhode Island,' Lily Bonner said as they stood on the quayside waiting for Lily's husband, Marcus, to take them in his carriage to Fifth Avenue.

'Does that mean another sea voyage?' asked Bronwen fearfully and was relieved to be told that they would be driving a couple of hundred miles northwards and that was all.

'Many of our friends and neighbours will still be wintering here in New York,' Mrs Bonner explained. 'I simply can't wait to go to all the parties. Can you imagine the envy on everyone's face when they see my wonderful new gowns?'

Bronwen stared at her in dismay. 'It's doubtful if any of them will fit you,' she warned. 'In the last three weeks you have…' she searched desperately for the right words '…grown much fuller.'

'I sure am aware of that! You'll have to let out the seams and then take them back in again after I've been delivered.' Lily beamed, patting her enlarged stomach.

Catching her first glimpses of New York from the carriage, Bronwen thought the four-storey brownstone houses in the heart of the city, though elegant, disappointing.

The Bonners' house in Fifth Avenue, however, was a double mansion, lofty and spacious. Her room was magnificent. Two doors led off it, one to a bathroom and the other to a good-sized room decorated in white, and in the centre was a magnificent cot trimmed in white satin and lace, ready for Lily Bonner's baby.

Bronwen found her life in America unlike anything she had imagined. As nursemaid-to-be she'd expected to spend most of her time in her rooms, filling her day with sewing chores and getting ready for the baby, but Lily asked her opinion on a myriad of domestic matters and, more often than not, accepted her advice.

Accompanying Lily on social outings became a pleasure rather than a chore. Lily gave her half a dozen of her own dresses and told her to alter them to fit; she introduced her to friends and neighbours as though she was an equal. As Lily's confinement drew nearer, Bronwen found she was being treated more and more like a friend.

'You're quite sure, honey, that you'll be able to cope when this baby arrives?' Lily would ask almost daily. 'I have no experience of babies at all!'

'Of course! I looked after my brothers and sister after my mother died, and I brought my youngest brother, Ifor, up from the day he was born.'

Bronwen was tempted to confide about her own predicament. It would have been a relief to share her secret with another woman. At night, in the privacy of her comfortable bedroom, she studied her changing shape in the cheval mirror. The way her waist was thickening and her breasts enlarging alarmed her. She couldn't ignore her condition for much longer. She had already felt the fluttering tremors beneath her heart as the child within her made its first feeble movements.

But it would be unfair to trouble Mrs Bonner in her present condition. When the baby was delivered she would be so over-joyed that, hopefully, she would accept the news with much greater understanding.

The fact that Lily Bonner would be so dependent on her in helping to care for the new baby and therefore unlikely to dismiss her on the spot also had a bearing on Bronwen's decision.

Lily Bonner's baby was born on the last day of July 1912. The physician, Dr Whitehead, accompanied by a nurse and a midwife, attended her as soon as she went into labour.

Bronwen was at Mrs Bonner's side, doing all she could to soothe and calm her. Afterwards she was adamant that it was only Bronwen's devotion that brought her through the terrible ordeal. Nothing had prepared her for such a traumatic experience.

When Bronwen went to inform Marcus Bonner that he had a daughter and that his wife was asking for him, the look of fury in his blue eyes was so intense that Bronwen was taken aback.

'A girl! I wanted a boy—a son and heir.' His tone was savage. He took a long hard swig from the whisky bottle at his elbow, then held his head in his hands.

Realising that she was watching him, he made a belated effort to extricate himself from the situation. 'Forgive me. I was carried away…' He bit his lip.

So great was his disappointment and frustration that the baby was not a boy that Marcus remained in his study, drinking and brooding, for the rest of the morning. By the time he went in to visit his wife and the new arrival, he was completely befuddled.

There was no question of Lily feeding the baby herself. For several days she lay prone in the huge bed, unable even to take food unaided. It was left to Bronwen to see to the infant and to find a suitable wet nurse.

And Lily was emphatic that she was much too old ever to undergo such an experience ever again.

Although Marcus accepted the many congratulations, he was furious at Lily's refusal to consider having another child. It meant that his chances of inheriting Lily's wealth were negligible.

As her strength returned, so Lily's maternal instinct developed and she was briefly besotted by her baby daughter.

'Have you ever seen anything quite so beautiful as my darling little Poppy?' she burbled as she pulled the lacy shawl to one side and gazed lovingly at the tiny oval face. 'Look at her delicate hands, her beautiful eyes.'

She extolled the baby's virtues daily until Bronwen saw that Lily was becoming exhausted and insisted on rest.

'Yes, perhaps you're right,' Lily would sigh, lying back on her silken pillows. 'I'm most grateful to you for the devotion you've shown me over the past weeks, you know!' Tears of gratitude shining in her grey eyes, Lily grasped Bronwen's arm. 'Promise me you'll not think of leaving me.'

'Well…'

Bronwen's slight hesitation brought a look of horrified concern to Lily's face.

'You're not homesick for Cardiff, are you?'

'No, no, it's nothing like that.'

'Then why can't you give me the assurance I'm asking for?'

'I…I don't know how to explain.' Consumed by misery, Bronwen kept her gaze on the baby, fussing with its shawl.

'You must! I won't rest until you assure me you will stay. Are you unhappy here? Has someone said something to upset you? Are you finding the work too hard?' Lily Bonner's voice grew shriller with each question.

'Please, it's nothing like that.' Colour stained Bronwen's cheeks. 'I…I don't know how to tell you…I've tried several times…I… I'm pregnant.'

Mrs Bonner stared at her in consternation. She had been so concerned about her own figure, longing for the day when she would return to her normal size, that she hadn't noticed the changes in Bronwen. She looked at the girl standing by her bedside in utter disbelief.

'Who is the father? When is it due?'

Lily Bonner listened to Bronwen's story with compassionate murmurs even when Bronwen admitted that she'd known she was pregnant before she left Cardiff. When she explained that the baby's father had been one of the seamen who'd drowned on the *Titanic* there were tears in Lily's eyes.

'Honey, this is so tragic! So what are you planning to do?'

'I don't know.' Bronwen hung her head to hide tear-filled eyes. She felt as if her entire world was caving in. Coming to America with the Bonners had seemed perfect, but now she was not so sure. If the Bonners turned her out, then she would be friend-less and utterly alone in a strange country.

'Do you want to return to Cardiff?'

Bronwen looked up, startled, brushing away her tears with the back of her hand. 'There is no point in my doing that! My father won't give me house room if he knows I'm pregnant.'

Lily Bonner's heart leapt as she realised the situation could be turned to her advantage, providing she handled it carefully.

She'd found Bronwen such a source of strength and comfort during her confinement. She'd been quick to realise that, adorable though her baby might be, she would make a consid-erable difference to her lifestyle. She had no illusions about the colossal amount of work involved in raising a child and the sac-rifices she would have to make.

Although she'd decided she was much too old to embark on motherhood again, she was far too young to sacrifice her social life in order to be a devoted mother. She needed a deputy and Bronwen was the ideal person, though Bronwen was not yet twenty and quite attractive so might want more from life than to be a surrogate mother.

But now, so it seemed to Lily, Bronwen would be more than ready to fall in with her wishes. With a child of her own on the way, she needed the security of a permanent home. If Lily gave her that, then she would be able to count on Bronwen's loyalty.

She took Bronwen's hands. 'You poor child! You should have confided in me weeks ago,' she admonished. 'Now that you have told me, I will do all I can to help you.'

'I can stay and look after Poppy?'

'Of course! You must think of this as your home.'

'You mean…you mean even after my baby is born?'

'Yes, honey. That is exactly what I mean. You see, I want you to take full charge of my darling Poppy until she is a full grown girl. You can look after your own baby at the same time. I will make sure you have everything you need. Your baby can share a nursery with Poppy, both here in our New York house and in our home at Rhode Island.' Lily beamed. 'Now, isn't that just the most perfect solution?'

'I…I don't know what to say.' Tears of relief and gratitude streamed down Bronwen's face. She'd never dreamed of such generosity. She caught at Lily Bonner's hand, fervently kissing the back of it. Blinded by tears of gratitude, she didn't see the look of triumph on Lily's face.

From the moment Dr Whitehead said she was fit enough to make the journey, Lily Bonner began making plans to leave New York. The heat was already becoming oppressive. She couldn't wait to move to their summer residence in Newport, Rhode Island.

'You'll like it there,' she assured Bronwen. 'Breezes straight off the sea, sandy beaches, green lawns, glorious copper beech trees and some of the most fabulous mansions you have ever set eyes on.

'The social scene in Newport is hectic; I shall need two or

three different outfits each day so do remember that Poppy is not your only responsibility. I brought you to America so that you could be my dressmaker and now that I'm starting to regain my figure you're going to have plenty to do.'

Far from finding Rhode Island relaxing, Bronwen found her days so busy that she could scarcely fit everything in.

Dinner was always a grand affair and usually taken on one of the steam yachts, and Lily's dress always more glamorous than the one she'd worn at luncheon.

When dinner was followed by a grand ball Lily wore one of her more elaborate gowns. Marcus would be in full evening dress and very often they didn't return home until the early hours of the morning. When Bronwen took Poppy along for her daily visit, Lily and Marcus were usually far too tired to give more than a cursory glance at the mewling bundle.

Lily was secretly disappointed that the baby was still so uninteresting. She looked forward to when Poppy could walk and talk. She ached to dress her up in pretty frilly dresses and bonnets, and show her off. Until that day, she embarked on a round of social engagements, determined to squeeze every vestige of pleasure and enjoyment she could from life.

Bronwen begged her to spend more time with the baby but Lily remained adamant.

'She's too young to know whether I am at her side.' Lily laughed. 'Anyway, honey, you are much more of a mother to her than I could ever be.'

Finally Bronwen, who was so advanced in her own pregnancy that she was bulky and clumsy in her movements, pointed out that she was finding it difficult to pick Poppy up and cuddle her, hoping that Lily would respond by spending more time with the baby. Instead, Lily engaged a nursemaid, ignoring Bronwen's protests.

'You'll need someone to help you, honey, when there are two

babies to look after,' Lily pointed out. 'It would be much better for the girl to start now, and for Poppy to get used to her before your baby arrives.'

Bronwen went into labour on a hot, humid day in late September, only a few days after Lily had decided that they would return to New York at the end of the week.

At first, Bronwen thought that the dull ache at the base of her back had been brought on by the additional lifting and stretching as she'd packed the clothes and nursery items that Lily wanted.

Lily, dressed in a navy-and-white-striped taffeta dress with a matching parasol to shade the enormous bright blue floppy feather hat that almost hid her face, was just setting out with Marcus for a luncheon date. Marcus was furious. 'Tell her we are due to join friends within the half hour and that you'll be back around three o'clock,' he snapped, consulting his gold hunter.

'I can't do that!' Lily protested. 'Bronwen never left my side all the time I was in labour.'

Marcus glared. 'Oh, come on, honey, she's merely a servant and this is an important social occasion.'

Lily glared. 'Just because you never showed the slightest concern when I was in labour, never even came near me, not even when my pains were at their very worst...'

'I couldn't bear to see you suffer,' he prevaricated, his handsome face dark with anger.

'Indeed? Well, I can't bear to simply walk away and leave Bronwen to suffer on her own,' she told him sarcastically.

'Women of her type don't suffer as you did. They...they just get on with it. It'll all be over in an hour or so.'

'In that case, go on your own to lunch and I'll accompany you to the ball tonight.'

Turning on her heel, Lily made for Bronwen's bedroom, leaving an angry Marcus in the hallway.

When Marcus returned from luncheon it was obvious to Lily that it was not going to be over in time for her to accompany him to the ball.

'Please,' Bronwen begged in between her pains, 'there is no need for you to miss the ball.'

But Lily staunchly refused. Bronwen was in such a terrible state of agitation that she seemed to have lost the will to cooperate with the midwife's instructions.

Towards dawn, when she was overcome by utter exhaustion, the child finally entered the world.

As the baby's first plaintive cry reached her, Bronwen closed her eyes and it was as though from another world she heard Lily telling her that she had a baby girl.

As the small body was placed into her arms Bronwen forced herself to look at her daughter. It was like looking at a replica of Elwyn's face.

'Lovely! It's a wonderful feeling when it is all over, isn't it?' The warmth in Lily's voice brought tears of relief and joy to Bronwen.

'It is indeed!' Bronwen breathed. 'Thank you for staying with me,' she added, grasping Lily's hand.

The two babies became the centre of both women's lives. Once Marcus had taken himself off on one of his interminable business trips the entire household revolved around the nursery, everything planned to fit in with the children's routine. Lily even abandoned her social whirl, devoting her time and energy to Poppy.

'You're missing out on all the parties,' Bronwen remonstrated when Lily turned down countless invitations to go out.

'I'm doing what I want to do.'

'If you tried on some of those wonderful dresses hanging in your wardrobe I'm sure you'll want to change your mind and decide after all to attend the suppers and balls.'

But the dresses, together with petticoats of satin, lace and taffeta, dozens of pairs of elbow-length white gloves, lace collars and ruffles and elaborate matching hats, remained hanging in the wardrobe.

Lily was far more concerned that there were enough pretty dresses and gowns for the two babies, and lace-trimmed bonnets to shade their delicate skin from the sun's rays. She made no distinction between the clothes selected for Poppy and those for Gemma.

Since Poppy was slight and small for her age, and Gemma larger than average, they were often dressed alike. Lily enjoyed nothing better than shopping in Fifth Avenue, returning with identical outfits for the two babies. When Bronwen protested at her extravagance she waved such remarks aside.

'Furthermore, from now on I want Gemma to address me as Aunt Lily and I want Poppy to call you Aunt Bronwen.'

For a long moment the two women faced each other, both stubborn and determined, battling with their own thoughts.

'If that is what you wish,' muttered Bronwen, her face a dull red.

'While Poppy is growing up I want her to feel part of a warm, loving family and I have more confidence that you'll provide the right sort of atmosphere than in Marcus ever doing so.'

Bronwen had already wondered about Marcus's long absences. Not that Lily was in the least melancholy! In fact, she seemed to be much happier when Marcus was away. It was as if Poppy fulfilled her life completely.

It did worry Bronwen, however, that Lily wanted Gemma to be included in Poppy's luxurious lifestyle. At the back of her mind lurked the fear that if anything happened to Lily, then she and Gemma might be banished from the Bonner household and, having been brought up in the lap of luxury, that would devastate Gemma.

Yet was it right to deny the child such a wonderful chance? Her mind raced ahead. Once nursery days were over, there would be private lessons, tuition beyond her wildest expectations.

Gemma would always be surrounded by luxury. She would sleep in a feather bed with the smoothest cotton sheets and lace-edged pillows. She would eat the best food, ride out in a carriage, go horse-riding or bicycling in the park, holiday each year at Newport, Rhode Island.

'Good. That's settled, then. There's only one other thing…'

Bronwen's heart missed a beat as Lily paused and frowned heavily.

'For the sake of the children, I want you to call me Lily and I shall call you Bronwen.'

'Oh, Mrs Bonner, you are my employer!'

'I am! So that is an order.'

Her tone was so crisp and authoritative that Bronwen found herself nodding obediently.

'Well, don't look so disapproving,' Lily said, laughing.

'If you are quite sure.' Bronwen let out a long sigh. 'It's going to feel very strange at first.'

'You'll soon get used to it.' Impulsively, Lily hugged her.

That long hot summer in Newport, Rhode Island, bonded the friendship between the two women and the two children. When they returned to their house in Fifth Avenue, the two babies, now inseparable, were moved into a more spacious nursery.

But when Marcus came home from Thanksgiving to New Year the routine changed to accommodate his presence and his interests. More and more, Bronwen was left looking after both little girls while Lily accompanied Marcus on a round of dinners, suppers, theatre trips and balls.

Marcus rarely came into the nursery unless he was looking for Lily, and when he did they would both leave almost instantly and their voices would be raised in anger the moment they were outside the door.

Bronwen knew that they quarrelled about the amount of time

Lily spent in the nursery and that Marcus resented the fact that the son he'd dreamed of had not materialised. He had no real interest in his daughter. Furthermore, he didn't approve of Gemma being treated as an equal.

Bronwen worried about this so much that she began to wonder whether it might be better for Poppy and Gemma to be separated now, while they were both too young to realise what was happening. She knew Lily would be upset, but hopefully she would understand and accept that such a decision ought to be taken.

But what would happen to her and Gemma if she left the Bonner household? Thousands of miles from home, she had no friends in America. Her wages had been generous and she had spent very little but, even so, she was doubtful that she had sufficient to pay her passage back to Cardiff.

And who would look after Gemma if she was seasick from the moment the ship left New York until they docked in Cardiff, as she had been on her trip over? What if their ship sank like the *Titanic* had done?

And then Marcus once more announced that he was going on a business trip for at least three months, probably much longer. And that he expected Lily to go with him.

There were several protracted discussions. Marcus was insistent that Lily should accompany him, not only on this occasion, but whenever necessary in the future; he was equally adamant that Poppy should be left at home.

'It is a hard decision,' Lily confided in Bronwen, 'but Marcus does need a hostess, you know, business dinners and so on. As long as I can be sure that you will always be here to take care of my darling Poppy, then I feel that my wifely duties should take precedence.' Her eyes were alight with excitement.

On the day of their departure she took her place beside Marcus, raising her handkerchief in farewell to Bronwen, who was standing at the nursery window holding both babies and encouraging them to wave goodbye.

The moment the cab turned the corner, still clasping Poppy under one arm and Gemma under the other, Bronwen twirled round the room with them.

Why had she worried? The nursery had, once again, become the centre of the universe, not only for the two babies, but for her as well.

And, so long as dear Lily remained so changeable, her need for Bronwen would guarantee that it always would be.

Trisha Ashley

Trisha Ashley was born in St Helens, Lancashire, and now lives in the beautiful surroundings of North Wales. She is the author of three historical novels and nine contemporary ones, the latest of which is *Wedding Tiers,* published by Avon, HarperCollins, though she is happy to say that her own wedding day was a bit less wacky than some of the ceremonies in this book… She has a website at www.trishaashley.com where she would love you to sign up for her newsletter, *Skint Old Northern Woman,* so you can get all the news from Trishaworld on a regular basis.

Tipping the Scales

She came up in the fishing nets, her cold, clammy skin like translucent pearl, naked apart from long silvery hair that clung like wet seaweed right down to the iridescent scales of her tail.

The crew conferred as she sat on the deck, watching them with aquamarine eyes, crunching the best of their hard-won catch between sharp, pointed white teeth. One of them, faster than the others and scenting a profit, caught her as she was about to slither back over the side.

She bit him, too, for his trouble. But she seemed happy enough in the hold, the men wary as they packed the fish with ice and sailed for port, fast.

A tall young man awaited them on the jetty, black curly hair blowing in the wind, eyes the turquoise of a Caribbean Sea. When they brought her up on deck, swathed in a mackintosh, he smiled dazzlingly.

She remembered her grandmother's stories. 'Are you my prince?' she asked, the first words she'd spoken. 'My destiny?'

'That's right, darling,' he agreed, handing the skipper a bundle of coloured paper.

He drove her through the early morning light to the fairground by the beach and pulled up outside some wooden doors.

'You'll be safe here,' he said, carrying her into a large room that smelt of stale seawater, algae and despair. When he switched on the light, great glass tanks cast watery shadows onto the walls and strange shapes moved within each one—except the last.

'There's something fishy going on,' she said, puzzled.

'Not on, *in,*' he replied, heaving her over the side with a splash.

'Don't leave me here,' she mouthed, bubbling, but his smile now reminded her of a barracuda.

'Sink or swim—my aquarium needs you. You put on a good performance for the punters and you'll get all the fish you can eat. Watch this.'

He drained one side of the tank opposite until a large grey seal sat in little more than a puddle…then, with a sudden shimmer, it changed shape to a slender young man with dark sad eyes.

'I'll leave you to get to know each other—at a distance,' he said, laughing, and left them in the aqueous half-light.

They sat on their fibreglass rocks, their eyes meeting through thick glass. 'He's the Owner,' explained the sealman. 'He does that every hour when the aquarium is open and humans pay money to come and watch.'

'How did he catch you?'

'Greed—I took the bait.'

'I thought he was my prince until he put me in stale water,' she said bitterly. 'I'm fed up to the gills.'

'He feeds us dead fish, too, and never cleans out the tanks. But you have to do what he says, or he will hurt you.' The sealman shuddered, his eyes going dark with remembered pain.

There was a hammering. 'What's he doing?' she asked.

'Changing the signs outside, at a guess. You'll be the star attraction now.'

'I want a mirror and a comb,' she said sulkily when the Owner came back in.

'You've got them—they're in that plastic clam shell over there. Now, you keep sitting on that rock and swish your tail occasionally…'

She slapped the water with it, drenching him from head to foot.

'You do that again, and there'll be no fish for *you* today,' he said, giving her an evil look. 'And after the aquarium's shut, I'll teach you some manners!'

When he'd gone to change she looked around her and sighed. 'How far from the sea are we?'

'Not far—when the front door is open you can smell the tang on the breeze. If there wasn't mesh over my tank I'd have been out of here in a flash and running down the beach—I'm sickening for the fresh, salty sea.'

'I couldn't run,' she said sadly. 'If I got out, how could I slither so far? My scales need oiling already.'

'I'd carry you; I wouldn't leave you here. But it's no use—the most we can hope for is that one day he will put us in a tank together.'

There was a sliding of bolts and a flood of light from the front of the aquarium. 'Hush, here come the visitors,' he warned. 'But if you put on a good show, perhaps he won't be angry with you later.' His tank filled with water and, with a flick of his flippers, he began to circle.

She watched as the crowd gathered, his tank was emptied again, and the sealman reappeared.

'How does he do that?' a girl asked.

'It's just a hologram projected in there; it's not real,' her boy-friend told her.

'He *looks* real,' she said doubtfully. 'And what about *her?*'

He shrugged. 'It's a woman wearing a mermaid tail, that's all. It's not even well made—look, you can see the join.'

The mermaid bared her teeth at them in a sharp smile and they stepped back nervously. She took up the mirror and began to untangle her silvery hair, humming.

The unearthly hum grew louder…and louder…until it became a strangely beautiful song that held the visitors fixed, en-thralled, to the spot.

Her voice rose higher: the glass walls of the aquarium began to tremble, the water rippled and the fish fled to their farther corners.

The sealman knew the power of that song.

'What's that racket?' the Owner demanded. He clapped his hands to his head. 'My eardrums! Stop it—stop singing *now.*'

But it was too late: everything rang and shimmered and swayed and trembled—and cracked. Great cascades of water poured out of every tank, swirling a flotsam of visitors, fish and the Owner towards the door.

The sealman, stepping gracefully over the shards, carried her out of the back door and towards the distant sea. The morning sun reflected off their nacreous skin and flashing scales. The crowds fell back, the beach road traffic stopped, the donkeys ran away and the kites tangled.

From behind came a sudden shout of, 'Stop them!'

This was beyond optimistic: for a seal, he ran fast. The waves were to his waist before anyone even reached the edge of the sea. Then there was a splash as they dived—cool, smooth bodies entwined, twisting and turning into the depths.

He gave her a passing unwary fish, salt fresh.

'*You* are my prince,' she said and, as a mark of her favour, bit the offering in half and gave him the head to seal their union.

Carole Matthews

Carole Matthews is an international bestselling author of hugely successful romantic comedy novels. Published in twenty-four countries, her unique sense of humour has won her legions of fans and critical acclaim all over the world. Latest bestsellers include *The Chocolate Lovers' Club, The Chocolate Lovers' Diet, It's a Kind of Magic* and *All You Need is Love. A Minor Indiscretion* and *A Compromising Position* both reached the top five in the *Sunday Times* bestseller chart. *You Drive Me Crazy* reached number eight in the original fiction charts. *Welcome to the Real World* was short-listed for the Romantic Novelists' Association Romantic Novel of the Year. *The Difference a Day Makes* and *That Loving Feeling* are out now.

When she's not writing novels, television or film scripts she manages to find time to trek in the Himalayas, rollerblade in Central Park, take tea in China and snooze in her garden shed in Milton Keynes. For regular news, competitions and short stories go to www.carolematthews.com or if you want to chat to Carole you'll find her on Facebook and Myspace.

A Weekend in Venice

It was already spitting when I left the hotel after an uninspiring breakfast of dry white bread and tasteless, rubbery cheese. Now the rain has settled in, not planning on blowing over in a pesky squall. This downpour is shaping up to give us a bad-tempered soaking and I think the bread at breakfast might be the only dry thing I see today. The sky is draped heavily over the tops of the ornate buildings. Venice in September, I hoped, would be full of sun, full of fun. Instead, it's full of tourists and full of water.

Winding through the maze of narrow backstreets, cobbles slick with rain, I make my way to St Mark's Square to find my tour guide. She's already in full flow, speaking to a huge group of Japanese tourists when I arrive. The guide is older than me, maybe ten years, but she's unutterably stylish—the chic that older Italian women do so well. There's a red silk scarf tied jauntily around the hips of her tight black jeans and she's carrying a matching umbrella that she hasn't put up despite the rain. Instead, she shelters under the arches around the damp façade of the

Doge's Palace while her tour group listen patiently in the pouring rain. My Japanese companions may be untroubled, clothed as they are in bright yellow rain capes, matching hats and shod in makeshift tie-on wellingtons that are being sold on the corner of every sodden street. I, in my summer-weight pea coat from Monsoon—how appropriate—and heeled suede boots, am less so.

The guide, Silvana, drones on for far too long about the historical importance of Venice as a trade route while the Japanese nod vigorously and we all get wet. My attention drifts. St Mark's Square is unusually empty, the outdoor cafés closed up, chairs stacked. Even the droves of streetwise pigeons have gone into hiding.

I should have been in Venice with Jerrard. The weekend was to mark our fifth anniversary together. We met at a conference on The Ethics of Green Marketing, which seemed so terribly dull a start to a love affair. To counteract this, we always went somewhere extravagantly romantic to celebrate the ticking off of another year together. Except this year we didn't. This year Jerrard felt that our relationship wasn't going anywhere. He felt 'the whole thing' had become stale. We should spend some time apart. *I* felt he meant he'd found someone younger and more obliging. Someone who didn't nag about leaving the remnants of his beard in the bathroom sink or make him pull his weight with the household chores. If he had met someone else, he wouldn't say. But he moved out, anyway.

I couldn't bear to see the weekend go to waste—call me frugal. As Jerrard did on many occasions. If I had been Jerrard, I would have gone to Venice anyway, hoping that it might reignite the spark that had been long missing. If that spark had still remained elusive, then I'd have called a halt. There's an etiquette to these things that he failed to understand. Take someone else, he urged. A salve to his conscience, perhaps. I didn't want to come with someone else. I wanted to be here with Jerrard. I wanted him to call me at the eleventh hour and sigh with relief when I told him that no, no one else had taken his place. No one else *could*.

Of course, he didn't call. He's walked out of my life without looking back to see if I'm okay, if I'm surviving without him, if I'm still in love with him. I am.

Inside the Doge's Palace, we trail around after the fragrant Silvana, through the crush of wet, doggy-smelling people, trying to admire the dark beauty of the Tintorettos while outside the rain gets heavier and heavier. Outside, great plumes of water spray from the mouths of the grimacing gargoyles on all corners of the roof, showering into the courtyard below, and it's easy to see why Venice is slowly being consumed by the rising tides.

The next part of our tour is supposed to be St Mark's famous Basilica. As I splash through ankle-deep puddles, thoroughly ruining my favourite boots, Silvana tells us with an insouciant shrug that the church is closed due to flooding. A high wind shouldering the waves across the lagoon has added its power to the rain and our tour is to be curtailed.

I booked the tour because I didn't want to mooch around Venice alone and lonely. Being in a group would give my emotions the shelter they required. It's not to be. Anyway, to be honest, the incessant chatter and clicking of camera shutters are not exactly enhancing my Venice Experience.

I decide to seek solace in a restaurant. A glass of good Rioja, some tiramisu and maybe a hot frothy cappuccino will restore my flagging spirits. Empty gondolas are tied up at the moorings: black, mournful, bobbing angrily at their enforced idleness. Their po-faced gondoliers are holed up in neighbouring cafés, conspicuous in their striped jerseys and comic boaters, thinking of all the tourists they've failed to ensnare, all the euros that haven't changed hands, how many times *O Sole Mio* hasn't been crooned. Today, Venice has pulled down its designer-labelled trousers and has bared its bottom at the tourists.

Cowering beneath my ineffectual umbrella, my long blonde hair plastered to my head, I find a pizzeria with steamed up windows and a cheerful hum of conversation. I think I'm lucky to score the last table until I find I'm sitting next to two American couples who talk in loud voices about 'doing Europe'. Today is Monday, so it must be Italy. Tuesday is France. Monday, England. My pizza is soggy, my wine is sharp, my tiramisu synthetic, my coffee and the service both lukewarm. The urge to phone Jerrard and cry is almost unbearable. Thank goodness the wine is awful, otherwise I might be tempted to down a whole bottle.

When I can linger no longer, I tip the waiter meanly as a small revenge for his indifference and head out into the downpour once more. The weather doesn't seem to be deterring the crowds and I squeeze my way towards the Rialto Bridge and the sanctuary of my hotel. On my bedside table there's a good book, a romance—and right now I need a happy ending. I'll have a hot bath, chill out, try not to think about what Jerrard's doing and read about the tangled love lives of others.

The steady stream of tourists thins to a trickle as I take the lesser-used backstreets to my hotel. The rain is worse. I look up, dodging the drips from my umbrella's spokes and don't recognise my surroundings. Somewhere in my haste, huddled down, I've missed my turning. There's a little shop that I should turn by, its window filled with carnival masques in red, black and silver—exotic, opulent, erotic. Each time I've passed I've stopped to drool over them but their prices are way beyond my meagre budget. I'm in a similar courtyard by a metal bridge but not the right one and now I don't know which way to go. My feet are cold, numb. My map, like my romantic novel, is on my bedside table. I hate this city. The rain is too heavy, the people too grumpy, the canals too smelly, the prices too extortionate, the pigeons too many, the pasta too fattening, the tourists too stupid. Tears run down my face. I'm alone and lost in Venice and I don't know what to do.

When I've done enough snivelling, I look up and try to get my bearings. Come on, Beth, get a grip, I chide.

Across the courtyard, there's a smart house. Its front door is bright red as are its balconies—surreal highlights in an otherwise monochrome scene. A small motorboat bobs by the door, next to a chalkboard, which has a phrase scrawled on it in a variety of different languages. The lettering is rapidly disappearing as fat drips of rain run down it. I can just about pick out the English version. *Models Required,* it says.

The door is ajar. Perhaps someone can tell me the way to my hotel. Before I can think better of it, I fold my umbrella and push open the door. The hall is dimly lit but warm and only serves to make me realise how cold I am. I shiver and call out, 'Hello.' My heels click on the caramel-coloured Venetian marble floor, echoing through the hall. 'Hello.'

A door opens and a tall man stands in the frame. The room behind is light and airy so I can't see his face. He says, 'You've come for the modelling?'

'No, no,' I answer. 'I'm lost. I'm looking for the Hotel Segusa.'

'Ah,' he says. 'Then you are very lost.'

'It's the rain.' I shrug as if it's an explanation. Nothing to do with my inability to remember to carry my map, of course.

'You are very wet,' he remarks. 'And you look cold.'

'I'm both.'

'Then come into my studio. Sit down. Wait. The rain will stop.'

'I don't want to disturb your work.'

'I am not working,' he says. 'I have no model. No muse. I am playing.'

It's tempting. My curiosity is piqued and the ancient radiator churning out heat is appealing.

He opens the door wider, light floods over him. His hair is dark and curling. His body is long, lean, athletic. A black T-shirt and jeans cling tightly to him, outlining his muscles and his slim hips. His skin is olive, a native, and when he smiles the room lights up some more. 'Come.' He beckons with slender artistic fingers.

Hesitant, I follow him into the studio. The room is bright white; the roof is made of glass and looks tear-stained with the rivulets of rain. There's a huge black leather couch and a large easel standing at one end. Behind, another enormous window with a view over the bleak slate-grey canal. A table filled with paints stands next to the easel.

'Oh,' I say. 'You're an artist.'

He laughs.

'I mean…well…you don't look like an artist.' He doesn't exactly comply with the typical image of starving artist in a grotty garret. I thought he was a photographer—that kind of studio.

'I don't know what an artist is supposed to look like.' His Italian accent is tinged with an American twang and I wonder if he's spent some time overseas. 'I'm Marcello.'

He holds out his hand and I take it. 'Beth.'

'I have coffee, Beth. Would you like some?'

'Please.'

There's a small kitchen area at the far end of the studio and Marcello goes to busy himself with making coffee while I stand and drip self-consciously on his floor.

'Take off your things,' he says to me. 'Be more comfortable.'

If only I could. I look round for something to do with my umbrella.

'Let me.' Marcello comes back with two cups of coffee, which he puts on the table with his paints.

I hand the umbrella over.

'Now your jacket.' I peel the wet sleeves away from my arms. Beneath it my T-shirt is soaked.

Marcello tsks at me. 'A cold will take you to your death. Off, off. I will find you a shirt.'

'But…I…'

'I work with naked women every day,' he says with a casual shrug. 'I am not shy.'

But I am! Before I can voice that particular thought, he's off, dumping my umbrella in the kitchen, hanging my coat over the back of a chair.

I have goose pimples on my arms and probably over the rest of my body. To distract me, I take in the artwork on the walls. There are, indeed, a lot of naked women, beautifully displayed, open, wanting, sensual.

Marcello returns and tosses a shirt at me. It's warm, dry. He shrugs again. 'What else are you going to do this afternoon? Take off all of your clothes. When you are warm again and we have drunk our coffee, I will paint you.'

My arms fold across my chest in an involuntary movement. 'I don't think…'

'You must not think at all,' he instructs. 'You must just do it.' Then he gives me my coffee cup.

Maybe Marcello has drugged me because as soon as I finish my coffee I'm so terribly tired, my limbs are leaden and I don't have the wherewithal to move. But, frankly, I don't care what he's done to me. Even though he's a stranger, I somehow feel safe here, in a warm cocoon. Maybe it's just relief that someone has taken control. My eyelids feel heavy. The rain clearly has no intention of easing up. It pours in torrents down the windows, drumming rhythmically, cutting us off from the world. He's left the room, my clothes are uncomfortably damp, so, tentatively, I tug my T-shirt over my head. Back to the door, I hurriedly unhook my bra and slip on his shirt. It's warm and soft, comforting on my chilled skin.

I pull off my boots. They're ruined, wet through, but, at the moment, I don't care. Wriggling my jeans over my hips, I'm relieved to see that the shirt falls to mid thigh and covers me with reasonable modesty.

'Sit down,' Marcello says when he comes back. 'Just relax.'

I edge onto the black sofa, curl my legs under me and try to look casual. He laughs at my discomfort. 'Pretend I am not here.'

How can I when he's staring at me so intently? I let my head fall back against a pillow. He goes to stand behind his easel. Then the reality of the situation hits me and I sit up straight again. 'I can't do this,' I tell him. 'Really. I'm far too strait-laced.'

Marcello smiles at me. 'I don't know what strait-laced is, but it sounds very nice to me.'

'I must go.'

'Wait,' he says. 'Now that you're here, I cannot let you go.'

A thrill of panic runs through me. He holds out a hand. 'Don't move. Don't move. I will make it all better.'

He reaches behind him and draws out a carnival masque from under a black sheet. I gasp. The eye-piece is feline, covered with rich red velvet the colour of a Venetian whore's lips. It's thickly encrusted with sequins and ruby red jewels. Above it, plumes of feathers stand proud, ruffling of their own volition. It's menacing, marvellous. Exciting and erotic. 'That's fabulous.'

His smile is indulgent. 'I knew you would like it.'

I wonder, has it been worn before, maybe by some glamorous woman dancing and posing her way through the streets of Venice, entertaining the crowd.

Marcello hands it to me. 'Put it on.'

'I can't!'

He looks bemused. 'Why not?'

It looks too mysterious, too daring and I'm strangely nervous of its allure. I'm not sure that I'm worthy of it. 'I don't know.'

'It will suit you,' Marcello assures me.

So I brush back my damp hair and put it on. It moulds to the contours of my cheeks, the bridge of my nose. Its weight is re-assuring. I look at him through the slits of the eyes and feel like a different person entirely.

'Get on the couch.'

Much to my own astonishment, I obey. Marcello arranges black pillows around my shoulders.

'Take off that shirt.' From nowhere, Marcello produces a sheath of blood-red crushed velvet. 'Drape this over you.'

I strip off the shirt and do as instructed, covering my breasts with the fabric.

'Leave them bare,' Marcello says. 'I want to see them.'

Lying back on the sofa, my head on the pillows, I let the fabric fall to my waist.

'Pull it high,' he says. 'High on your legs. Your thighs are magnificent.'

I don't think anyone has ever told me that before. My hands inch the velvet higher.

'Great,' Marcello murmurs. 'Wonderful.' He picks up a paint-brush. 'You look beautiful. *Bella, bellisimo.* Think amazing thoughts.'

I lie back on the pillows, breasts and thighs bared, arms lifted above my head and wonder what Jerrard would say.

'The light is gone. I can paint you no more.' Marcello puts down his brush. 'I can only remember you with the light of my eye.'

I'm tired, woozy, the hours have gone by while I've lain here, my mind in happy freefall. I try to sit up. 'I must go.'

'No.' Marcello sits by me. 'First I must love you,' he tells me. 'Then I must feed you.'

He laughs at the surprise on my face. Then he shrugs. 'It is the Italian way.'

Taking the soft velvet in his hands, he caresses my breasts with it, making my back arch. He strips off his clothes effortlessly as he covers me with kisses, murmuring, *'Bella, bella,'* as he does. Then, when he is naked and above me, he takes the strip of velvet and binds my wrists together as he holds my arms above my head. I want all of him inside me. More, more, more.

Then we twist together and I straddle him. I unbind my wrists and slip the velvet over his eyes while my tongue travels his body. The feathers on my masque shiver with excitement, ripples tensing and thrilling until I throw my head back and moan with pleasure.

For a long time we lie, Marcello's arms around me. The drumming of the rain has finally stopped. The silence is comfortable and welcome. Then Marcello says, 'And now, I promised I would feed you. I must do so.'

He eases away from me and pads, still naked, to the kitchen. I stare at the ceiling, spent, exhausted, exhilarated, not knowing what to think. When Marcello comes back, he brings a platter with bread, cheese, Parma ham and figs. Then he brings a bottle of wine and glasses.

Somewhat reluctantly, I sit up and take off the masque. 'I feel like another woman in this.'

'No.' He takes my hand. 'I think you feel more like yourself.'

We curl against each other. I'm ravenous. It's as if I haven't eaten properly for years. The cheese is rich and smoked; the bread fresh, crunchy; the ham salty on my tongue like Marcello. He drizzles red wine from his fingers over my breasts and laps it. The juice of the figs runs down my chin and I giggle as he kisses it away.

'Can I see the painting?'

'No,' he says. 'Not yet.'

'But when? I leave tomorrow.'

'You will know.'

'How?'

'Be patient.' He puts a finger to my lips and doesn't say any more. When we've finished the food and drunk our fill of the wine, I get dressed. My clothes are still damp. I pull on my jeans and, after the warmth of the studio, they feel deeply unpleasant against my skin.

'Keep the shirt,' Marcello says.

I can smell the scent of his body on it. I try very hard to catch a peek of the painting, just a tiny glimpse, but my artist is having none of it. He steers me away to the other side of the studio.

'Well,' I say, when I'm fully attired once more and have my soggy umbrella to hand, 'that was a very interesting afternoon.' Much better than some fusty old church.

'Take this, too.' He gives me the carnival masque.

I say, 'This must have cost a fortune.'

'Take it,' he insists. 'It will always remind you of the time we have spent together.'

'I'd like that.' I give him a peck on the cheek as I clutch the carnival masque to me.

'Give me your telephone number.'

I scribble it on the piece of paper that Marcello offers. 'Now you'd better tell me how to get back to my hotel.'

At the cherry-red front door, Marcello gives me meticulous directions. I kiss him goodbye. This time a long, lingering kiss. My fingers trace the contours of his face, committing them to memory. 'Thank you.'

'It was my pleasure.' We kiss again and he runs his fingers through my hair. 'I would like to spend more time with you, *bella* Beth,' he says, 'but I have things I must do.'

'I understand.'

Then I leave. The night is cool and fresh. My steps are brisk on the slippery streets, light and carefree. I'm heading back towards my hotel, glad that I'm no longer lost.

The next day the sun is full and high in the sky. I take my breakfast by the open windows of a Juliet balcony and watch the diamonds of sunlight glitter on the surface of the Grand Canal. In my dark shuttered room I slept like a log, alone in my double bed—a deep sleep filled with colourful dreams. In full carnival regalia I was parading through the streets, all eyes on me wearing my wonderful masque, low-cut dress with bustle and silk slippers on my feet, Marcello in black velvet, his hand held tightly in mine. I awoke refreshed, light in spirit and smiled at the masque propped up against the alarm clock on my bedside table.

Now I'm anxious to greet the day. And what a day! The gondoliers are back out in force, their songs ringing out across the water. The tourists are already thronging towards the Rialto Bridge. I finish breakfast—fresh warm bread this morning—and head back to my room.

Carefully folding Marcello's shirt, I slip it into a plastic bag that I find in the bottom of my case. This time, as well as my umbrella, I take my map. My destination is Marcello's studio. My excuse: I have his shirt to return.

The tourists move at a snail's pace, shoulder to shoulder, through the ribbons of streets and the tiny arched bridges, stopping to gawp in the shop windows at the masques, the jewels, the handmade paper and quill pens. I break my journey only to buy chocolate-covered nougat, Torrone Classico, from a gorgeous chocolate shop that makes me salivate.

Retracing yesterday's steps, I eventually find myself in the small square by Marcello's studio. Today, there's no chalk board outside and the cherry-red door is firmly closed. The bobbing boat is gone. A cold dampness encircles my heart despite the increasing heat of the day. Without hope, I knock at the door and am greeted by silence. I wait patiently and knock again. Wherever Marcello is, he clearly isn't here.

Folding the plastic bag containing his shirt as small as I can, I leave it tucked down beside the door, hoping that Marcello finds it still here on his return. I want to keep the shirt to remember the scent of him but that seems too pathetic, too sad. I don't know what I wanted in coming back to his studio. Perhaps to check that it really did happen. Or did I think that we could have had another wonderful day together? Yes, I confess, I did. But it was as much of a dream as my glorious vision of the carnival was in my sleep. Perhaps Marcello will call me one day. But, somehow, I doubt it.

So now I have the day to myself. I let the crowd carry me along aimlessly and, eventually, we burst into St Mark's Square. Today it is full of pigeons, full of tourists, full of couples holding hands. Blowing my budget, I sit outside Florians Caffé sipping a chilled Bellini and listen to the soaring strains of the tail-coated violinists, the sun bronzing my face. I eat a piece of my Torrone to give me a sugar rush, to give my spirit a lift.

In the square a mime artist poses for the Japanese tourists, who never, ever tire of taking photographs. She's dressed in a cheap, hastily put together carnival costume and a flimsy masque that is nothing compared to the beauty of mine. I smile contentedly. I'm not going to let the fact that Marcello isn't going to feature in my plans spoil my last day in this city. I have churches to see, paintings to marvel over, many paninis to eat. Tonight, I fly back to London and have wonderful memories and an exotic carnival masque as souvenirs.

Back at work, the relentless push towards Christmas is turning us all into mad things. I have endless marketing proposals to finish, tight deadlines, even tighter budgets. My weekend in Venice seems long ago, Marcello a distant and wonderful memory. Any beneficial effects dissipated just as soon as I returned to the daily grind. Only the rich, ruby-red carnival masque smiling enigmatically at me from my bedroom wall reminds me that it ever happened at all.

Every night I go home late, flop in front of the television and watch *I'm A Celebrity…Get Me Out of Here!* I enjoy the delights of a microwaved meal on my lap and a large glass of anything remotely alcoholic.

I moved out of the flat that I rented with Jerrard into somewhere less salubrious and more affordable. Switching on the television in my cramped living room, I settle down to my night of wild entertainment. The news is on before *Celebrity…*and I let the doom and gloom wash over me in the same way as I let the taste of my tepid luxury seafood pie wash over my taste buds, helped down with a passable white. Then an image on the screen arrests my attempts to pretend I'm enjoying this meal. I grab the remote and turn up the sound.

'World-famous Italian artist, Marcello Firenz, is in London this week for his first exhibition in five years…'

I tune out as I see Marcello on my television screen, in my lounge. I'd know him anywhere. He speaks into the reporter's microphone, thrust into his handsome face, but I don't hear what he's saying—I simply watch his hands rake through his dark curls and remember when I did the same thing. Marcello disappears and the newscaster moves on to another story. *Famous* Italian artist. I know Marcello Firenz's name—who doesn't?— but I had no inkling that he was *my* Marcello.

My heart's pounding as I jump up and search for this week's issue of *London Lifestyle.* Flicking wildly through the pages to the events section, I scan the listings until I see Marcello's name. His exhibition opens to the public tomorrow night at a gallery that I've never heard of. My pounding heart halts abruptly. The exhibition is called *Carnival*.

I have no idea how I get through the next day at the office. I can't wait to get to Marcello's exhibition. My smartest suit has been hauled out of the back of my wardrobe and I've retouched my make-up a thousand times, spending so much time in the ladies' loos that my colleagues probably think I've got some hideous stomach bug. The ruby-red carnival masque is in a Sainsbury's carrier bag, plumes spilling over the top. I've taken it out and looked at it as many times as I've put more slap on. The afternoon drags interminably and the minute the hands of my watch hit six o'clock I'm outta here.

I take the packed rush-hour Tube to the chi-chi gallery, which is in a smart backstreet in Bloomsbury. A gaggle of people, champagne in hand, cluster around the door. I pull up short. In the window is a magnificent full-size painting of a harlequin in a carnival masque, bright, vibrant, dancing. Despite the cold, my palms are clammy with sweat.

Pushing through the crowd, I make my way into the spacious white rooms. A waiter thrusts a glass of champagne into my hand and I down it gratefully. Juggling my carrier bag with its escaping plumes, I take some tiny canapés and eat them without tasting. Marcello must be here, surely, but I can't see him. He never did call me and, to be truthful, I never really expected him to.

The first room is filled with large canvases of revellers in gaudy costumes; men in luscious capes wearing masques with obscenely pointed noses; women, breasts spilling from their lace-adorned dresses cover their eyes with feline masques. My mouth is dry as I marvel at Marcello's skill. Murmurs of approval ripple through the crowd around me. I make my way through the rest of the gallery; the paintings become more erotic, the masques more elaborate, more sinister, more beguiling.

There's a crush to get into the final room. A buzz of appreciative murmurs hangs in the air. I wind through the crowd, picking my way forward. 'Excuse me, excuse me. Thank you. Excuse me.' Then, when I finally manage to squeeze through the doorway and into the room, I get my first glimpse of what the art-lovers are staring at. I freeze and stare at myself.

That's me. Up there on the wall. Thirty feet wide and twenty feet high. My breathing arrests in my chest. I go hot, cold, hot again. It's really me. I am magnificent, voluptuous, provocative, sex personified. My breasts are full and inviting. My thighs milk-white, parted. The red velvet is draped between my legs, veiling and yet accentuating the delights that lie below. No wonder Marcello wanted me. I'm a whore, a jezebel, a harlot, a scarlet woman, a temptress offering her goods for her chosen man to try. Beneath the disguise of my carnival masque there's a hint of a sensual, knowing smile. I never realised that I was such a fabulous being. Who'd have known that this darkly sexual person was locked inside of me?

The crowd thins. I feel a hand at my elbow and spin round.

'She's a beauty, isn't she?'

My eyes widen and the room rocks slightly under my feet. This was the very last person I was expecting to see. 'Jerrard?' I manage to say. 'What are you doing here?'

'Admiring the artwork,' he replies coolly.

I gulp. I haven't seen Jerrard since he walked out on me, the week before I went to Venice. Not one single phone call to find out how I was faring. To see if I had gone away without him. Well, now he knows that I did. Now he can tell that I had a rather interesting trip.

His eyes are locked on the painting. He's finding it hard to tear his attention back to the real life me. My cheeks are hot and flushed. Good grief. What on earth is he going to say? I hide my carrier bag behind my back.

'This guy is a genius, isn't he?'

I nod, mutely.

Jerrard sighs contentedly and there's wonder in his voice when he says, 'Every brush stroke on the canvas is vibrant, alive.'

'Mmm,' I agree vaguely. Not quite as alive as the same woman standing next to you. I just wish he'd make his comments now and we can get this over with. I've never much cared for Jerrard's cat and mouse games. He must realise that this is what I did in Venice without him.

'What a beauty,' he breathes again.

And I am. I'm naked for all to see. Jerrard and I were together for five years. Surely he must recognise those breasts, those thighs, that come-hither look? Can he not see the woman he knew so intimately right in front of him?

Finally, Jerrard drags his eyes away from the painting. 'I'm sorry I haven't called,' he says. 'I meant to.'

I shrug. He has absolutely no idea that this wanton woman displayed in front of him is me!

'I heard that you had a good time in Venice.'

'Yes. I did.' I let my gaze fall on the painting and smile.

'Did you like the art?'

'Fabulous. I learned a lot.'

'Did it rain?'

'On one particular day, it never stopped.'

'How terrible.'

'Not at all,' I say. 'I still managed to amuse myself.'

'Look, I'm sorry about what happened between us,' Jerrard says. 'Perhaps I was a little hasty.'

Ah. So, it hasn't worked out with the nubile young bit-of-stuff.

He takes my hand. 'Do you have plans? Can I take you to dinner?'

I glance up at the massive canvas again and I see a woman who's powerful, self-assured, independent, confident. This is a woman who could do anything. She could give up her dreary job, move from her dreary flat, find herself a wonderful man, have herself a wonderful life. This is a woman who could rule the world. I slip my fingers out of Jerrard's grasp. I hear myself say, 'I don't think so.'

Jerrard looks put out.

'I loved you, Jerrard, but our time has passed. I'm a different woman now. And I don't believe that you ever really knew me.' How can I begin to explain to him that a man who knew me for barely an afternoon saw so much more than Jerrard ever would? And one day I'll find a man who will see me like that again.

At the front of the gallery, someone claps their hands. 'Ladies and gentlemen,' he says. 'Mr Marcello Firenz!'

Marcello takes centre stage. He's as strikingly handsome as I remember. 'Thank you for coming this evening,' he says. 'It is very good to be back in London after such a long time…'

As Marcello continues his well-rehearsed speech, I turn and see that Jerrard has slipped away from me and I have no desire to go after him.

'So, be my guests,' Marcello continues. 'Have some champagne. Eat. Look at the paintings…'

The assembled audience applauds and then moves out into the other rooms. Marcello has a clutch of people around him. It's now or never. Shall I go and say hello, tell him that painting my portrait is the most wonderful thing that anyone has ever done for me? Or should I just melt into the background? He's laughing, enjoying the plaudits, comfortable with the adoration of his admirers.

'I'd love to buy this painting,' I hear a man say to Marcello, gawping up at me on the wall. 'It's magnificent. Your best work.'

'Ah, this one,' Marcello says, his full mouth parting in a languid smile. 'This one is not for sale.'

The man moves away, slightly disgruntled at having his retail therapy thwarted. Marcello is momentarily alone and I inch forward—not the brazen harlot now but shy and unsure. As I near, a woman joins him. She's dark-haired, beautiful and I wonder if he's painted her, too. Perhaps she's his wife, maybe a lover. He slips his arm casually round her shoulders and plants a tender kiss on her forehead. I get a vision of his lips against mine and can almost taste his kiss. Ah, well. I should go. Then, as I turn to leave, Marcello's eye catches mine. Electricity crackles between us. I smile, mouth 'thank you' at him and quickly make my way out of the gallery.

The night has turned cold as I step into the street but it can't take away the warm glow inside. Marcello and the glorious afternoon we spent together in Venice will always be one of my most precious memories. I'm still clutching my carrier bag with the masque. This beautiful disguise will serve as a treasured and tangible reminder. A tear comes to my eye but I won't be unhappy. I wonder where the painting will hang, who will look at it and what they will think of the woman in the ruby-red carnival masque. I'll look back at the masque in my old age and think of a time when I was young, reckless, daring and extraordinarily beautiful.

A time when a weekend in Venice changed my life.

Louise Allen

Louise Allen has written thirty historical romances for Harlequin Mills & Boon, all but one set in the Regency period. She began while working as a property manager but has now been writing full time for two years. Her latest book, *The Piratical Miss Ravenhurst,* completes her six-part series, *Those Scandalous Ravenhursts,* and in 2010 she is contributing two stories to an eight-part Regency continuity published by Harlequin Mills & Boon.

She has a large collection of Regency fashion prints and loves researching, whether it is on the battlefield at Waterloo or walking through London guided by an 1814 map.

Her aim is to create heroes and heroines who will reach out to a twenty-first century reader while staying true to their Regency world. Passion…from the past into the present. www.louiseallenregency.co.uk

Guinea Gold

'She is very lovely, is she not?' Thea looked up at the tall stranger who had strolled into the chaperones' corner and whose eyes moved from the dancing figure of her daughter to her own face. 'You are to be congratulated, Lady Wilmott.'

'Why, thank you, sir, but I can claim little credit, except perhaps for her colouring: my daughter must own the praise for her sweetness and her grace.' This was no time for reticence or false modesty, not when a young lady was to be launched upon her first Season. But who was the admiring gentleman, other than an elegant sophisticate at least twice Camilla's seventeen years?

'You do not recognise me, ma'am?' He smiled and something flashed through her memory from long ago: laughter, a tear or two, a hesitant kiss, a clumsy boy with feet and hands still to grow into.

'Perhaps…' Thea shook her head. 'You remind me of a boy from my first Season. Lucas Randall…' His mouth curved again into a mischievous look that sliced eighteen years from his age and she gasped. 'Why, it is you! And you are grown up—oh! What a foolish thing to say; of course you are.'

And how unfair it was that a gangling youth grew up to this fine maturity, with the silver at his temples lending gravitas and the lines at the corners of his eyes adding charm, when for a woman of thirty-six those first betraying flags of age merely rendered them invisible.

'You joined the diplomatic service, did you not?' So long ago, those unspoken messages sent in a glance, a touch, an untutored, instinctive caress. Nothing had been said. How could there be when she had been so eligible and so dutiful and he'd been a penniless younger son, with nothing but his way to make in the world?

He had known it was impossible, just as she had. Yet there had been that one moment of rebellion when he had held out his hands to her, his heart in his eyes, and she had known what he was asking. *Come with me.* She had hesitated, wanting him so much, so very frightened. As she'd taken long seconds to find the courage, he had turned away, his eyes shuttered, and left her to her duty and her destiny.

And so there was nothing to give her the lie when Papa had told her of the flattering offer that had been made for her and asked, 'There is no one you have set your cap at, I trust, my dear?' *No,* she had answered; there was nothing to prevent the very proper marriage of the well-dowered daughter of an earl to a mature man of wealth and influence, nothing to cause a scandal.

'I did.' She started, brought back to the present by Lucas's deep voice. A man's voice now. 'The diplomatic service is a suitable occupation for the younger son of the family, is it not?' He stood beside her spindly gilt chair, relaxed, his eyes following the laughing girl down the length of the set. 'I went abroad—India to Spain to the West Indies, then Brazil and lately the Congress. England seems the foreign country to me now.'

'But you are back for good?' How warm it was, the long

ballroom so crowded, so noisy, so brightly lit. Her fan was little help, not for the colour in her cheeks, not for the drumming in her pulse.

'Indeed. I have been honoured with a title and lands marching with the small estate I have built up over the years. I am the Viscount Randall now; it is time to settle down.'

'And to raise a family?'

'Yes. Of course, one requires a wife for that pleasant duty.'

Camilla, laughing, paused in the measure, chattering to her partner while they waited for their turn to promenade. 'My father always held that a man in his thirties should marry a girl before she is twenty, that it is a very suitable age difference,' Thea remarked. *A mother knows her duty and it is absolute: marry your daughter, and marry her well.*

'You followed his guidance yourself, of course, Lady Wilmott.'

'Papa was always wise in matters of that kind.' *Wise and firm and well-meaning.* She had understood very clearly where her duty lay.

Lucas opened his dance card and glanced at it. His fingers were brown, as long as she remembered, but now his whole body was grown and muscled and those big hands fitted. Once they had touched her hair. She had felt them tremble. What had he said, stumbling over the words? *Your hair is the gold of guineas in the candlelight, shining and precious.* And he had turned and left, perhaps, like she, unable to cope when emotion tore away the pretence of their flirting to reveal naked feeling beneath.

Thea made herself look away, stirring uneasily on the hard upholstery.

'There is a waltz shortly, I believe.'

So now he had asked. All that would follow was inevitable, for how could he fail to be enchanted by Camilla? The next few months flashed before her eyes: the betrothal, the shopping, the planning, the wedding, the future... Her future. What would that hold? Loneliness and nothing to distract her from her memories.

For eighteen years she had had her husband and her daughter to fill her life, give her purpose, make her forget that once she had wanted something, someone, of her own choosing.

How very strange to have a son-in-law one's own age. This man, of all men. There would be grandchildren, of course, and they would look just like the children she had once dreamed of having with Lucas. Children with her golden hair and his hazel eyes. Tall sons and laughing daughters. The dance floor in all its glittering colour blurred and she closed her eyes for a moment.

'A waltz? Yes, there is.' Thea made a business of consulting the dance card. 'Camilla has been approved to waltz by two of the Patronesses.' The warm glow of maternal pride that her lovely daughter should have secured approval so easily warred with the knot of shameful chagrin twisting inside. 'But there is another set yet, Lord Randall, and Camilla is engaged for that. Perhaps you would like to return—'

'I will wait here, if that is acceptable, ma'am?' At her startled nod he took the chair next to her, his height and strong body incongruous on its fragile frame. 'Unless you are awaiting a partner? I should not monopolise you.'

'Me? Oh, no, my lord, I am here *en chaperon*. I do not dance.'

'No?' He fell silent, watching as the music stopped and Camilla was claimed by yet another young man for the next set. They were falling at her feet, helpless, and she was glowing with the attention. Thea knew she should be stricter but memory and regret made her heart soft and her judgements indulgent. Soon enough for duty and decorum and to put dreams away in lavender.

'Were you happy?' They both spoke at once, the same words.

'You answer, my lord,' Thea insisted, fluttering her fan. 'Were you happy so far from home for so long?'

'Not at first, no,' Lucas said. 'But I would not have been happy anywhere in England, so better to go away from the source of my unhappiness. I learnt fulfilment and satisfaction in time. I taught myself to be happy again, at last.'

'Why were you unhappy here?' The noise of the room was far away now, the dancers blurred, the music a faint murmur on the edge of hearing.

'Because my heart had been broken,' he said with that smile, challenging her to take his words seriously, defying her to feel sorry for him. 'Now, your turn.'

'I was…content.' Thea chose the word with care, despite the turmoil he had thrown her thoughts into. 'Lord Wilmott was kind to me; my father was no doubt right about the benefits of an older husband. He died two years ago of a heart condition, poor man.'

'Poor man, indeed. But he had the felicity of a happy marriage and a lovely daughter. How very like her mother she is.'

There was no answer to that. He had fancied himself in love with her once then, when they had hardly been older than Camilla was now, and he had believed his heart broken when she had married Arthur.

What had she believed then? Nothing? She had convinced herself that she felt nothing, believed nothing. Love had been too big a word, disapproval and disgrace too dreadful to be borne. She had not dared to hope for what might have been, shy little innocent that she was. Not like Camilla, that bold, confident, golden girl.

And now Lucas had come back, prosperous, titled, eligible and desirable. Oh, so very desirable, she saw now with the experience of marriage behind her. And there was the image of the girl he had fancied himself in love with so long ago, ripe for his plucking. He had only to hold out his hand, scattering those callow youths like a hawk amongst sparrows. How could Camilla resist?

Thea watched him out of the corner of her eye, saw the boy inside the man, felt the ache begin, knew the yearning had always been there, never acknowledged. Now she must put it back in that dark closet again, where it had stayed so safely all these years.

'Mama!' So soon. The dances had passed as they had sat together in silence and here was her daughter, her fate. 'Oh, I think I have danced my feet off!'

Camilla paused as Lucas stood up, her eyes widening at his height, the darkly handsome looks, his air of confidence. 'Sir.' Her curtsey was everything a mother could hope for, her modestly lowered lashes a chaperone's delight.

'Camilla, this is Lord Randall. My lord, my daughter.'

He bowed. Camilla blushed.

'Lord Randall is waiting to ask you for a dance.'

The orchestra struck up for the waltz. Couples began to make their way onto the floor.

'Yes, Miss Wilmott, I was hoping you could spare me a country dance a little later.'

'A country…' He turned to Thea as she stammered out the words. He stretched out his hand as he had once so long ago and his eyes dared her to follow him.

'Yes, when you and I return from dancing this waltz.'

'Me?' Thea stared into the hazel eyes, finding again the gold flecks, the long lashes, the humour and the tenderness as he looked at her. Her, aged thirty-six. Her, with the curves of a mature woman, a mother. Her, with the threads of silver in hair that would never be the gold of guineas again. Her.

'Yes, Thea. You. I have waited eighteen years for this dance.' Lucas held out both hands to her. 'Have you?'

The mother said *no*. The chaperone said *no*. Thea put her hand in Lucas's strong brown clasp.

'Oh, yes, Lucas. Oh, yes.'

Sue Gedge

Sue Gedge taught Drama in London schools for twenty years before taking retirement in order to concentrate on writing. Her short stories have been published in *All Hallows, Supernatural Tales* and *The Silent Companion,* and her play, *A Present from Cookham,* about the painter Stanley Spencer, was performed at the Lilian Baylis Theatre, Sadler's Wells.

Sue studied Creative Writing at Birkbeck College, London and has appeared twice at the live reading event, *Writloud,* at RADA. Her first novel, a romance with a dark supernatural twist, *The Practical Woman's Guide to Living With the Undead,* can be read on the HarperCollins website www.authonomy.com

Holiday Snaps

'So.' The woman in the grey dress spoke tonelessly into her microphone. 'I am Nadia, your guide. We are in Nevsky Prospekt. On your right, you will see the Palace of Count Stroganoff. The Palace was built in the eighteenth century for Count Stroganoff, who is remembered today for the dish of beef which still bears his name. Boeuf Stroganoff.'

Carrie glanced up from her book and through the grimy window of the tourist bus at the flaking façade of the dull square building. Its cream, brown and green stripes gave it the appearance of a block of cheap, synthetically flavoured ice cream. The Palace was not at all beautiful and, as her husband Morris leaned over and lifted the viewfinder of his Nikon to his eye, she suppressed a sigh and returned to her reading of *Anna Karenina*.

1974. Still in the grip of the Cold War, the city that had once been called St Petersburg was known as Leningrad. Carrie could hardly believe that it was the same place where Anna Karenina had fallen in love with the handsome, dashing Vronsky. As she read, she imagined sunlit, tree-lined streets and elegant squares, but when she looked up at the real world everything was grey and dispiriting. The River Neva was sluggish and brown, the food in the hotel consisted of nightly portions of breaded force-meat and tinned peas, the wide, dusty streets were thronged with joyless people: shuffling, grim-faced old women carrying brown paper packages, dark-suited officials out of whose way you must side-step without dissent and young men in grey trousers and white shirts who accosted you. 'Change money? Chewing gum?' Tickets for the Kirov ballet were not available, coupons must be produced for all meals and excursions, the bath water in the hotel was a suspicious shade of bright orange and there was a grey linen blanket on a stained white cover on the bed. In the Ladies toilet, just off the hotel foyer, an old woman in black, a *babushka,* sat under an antique chandelier using a pair of large scissors to cut pieces from a roll of coarse fawn-coloured paper that she kept jealously on her lap, occasionally and with reluctance meting out portions of this Russian excuse for toilet tissue to those bold enough to ask.

Carrie was oppressed by Leningrad. The air was humid and stifling. According to the guide book, Peter the Great had built the city on a malarial swamp and hundreds of the peasants he had used as labourers had died in the process. Carrie was not surprised. She felt as though she could hardly breathe.

The bus pulled into the kerb.

'Here, on the River Neva,' Nadia announced, 'you will see hydrofoils. You are permitted to take photographs, although it is forbidden to record anything of military or strategic importance.'

'View number one hundred and forty-two.' Morris pressed the shutter of his Nikon. 'That almost meets my target for today! *The River Neva with hydrofoils.* Write that down in the notebook, will you, Carrie?'

Obediently, Carrie took the book and pen out of her bag. Inwardly, she winced. *Targets.* Morris seemed to live for them. She remembered that list she'd found in his sock drawer last month. It had been a neatly typed sheet of paper outlining his 'Five Year Holiday Plan'. The list began with their honeymoon trip to Florence, Rome and Venice, a holiday that had left Carrie feeling troubled and unsatisfied. 'You can't expect too much too soon,' Morris had said, but he had appeared to be enjoying himself as he meticulously ticked off all the frescos and paintings that he considered 'significant' in his guide book. The next year they had been 'Munro-bagging' in the Highlands of Scotland and the year after this, judging from the Five Year Plan, there would be more 'Munro-bagging'. She should have known that one climbing expedition wouldn't be enough for Morris. Hadn't he explained that there were two hundred and eighty-four mountains in Scotland which were over three thousand feet, and therefore classed as 'Munros'? He had set himself the target of 'bagging' every one. Just as, at this moment, he was making a determined effort to take twice as many snaps as the senior partner at the bank had taken on *his* tour of the USSR last year. Morris really was quite… Carrie blinked furiously. No, not now! She couldn't bear to think about it!

'And, on the other side of the river,' Nadia announced, 'you will see the Institute where the famous scientist, Pavlov, conducted his experiments with dogs.'

'View number one hundred and forty-three, make a note, Carrie.' Morris lifted his second camera to his eye. Carrie felt a sudden stab of irritation as she jotted down 'Pavlov Institute' in the book, smiling as she realised that he was focusing on entirely the wrong building. She decided not to tell him. He would only get annoyed.

As the bus moved on, Carrie noticed a young couple sitting

on the opposite side of the aisle. They were both bronzed and slim, the man in a white T-shirt and jeans, the girl with her long black hair tied up with a shoelace. The man was running his fingers up and down the girl's spine playfully. They looked happy, chatting together cheerfully about the awful food in the hotel yesterday and how there was no good boeuf stroganoff to be had in Leningrad today. They were Australians, judging from their accents. Carrie's stomach flipped. Listening to those accents reminded her of Bruno—Bruno, whom she'd determined to put out of her mind. Bruno, with his sun-bleached hair and gorgeous smile. Bruno who…*oh!* This was unbearable.

'Get the wide-angled lens out of my bag for me, will you, Carrie?' Morris said. 'I'll need it when we arrive at the fortress.'

She had been married to Morris for just over two years now. At the time, marrying Morris had seemed the most sensible thing to do. And her family had approved. *'Morris will be good for Carrie; he's steady and earning a good salary. Carrie needs someone like him—dreamy, impractical Carrie, always with her nose in a book…'*

Matchmaking. It was bred in their cultural tradition, in their roots, even if times had changed since Carrie's grandmother had emigrated from Minsk to Mile End. That big family party where they'd been introduced to each other and then Morris arriving at her parents' door in his new car, ushering her off to the best restaurants. He'd bought her roses, expensively wrapped, from a Bond Street florist, although they had been oddly devoid of scent.

'You could do worse than marry Morris,' her mother had said. 'You're not too young. *I* was married at eighteen. And it is not as if you're going to university now.' *Not after I failed to get those grades,* Carrie had thought with a pang of self-recrimination.

'You spend too much time reading books,' her father had said, kindly but firm. 'All that lovey-dovey stuff! Life's not like that, you know. You have to be practical in the real world.'

She'd been so depressed that summer, filled with a sense of failure. And then Morris had proposed and for a while she had truly believed that he was the one who…

The bus came to a halt.

'We have arrived at the St Peter and Paul Fortress.' Nadia replaced her microphone in its holder. 'Here, we will visit the Tsar's prison.'

'Keep up, Carrie—don't lag behind!' Morris called back as the party made its way to the entrance.

Keep up, Carrie. That was what he had yelled at her repeatedly on that hateful Munro-bagging trip last summer. Carrie remembered, with a shudder, the fatty wobble of his thighs as he'd charged up the mountainside in his shorts, running ahead, apparently determined to be the first person in the party to reach the peak. Morris hadn't looked good in shorts.

Nadia led the way into a narrow, blackened cell. 'In here, the Tsars imprisoned those they considered enemies. And, out in the courtyard, they held executions.'

'Jeez!' The young Australian man whistled through his teeth. 'Not exactly a comfortable bed, eh?' He pointed to a bare iron bedstead with rusty slats.

That accent again. *Oh.* Maybe the couple came from Queensland, like Bruno. Beautiful Bruno, with his sun-bleached hair and his sexy smile, his perfect body that looked good even in the *lederhosen* that was obligatory for his job as a singing waiter at the Austrian restaurant off Drury Lane. Bruno, who sang *Roslein* and *Danube So Blue* in a perfect tenor voice. Bruno, who was going to be a professional actor and singer one day. Bruno, who had *looked* at her that very first time when she'd gone to the restaurant with the others from her writing class at the City Lit. Bruno, who, finally, had asked if she'd like to meet him for a drink, or maybe a trip to the theatre? Carrie still felt sick when she remembered the stricken look on his face at her reply. *'I can't, I'm married.'*

How could he have known? Every time she'd visited the restaurant she'd slipped her wedding ring away in her purse. But
still they'd been able to meet—not on a date, of course—Carrie
hadn't wanted to cheat on Morris—but she *had* stayed behind at
the restaurant after closing time for coffee. And, during their time
together, it had become so clear that if only she hadn't met
Morris first, then… Why did life have to be so unfair?

'Now we will return to the bus,' said Nadia. 'This way.'

The party turned and trooped out into the yard where the
Tsar's enemies had been shot. Carrie stared at Morris, who was
taking a reading from his light meter of the dark, high walls of
the prison. How ridiculous he looked, like a badly trimmed
Christmas tree, with those two cameras, light meter and col-
lapsible tripod slung round his neck. Why had he bought such
silly holiday clothes, those baggy white trousers, garish checked
jacket and broad-brimmed hat, and grown that beard, so strag-
gling and gingery, accentuating the arrogant thrust of his jaw?

'Monday week,' he announced, without turning to look at her.
'Once we're back home. Thought we'd invite a few people from
work round for cheese and wine, and then we can show them
our holiday snaps.'

Our snaps? Carrie thought. Aloud, she said, 'Not on a
Monday. That's my writing class.'

'Oh, that!' Morris shrugged. 'You ought to give that up. You'll
never make it as a writer. All you ever do is write drivel, for the
most part.'

And he lifted his Nikon to his eye, supremely unaware that,
with that statement, he had killed the last vestige of moral obli-
gation that had been keeping his marriage together.

Carrie was flooded with joy as the full realisation hit her.

I don't love him, she thought. *I've never loved him!* It was the first time she had dared to let the words form themselves in her head. *I don't love him!* Excitement, liberating and joyous, thrilled through her body. *I don't love him! And if I don't love him, then…*

Then I can leave him!

There was no need to feel guilty. Morris would survive. He'd never wanted *her*, had he? He'd wanted a wife, so much *was* true. But not, as it turned out, one who spent every night banging away on an old Olivetti portable, trying to write novels and stories that were *drivel, for the most part*. Well, he was wrong there! Bruno had read the entire first draft of her novel. Beautiful Bruno, with his sun-bleached hair, took her seriously and listened when she was talking or reading her work out loud. Bruno wanted *her*. Bruno looked at her in *that way*. Bruno, whom she longed to kiss and whose hands would be soft and who would…*oh!*

The Australian couple were walking in front of her. The man's arm was round the girl's shoulders and they were laughing. Carrie followed them back towards the bus, almost skipping along the cobbled walkway as she left Morris and the dead weight of the stone walls of the Tsar's prison behind her.

'So.' Nadia picked up her mike. 'On your right, you will see the houses built by Rastrelli, the Italian architect employed by Peter the Great, who…'

'Hey!' the Australian girl interrupted. 'We've left someone behind.'

'Who?' Nadia looked around her wildly.

'This young lady's boss.' The girl flipped her hand towards Carrie.

'He's not my boss, he's my husband,' Carrie said. She was glad no one seemed to hear her admit this. The bus pulled up at the side of the road, brakes screeching.

'Oh! In fifteen years as a guide, I have never lost a tourist!' Nadia wailed, her façade of Soviet cool broken at last. The party gathered round her, anxious to offer reassurance.

'I'm sorry,' Carrie admitted, getting out of her seat. 'I didn't notice he wasn't here. He must have got left behind, taking photographs.'

Or maybe he's been taken to the Lubyanka, she thought, *for taking a snap of something of strategic importance.* She dismissed the idea. Of course they wouldn't do that to an ordinary tourist.

'Please…no, *niet.*' Nadia bent her head down, twisting her hands in her lap. 'Do not complain. I have good job with Intourist. I support my mother and grandmother.'

'It's all right,' Carrie reassured her. Suddenly, she felt sorry for this woman, no more than a girl really. 'He'll find his way back to the hotel.'

'Yes, there are many taxis,' Nadia agreed, looking up with a faint smile. 'And, when he returns, we will greet him with joy, just as Lenin, the founder of our state, was greeted when he arrived at the Finland station!'

'Our guide seems to think she cracked a joke!' the Australian girl whispered to Carrie as they settled back in their seats. 'She's lightening up!'

As Carrie looked through the window of the bus it seemed to her that the whole world was lightening up. How could she ever have thought Leningrad ugly or dull? She could see sun-touched plane trees and pastel-coloured buildings, lit by a warm, soft haze. Such a funny, endearing place—that rough loo paper, the dear old *babushkas,* the hilarious confusion over meals and coupons!

Morris would be angry, of course, fury would be darting from his little mud-coloured eyes when he finally got back to the hotel. And she would have to tell him it was all over between them. Still, he'd be more upset by the inconvenience than anything else. And Morris would find someone else. Someone who wanted to go 'Munro-bagging', perhaps. But he didn't need *her. Drivel, for the most part…* How *could* he have said that? Calmly, she reopened her copy of *Anna Karenina.*

'Good book?' The Australian girl leant across the aisle.

'Brilliant! It's a love story. Anna leaves her ghastly husband and runs off with Vronsky. But I'm afraid it's going to end in tragedy.'

'Jeez!' The Australian girl whistled. 'She's a woman, so she has to suffer, eh? Well, it needn't be that way, eh? Not this end of the twentieth century!'

'No,' Carrie agreed. 'It needn't.'

Love, Carrie thought as she settled back to her reading. What was it? Something, perhaps, to do with the way she was feeling right now. Such excitement. Such optimism. And she was still only twenty-two... There was so much time ahead of her!

She slipped her wedding ring off her finger. In another week she would be back in London. Soon she would see Bruno again.

Rosemary Laurey

USA TODAY bestselling author Rosemary Laurey is an ex-pat Brit, retired special education teacher and grandmother who now lives in Ohio and has a wonderful time writing and letting her imagination run riot. A split personality author, Rosemary also writes erotica as Madeleine Oh and fantasy as Georgia Evans. Her most recent book is *Bloody Right,* August 2009 (Georgia Evans). Please visit her websites: www.brytewood.co.uk, www.rosemarylaurey.com and www.madeleineoh.com

Nightwalker

For two days and a night they forced her to walk, yanking the rope around her wrists when she stumbled. She'd longed for a chance to rest, but now they'd stopped Mary Chartley learned what hell looked like.

Tied and helpless at the edge of the clearing, she watched the dark silhouettes of her captors against the fire. Their flickering, distorted shadows resembled devils from the pit. And she was cast in its depths.

There were only two now. After an argument, the other three had taken the little ones and branched off on a different path about noon.

Cold fear curled deep inside. This had been a tale of horror since the moment she'd left church with her family and the Indians had attacked: shouting, killing and snatching captives before the men could run for their guns.

Her two younger brothers, along with little Anne Worple and Jimmy Payne, had been captured. The savages had snatched

Jimmy from his mother's arms as they'd killed her and forced them all to a running march, prodding the little ones and ignoring their tears. Mary had done her best for the children but their cries, as they were all carried off at the fork in the trail, still echoed in her ears.

She could do nothing for them now and she had little doubt about what her captors planned for her. Thank heavens the children wouldn't witness her shame.

At fifteen, Mary Chartley knew too much of the harshness of pioneer life to cherish illusions. The shocked whispers and shaken heads of her mother and the other women had taught her what happened to Indian captives.

Mary shut her eyes and prayed for strength to endure.

She'd made herself strong to buoy up the little ones but, now they were gone, despair washed over her like a bitter tide. Would she ever see her home again? Did she want to, knowing she'd return humiliated, whispered about and pitied? Or, worse, with child.

She curled her legs up under her and rested her head on her bound hands.

A voice grunted at her in a language she couldn't understand and she looked up at one of her captors. His face expressionless, his mouth hard and his eyes cold, he held out a drinking flask.

Thirst! She was parched but knew to take only a sip, remembering how poor little Jimmy had gulped water in his thirst and been cuffed so hard he'd fallen. She held the water in her mouth before swallowing it very slowly. She dared another glance at her captor. He nodded approval and offered her a second sip. So she wasn't being left to die of thirst. Yet.

She held the second mouthful until the water warmed against her tongue. It might be morning before they offered more.

As her captor returned to the fire a third Indian emerged from the woods. She'd seen him before. During the long march he'd appeared two or three times, unnerving her by his intent stare.

Now, thank heaven, he didn't even glance her way. Just offered the others a brace of bloody rabbits and joined them.

She tried to sleep, to rest while she could, but she watched her captors clustered around the fire. Anger burst deep inside. They were warm and anticipating a supper of succulent roast rabbit whilst she was bound wrist and ankle and shivered in the night.

Driven by longing for warmth, she dragged herself towards the glow of the fire.

Three pairs of dark eyes turned in her direction. No one spoke or moved, so she continued until she sat at the edge of the fire, across from her abductors and the new arrival.

After seemingly amused glances her way, they resumed their whispered conversation. Why did they whisper? She couldn't understand a word they said. Perhaps the still of the forest impelled quiet. Were they cautious about pursuit? No, they'd never have stopped to light a fire if there was a chance of her rescue.

Her spirits sank but at least she was miserable in the warmth. She curled up on her side and took comfort from the fire.

She was half dozing when two moccasined feet came into her line of vision. She pulled herself upright and looked up at a harsh, unsmiling face as he tossed a leg of rabbit into her lap. The roasted meat burned through her skirt but the aroma had her mouth watering. She had a hunger that a skinny leg of wild rabbit would never satisfy, but it would have to. She picked up the meat, not an easy task with bound wrists, and ate slowly, savouring, taking tiny bites and making it last as long as possible.

The others ate. Or, rather, her two captors ate. The third just talked, casting glances her way from time to time in a way that made her face burn. Hunger and the drive to survive had her scraping off every last shred of meat. She sucked the bones until all taste was gone, then licked her fingers clean. Who knew when, if ever, she might eat again?

She was offered another taste of water before the newcomer produced a pouch of stones and all three set to gambling with occasional grunts, laughs and guttural words.

They ignored her completely and nothing could please her more.

Mary settled back on the ground and watched from under her lids. The newcomer was dressed, like the others, in skin leggings, a tunic and moccasins. His hair, too, was dark and braided, but there was an air of difference about him, a separateness. Was he from another tribe, just joined with them? But he'd brought the rabbits. Without them they'd have had nothing to eat.

He seemed stronger. Not taller, but he moved with assurance and little of the care and caution she'd observed in her captors.

She again tried to sleep, thinking of the inevitable forced march in the morning, but the sound of the trio across the fire kept her awake.

There was an indignant shout—someone had lost, it seemed— and laughter. A knife and a beaded pouch changed hands. After discussion and a couple of glances in her direction, the betting continued. At last, the warmth and exhaustion took over and Mary dozed.

Until a tall figure stood over her. 'Sit up.'

She sat, blinking at the firelight and the fringe on his leggings. His hand closed on her wrist in a firm, but not cruel, grasp. There was purpose and determination in the dark face and it took all she had to tamp down her fear.

She gasped as a knife gleamed in the firelight and the cords binding her wrists fell to the ground. Why? Another, equally precise and swift, slash and he severed the cords binding her ankles. Tucking the knife in his belt, he took her upper arms and lifted her to her feet, holding her as her legs wobbled with the returning circulation.

There was no cruelty there or harshness in his dark eyes. Not even pity. Just quiet, careful assessment, such as her father wore as he tested her and her brothers on their Bible verses on Saturday nights.

'I am Nightwalker,' he said. 'And you are mine.'

Her frisson of fear faded as he smiled. Would he smile if he planned her ill? She held his gaze. 'And I, sir, am Mary Chartley.' What sort of name was Nightwalker? 'You speak English, sir.'

'I speak many tongues, Mary Chartley. Did you understand me? I won you. A fair exchange for the loss of a knife and a pouch of tobacco, I think.'

Won her for what? 'Why?'

'Why?' he repeated, still holding her arms, his hands cool against her skin and the glint of something—amusement, curiosity—in his eyes.

'I mean, why did you lose your possessions for me?' As she asked, she knew. Or feared she did.

'I thought you deserved more than a life as a slave.'

But was her future now any better? 'And you offer me what, sir?'

'Nightwalker,' he said. 'I am Nightwalker.'

Whatever that might be. 'What do you offer me, Nightwalker?' Her legs felt better now, stronger, as she squared her shoulders and prayed for courage.

He met her gaze with sombre eyes. 'I offer you a choice, Mary Chartley. As of this night of fear, would you live or die?'

That was her choice? Yes, she read it in his eyes. If she wished to be spared the future, he would kill her and, she sensed, mercifully. Her throat went dry. She swallowed but was too parched for it to help. He would spare her shame and humiliation and a life of slavery, but in doing so, end all hope.

'The night wears on. What do you choose, Mary Chartley?'

Whatever lay ahead, there was only one choice. 'To live.'

His teeth shone in the firelight. 'As I had hoped. You're worthy. Come.' He took her hand and led her across the clearing, past the pair seemingly sleeping now, by the fire and into the darkness of the trees.

She should be frightened, terrified—alone in the woods, far from anywhere.

Nightwalker now owned her.

And fear was overtaken by curiosity. Who was this man? She stumbled in the dark, but he caught her as if the darkness gave him no difficulty.

'Afraid, Mary Chartley?'

'Yes.' Who would not be?

'You may change your mind.'

To accept oblivion in his hands. 'No!' Her voice was shaky but her resolve firm. 'I am afraid, but to choose death is the coward's way.'

'I was right,' he said in the stillness. 'Come.'

He led her deeper into the woods. She should be petrified by now but, for reasons she couldn't fathom, she trusted him, felt safe, protected.

'Where are we going, sir… Nightwalker?'

'Here,' he replied. 'No need to go further.' He stilled, hand at the base of her neck. 'It is time. Are you still sure, Mary Chartley? I offer you a life without death.'

'Impossible.'

In the darkness she sensed the curl of his mouth and the glint in his eyes. 'It is the way of the Nightwalkers.' He pushed aside the tattered neck of her Sunday best gown and brushed his mouth on her shoulder. A strange lassitude washed over her. His touch was not unpleasant. Scarcely unwelcome.

And he bit.

At the stab of pain she cried out, would have broken away, but he held her, and on the heels of the fading hurt came a new sensation: a sweetness, a strange, soft pleasure that echoed within her and grew and swelled until she trembled in his arms as a wanton joy enthralled her. She was giddy and close to fainting when he lifted his mouth away.

'It is begun,' he said. She gasped again as he bit his own wrist, tearing the flesh open until he bled. 'Taste.' He held his wrist to her lips.

Her reason and a lifetime of teaching told her to refuse such blatant barbarity but a strange emotion, an inexplicable need and attraction drew her on and she licked his wound. The taste was strange and thick. It should have been repugnant but she saw his smile and an unfamiliar desire roared in her consciousness. She wanted this contact with him. Yearned for it. Needed it. She ran her tongue over the tear in his skin, tasting his strength. He pressed his arm to her mouth, holding her head steady.

'Enough for now,' he said. 'You must return to the warmth of the fire.'

Taking her hand, he turned her back towards the glint of firelight in the distance. She stumbled, her legs buckling, so he swept her into his arms and strode back through the trees, brushing aside branches. She leaned against him, unafraid of the dark and the strange sensations still coursing through her. She sensed her old life was further behind her than ever.

Once back by the fire, he set her on the ground and covered her with an animal skin.

'Once more,' he said, as he held out his arm to her. In the firelight she saw no trace of his earlier wound, but he bled anew as he ripped his flesh.

What was done in the dark seemed even more wanton and pagan in the firelight, but he insisted and she had no desire to refuse. 'It is life,' he told her. 'You must taste of life to live.'

When she'd taken enough to satisfy him, he lay down beside her, his arm on her shoulder. 'Sleep, little one,' he said. 'I must leave soon, but I will return.'

★ ★ ★

She awoke to daylight, a fire gone cold—alone.

Nightwalker had disappeared and the other two had packed their belongings and left. But where was she? Miles from home and the memory of last night still clear and shocking.

And she was ill. Her head throbbed, she shook with fever and her limbs ached.

Was she going to die alone in the woods? No. The memory of Nightwalker's promise to return stayed clear as she shivered. She was burning with heat and thirst. She stood unsteadily, wrapping the skin around her shoulders and listened. She heard the birds in the trees and little creatures underground beneath her feet, the sap in the trees and the rustle of undergrowth as an animal crept back to its lair. And the sound of running water.

Parched, she stumbled through the woods, heading towards the sound. Dragging her skin blanket with her, tripping over roots and rocks, pressing on towards the ever increasing roar of blissful, needed water.

It was a waterfall and a swift-flowing stream, enough to quench her raging thirst and quell the heat that burned inside her. Dropping the blanket on the bank, she plunged in, clothes and all, and lay down in the water.

Oh! The blissful, cool, glorious water. Lying on the pebbles, she soaked up the sensation.

She was better, but not yet well. She stood and waded to the bank, picking up the skin and stepping back into the water, to wade upstream until she was in the shade of an overhanging tree. The pain behind her eyes eased.

She stripped off her clothes—or all but her chemise and drawers—and spread them in the sun, stepping back into the shade as soon as she could to ease her aching head. Wrapping herself in the skin, she sat down, her back against the tree trunk, and dozed.

About mid-morning, judging by the sun, she awoke, once

again sweating and shaking. Casting aside her blanket, she slid back into the river to ease the burning across her skin. Three more times she woke sweating and cooled herself in the stream. Until, as the sun lowered behind the hill, she sweated no more. She was no longer too weak to walk. In fact, a wild energy coursed through her; she felt she could run, race the river and fly.

There were still several hours of twilight before full dark. She pulled on her now dried clothes and was hooking up her waist when she started at a sound. Something other than the activity of the trees, the creatures of the woods and the river that had kept her company in her sickness.

She turned, ready to flee, and saw Nightwalker on the opposite bank.

A wild surge of joy had her smiling and waving at him. Why? Without him, she could have returned home. But, seeing him, she had no wish to try.

He ran across the river, seeming to skim the water.

'You came back, like you said you would.' She saw him more clearly in the twilight than she had in the night. He was tall, dark-skinned as the other Indians, his hair in twin braids and his eyes dark as pitch but, when he smiled, his eyes crinkled at the corners and light glimmered in their depths.

'Yes,' he replied. 'Will you come with me?'

'Where will we go?'

'Everywhere. As Nightwalkers, the world is ours.' Everywhere? She'd already passed the palisades that marked her home and her known world. With Nightwalker, she'd go beyond the forests and the great rivers the grown-ups talked about, into the wild uncharted territories and beyond. 'Will you come, Mary Chartley?'

He always asked. Never told or ordered, like her father or her cousin's husbands. Going with Nightwalker meant a joining as if they were man and wife; she knew that without being told. She also knew from last night that there was more between them than ever between man and wife sanctioned by church and convention.

She smiled. 'Yes, Nightwalker, I will come with you.'

He beamed. 'I knew when I first saw you, protecting those children, comforting the little one who cried with fear. You were worthy.'

One day she'd ask what he meant by 'worthy'. For now, she stepped close. Very close. She was aware of his height, his strength and power and his sweet male scent. 'I will come,' she repeated.

'You will not need these,' he said, touching her tattered bodice. 'I have better clothes for you.'

He undid the bundle he'd carried under his arm and unrolled leggings, moccasins and a tunic of soft deerskin.

She stripped off her torn and wrinkled clothes, discarding even her drawers and bodice without a trace of the shame she expected to feel at her nakedness. He helped her with the unfamiliar lacing on the leggings before she pulled the tunic over her head. The soft moccasins fitted perfectly. Her old clothes he left under a rock.

'There is one more thing you must do,' he said. 'Twice you tasted of me. There must be a third time and then we will walk the night together.'

This time she felt no reluctance. As he opened his arm and his blood flowed, her mouth watered with anticipation. She wouldn't think. Couldn't. Wild need and a strange, deep instinct drove her as she fastened her mouth on him and tasted with a hunger and rampant desire for this closeness. She suckled like a babe at the breast, but this was so much more: greater, sweeter, headier. She tasted his power and endurance as his strength flowed into her veins, until he wiped her lips with the pad of his thumb.

'And now, Mary Chartley, you must have a new name for your new life. I first saw you in twilight. Come with me, Twilight.'

She took his hand. 'Yes, Nightwalker.'

'Let us go,' he said. And together they walked into the darkening shelter of the woods.

Charlotte Betts

Charlotte Betts discovered a passion for writing after her five children had grown up and left her in peace. Demanding careers in hotel design and property force her to be inventive in finding time to write but she has achieved seven novels in eight years. One of her short stories was published in *Scribble* and others shortlisted by *Writers' News* and *Real Writers*. She has won first prize in five short story competitions and wrote a regular column on interior design for the *Maidenhead Advertiser* for two years. She is a member of WordWatchers www.wordwatchers.net and the Romantic Novelists' Association.

Violets and Vivaldi

The sound of the flute came from nowhere, the liquid notes of Vivaldi teasing and tantalising, like a call to play. Charlie stood motionless on the snowy cobbles, listening. Then he saw her. Swaying gently as she played, framed by the carved stone window surround, slender figure backlit and her cloud of blonde hair like a halo. He couldn't see her face but from the way she moved he knew she was beautiful.

He listened for the next thirty minutes, the music washing over him, transporting him to another place. He didn't realise how chilled he had become until she ceased playing, leaned forward to close the casements and disappeared.

Blowing on his frozen fingers, he stamped his feet, feeling like a child who'd had a precious toy snatched away. It was only his second day in Prague but he'd already fallen in love with the Old Town and he knew he'd never forget the girl with the flute.

The following morning Charlie took the bus from his hotel

to his new office. Inside, just as the lift doors began to close behind him, a blonde girl in a short skirt slipped through the gap.

'Hi!' She smiled, demonstrating the USA's superior quality of orthodentistry. 'You new here?'

'I arrived at the weekend,' he confessed.

'I work just along the hall. Real estate. Have you gotten an apartment yet?' He shook his head. 'I'll come get you at lunch,' she said firmly. 'Now, don't you worry about a thing; you'll soon be in a darling little apartment of your own.' She patted his arm, flashed her perfect teeth again and walked briskly away.

Nancy turned up at his office at noon and led him into a small restaurant, ordered lunch without consulting him about what he liked and spread out a sheaf of apartment-to-let details. 'You'll like this one,' she said. 'It's near the Old Town but it's expensive. Or this one has better than average Czech facilities.'

He studied her manicured nails, immaculate make-up and felt an urge to muss up her shiny hair. So much perfection was daunting.

Nancy crossed her legs in their short-short skirt and adroitly extracted all information about his prospects, which she seemed to find acceptable. Within a few days she had organised his life. She installed him in a sunny apartment with parquet floors and high ceilings, arranged a laundry service and introduced him to her friends. She made love as efficiently as she did everything else.

One Saturday afternoon Nancy went shopping with her girl-friends. As usual, whenever he had time to himself, Charlie headed for the street where he'd heard the girl with the flute. The window had always been firmly shut. But now, as he turned the corner, he heard an enchanting ripple of sound, the rise and fall of the music like laughter. And there she was, her slim figure framed by the window, just as he remembered her.

He stood rooted to the ground as he watched her, drinking in every note and engraving them on his heart. When she finished the last melody and closed the casements he was bereft.

Aimlessly, he walked on down the street until he came to a café where he sat in the fuggy warmth, sipping espresso and slivovice and trying to understand the malaise that had descended upon him in the past weeks.

Last night, Nancy had talked about moving in with him. He wondered how long it would be until she started talking about flatware and fancy dinner services. He knew he didn't want to end up living in Minnesota but, in the face of her determination, thought it would be inevitable unless he took a grip on things. Gloomily, he stared out of the café window. And there, hurrying along the pavement, was the girl, carrying a flute case. Mesmerised by the swing of her blonde curls, Charlie watched open-mouthed as she pushed open the door.

Without pausing to think, he stood up. 'Excuse me,' he said. 'May I buy you a coffee?' She looked at him consideringly, her blue eyes clear as spring water. 'I heard you earlier,' he said, blushing. 'You play beautifully.'

She hesitated, pushing the mass of hair off her face. Her pink and white skin was refreshingly bare of make-up.

'Thank you. Cappuccino, please.' She held out her hand. 'I'm Anna.'

Charlie sat down beside her, unsure of himself.

Silently she looked back.

'Have you played the flute for long?' he asked at length.

'Nearly all my life.' She smiled and he relaxed a little. 'But it is not always easy to find work. There are many musicians in Prague.' She shrugged. 'I will play tonight and tomorrow. Then nothing. I must find other work.' She stared down at her hands. 'May I have something to eat?' she asked suddenly.

'What would you like?'

'Anything.'

He went to the counter and carefully selected a strudel decorated with a snowy drift of sugar.

Silently, she devoured the last morsel, then smiled as she noticed him watching her. 'Sorry, I haven't eaten today.'

'I'm glad you enjoyed it.' He wondered if she hadn't eaten because she had been too busy or because she was broke. They chatted about the Velvet Revolution, the tourists and Vivaldi. Her laughter was as captivating as her music and before long Charlie felt he could hardly remember a time when he hadn't known her.

'What time is it?' she asked suddenly, looking out at the darkening streets.

'Half past four.'

She gasped and began buttoning her coat. 'I'm late for rehearsal.'

They tumbled out of the smoky café into the freezing air outside. Charlie took her hand and they ran through the twisting streets, over Charles Bridge spanning the wide Vltava, ducking down alleyways, feet slithering on the icy cobbles, slowing only to let a tram rumble past. At last they stopped outside an ancient church.

'Goodbye,' she said.

He noticed that there were snowflake diamonds on her hair. 'May I see you again?' he asked.

She leaned forward to kiss his cheek but he turned his head and felt her warm lips on his. 'Come to the concert,' she said, disappearing through the doorway. He lifted icy fingers to his mouth, which burned with the memory of her kiss.

Chattering, Nancy, Emmy-Lou and Eugene followed him out of the church. Charlie walked silently, hands thrust deep in his pockets as he tried to hold onto the music he still heard in his head.

'Let's get outta this cold,' Nancy said.

'I'd like to wait and see Anna,' said Charlie.

'He met one of the musicians this afternoon,' Nancy said to Emmy-Lou. 'The girl with the flute.'

'She was kinda cute,' said Eugene, giving Charlie a knowing nudge.

'I thought there'd be an orchestra, Charlie,' said Nancy accusingly, 'not just a trio.'

Charlie caught sight of Anna exiting from a small side door. 'Hello!' he said. 'The concert was wonderful.'

'I'm glad you liked it.'

'Introduce me to your little friend,' Nancy said, firmly taking hold of his arm. The two girls eyed each other, both blue-eyed and blonde but worlds apart.

'This is Anna,' said Charlie.

Anna held out her hand and Nancy touched it with the tips of her fingers. 'The others are waiting,' she said, pulling Charlie away.

He looked back over his shoulder. Anna smiled at him and he wasn't sure if it was with pity or scorn.

The following evening Charlie sat in the church watching Anna play again, his heart contracting at her total concentration. Outside, he handed her a bunch of violets and, smiling, she buried her nose in their velvety petals, inhaling the delicate scent. Afterwards, they ate duck, stewed cabbage and dumplings in a nearby restaurant.

'Have you found work?'

'Not playing music.' She looked infinitely sad and his heart bled as he imagined the waste of her talent if she worked in a shop or waited on tables.

'You'll find something soon.'

She shrugged, the flickering candlelight illuminating her melancholy face.

Outside, in the dark, arcaded street, Charlie took her in his arms and kissed her.

She clung to him. 'Oh, Charlie! If only it could always be like this.'

'Why can't it be?'

Entwined, they walked through the echoing streets until they reached her apartment building. They climbed the four flights of crumbling stone stairs, stopping to kiss on each landing. Anna unlocked the door and they fell inside.

'Stay with me, Charlie,' she whispered as he buried his face in her hair.

Nancy took Charlie to a new restaurant in the Old Town. Sitting under a vaulted ceiling, they ate fois gras on hot toast by candle-light. Nancy thought it was romantic and so it would have been with the right person, thought Charlie, thinking of Anna. Indeed, she'd barely left his thoughts. He knew it was ridiculous, but people did fall in love at first sight or, in this case, sound, didn't they?

'Are you listening to me, Charlie?' demanded Nancy.

He was still trying to work out how he was going to tell her he didn't want to be with her any more. 'Sorry?'

'I said Mom and Pop are coming to visit. Won't that be nice?'

Charlie didn't think it would be nice; he'd heard all about Hiram J Hinkmeyer the third.

'They're dying to meet you.' Nancy smiled coyly. 'They thought they should take a look at you, as we're such an item.'

Charlie chewed his toast, which seemed to have turned to sawdust. Across the restaurant an elegant young woman, blonde hair caught up to show her profile, gazed into the eyes of a fleshy German businessman. Charlie didn't recognise her at first because of the heavy make-up. This was an Anna he didn't know.

Nancy noticed him staring at the couple. 'Gross, isn't it? These Czech girls take advantage of the ex-pats.'

Charlie was frozen into silence, watching as the German pinched the soft bare skin of Anna's arm, then moistly kissed her fingers, not noticing how she shrank from him. He scratched his fat belly and called for the bill.

Anna rose from the table and made her way down the stairs.

'I just love this dinnerware,' said Nancy. 'Perhaps we could find something like it.'

'Back soon,' said Charlie. He hurried down the stairs and waited until Anna came out of the cloakroom. 'What do you think you're doing?' he muttered, grasping her arm.

'Charlie!' She had been crying, even though she'd tried to conceal it with fresh make-up.

'Is this the new job you talked about, going with fat old men?'

'I have to eat, Charlie!'

'I'll give you money.'

'Then you are no better than him,' she said flatly.

He gasped as if he'd been kicked in the stomach. Tears and mascara ran in black rivulets down Anna's cheeks but then he noticed, pinned to the shoulder of her dress, the little bunch of violets he had given her. Gathering her to him, he smothered her with kisses. 'Marry me!' he demanded. She stared at him, eyes drowned and huge. 'Stay here!' He ran back up the stairs.

'Are you OK?' asked Nancy. 'You ran off pretty quick. I was just asking if you like this cute dinnerware.'

Charlie sighed. 'Nancy, I hate the dinnerware and I don't want to live in Minnesota. You must know that we're not right for each other. I should have stopped it before. I'm sorry but I'm going to marry Anna.'

'But Mom and Pop are coming out especially to meet you.' Her eyes were perfect circles of astonishment and, for the first time since he'd known her, she looked unsure.

He stood up and kissed her cheek. 'Thanks for everything but really it is better this way. Goodbye, Nancy.'

The German was drumming his fingers on the tablecloth and glancing at his watch.

Charlie ran lightly down the stairs to where Anna was waiting for him. She had let down her hair and scrubbed her face clean. He took her hand and, laughing like children, they made their escape through the kitchens and out into the street.

Elizabeth Chadwick

Elizabeth Chadwick's first venture into fiction was telling herself a story about fairies when she was three years old. Inspired by a programme about knights in armour, she wrote her first novel in her teens. Her work was spotted by leading literary agent Carole Blake and Elizabeth's first published novel *The Wild Hunt* won The Betty Trask Award. Four of her novels have been shortlisted for the Romantic Novelists' Association major award. She is translated into sixteen languages. Elizabeth is renowned for her ability to bring the past to life and her biographical novels set in the Middle Ages have won extensive acclaim. *The Scarlet Lion* was nominated by the Historical Novel Society as one of the landmark historical novels of the decade. Visit www.elizabethchadwick.com to find out more.

A Clean Start

Summer 1149

Sleeves rolled back exposing broad red forearms, Florence heaved a bucketful of scalding lye solution into her washtub to mix with the cold water drawn earlier from the well. Humming to herself, she tested the temperature with a rapid swish of her fingers and stooped to the willow laundry basket. Her lord and his wife had two sons and a baby in the cradle and, what with tail clouts, swaddling bands and the ordinary tally of shirts, chemises, towels, sheets and bolsters, there was always washing to do. If Florence grumbled about her workload, it was usually with good nature, for there was great satisfaction in turning a bundle of stained, stale linens into neatly folded parcels, soft, clean and snowily fresh. She boasted that there was no stain she could not remove.

As she churned the first batch of garments in the lye water, she watched youths training with spears and shields on the sward nearby. Her son, Adam, was prominent among them and one of the most aggressive, despite being one of the younger ones. Florence bit her lip. His father's death in battle four years ago had hit him hard. His grief and bitterness had turned to anger and all he wanted to do was fight and have revenge. People said that his anger was better out than in and that in time he would change. All youths went through such phases. Would she rather he clung to her skirts and shrank from the world?

Water sloshed over the side of the tub and wet her skirt. Adam had lost his father and she her husband, her provider, her mate. He had been a serjeant, an ordinary soldier, beholden to Lord John FitzGilbert the Marshal. One day he had ridden out behind his lord, and had not come home. He was buried in a communal grave near Winchester with all the others who had died on that day. She had no tomb at which to mourn. Lord John had returned badly wounded and life had changed for ever, even while it went on the same. She received a decent wage for her laundry work and she was entitled to eat and drink in the hall and have light for her small dwelling beside the kitchens. Her son was clothed, fed and was now receiving training at Lord John's behest. He worked as a groom's lad in the stables and when he wasn't tending to the horses by which their lord set such store, he was practising his weapon play so that when he was old enough and sufficiently skilled he could take his father's place among the foot soldiers. Florence prayed every night that by the time he was old enough to march out with an axe in his belt and a spear in his fist the war would be over. Adam would rise to a senior groom, would marry and beget grandchildren to comfort her old age. However, for the moment there was no comfort. Only raw anxiety.

Florence removed a shirt from the lye tub and began pounding it with a mallet to loosen the grime around the neckline and cuffs, her solid red forearms shaking with each blow. She found this part of the process immensely satisfying. A vigorous bout of linen bashing was guaranteed to dissipate most ills.

On the wall walk, the watchman suddenly blew his horn and bellowed urgently down to old Matthew, the gatekeeper. Florence ceased her pounding. Her anxiety blossomed into fear and her stomach began to churn as the great wooden doors swung wide. Moments later Lord John pounded into the bailey with his troop, filling the yard with the flash of mail, the colours of shields, the powerful smell of sweating, hard-ridden horses. A couple of saddles were empty and they had wounded among them, too. Lord John flung down from his stallion and began issuing rapid commands. Florence swallowed the lump of panic in her throat. Half of her wanted to run away and hide, but the other half stood its ground as the injured men were borne away for tending and someone was sent running for the priest.

Adam joined her as the crowd dispersed, his face pale with shock and his eyes dark and wide. 'It's Prince Eustace's men. They've burned Rockley and our men were too few to hold them off.'

Florence bit her lip. Rockley was one of their lord's settlements on the Marlborough Downs, although there wasn't much there beyond a couple of shepherding families and their flocks. 'What about the people?'

'Fled to safety, but most of the sheep have been slaughtered.' His tender young hand clenched around the haft of his spear. 'I could have helped. If we'd had more men…'

'You are not trained,' she snapped, her heart pounding. 'Look what happened to those who did fight. Look what happened to your father.'

He said nothing but a mulish expression crossed his face. 'There are horses to see to,' he said abruptly, and turned away.

Florence's hands were trembling as she picked up her mallet and resumed hammering, although she could barely see the garment through a blur of tears. This wouldn't do, she told herself; this just wouldn't do. She bundled a chemise into the rinsing basket, then suppressed a cry of alarm as she saw Lord John standing to one side, watching. Hastily she curtseyed. He bade her rise with a swift gesture. He no longer wore his mail shirt, but still retained the padded undertunic, streaked with grease from the iron rivets of the former. The upper left side of his face was terribly scarred where molten lead from a burning church roof had dripped onto him and taken the sight of his eye. His right eye, however, missed nothing. He had everyone's measure, from his senior knights down to the smallest pot boy pissing in the kitchen fire when he thought no one was looking. Just now, that measuring gaze was fixed implacably on her.

'I have a task for you, Florence.' He handed her a bloody linen shirt. 'I want you to get this clean.'

She was taken aback because usually one of the under-chamberlains would have brought such a request to her. It obviously wasn't Lord FitzGilbert's garment; there was no embroidery and the linen was less fine. Still good quality, though. The lower right arm was heavily stained and the sight of the brown dried blood made her stomach churn.

She tried to sound brisk. 'I will do my best, sire. Salt and plenty of pounding should do the trick.'

He gave a curt nod. 'I trust you to do your work well. The man who owns this lost his hand to save my life. He deserves what I can do for him.'

Dipping another curtsey, she thought it a strange thing to say. Why was it of benefit to its owner, that Lord John should bring the shirt in person? Because it was an honour? But who was to see? Who would know?

'When you have done, bring it to Hugh Fergant in the soldiers' dormitory,' Lord John added. 'If he has other items to be washed, then I will see you paid.'

'Hugh Fergant is the injured man, sire?'

He nodded and started to turn away, then paused. 'He has no kin, so he is in our hands. I will not have him suffer for lack of good tending.'

'Yes, my lord.' Florence looked at the shirt. Hugh Fergant was new to the garrison and generally kept to himself, so she did not know him beyond a distant glance. She wondered if he would die. Was she washing a dead man's shirt? The thought made her shudder.

She scrubbed and pounded, rinsed, scrubbed and pounded again until her hands were sore, her arms burning and the sweat ran down her face like tear streaks.

Hugh Fergant's bed was in the soldiers' dormitory—a wooden building beside the great hall to house the mercenaries to defend the keep. Florence made her way past the row of straw-stuffed pallets and sleeping spaces until she came to the one at the end, set beneath a window embrasure.

Fergant was propped up against several pillows and when she arrived was dozing, so she was able to study his beard-grizzled features without being scrutinised herself. Like her, he was old enough to have lines on his face and a seasoning of grey in his dark hair, but sufficiently young for his flesh still to mould against his bones. There was a slight bend in his nose, indicating it had been broken and had mended awry. His right arm was bandaged to the wrist and that was where it ended. No hand. No fingers.

'I suppose I must grow accustomed to being the butt of stares,' he said.

Florence jumped. 'I thought you were sleeping,' she said, feeling flustered. 'I didn't want to disturb you.'

'And do you always creep up on men to stare at them when they're asleep, mistress?' His eyes as they struggled to focus on her were the colour of mud, dark and fogged with whatever he had been given to dull the pain. Sweat glazed his brow.

Florence summoned her dignity. 'Lord John asked me to bring your shirt to you and take any other laundry you had.'

'Lord John is uncommonly generous,' he said sourly.

'Yes,' Florence replied, her own lips prim. 'He is.'

He dropped his gaze to the folded shirt she was still holding. 'At least he expects me to live to wear this again.'

'Unless you take the wound fever, why shouldn't you?'

He clenched his jaw and looked away from her. 'What is there for me now, a soldier who cannot hold a sword?'

Florence drew herself up. 'I had a husband once. Would that he had had the opportunity to decide such a thing.'

'And what do you think he would have chosen?'

The question was like a slap and made her suck in her breath. Without a word, she turned and walked out. Once in the fresh air, she inhaled deeply, clearing her lungs of the enclosed weight of the soldiers' quarters. She felt weak, sick and shaky. Angry, too. At Hugh Fergant, at her lord for putting this burden upon her, and at herself most of all. She had thought she was done with mourning, but pockets of grief still lurked in dark, hidden corners. What indeed would her husband have chosen? She didn't know, and she never would.

Looking down, she realised that the shirt was still in her hands and she had not taken Fergant's soiled laundry. Lips tight, Florence turned round and marched back into the building, her skirts billowing with the vigour of her step.

He was slumped back, his eyes squeezed shut and his mouth drawn tight with pain. She placed the folded shirt on his bed. 'Sometimes it is not the things that are taken away, but the things that remain that define a man,' she said, her tone peremptory.

He didn't open his eyes. 'Does that apply to a woman, too?'

Florence grabbed the bundle of soiled linens at his bedside and stalked out. When she set to work on her laundry, it was with a renewed will and angry relish.

★ ★ ★

Four weeks later, Hugh considered his bandaged arm. He would not think the word 'stump' for the place where it ended. He would not dwell on the fact that a month ago there had been a hand and fingers that knew the pleasure of holding a weapon and lifting a cup. There was no point thinking that way. He gave a wry grimace. The laundress had been right. It was indeed what remained that defined a man.

It had taken him an age this morning and much fumbling and cursing before he'd succeeded in fastening his hose to his drawers, but he had managed. Another small triumph and a salutary lesson in how much he had taken for granted. Having donned his tunic and smoothed his hair, he picked up the small carved pot he had asked one of the men to obtain for him in the town. It rested in his palm, solid and delicate at the same time, and the feel of it made him smile before he closed the fingers of his good hand over the scrollwork on the lid and left the dormitory.

Florence was in the yard, bustling the dust from her laundry shelter with great sweeps of a besom broom. Hugh watched the robust motion of her arms and a pleasant warmth suffused his solar plexus. Although she was frequently prickly, he had come to value her visits during his convalescence, and he dared to think that she might have enjoyed them, too, despite their rough start. Drawing a deep breath, he strolled across the yard, feigning a nonchalance he was far from feeling.

At his approach, Florence ceased her sweeping and pleasure brightened her face. She had strong features—a big nose, square jaw, thick black brows. Everything about her was stalwart but, amid all that vigorous practicality, her eyes were surprising, like agate jewels flecked with green and amber and gold.

'A fine morning,' she said. 'Are you feeling better?' Her smile of greeting exposed white teeth; one of the front ones had a chipped edge.

Hugh shrugged. 'I am managing, mistress, and for that I have you to thank.'

'For doing your laundry?'

'For shaking me out of my self-pity and being good company.' He cleared his throat. 'I wanted to tell you that my lord has offered me a post as gatekeeper. Matthew is feeling his years and my lord wants a younger man to learn the duties and take over in the fullness of time. It's a task that a determined man with one hand and a hook can accomplish well enough.'

'I am pleased for you!' She leaned forward to touch his arm, those wonderful agate eyes bright.

'I wanted to give you this.' He held out the pot and watched her face change. She already had a ruddy complexion but now a flush lay on it that reminded him of a Damascus rose.

Biting her lower lip, she took the pot from him gingerly in one large work-roughed hand and uncapped the lid with the other. A warm, sensual perfume wafted from the pale unguent within.

'It's a rub for softening the skin. I thought you would like it.'

She said nothing for a moment and then she gave a small laugh, although her chin quivered. 'I do. Indeed I do. But I think it is a lost cause on a laundress.'

'There is no such thing as a lost cause, as you told me yourself, and as Lord John would tell you, too.' Hugh hesitated, then added on a more intimate note, 'It is good to have special things in the world.'

Florence blushed again, then smiled in such a way that he thought he had never seen anything so beautiful in his life.

Although busy over her laundry vat, Florence still found time over the weeks to watch Hugh learning his new trade with Matthew the gatekeeper. Hugh's manner was deferent and respectful in order to soothe the old man's pride. Matthew was prickly and authoritative, but they seemed to be rubbing along well together.

Smiling a little wryly, Florence looked down at her hands which, as usual, were red and chapped from their immersion in hot lye solution. Not all the perfumed unguent in the world was going to make a difference. Yet, in other ways, she had not felt the same since dipping a first tentative forefinger in the pot to make the luscious scent of roses bloom around her.

Her son paused at her side on his way to battle practice. 'I don't know why you're so taken with him,' he growled.

Florence gave her son a look of mingled anxiety and exasperation. 'He is a good man. He's doing very well at gate duty.'

'Hah!' Adam snorted. 'He's just letting Matthew order him around.'

'He's letting Matthew teach him the job, which is as it should be, and he's being careful of Matthew's pride.'

Adam's lip curled. 'He's a useless cripple,' he said viciously.

Florence gasped at her son's venom. 'How dare you say such a thing? I am ashamed of you!'

Adam's complexion reddened. 'You should be the one ashamed, Mother. It makes me sick to see you fawning over each other. My father was twice the man he is. Do you think he would have approved?'

'Your father is dead,' Florence snapped, wondering how many more times she would have to say those words and feel the cut. That, too, was like an amputation. 'Life has to go on.'

'He's useless!' Adam reiterated, his voice holding a desperate wobble. 'Lord John only keeps him out of pity.'

A hard hand gripped Adam's shoulder from behind. The fingers were long and elegant and the middle one was adorned with a gold ring set with a green beryl. Adam spun round, stared upwards, then bowed his head. Florence dropped a curtsey. 'My lord.'

Lord John transfixed Adam with a fierce one-eyed stare. 'Better men than you put bread on the table,' he said. The pitch of his voice was normal, but each word was as clear as ice. 'Hugh will learn to fight left-handed, as I have learned to fight without half of my vision. When you have his bravery, then you will not need to criticise. Then I might think you worth something.'

Adam flushed scarlet. The Lord Marshal gave a brusque nod and strode off towards the stables.

Florence reached for her son but he shrugged her off and stamped away in the opposite direction.

Sighing, Florence returned to her laundry, resolving that she would speak to Adam once her work was finished and he had had time to think. The matter had to be resolved before it could fester further.

Sniffing back tears of humiliation, determined he would not openly cry, Adam gathered his belongings. He felt foolish and humiliated. He refused to stay where he wasn't wanted. Barons were always looking to hire warriors and Lord John wasn't the only one around. He could use a spear as well as any man—better than many. He was tall and strong for his years. They'd want him in Devizes or Winchester for certain. After a glance over his shoulder to make sure no one was looking, he opened his mother's clothing chest and rummaged past her chemises and folded gowns until he found the pouch containing his father's large silver cloak brooch. Adam tipped it into his hand, stared at it for a moment and then secured it to his mantle, high on the shoulder in the style of a warrior. He told himself it wasn't stealing. He was only taking his rightful inheritance. Nor was it stealing to take his father's shield from the wall behind the bed box, or the long knife with the tabby patterned blade that had belonged to his grandfather. He wasn't going to leave them behind for Hugh Fergant to use.

The gates were open and Matthew dozed by his watch fire. There was no sign of Hugh. Adam felt a surge of satisfied contempt. Fine guards these were. If he was an invader, he could have ridden in and massacred everyone.

Three beggars huddled in the lee of the castle wall, awaiting handouts of bread from the almoner. They were so much a part of the landscape and Adam was so caught up in his own discontent that he paid them scant attention.

However, they were not so dismissive of him, nor the silver cloak brooch glittering on the crest of his shoulder…nor the fact that he appeared to be alone.

Hugh returned from an errand to the stables and stood by the gate, observing the bustle in the outer ward. Florence had just carried a basket of washing across to the drying frames near the well. He admired her strong, ample curves, imagining himself in possession of all that generosity. Behind him, old Matthew hawked and spat into the fire, making it sizzle and hiss. 'Yon laundress's lad's gone off as if he means business,' he remarked.

Hugh turned, a cold prickle between his shoulder blades, the same one he always felt before a battle. 'Gone where?'

'Didn't say.'

'How long since?'

The gatekeeper pointed at a spot on the wall behind him. 'Since the sun shadow was there. Looked to me as if he was going some way. He'd got a spear and shield with him, and he was wearing his cloak.'

Hugh shook his head in exasperation. 'Why didn't you stop him?'

Matthew shrugged. 'Not my business.' His eyes gleamed. 'Thought you might find it easier to be rid of him, anyway.'

Hugh clamped his jaw on the retort that Matthew's wits were addled if he thought such a thing would help his relationship with

Florence. Muttering an oath, he hastened to the stables and ordered one of the grooms to saddle his bay gelding. 'Make haste!' He cursed that he could no longer fasten buckles and cinches himself.

'The lads have been riding him while you've been sick,' the groom said. 'He's still got a bit o' stable belly, but he'll do.'

Hugh gave a brusque nod and set his foot to the stirrup. 'He'll have to.'

It was simple enough to guide a horse one-handed and Hugh was an accomplished rider. A man had to be to follow Lord John. Even so, he felt vulnerable as he rode out of the keep gates. A part of him knew that this was outright folly. What was he going to say to the boy? What if it came to blows?

A few enquiries at the gate, abetted by his own instincts, set him on the track across the Downs towards Devizes, which was the nearest town of any size. The route was beautiful now, in the summer, the grassland lush and the sheep grazing, their lambs gambolling in groups or stretched out sleeping on the cool green grass. In winter, the road could be a lowering bleak place, beset by bitter winds and drifting snow against the great grey standing stones that had been built by giants.

He rode into a dip, rounded a sharp turn in the path and stared in momentary shock at the sight of Adam being menaced by three ragged figures.

'*Hah!*' he cried to his gelding and dug in his heels. He pulled his cloak off over his head. The men turned to the noise of pounding hooves but Hugh was already upon them. He threw his cloak over the man to his left, rode down the middle one and put the horse between the youth and the third attacker.

'Put your foot on my stirrup!' Hugh bellowed.

Pale as whey, the lad set his foot over Hugh's. The latter's powerful right arm and strong hand grasped him and hauled him up. 'Go, Bayard, go!'

The gelding, a twelve-year-old veteran of many skirmishes, responded to voice and heel with a speed that left the attackers floundering. A glance over his shoulder showed Hugh that the man he had ridden down had not risen again. He had lost a decent cloak and the boy had sacrificed his shield and spear, but a patrol party could easily recoup them.

'How did you know to come after me?' Adam asked.

Hugh reined the gelding to a brisk walk. 'It's my duty as gate-keeper to know all that comes and goes.' Hugh decided not to mention old Matthew's part. It better served his purpose to have the youth think him omniscient. 'I thought you had backbone enough to stay.'

The boy's jaw tightened with defensive pride. 'Why should I?'

'Why should you leave? Because of this?' Hugh raised his handless arm. 'I have no choice but to live with this for the rest of my life but I intend to make the best of it. Do you know how easy it would be to go and whimper in a corner?'

There was an uncomfortable silence.

'I have no quarrel with you,' Hugh said.

The boy's expression contorted as he struggled with a dilemma. 'Back there,' he said. 'You knew what to do.' There was grudging admiration in his voice.

'I've fought enough battles, lad. You don't follow Lord John if you can't handle yourself.' He took his hand off the rein to grip the boy's shoulder. 'You'll know what to do next time, too.'

Adam swallowed. 'Yes.' And then in a subdued voice, 'Thank you.'

Hugh said nothing, but a feeling of warmth at his core made him smile.

Florence was waiting anxiously and as they dismounted she flung her arms around both of them, weeping with relief. Scarlet, Adam stood like an effigy in her embrace.

'Don't fuss, woman,' Hugh said with a conspiratorial man to man glance at Adam. 'All's well.'

Adam nodded and scuffed the ground with his boot soles.

Florence, seeing that some kind of peace had been made between them, held her tongue, although she noticed that Hugh was missing his cloak. Doubtless, she would hear the story in the end.

That evening, Florence took a chicken pasty and a jug of ale over to the watch fire. Old Matthew was snoring under a canvas shelter, but Hugh was hunched over the flames, now and then feeding them with firewood and lumps of charcoal.

'How's Adam?' He made room for her on his bench.

'Asleep. He says you saved him.'

Hugh rested his forearms on his knees. 'He's learned some hard lessons but all to the good. Best to let it rest and move on. It's a new day tomorrow.'

Florence held her hands out to the fire. 'The signs say it will be fine.'

'Good washday, then.'

Smiling, Florence watched him unwrap the pasty, dextrous despite his handicap, and then take a full, appreciative bite. She wanted that kind of hunger to fill her life again...desired it. 'I think my lord intentionally gave me your shirt,' she said thought-fully.

'He always pays his debts with interest,' Hugh agreed once he had swallowed. He wiped his hand on the cloth and took her right one within his grasp. 'If the weather's set fair for the next few days, perchance there'll be time for a wedding, too.'

'Perchance,' Florence agreed and, leaning her head against his shoulder, watched the sparks climb on ropes of smoke towards the stars.

Katie Fforde

Katie Fforde is the chairman of the Romantic Novelists' Association in this, its fiftieth anniversary year.

She lives in the West Country with her husband and some of her three children. She writes novels that are about real women living contemporary, although not always conventional, lives. The love story is a major part of each book and she also likes to explore a new theme or profession every time. Her books have been translated into several languages. Her most recent novels, *Going Dutch* and *Wedding Season,* reached the *Sunday Times* bestseller list and her new novel, *Love Letters* is available now. She is currently writing her sixteenth novel, part of which is set in America. For more information about Katie and her novels, visit www.katiefforde.com

The Secret Life of a Good Woman

Amanda looked anxiously up and down the road, indicator flashing. She wasn't only looking for traffic, but for people. But only a dog from behind a gate saw her pull onto the main road.

'I could be going to Waitrose!' she castigated herself. 'No one can see the overnight case in the boot! Stop panicking!'

But the guilt was overwhelming. She almost pulled over to make a phone call, cancelling the whole thing. But she didn't.

Did other women of her age sneak out like a grounded teenager? Not women like her, surely. She was a good woman; anyone who knew her would say that. She'd either run or helped run every organisation from toddler group to the Soup Club.

She put the radio on to distract herself from the enormity of what she was about to do, but she didn't hear it. 'I'm on the church flower rota! And I'm sneaking off to a hotel with sexy underwear in my case!'

She knew no one would believe it if the news got out—she

didn't even believe it herself. But she was a good woman about to do something that felt very bad.

Buying the underwear had involved cloak and dagger Internet shopping. She couldn't go into the local sexy underwear shop and buy French knickers because a friend of her daughter's owned the shop.

It wasn't just buying the stuff that was tricky; it was hoping it would arrive while her husband wasn't around. It was Russian Roulette—with knickers!

She got to the crossroads and saw her neighbour's mud-spattered Peugeot. She smiled and wiggled her fingers in greeting. Sweat glazed her face. Guilt or a hot flush? There was no way that Elsa Babbage would buy French knickers, even if she knew what they were. She wouldn't have struggled into several different pairs, trying to find one that didn't end just under the fold of her stomach. Underwear makers had no sympathy for the older woman. They didn't accept that even though you were approaching the menopause at a rate of undignified knots you might want to wear something other than Sloggis under your stretchy crimplene trousers. Just sometimes one wanted—or even needed—to break out of the uniform considered appropriate for 'women of a certain age'.

And then there was the basque. Amanda had her heart set on a basque or a corset but, in spite of an exhaustive search, she couldn't find anything you could put on single-handed. What was the point of that? When she made tactful enquiries—of course she was seeking the information for 'a friend'—the sales assistant invariably said, 'But men love pulling on those strings to get that wasp-waisted look!' That may well have been true, but it was no help to Amanda.

She slowed right down as she came into the town, trying to look as if her head was full of organic vegetables and wholemeal pasta. She passed the little shop where she bought her tights, regretting that on this occasion she couldn't use the help of her favourite pull-you-in, pull-you-up ones that could make flesh that was more the colour of uncooked pastry than rose-pink or pale gold look at least superficially smooth. No, she had decided to eschew tights and had investigated hold-ups, as recommended to her by the woman she did church flowers with. It had been particularly hot and hold-ups were a lot cooler than tights, apparently. Amanda couldn't quite bring herself to go for stockings; that would be just too—well, sexy. Hold-ups had a utilitarian name and therefore, in spite of the lace tops, were just about acceptable.

She noticed someone she knew going into From Top to Toe, the hairdresser-cum-beauty parlour. She was probably going in for a 'man and ped' just because she had a big 'do' coming up.

A couple of days ago Amanda had slunk in there, feeling like an underage teenager going into an off-licence to buy alcohol. It had been ridiculous; they knew her well, she'd had her legs waxed in summer, from the knee down. The tricky part was that the woman who always looked after her at the beauty parlour knew this—they had discussions about women who always liked to be hair-free and those, like Amanda, who were a bit more sloppy about it. So why was she asking for a 'high leg wax' now?

In the event she hadn't had to lie. She just said that a friend of hers had a swimming pool. And she had! The fact that this friend hadn't asked her to swim in it was neither here nor there. She might ask her at any moment! Amanda had to be ready, hadn't she?

Now she was away from her immediate area Amanda stopped feeling so worried about being spotted. She only had to gnaw on what she was about to do, with her sexy underwear in her suitcase, her body exfoliated and hairless—almost—her eyebrows shaped, her finger and toe nails professionally painted.

She did feel incredibly sexy and wondered if her extreme nerves about the whole thing were partly responsible for her turned-on state. It was all so out of character for her, as if she'd taken on a new personality—one more dashing than she had ever been before.

Then she had a minor panic attack that brought on a flush that was definitely menopausal. Supposing he was already there when she arrived at the hotel? Could she say, *Excuse me, I need to take off my Sloggis and put on my French knickers?* No! Should she find a public convenience and struggle into it all while not letting anything touch the probably filthy floor? No!

Then she calmed down. It would be perfectly reasonable for her to say, *I'll just get myself settled in and meet you in the bar.* That would be fine, perfectly normal. The trouble was, she didn't know what was perfectly normal. She had never had what used to be known as 'a dirty weekend'.

She was a complete innocent when it came to all this. She may have had three children but she felt almost like a virgin.

There was a car drawn up in front of the hotel. It could have been his—she had no way of knowing. He was coming straight from the airport; he might have hired one or he might have got a taxi. She parked next to it and panicked all over again. She didn't have to do this. She wanted to—very much indeed—but if her nerves overcame her she could just drive home and send a text explaining. Mentally, she was torn in two—was she a sophisticated woman of the world to whom this sort of thing was natural? Or was she 'good old Amanda' who was more used to organising a bring-and-buy sale or a charity auction?

She took some calming breaths. The bring-and-buy sale might not have produced a film of perspiration but going to a swanky hotel in the middle of nowhere definitely had. As she pulled her top away from her to cool herself she caught a whiff of her new perfume. Would he like it as much as she did? And, if he didn't, could she wash it all off? Aware she was creating things to panic about, she gave herself a talking-to. This had been planned for weeks and weeks. She'd spent hundreds on her failed attempts at getting nice French knickers; she couldn't waste all that effort. She was so nervous she could hardly make her legs carry her out of the car and up the steps of the hotel.

He happened to be in reception when she came in. Her heart leaped, preventing her from speaking for a few seconds. He looked so—elegant. It must have been a new suit, she decided, worn with the shirt that made his eyes as blue as the sea. Then she smiled and moved her lips, working some saliva into her mouth so she could speak. 'I'll just check in, get unpacked and meet you in the bar, okay?'

'Don't be too long,' he said, his eyes glinting with impatience.

She realised his anticipation was as great as hers and the thought made her hand shake as she signed the register and struggled to remember her car registration and postcode. But as she walked up the staircase, behind the receptionist, she put a wiggle in her walk because she knew he was looking.

Putting on the French knickers, the hold-ups and the bra designed for maximum cleavage helped a lot. Before she put on her favourite black dress she looked at herself in the mirror. She did look sexy. She didn't look fat—or, at least, only reasonably so. The hold-ups did something to her legs and the lace of her knickers made her thighs look curvy rather than lumpen. She sucked in her tummy, she put her hands on her hips and she posed. Yes, she had made the transition from Good Woman to Sex Kitten and she loved it. Putting on her high heels made the transformation complete.

But even Sex Kittens could feel nervous, she discovered as she joined him in the bar.

'What would you like to drink?' he asked.

She couldn't decide; all she knew was that she wanted as much alcohol as possible without her having to order a whole bottle of something.

'Maybe madam would like a cocktail?' said the barman, handing him a menu.

His eyes flicked over it quickly, efficiently. 'Have a Cosmopolitan. You'll like that.'

Amanda nodded. Did he have other ideas about what she might like? she wondered. Plans for what might happen later?

'If you don't like it, you can have something else,' he said when at last her drink was ready.

She sipped it. 'It's delicious.'

'Good. I'll just have a small whisky.'

They took their drinks over to the fire, Amanda's high heels making her wobble a bit on the thick pile of the carpet. She still wasn't sure she would be able to get through this but, she realised, if she finished her drink there was no question of her being able to drive home. Down that Cosmopolitan and you're committed, she told herself.

When he offered her another one, she said yes.

Conversation flowed through dinner—he really was very entertaining and made her laugh a lot. But she didn't drink much wine. Now she was no longer so nervous she didn't want to lose her head any more than she already had done. She wanted all her senses to be on full alert for what would come later.

'I didn't know sex could be like that,' she said afterwards, when she'd made them both a cup of tea.

'Well, it can. I'm glad you liked it,' he said, his eyes crinkling in amusement at her enthusiasm.

'I just loved it. The thing is, I'm not sure I'll be able to keep all this a secret.'

'You must. You mustn't tell anyone. This is just between us. And I want to be able to do it again.'

She sighed deeply, all her guilt soothed away by pleasure. In all her married life she had never had sex like that before. It was amazing, shocking and utterly wonderful. He made her feel like a sex-goddess, a young sex-goddess, not a menopausal Good Woman. She'd loved it—from the moment he'd unzipped her dress and kissed the back of her neck to when he'd removed one of her stockings from the light fitting. Neither of them was quite sure how it had got there.

Amanda was on the telephone. 'Susie, I have to tell someone. The most amazing, fantastic thing! Every woman should do it. It should be on the National Health!'

'Golly, Amanda! What have you been up to? You sound all sort of...well, I don't know...'

'Loved-up?'

'If you must use that expression, I suppose that's what I mean.' Susie sounded very disapproving.

Amanda didn't care. She just had to confess all to someone. 'It took ages to organise; I spent thousands—well, hundreds almost, on sexy underwear—'

'Amanda!' No longer just disapproving, Susie was horrified.

'We went to the most amazing ho—'

Too late she realised her husband was behind her and had probably heard at least part of her conversation with Susie.

'What?' demanded Susie from the other end, unaware of the catastrophe that had befallen her friend.

'We went to an amazing ho-down,' said Amanda weakly, almost laughing at the pathetic-ness of her last-second substitution. 'You know what a ho-down is? It's American—a sort of dance...'

When she ended her conversation with Susie, her husband was still there, waiting.

Arms folded, he looked down at her, his expression stern. Amanda had no way of telling how much he'd heard, of how much trouble she was in.

'What was all that about?'

She dropped her eyes.

'I thought we'd agreed to tell no one!'

Amanda came up to him, smiling guiltily. 'I'm sorry, I just couldn't resist. It was so fabulous.'

He ruffled her hair, then took hold of her chin and kissed her. 'We'll do it again soon, I promise. You're a naughty little thing, you know.'

Amanda sighed in blissful reminiscence. 'I know. It's such a lovely change from being a Good Woman.'

Sophie King

Sophie King has written five novels, all of which are published by Hodder & Stoughton. They include the best-selling *The School Run, The Supper Club* and her latest novel *The Wedding Party*. All her novels are aimed at women—and some men—from teens to grannies. She specialises in dysfunctional families—both in practice and on paper—but her page-turning novels will make you laugh as well as cry. Sophie also teaches creative writing at Oxford University and is the author of *How to Write Short Stories for Magazines and Get Published* (How To Books). Her real name is Jane Bidder. Find out more at www.sophieking.info

Word-Wise

'What's envy, Gran, and why is it green?'

Not another question! I looked up from the cooker, where I was cooking spaghetti bolognese for Molly's tea, and tried not to sigh. Ever since my granddaughter had arrived, she hadn't stopped asking things. I'd forgotten how her mother had done the same. I seemed to have forgotten a lot about extremely bright six-year-olds.

'Envy is when you want something that someone else has— but it's not exactly green,' I answered, wondering whether the spaghetti was ready yet. To be honest, I'd got so used to living on my own that I'd stopped making proper food and made do with toast or a bowl of soup. 'Where did you hear that, anyway?'

She tossed one of my magazines aside. 'It was in this. Why can't we say something is pink with envy? That's my favourite colour.'

Yes, everything Molly possessed was pink, from the duvet cover she had brought with her to her jogging suit. 'If someone is happy, they're in the pink,' I added, carefully spooning a slushy mush onto the Peter Rabbit plate which my daughter had had as a child.

Her eyes—so like my daughter's—widened. 'Why?'

I'd walked into that one all right! 'I really don't know, Molly. The English language is funny. Now, why don't you eat up your supper?'

She eyed her plate suspiciously and I didn't blame her. I wouldn't fancy it myself. 'Do you think I could have a nice boiled egg?' she asked in a quiet voice. 'Mummy often makes me one for tea.'

'Of course, poppet.' Heavens, her eyes were beginning to look watery again. 'I'm pretty certain I've got one…'

I rummaged through my fridge. Really, I ought to get round to sorting it out. There was all kinds in here; half eaten packets of crispbread which had got damp round the edges. Out-of-date yoghurts. An empty butter tub. Now I had someone to look after, I ought to be more organised.

'I'm afraid I'm out of eggs and the corner shop is closed…'

'You could borrow one from your neighbour,' piped up Molly. 'I was talking to him over the fence before tea.'

'What?' I hadn't spoken to the man next door since he had cut down that lovely tall hedge that had given me my privacy. All right, so it was on his side but that wasn't the point.

'How can a hedge have a point?' interrupted Molly. 'It's flat on top.'

I hadn't realised I'd been talking out loud. 'But…never mind. Look, I'm sorry, darling, but I don't speak to the man next door ever since I gave him the cold shoulder.'

'Gave him a cold shoulder?' Molly jumped up and gave me a sympathetic cuddle. 'Poor you! My friend Julie's gran's only got one proper hip. The other one's plastic. Did you get a plastic shoulder when you gave away your cold one?'

I wasn't sure how much more I could take of this. Whoever invented these phrases or idioms or whatever they're called? It's only when you start trying to explain them to a child that you realise how daft they are. 'Why don't you go and play outside while I rustle something up for tea?'

For one awful moment I thought she was going to ask me what 'rustle' meant but off she went, into the garden, clutching her new doll, which my daughter had given her as a goodbye present. Now, what *was* I going to make her? Ah, there's a tin of baked beans here…

'I've got an egg!' Molly came rushing in through the back door, her face flushed with excitement. 'Look! In fact, Mr Jeffrey gave me two. He said he hoped it might mend fences but I told him that you were all cross because he cut the hedge down, not his fence.'

Honestly! The cheek of the child—not to mention my neighbour. 'You didn't ask him for these eggs, did you?'

Molly put her head on one side and gave me a lovely smile, just like her mother used to at that age. 'Well, we started talking and I said I was waiting for my tea but that all you had in your fridge was a mouldy packet of crispbread and what I really wanted was a nice boiled egg like Mummy gives me and he said he had plenty of spare eggs.'

Great! Now I'd have to replace them. Well, I'd just put them on the doorstep and sneak away.

The following day it was too wet for Molly to go into the garden. 'It's raining cats and dogs,' I remarked, looking out of the window.

My granddaughter wiped mist off the windowpane. 'I've always wanted a kitten,' she said wistfully. 'Mr Jeffrey's got one. Do you think if I go out in the rain I could catch one before it fell to the ground?'

'No.' I was getting ready to go to the shop so I could replace those eggs as soon as possible. 'It's just a way of speaking. We don't really mean that animals come down in the rain.'

'Then why do we say it?'

I felt like banging my head against the wall.

My granddaughter tugged at my hand. 'Can I come to the shops?'

Well, I wasn't leaving her here alone, was I?

'Mr Jeffrey said he'd like to build bridges,' chattered Molly as we walked briskly in our raincoats, me holding the umbrella over her. 'Is that difficult?'

My mouth tightened. 'Very.'

'I'd like to build aeroplanes when I'm older. I wouldn't mind building bridges as well but I'd like to start with planes first.'

The shop was packed when we got there but we still managed to get the kind of food that Molly liked. Eggs, of course, and pizzas and chocolaty things that you put in the toaster which I'd never seen before and...

'Mr Jeffrey! Look! He's in the queue. Hello, it's me! Molly from next door.'

I didn't know where to look.

'Morning, Jilly.' The wretched man was doffing his hat and chatting as though we did this every day. 'How are you?'

He wasn't getting away with that. Not after what he'd done. I pretended to rummage through my trolley.

He grinned. 'Still acting cool as a cucumber, eh?'

'Gran's not a cucumber,' butted in Molly indignantly. 'She's much prettier than that. Anyway, it's not her cucumber that's cool. It's her shoulder but she doesn't have it now because she gave it to you.'

The look of total bewilderment on his face was almost worth bumping into him for.

'You know, there's no need to see red after all this time, Jilly.'

'What does...'

'Shh,' we both said.

'Actually, I have every right.' I looked up at him, facing him squarely in a way that I hadn't done for some time. 'And, as you well know, Jeffrey, it wasn't just the hedge.'

A flash of guilt crossed his face. 'You don't have to make a meal out of it.'

'Oh, that's a good idea,' burbled Molly, slinging the contents of my trolley onto the sliding belt. 'Can we all have a meal together tonight? Mr Jeffrey is really good at pizzas. His granddaughter likes them, too.'

I couldn't help myself. I didn't mean to but it just came out. A small smile, which Jeffrey caught sight of and which made him smile himself. 'She's a right case, isn't she?'

'I'm not a suitcase. I'm Molly. Look! The rain's stopped. Does that mean I won't find a kitten after all?'

Jeffrey raised an eyebrow questioningly. 'Don't even ask,' I whispered. Somehow, by now, we were walking down the road together.

'Look,' said Jeffrey quietly. 'About that time we were meant to go out for supper, to make up for that hedge business…'

'You mean when you stood me up.'

Molly skipped in between us indignantly. 'Why did you have to stand her up, Mr Jeffrey? Gran's not that old. She can stand up on her own, although Mummy says…'

'Shh,' we both said again.

'Something came up.' Jeffrey was looking more and more uncomfortable and a trickle of sweat began to run down the side of his neck. 'Actually, I had to look after my grandson at the last minute and I'd lost your phone number so I couldn't ring you. I tried to explain but you wouldn't listen.'

My daughter always used to say that. I do hope she's all right.

'I don't suppose,' said Jeffrey as we reached my house, 'that you'd give me a second chance?'

Should I? I have to confess that I've often looked over his hedge and wondered whether…

'Mummy!' yelled Molly, breaking free of my hand. 'Look! She's back.'

And so she was. Two days wasn't very long for a honeymoon

but my daughter had said she didn't want to be away from Molly for any longer and, besides, she was still worried that Molly might find it hard to have another daddy. But, from what I could see, with the way Molly was swinging between my daughter and her new husband, it might just be better than we'd both hoped.

'I'd better go,' said Jeffrey, even though a hopeful note in his voice suggested otherwise.

'No, wait.' My hand reached out and caught his arm before I could stop it. 'Let's meet up later.'

Something below tugged at my skirt. 'Can I come, too, before going home with Mummy?'

Has that child got magic powers of hearing? I give up. All right, here's to supper. Who says three's a crowd?

Jan Jones

A maths graduate, former computer programmer and playgroup leader, Jan Jones writes contemporary romantic comedy, Regency romances, short stories and poems. She won the RNA's Joan Hessayon Award in 2005 with her debut novel *Stage by Stage,* which came about through her experience of chaperoning her daughter during a touring production of *Joseph and the Amazing Technicolor Dreamcoat.* When in Georgette Heyer territory, she uses her fascination with history to write a series of Newmarket Regencies (*Fair Deception, Fortunate Wager* etc.) set two hundred years ago in her nearest town. As with all writers, elements of her life also inspire her many short stories for women's magazines—one of which won the RNA Elizabeth Goudge award in 2002. This could be why she gets funny looks whenever she takes out her notebook during conversations in the bar.

Jan organises RNA parties and the annual conference and is firmly of the opinion that the RNA is the friendliest, most supportive organisation around. Jan's website is at www.jan-jones.co.uk

Love's Colours

They were all there, sprawled around the corner table in the Anchor as if I'd never been away. The familiar and the strange warred in me, feeding my hesitation as I leant my art case against the old oak settle. Behind me, through the open door, seagulls wheeled over the constantly changing sea, crying their freedom to the winds. Inside, the locals' after-work territory was as un-altered as the pink-faced jollity of the tourists.

My best friend Nikki and my older brother Sam were arguing as usual. Tom was there, Pete and Ella, Harry—everyone. And Adam, just coming back from the bar with a tray of drinks. Adam, who turned his head and saw me first.

There was just a moment when our eyes met and the world stuttered in its tracks and then he smiled as if I'd only been gone a day or an hour. 'Another half, Jason,' he called to the barman. 'Hi, Gina.'

Well, it was a welcome, if not the answer to a question I hardly

dared ask. My feet came unstuck from the floor. I moved—
forward into the room, and back fifteen months in time.

'Gina!' shrieked Nikki, scrambling over Sam in her haste.
'When did you get back? Why didn't you phone? God, you're
so thin! You cow!' She flung her arms around me.

I hugged her, tears starting in my eyes. 'I love you, too, Nikki.'

Then they were all talking at once, buffeting me with noise,
bombarding me with questions.

'Forget how to email, did you?' asked Sam over Nikki's head.

I was ready for this. 'You all got hand-painted postcards. What
more do you want? They'll be worth a fortune when I'm
famous.' It had been easier that way. If I'd talked to any of them,
even by email or MSN, I wouldn't have been able to hack it.
Nobody tells you about the hollow, lonely space in every great
adventure.

Beside me, Nikki was pouring news like the broken water-
spout I'd sketched in Rome. Holly had had a baby girl—I hadn't
even known Holly was pregnant. Jason's gran had finally died
and they'd found her mattress stuffed with twenty pound notes.
Denise had promptly dumped Tom—since when had they been
an item?—and hooked up with Jason instead. Sam and Adam's
lifeboat had rescued a soap star I'd never heard of. Nikki had had
her photo taken with him for the paper. The photo was on her
dressing table—signed—in a red plush frame and Sam was pretending he wasn't jealous. My eyes found Adam again. His
browny-yellowy hair still framed his face in thick, windswept
curls. He wore faded jeans and an ancient T-shirt, just as he had
the day they'd waved me off. He still looked totally, utterly, gut-
clenchingly desirable. Was I the only one who had changed?

A blonde woman in city clothes came through the door.
'Whatever is *this*?' she said, her laugh cutting ice-perfect through
the noise at our table. She nudged an elegantly shod foot against
my scuffed art case. 'Are we collecting for another jumble sale?'

We? My hackles rose, reappearing from under fifteen months of foreign travel.

Adam spoke for what may have been the second time. 'Hello, Trish.'

Nikki paused in mid-flow. 'Oh. Hi, Trish,' she said with a distinct lack of enthusiasm. 'That's Gina's.'

I got up, feeling shocked and strange all over again. My art case is large and unwieldy and incredibly heavy but my friends had clubbed together to buy it when I was awarded the Edith Warburton Young People's Travel Bursary and as such I fight very dirty indeed when it is threatened. For the last fifteen months it had been welded to my side. And I'd simply *left* it by the door of the Anchor.

By the time I'd hauled it to the table—apologising to a holi-daymaker who sportingly said not to worry, pet, one's only for insurance—the not-local blonde had inserted herself between Tom and Adam and was asking in a bright voice whose round it was.

'Mine,' said Nikki flatly. 'Gina, don't you dare get any paint-ings out before I get back.' Which, of course, was quite enough to make Sam open the flap.

'Hey, how did you get this cut in the side?' asked Tom, far more interested in the condition of the case than its contents. 'It's nearly through to the lining.'

'Naples,' I said. 'There was a handbag snatcher on a motor-bike slashing shoulder straps.'

Pete ran his hand in a proprietary fashion over the triple-stitched, full-grain belting leather. 'Bit off more than he could chew with this.'

'You're not kidding,' I said. 'He got his knife stuck and swerved into the path of a cab.'

Adam's hand jerked, spilling his beer. 'Messy,' he said.

'Yes,' I replied.

Adam was a few months older than Sam—and a whole world ahead of him in experience. He'd run away to sea at seventeen and returned six years later with enough money to set up a carpentry workshop on the quay. Now he made carved boxes and plaques and wooden flower bosses for tourists—and chairs he designed himself that you could live in for ever. The old people nodded and said they'd known he would settle down, but often I'd watched him gazing out at the wide, endless sea, his unreadable eyes an exact match for the grey-green water.

The blonde woman moved impatiently. She had flawless chiselled hair and a complexion to die for. Ella, by far the most stylish of our group, looked provincial and unsophisticated in contrast. I didn't dare think what *I* looked like.

'Knew we were right to go for something substantial,' said Tom, patting the case with satisfaction.

Substantial? It was like Fort Knox, that case. I'd kept *everything* in it since I'd had my purse snatched out of my hand in the very first queue at Le Havre.

'Ugh, is that the Seine?' said Ella, wrinkling her nose at a view of Notre Dame. 'It's really dirty. Didn't you do anything nice, Gina?'

'Oh, you're a *realistic* painter,' murmured Trish. I had to admit I was impressed. A put-down in one word.

'It pays the bills.' Actually, it didn't. Any more than my untamed seascapes did. At least, not yet. Which was why I painted the other sort, too. 'Here you are, Ella. Greek waterfronts in pastels. I thought I might try the same technique on the passing trade here next summer. What do you think?'

'Oh, yes,' said Ella. 'These will sell.'

Trish's lip curled.

'Is this Cannes?' said Sam, gazing at another sketch in disgust. 'Look at the money tied up to that quay! Bet you never even saw the boats go out.'

'No, but one guy bought a painting I'd done of his yacht, bless him.' Just in time, too. It had fed me for a fortnight.

'What are all these little holes?' asked Pete, still checking out the case.

'That's where the kids I was nannying for in Barcelona used the bag as target practice for their potato gun.'

'Nannying?' said Nikki, putting the drinks down on the table and accidentally catching a corner of the tray on Trish's sleeve. 'Oh, yuk, why?'

I grinned. 'Duh! Because money doesn't go as far around Europe as it did in Edith's day and people weren't always buying my pictures, especially over the winter. I had to do all sorts of part-time jobs to get by. Washing up in Sorrento was best. All day to paint—you could just *eat* the light there—and then the punters in the bar too drunk to notice the smears on their glasses in the evenings anyway.'

Trish shuddered and turned to Adam.

'Where else did you go?' demanded Nikki.

'Valencia. Florence. Sardinia.' I swallowed, remembering. 'Tunisia.'

'Now *this* is pretty,' said Ella, pulling out another painting.

I groaned. 'Venice. Everything you do there looks like a Canaletto copy.'

Trish's mouth pursed in a *you said it* kind of way. She crossed her legs in a graceful fashion, which brought her arm two inches closer to Adam's.

'Funny shape boat,' said Tom, peering closely at the painting.

My throat closed up again. One of the things that had kept me going was imagining my friends' comments as I painted. I'd known Tom would say that.

'It's a gondola,' said Adam. 'They're built symmetrical so they can be poled in either direction.'

I'd known he would say that, too.

'Oh, have you been to Venice, Adam?' cooed Trish. 'Do tell.'

'Who is she?' I muttered to Nikki under a burst of noise.

'Bloody London photographer,' Nikki muttered back. 'Come down to run the Quayside Gallery.'

I stared at her, appalled. The Quayside was where my paintings were due to be displayed as part of the Edith Warburton thing. It was supposed to be my big break. Trish would probably hang my entire portfolio in the loo.

Nikki shrugged sympathetically. 'She's got some really crap arty ideas. The first thing she did when she took over was a God-awful photo-feature on the lifeboat. All black and white and enigmatic. It took weeks to shoot and Sam said she kept getting in their way, even when they were on a call-out! Then she blew the prints up life-sized and splattered them around the entrance foyer "as a tribute to our local heroes".' Nikki lowered her voice still further. '*And* she tried to sink her hooks into Sam. When he wouldn't bite she moved on to Adam. She's got some of his furniture on show in the gallery.'

Pain hit me without warning. I bent my head until it went away.

I had no rights, but that didn't stop me hoping. It didn't stop me whispering small, soundless prayers as I pushed myself against the wind early next morning. A frisson feathered my chest when I saw Adam standing alone on the bluff, gazing out to sea, sweatered in cream-coloured Aran. *Oh, please. Oh, please. Oh, please.*

That sweater was my present to him two Christmases ago. He was here where we used to meet. I had palmed a wooden rose from his workshop when I'd given him my seascapes to mind, and on the ferry I'd found an identical one tucked into my art case. Did it mean anything now? Or not?

Clouds scudded overhead, heralding autumn.

'Hi,' I said, coming up behind him.

Below us, a hardy jogger pounded along the beach. Adam

smiled at me, as casual as he had always been. 'Hi,' he said. 'How are you, Gina?'

I stared at him, thrown by the mundane question. That was what came of psyching yourself up with prayers. I pulled myself together. 'Okay, I think. Some of it…some of it wasn't very easy.'

'Life isn't.'

He would never ask. Just as I hadn't questioned him about his own missing years. But then I'd been barely twelve when he left and only eighteen when he came back. Eighteen, restless with unfulfilled talent and ripe for falling in love. 'I made a bad mistake in Sicily,' I said abruptly. 'Woke up in Tunisia. I had to work as a topless waitress for a month in a hole-in-the-corner bar to get the ferry fare out.'

He looked sideways at me, considering. Then returned his gaze to a distant freighter. 'I shopped my crew-mates on my final trip. They were smuggling drugs. The workshop was the reward money.'

It explained a lot. Suddenly everything welled up in me. 'Adam, why did you encourage me to apply for the bursary? Why did you want me to go? You practically forced me! I thought we…' I swallowed and looked away. 'All you had to do was say the word.'

The wind rushed past. 'I know,' said Adam on a thread of a breath. 'And I wanted to. Never think I didn't. Not saying that word was the hardest thing I've ever done.'

'Why?' It was almost a wail. I could hear the pain and betrayal in it and hated myself for giving my feelings away.

'Because, sooner or later, it wouldn't have been enough. I'd been there, remember? You'd get restive, wondering what you were missing, and by then it would be too late to mend things between us. I already knew where my work lay, where my heart belonged. You didn't.'

Was he saying what I thought he might be? I didn't know. I didn't know anything any more. Both of us were so dreadful with words. I jerked my head towards the lookout shelter. 'I've got something to show you.'

The shelter wasn't much—three sides, a roof and a bench—but it cut off the worst of the wind and gave an illusion of privacy. The world shrunk to being just him and me. I tugged my sketchbook out of my pocket and passed it to him. I was shaking and nearly nauseous at the thought that I might be wrong but I had to make him understand.

Adam raised an eyebrow. 'I saw your paintings last night.'

'Not these,' I said. 'No one's seen these.' I opened the cover. 'This was in Le Havre the first day. I'd had my purse stolen. I was scared and alone and I sat on the wharf with the art case heavy on my knees, remembering everybody's pride when they gave it to me. I watched the ferry leave for home and I squeezed your rose so hard it made ridges on my fingers. And I drew this through my tears.'

He looked at the sketch. A stillness came over him. 'That's not the ferry,' he said. 'That's Start Point. With the wind rising from the west.'

Was he getting it yet? I turned the page. 'This one I drew in Marseilles.'

He looked at it, then up at me, then back at the drawing again. 'Fairhaven Strait,' he said slowly. 'At the beginning of winter.'

He turned more pages. 'Alicante,' I said as he flicked over Ness Headland when the spring tides were in. 'Genoa,' I added as he paused at Withy Lighthouse, its beacon cutting a path of light through driving rain. 'Corfu,' I murmured when he stopped at our own shuttered harbour on a close-of-season Sunday.

He raised his eyes, sea-grey, sea-green, blank with shock. 'Gina, did you not have the right colours in your pencil tin for the Mediterranean?'

I'd stopped trembling now. It was done. For better or for worse. 'I had them in the tin, Adam,' I said steadily, 'but they weren't the colours in my heart.'

'Oh, dear God,' he whispered. 'I got it wrong.'

'White horses on the waves—' I put a hand on his Aran jumper. 'Cloud-streaked sky—' I brushed his jeans. 'Yellow ochre for the shore—' I threaded my fingers through his unruly hair. 'Grey-green sea—' I touched the tiny crow's feet next to his eyes. 'You weren't wrong, Adam, not completely. I did need to go, but my core is here and these have always been my real paintings. The others are just bread-and-butter stuff.'

'We all have to live.'

But his eyes weren't on what he was saying and there was hope, fast and bubbling and unstoppable, in my chest. I had to know one thing, though. 'Including you. Nikki says Trish has your furniture in the gallery.'

'Business, that's all it is.' He stood and held out his hand to me. 'I've never been deceived by surface veneer, Gina. My benches are in the Quayside—but my walls are covered with your seascapes. I love every wild, stubborn, uncompromising brush-stroke and there hasn't been a single day since you left that I haven't cursed myself for a fool and prayed for you to come back.'

I let him pull me up. His arms circled my waist. 'Are you staying, now?' he asked.

I looked at him. 'With you, Adam?'

He smiled. 'With me.'

I lifted my lips to his, fitting into his body, love flooding me, properly home at last. 'Yes,' I said. 'Yes, I'm staying. Here. With you.'

Janet Gover

Australian by birth, Janet Gover has travelled around the world as a journalist and broadcast consultant. Her work has appeared on major national and international television networks in Australia, Asia and the UK. Her first fiction was published in 2002. Since then, her short stories have regularly appeared in women's magazines in the UK and Australia. *Waiting for a Wish* won the RNA's Elizabeth Goudge Trophy in 2007. Janet is a graduate of the RNA's New Writers' Scheme. Her first novel, *The Farmer Needs a Wife,* was published in January 2009 by Little Black Dress, her second in December 2009. Read more about Janet and her work at www.janetgover.com

Waiting for a Wish

Three days before his tenth birthday, Peter saw a fairy by the canal at the bottom of his garden.

It was on one of the long June evenings that would remain an indelible childhood memory. He was sitting at his small desk in his bedroom at the back of the house, staring out of the window and not doing his homework. The book in front of him had his name written in large blue letters on the cover. Peter Aitkin. His mother had written that on the first day of school.

From their places on the brightly coloured curtains, Luke Skywalker, Han Solo and R2D2 stared out of the window in much the same unseeing way that Peter did. Peter wasn't really interested in *Star Wars* any more but his mum had made the curtains. Now that she was gone, there was no one to make new ones.

The back garden was long and narrow, just like all the others in the street. There was a wooden shed, where his father kept the lawnmower and his tools and a glasshouse where his mother had grown flowers and vegetables. The glasshouse was empty now. This year, Peter was almost tall enough to see over the fence without standing on his father's wheelbarrow. Behind the fence was the canal and on the other side of the canal was another garden that was very different to his.

This garden was huge, with broad neat lawns and tall trees. Colourful bushes flowered in the spring beside gravel paths. In the distance, he could see a big white house. Some nights, the house and the garden would be filled with bright lights and he could hear music. But he never saw any people. The house was too far away and the people at the parties never came down to the canal.

The night he saw the fairy was one of the party nights. Music floated down from the big white house. The lights glinted through the trees, although there was still daylight left. He was staring out across the canal, not really looking at anything in particular. Suddenly she was there.

She was dancing on the green lawn, close to the canal. He knew she was a fairy because she had wings. They were pale and soft and flapped a little as she moved. Her hair was long and straight and fair, flowing down her back like silver as her tiny bare feet flitted across the grass. She spun slowly, her arms spread wide as if to welcome the moonlight. She was beautiful.

Peter pushed a lock of dark hair out of his eyes. He opened his window and leaned out for a better look.

She stopped dancing, smiled up at him and waved.

He waved back, then pointed down at his own garden. Would she understand? Hoping she would wait for him and not fly away, Peter turned away from the window and slipped down the stairs. From the living room, he could hear the sound of the football game his father was watching on television. Quietly he opened the back door and crept out into the garden. He closed the door ever so carefully.

The evening air was cool and fresh. Peter breathed in the rich smell of the lawn his father had mowed that afternoon, trotting down to the back fence. Holding his breath, he peered over the top of the fence.

She was still there, waiting for him. She looked a lot like a very pretty girl with long blonde hair and a pink dress. But little girls don't have wings.

'Hello,' Peter said.

'Hello.' Her voice sounded like bluebells in the forest.

'What's your name?'

'Annabel. What's yours?'

'I'm Peter.' He hesitated for a moment, then asked, 'Are you really a fairy?'

She laughed. 'Of course I'm a fairy.' And she twirled to show him her wings. Her pink skirt twinkled as if there were stars sewn into it.

'Come over here and play with me,' Annabel said.

Peter very much wanted to. He might be able to climb over the fence, but the canal was another matter.

'I can't cross the canal,' he told the fairy. 'And besides, I'm not really supposed to go out at night.'

'Why not?' Annabel asked. 'It's very pretty in the garden at night.'

'Dad doesn't like me to be outside on my own. Not since Mum died.'

Annabel's smile faded and she looked sad. 'How did she die?'

'It was an accident. In the car,' Peter said. He couldn't say any more. He still sometimes cried when he talked about his mum, and he didn't want to cry in front of the fairy.

'What was she like?' Annabel asked.

'She had dark hair and dark eyes,' Peter said without even pausing to think about it. 'She always smelled like herbs—the ones she grew in her glasshouse. And at night she would sing to me.' Peter felt tears pricking the backs of his eyes. The other boys in his class at school would have laughed if he'd told them how much he wished he could hear his mum singing again. But a fairy was different. She would understand.

'I'm sorry, Peter,' Annabel said.

'That's OK.' Peter ran his sleeve quickly across his eyes. 'Do fairies have mothers…or fathers?'

A flicker crossed Annabel's face and, for a fraction of a heart-beat, her smile faded.

'Of course not, silly.' The smile was back, brighter than ever. 'Fairies don't have families. Fairies have a queen. One day I'm going to be Queen of the fairies. I'll have a crown and everything!'

Queen of the Fairies—that sounded good.

'Well, if you're Queen, you're going to need a King.'

'Peter!' Before Annabel could reply, a loud shout from the house interrupted them.

'That's Dad. He's looking for me.'

'Will you get in trouble for being outside?' Annabel asked.

'No,' Peter said. 'It'll be all right. But I'd better go in now.'

'Goodbye, Peter,' the fairy called softly as Peter started running back towards the house.

He came into the garden and looked for her the next night. And the one after that. But he didn't see her.

On his birthday, Peter's dad gave him a shop-bought cake with candles on it. It wasn't as nice as the cakes his mum used to make but, when he blew the candles out, he made a wish just the same. He didn't wish for his mum to come back, because his dad had told him that could never happen. Instead, he wished for the fairy to come back.

He made the same wish on his eleventh birthday, but she never came back.

On his twelfth birthday, he wished for a new bike.

★ ★ ★

The two men walked in silence down the path to the station. Their footsteps on the gravel seemed too harsh amid the gentle night noises. Peter Aitkin paused and looked up at the sky.

'You know, Dad, you can't see the stars in London.'

'Are you sure you want to go back tonight?'

'I have to. I'd like to stay but I have meetings early tomorrow.'

They resumed their journey. Compared to the never ending rumble of the city, Peter enjoyed the almost silence of the village where he had spent his childhood. He didn't come here often enough. The three hour train journey from London was too daunting, his job too demanding, time too short. Tonight's dinner had been a special occasion.

'Diane's great, Dad. I really like her.'

'I'm glad that the two of you got on.'

Peter had made the journey to meet the woman his father was to marry. James Aitkin had been alone for two decades. Peter was pleased that at last he'd found someone kind and loving to share the rest of his life. Over a quiet dinner at Diane's house they had talked about the wedding. Peter was to be the best man.

'You don't mind that I'm selling our old house?' James asked.

'Of course not,' Peter assured him. 'You do whatever you want. It's been quite a while since I lived there.'

'I know. You've gone a long way from this little village. I hope you realise how proud I am.'

The two men hugged goodbye at the station entrance. Peter was two inches taller than his father, something he had never really become accustomed to.

Peter watched Dad walk back towards the cottage where his future wife was waiting. He felt nothing but joy for them. His father had found something that had so far eluded Peter. He had met any number of attractive, interesting women in London, but not once had he even come close to falling in love. It was almost as if his heart was on hold—waiting for something or someone.

Peter shook his head at such a fanciful thought. His thirtieth birthday was only a few weeks away and he should know better.

He took one last long look at the sleepy village. There were no thatched roofs or Tudor beams. No Norman church towers or ruined castles. His home town would never feature on a picture postcard. As a child he had hated the streets of identical homes and the small row of shops that didn't boast a single high street chain. Now he was a man, hate had turned to understanding and a sneaking affection.

Peter turned towards the station gate. Something had come over him this evening. Maybe it was the champagne he'd shared with his father and stepmother-to-be, and the emotional effect of planning a wedding. He had three hours on the train to get his errant thoughts back under control.

He walked through the gate and past the soft-drinks machine. Then he saw her.

She was dancing under the light at the far end of the platform. Her long blonde hair fell down her back like liquid gold and moved in time to the swaying of her body. She spun, arms spread wide and eyes closed, completely lost in the rhythm of music that only she could hear.

Peter was captivated. She was the most beautiful girl he had ever seen. He wanted to walk up to her. To talk to her. But he was afraid that if he approached he would scare her away.

As she swayed and turned, her light coat fell open, revealing a pale pink dress that glittered like stardust. She lifted her face to the sky and stardust fell around her, glinting in the platform lights like…like rain.

Peter dragged his eyes from the vision and looked up. The first few cold drops fell onto his face. Then a few more. Seconds later, the heavens opened.

Halfway down the platform, an overhanging tree offered shelter. Peter sprinted towards it, aware as he did that the girl at the end of the platform was running towards the same spot, a rucksack in her hands.

They almost collided as both ducked under the sheltering branches.

'Sorry.' Peter stepped back to make room for her.

She looked up with the greenest eyes he had ever seen and then reached up to remove her earphones. Shaking droplets of water from her hair, she pulled her iPod from her pocket and turned it off.

'Wow,' she said softly as she peered out at the rain. 'I'm really pleased this tree is here.'

'It won't shelter us for long,' Peter said. 'I think we should make a run for the ticket office.'

As he spoke, the branch above them shook and large drops of water splashed onto his face.

The girl laughed gently. 'You might be right.'

She set off at a run. Her feet seemed to fly down the platform. Peter followed behind, feeling almost clumsy as his large feet splashed in every rapidly forming puddle.

Just ahead of him, the girl's stride faltered as the rucksack tumbled from her hand to the platform.

'I've got it,' Peter said, sweeping it up as he passed.

They made it to the shelter of the deserted ticket office and Peter held out the rucksack. Something white and very soggy had almost fallen out of the open top. Something made of feathers.

'Rats,' the girl said, brushing ineffectually at the damage.

'Nothing serious, I hope,' Peter said, his curiosity getting the better of him.

'My wings,' she replied. 'They're so hard to clean.'

'Wings?'

She looked up at him and laughed gaily. That laugh floated around him and into him and wrapped itself around his heart.

'I'm a fairy,' she explained. 'Well, actually I'm a drama teacher but I entertain children sometimes as a fairy.'

'Ah.'

'What's the matter?' Her head tilted to one side as she smiled up at him. 'Don't you like fairies?'

In the distance, a low rumble of wheels and an approaching light heralded the arrival of their train.

She smiled up at him as she hefted the rucksack onto her shoulder. 'By the way, my name is Annabel.'

'I'm Peter,' he said. 'I don't dislike fairies. It's just that one broke my heart a long, long time ago.'

Maureen Lee

Maureen Lee was born in Bootle near Liverpool where her novels are set. She has been married to a lovely chap called Richard for an incredibly long time and they have three very grown-up sons. She has written twenty novels, seventeen of them sagas. In 2000, *Dancing in the Dark* won the RNA Romantic Novel of the Year Award; she has been shortlisted and longlisted for two other books. For the record, Maureen hates housework, is obsessed with anything to do with politics, loves shopping for clothes and lunching with friends. You can read about Maureen and her books at www.maureenlee.co.uk

The Kiss

It was December, seven days before Christmas, and the weather was dire. By four o'clock the sky was black, the rain a downpour and a fierce wind made the trees groan and the windows rattle in their frames.

Sarah turned on the lamp beside her daughter's bed. The lamp was cream with a lace shade. She returned to the rocking chair and glanced around the room, now softly illuminated with creamy light. It looked so pretty, but everything in Karen's room was pretty, from the frilled bedding and matching curtains to the pale lilac walls and white furniture. Karen had been allowed to choose everything herself.

Years ago, Karen would have come home from school and she and Sarah would be warmly ensconced in the kitchen, mouth-watering smells coming from the oven, while Karen did her homework or watched the portable television.

The motion of the chair increased as other memories chased through Sarah's mind. Karen starting school; in the Nativity play;

riding her first bike; the day she cut her head when falling off a swing. She recalled the pride she'd felt on speech days when her daughter won a prize; then arriving home with the news she'd got a string of O levels. The A levels had come two years later.

A less pleasant memory: the day five years ago when Karen had left for university. She'd got her degree, but Sarah had never dreamt she wouldn't return home.

'Oh, Lord!' Her eyes welled with tears. Gentle shadows cast themselves darkly over her lovely tearful face. Once again she glanced around the pretty room. How could Karen leave this for a dismal bedsit a hundred miles away in London? Even at Christmas, her daughter was only coming home for a few days.

Sarah rubbed her eyes. Roger wouldn't say anything if he noticed she'd been crying again, but she knew it made him uncomfortable. He'd accepted their only child leaving home with surprising equanimity. Sarah couldn't understand why he wasn't upset.

'Of course I'm upset,' Roger insisted when she rounded on him. 'But it had to happen, love. It was inevitable.'

Sarah hadn't thought so. She'd envisaged Karen marrying a local boy so they would see each other every day. But not only was Karen living away from home, she showed no sign of settling down. According to her letters, there was a different boyfriend every week.

'I'd better start on Roger's tea,' she muttered dully. She rarely prepared a proper meal nowadays. Tonight she'd make an omelette and open a tin of peaches for afters. Her conscience pricked. It wasn't enough to give a man who'd been on his feet all day, but she couldn't be bothered making anything more substantial.

But she stayed in the chair for another few minutes, listening to the wind lash the trees and the rain thud against the windows. It was a while before she realised her mobile was ringing downstairs. She leapt from the chair and ran to answer it.

'Hi, Mum,' came Karen's cheerful voice.

Sarah's heart missed a beat. 'Karen, love, where are you?'

'On my way to Liverpool Street station: I'm coming home.'

'For good? Are you coming home for good, love?' Sarah asked eagerly. She visualised her daughter's vivid face; Roger's dark eyes and her mother's blonde hair. People often remarked on the striking contrast.

Karen laughed. 'No, Mum. You always ask that. I've got a cold, I've a few days holiday due, so I thought I'd come early for Christmas. I'll probably catch the train that gets in at twenty-five past seven.'

'We'll meet you with the car, love.'

'There's no need, Mum. I'll walk. It's not very far.'

'Far enough on a terrible night like this and you with a cold! We'll be there.'

Roger Magellon noticed the light in his daughter's room with a feeling of foreboding when he parked the car in the drive. But, to his surprise, he could smell a real meal in the oven for a change and his wife was in the kitchen, eyes shining.

'Karen's coming home!' she sang. 'I said we'd pick her up in an hour.'

More than anything in the world, Roger wished that he could make her eyes shine the way they now did.

She went on, 'I hope you don't mind waiting for your chicken casserole, Rog, but I thought we'd have it together.'

It was an effort to keep his voice steady. 'I wouldn't mind normally, love, but it's the first night of the play. The curtain goes up at half seven. We need to leave in fifteen minutes. You promised you'd be ready.'

Sarah bit her lip. She had totally forgotten about the play. Roger had been a professional actor when they met, tall and charismatic with the look of a young Sean Connery and dreams of becoming a star. He'd had the occasional walk-on stage and television part but mainly supported himself with part-time jobs: waiting on tables, washing dishes, labouring.

He'd given up his dreams when Karen was born. Instead of being an actor, Roger had worked in an electronics factory in the small Norfolk town where they lived. He'd risen to foreman, but had never got over his love of acting. He had become a star, but only of the local amateur dramatic society.

'I'll pick Karen up myself and see the play tomorrow,' Sarah murmured.

'Tonight's special, Sarah, you know that,' Roger said stiffly. 'The Mayor will be there, the press. There's a seat reserved for you at the front.'

'But, Rog,' Sarah said reasonably, 'Karen's coming home. She's not well. She's got a cold. I called on my mobile and she's definitely on the train.'

'Karen has looked after herself perfectly well for the last five years! She has a key. Call and tell her about the play. She'll understand.'

'It's such an awful night.' Sarah thought of something. 'Oh, Rog! I hope you don't need the car!'

Roger felt himself shrink inside. He stared at his wife, as lovely now as when he'd fallen crazily in love with her a quarter of a century ago and given up his lifelong ambition to make her happy. He still loved her, but in a way she'd as good as left him. The Sarah he used to know no longer existed. Her spirit was down in London with their daughter.

'I don't need the car, no. Patsy Donaldson offered to pick us up.' He corrected himself. 'Pick *me* up.' It was obvious Sarah had no intention of going to the play. It was a new one, a Christmas thriller, written by a young local woman who showed great promise. First nights were always exciting but tonight was particularly so.

'I'll have a quick shower, then I'll be off.'

'I'll make some tea.' She'd hurt him, Sarah realised as she listened to his footsteps, heavier than usual, going upstairs. But it was essential she be there for Karen on a night like this. She'd turned on the radiator in her room and put a bowl of pot pourri beside the lamp. She hugged herself at the thought of having her daughter home until after Christmas.

Roger came down and sat at the table where Sarah had put a mug of tea. 'Thanks.'

They sat in silence until Roger said in a rush, 'Isn't it time you remembered, love, that you're a wife, not just a mother?'

'Roger, I—'

'Not only that, you're a woman in your own right. It's time you did something for yourself instead of wasting your life worshipping at the shrine of our daughter.'

'That's a horrid thing to say.' Sarah's voice shook. In all the years they'd been married, he'd never spoken to her like that.

'I just wish half the love you have for Karen was directed at me.'

A horn sounded outside. 'That'll be Patsy.' He got up without another word. The slam of the front door echoed through the silent house, sounding strangely final. Sarah hurried to look through the front window. She hadn't wished him good luck. He slid into the seat and Patsy Donaldson leaned across and kissed him on the cheek. There was a glimpse of her bright red hair before the door shut and the light went off.

It meant nothing, the kiss. If she'd gone with Roger, Patsy would have kissed her, too. Even so, it niggled.

Sarah was still thinking about it when she drove to the station, passing the brightly lit Town Hall. Christmas lights swung wildly in the gale. She parked the car, but was too on edge to sit and wait. She got out and went through the dark, deserted booking hall, turning up her raincoat collar and stuffing her hands in the pockets. Her hair blew around her head like a fan.

Patsy Donaldson was forty; lovely, elegant—*divorced*. And Roger was an attractive man, perhaps even more so now that his face was comfortably wrinkled, his black hair touched with grey.

In the far distance, the train could be seen snaking silently through the countryside, the windows tiny squares of orange. She imagined Karen in one of the orange-lit carriages. Soon, she would get off, Sarah would hug her, take her home, feed her, they would talk till long past midnight. Or she might prefer to go to bed, in which case Sarah would sit in the rocking chair, as she'd done so many times when Karen was little, watching her daughter sleep.

At the same time, she envisaged Roger in his dressing room at the Town Hall getting ready for the play. He'd so wanted her to be there, his wife. And she'd promised, just as she'd promised to pick up Karen.

Which promise mattered most; the one to Roger, or the one to Karen?

Sarah shuddered as a particularly violent gust of wind sent her staggering. Roger or Karen? Her husband or her child?

That kiss, innocent though it was, had jolted her, made her see things differently, think of Roger in a way she hadn't done for years. *'You're a wife, not just a mother,'* he'd said.

The railway lines were beginning to hum.

Roger had given up everything for his wife and child—his cherished dreams. A thought struck Sarah, making her gasp. Was it too late for him to take up acting again? If she got a job, supported him for a change…

The train was less than a mile away and approaching rapidly. Karen would have put her coat on by now, pulled her suitcase from the rack, be standing by the door. She was always one of the first off. Sarah bit her lip at the idea of her daughter's eager face searching for the car outside. If it wasn't there, she'd hang around, her cold getting worse, wondering why Mum and Dad were late. She would worry. Sarah couldn't bear the thought of causing Karen a single moment's worry. If only she'd brought her mobile she could call her now.

'Karen has looked after herself perfectly well for the last five years.'

Sarah glanced at her watch; twenty-five past seven. If she left this very second and drove like the wind, she might get to the Town Hall before the curtain went up. But not if she waited for the train. She thought—again—of the kiss. She'd lost her daughter, but in the way most mothers, eventually, lost their children. But if she lost Roger! She loved him. She'd forgotten just how much during the time spent pining over Karen.

She didn't realise she was walking out to the car until she found herself unlocking the door. As she sped away, she felt a moment of deep sadness.

For the first time ever, it was *her* leaving Karen behind.

Linda Mitchelmore

It's an ill wind that blows nobody any good and for Linda Mitchelmore it was losing her hearing to a viral infection that prompted her to write. She signed up to a postal short story writing course with *Writing Magazine* and has now had some one hundred and fifty short stories and serials published in national magazines in the UK, Sweden, South Africa and Australia.

For Linda, it has come full circle since she signed up for that short story writing course as she is now a preliminary judge for *Writing Magazine* competitions. Linda has been a member of the RNA's New Writers' Scheme for far too long, but alas she has not made it as a novelist—yet!

From Russia with Something Like Love

I was wearing a new dress that day. Cotton. Handmade on Mum's old Singer sewing machine, because just about everything was in those days. The dress had a boat-shaped neckline which, given what happened, was more than appropriate. It was darted back and front to the waist, with a full skirt and apple-green penny-sized spots on a white background. With it I was wearing heels—not very high at one and a half inches but the tips were like rapier points. The toes were only marginally less pointed. White leather from Freeman, Hardy and Willis. 29/6. A world away from lace-up school shoes and navy serge uniform.

Mum said I looked like a tart and surely I wasn't thinking of going out like that. Dad told me to 'wash that muck off your face before you leave the house'. I ran a flannel over my lips, which turned the pillar-box red lipstick to a more subdued rosehip.

'Hello.' A man's voice cut across the sound of waves flumping onto the shoreline, the wind and the screech of seagulls. I turned to see six sailors sitting on the sea wall. Two were wearing hats and I tried to read what ship they were from. Naval ships have always anchored in the bay from time to time.

'Don't talk to them!' my friend Shelley said. 'They're foreign. Russian.'

'How can you tell?' I mean, only one of them had spoken and only one word.

Shelley—who knew everything!—gave me a withering look. 'Because that's Russian letters on the hatbands. And, as you're in the B set for Current Affairs, it's probably missed your attention that we're in the middle of a Cold War.'

'No, it hasn't. And anyway, there's a policeman over there and he's not arresting them, is he?'

I took a step nearer the sailors but Pamela, who was always joined at the hip to Shelley, grabbed my arm.

'Don't, Karen!'

I shrugged her off. 'I'm only going to say hello back.' I smiled at the sailors. 'Hello. Welcome to Devon.'

'This dump!' Shelley snorted.

'Is nice place,' said the same sailor who'd said hello. 'You like ice cream?'

'Say no!' Pamela hissed. 'They'll spike it with something. Then they'll drag you under the pier and…'

'In broad daylight? Don't be stupid,' I said.

The sailor who'd spoken to us was talking in his own language to his mates now. Two of them slid off the wall. One of them counted up to nine on his fingers in English—six of them and three of us—and raised a questioning eyebrow.

'Yes, please,' I said. 'A whirly whip with a flake in it.'

'Karen!' my friends said together.

'Oh, relax! You can tell Mr Strutt on Monday that you've been furthering Eastern bloc/British relations.'

The sailors came back from the ice cream hut on the beach

with fists full of cornets dripping everywhere and we shared them around, laughing as we tried to lick the drips. Shelley and Pamela were relaxing a bit now. I took out my camera and got snaps of the sailors on the wall and one of Shelley and Pamela with their tongues stuck out, licking ice cream for England.

The sailor who'd spoken to me finished his ice cream and grabbed me by the waist and lifted me onto the wall. My petticoats sort of flew up around me and, what with the ice cream still in my hand and trying to stop my hair flying in the breeze, there was a fair bit of stocking top that got flashed. I tossed what was left of my cornet to a seagull and frantically began flattening my petticoats.

Shelley grabbed my camera and began taking photos. I was in the middle, three sailors either side. No one was going to believe this—Karen Arthur, who was just about the only girl in the class who'd never had a boyfriend, with six potentials lined up. The sailor who'd said hello put an arm around my shoulder and I rested my head against his neck.

'I am Gregor,' he whispered.

'Gregor,' I said, rolling the name around my tongue. All his mates were talking in their own language. If they were Russian then it was a surprise to hear their speech not sounding like German, as I'd imagined it would—all sort of guttural and hard, a bit sinister. The way they spoke sounded more flowing and French. 'Where are you from?'

'Leningrad.'

'Formerly St Petersburg. That's in Russia, Karen,' Shelley sneered.

'I know that, thank you very much!' Shelley's know-all attitude was beginning to get to me.

'Yeah, and we're going,' Pamela said. 'Our boyfriends wouldn't like it if they knew we were being chatted up.' She hoisted her bag halfway up her arm and sniffed haughtily. 'Come on, Shell.'

Well, they weren't being chatted up, were they? It was only me.

'You like walk?' Gregor asked as Shelley and Pamela scurried off. I had a feeling this was the end of our little trio, but I didn't care.

He made a V of his arm, resting a hand on the waistband of his trousers, and I slipped my arm though his.

It was all very innocent. Girls were still virgins at fifteen in those days and intent on staying that way. We walked the length of the prom and back, me clicking along beside Gregor in my steel-tipped heels. Lots of people looked at us and smiled, because we must have looked amusing—Gregor well over six feet and so blond, and me five foot nothing with café-au-lait skin and raven-coloured hair.

'We go on sand?' Gregor said.

I didn't think he meant as in lie down on it, so I slipped into the Ladies and took off my shoes and stockings.

Gregor jumped down from the prom and held out a hand to help me down. He didn't let go of it, either. The sand was warm and gritty between my toes and we giggled our way across the beach, making funny foot patterns. We made arches of our arms as we weaved ourselves around picnicking families and children bent over making sandcastles. The tide was coming in now and we paddled, the water warm as it slid over the hot sand. I couldn't resist the urge to scoop up a handful of sea water and flick it over Gregor. He didn't mind.

'I am sailor,' he said, laughing.

The sun was beginning to slide down the sky and I didn't want the day to end. So we went back up onto the prom and found a bit of space on a bench and sat squashed up together and shared a portion of fish and chips, Gregor with his arm around me, and me feeding him the hot, salty, vinegary chips. We wiped our hands on the chip paper and threw the wrappings in the bin beside our bench.

Then Gregor took some photos from the pocket of his uniform jacket.

'You live there?' I said.

He was holding a colour photo of what looked to me like a palace with gold onions and jewelled orbs on the top of ornate towers.

'No—' Gregor laughed '—this is Church of the Resurrection.'

He showed me photo after photo of beautiful buildings. And there was me up until now thinking Russia was all shacks in the woods and bread queues and bears and ice.

'Peter the Great Bridge,' he said, holding out another photo for me to look at. 'In spring big ice come down the river.'

'Like baby icebergs,' I said.

'When I no longer sailor,' Gregor said, 'I will be artist.' From his other pocket he brought out a whole sheaf of photos of artwork. They were wonderful. I was good at art but I never knew the Russians were, too—they keep a lot of stuff from you at school, don't they?

I sat looking at the photos.

'Is beautiful, yes?'

'Very,' I said.

'You visit?'

'I don't think so,' I said. My Dad worked on the lorries that tarred the roads—fat chance of a holiday to Russia or anywhere else.

'One day,' Gregor said.

'Maybe,' I said.

A horn blasted then, and I could see a launch nearing the pier. Sailors seemed to be coming from all directions—some with girls; a few of them obviously the worse for a few beers.

'My boat,' Gregor said.

'It's been a lovely day,' I said. 'Thank you.'

I had no illusions that this was going anywhere.

'Tomorrow?' Gregor stood up and stuffed his photos back in his jacket pocket. 'I see you tomorrow? Here?'

'After lunch,' I said.

Sundays were written in stone in our house—I knew I'd have lots to do before I could escape.

'My, my,' Mum said. 'We are full of energy this morning.'

I'd cleaned the grate and re-laid the fire. I'd stripped the sheets from the beds and put them in the copper to soak ready for Monday's wash. I'd cleaned all the vegetables for lunch, even though I didn't think I'd be able to eat a thing for excitement. And it was still only ten o'clock.

From the tone of her voice, I had a feeling Mum had guessed I was going out.

'Well, seeing as you're so far ahead with the chores, you can take this bit of an apple turnover to Maisie Evans.'

I groaned. Maisie Evans lived twenty minutes' walk away and I knew when I got there she'd find half a dozen things for me to do.

'You're going, no arguments,' Mum said.

So I ran all the way to Maisie Evans's cottage, delivered the apple turnover, cleaned *her* grate, re-lit *her* fire and helped her take down the kitchen curtains to wash them. And then I raced back again. I swear my feet hardly touched the pavement there or back.

Lunch was an agonisingly drawn out affair. Dad chose the time to quiz me about schoolwork and who my friends were and things like that. I wondered if he'd bumped into Shelley's dad in the pub and heard all about Gregor.

But eventually I got away. I was wearing the same polka dot dress as yesterday, so that Gregor would pick me out easily in the throng of holidaymakers, and because I didn't have anything else pretty enough to wear on a date.

But there was a sea mist hanging over the bay and I could barely pick out Gregor's boat. I couldn't see him anywhere, either. Perhaps he didn't understand the word 'lunch' and had given up waiting for me.

I sat down on the top of the steps that led up from the road to the pier and hugged my knees. The sea mist was making the air chill so I put my deeply unfashionable cardigan over my shoulders. I'd give him an hour to find me and then I'd go. The hour was almost up and the sea mist had begun to evaporate when I heard the putt-putt of Gregor's launch. He came running down the wooden pier, his hat in his hand, his white-blond hair flopping over his forehead. His eyes were just as beautiful as I'd remembered them; there was a shade of blue in my watercolour box—cobalt—and I thought if I were to paint him that was the one I would choose for his eyes.

'You wait for me,' Gregor said, holding out a hand to pull me to my feet.

'I did,' I said.

Our hands stayed locked together and I said would he like to go to Fairy Cove, and he said anywhere would do if it was with me. I almost swooned when he said that.

Fairy Cove was my favourite place. Hardly any holidaymakers found it because you had to scramble down rocks to get to it, and be mindful of the tide so you didn't get cut off.

I smoothed the pebbles away to make a softer place to sit in the sand below and sat down on my cardigan. Gregor asked if he could draw me in my polka dot dress. Drawing was better than photographs, he said—it had more feeling.

The afternoon was warm and I got quite sleepy sitting there—long enough and still enough for Gregor to make lots of drawings. I could tell he was good—very good. He said he would transpose the drawings to paintings when he got home.

The tide had turned so we moved nearer the path, ready to scramble up it at the last minute. We couldn't be seen by anyone from where we sat but Gregor didn't try anything on with me—it was enough for us to talk and smile and laugh and touch hands now and then. Shelley said that every boy she'd ever been out with couldn't keep his hands off her. Well, that was probably because she let them.

Gregor hadn't kissed me yet, but I knew he would.

The tide was almost up to our toes when Gregor took a tin from his trouser pocket. Not any old tin but one that seemed to be encrusted with sapphires. When he opened it, it was full of tobacco.

'No, thanks,' I said. 'I don't smoke.'

My mum would kill me if I went home stinking of fags.

'Not to smoke,' Gregor said. 'To have. For gift.'

He tipped the tobacco onto the beach, then blew in the tin to get rid of every last strand.

'I think you lovely girl.'

'Thank you,' I said as Gregor placed the tin almost reverently in my hands.

And then he cupped my face in his hands and kissed me on the lips. Shelley—who knew everything!—said I'd have to kiss a lot of frogs before I found my Prince. But she was wrong—I'd found my Prince first time.

The kiss went on and on and I seemed to know what to do even though I'd never been kissed before. Oh, Shelley and Pamela where are you now? And then I thought—no, this is just between us, Gregor and me. It will be my secret, something to smile inside about during Physics or when Mum and Dad are rowing like mad, making the windows rattle with their angry words.

'In Russia we give decorated tins to lovers so they do not forget.'

'Lovers?' I said. That meant *doing it* and no way was I going to *do it* with Gregor, not even for a tin decorated with sapphires.

'Lovers is wrong word?' Gregor looked hurt at my response.

'No,' I said. 'It's a good word.' Just the wrong time, I thought, but it would be too difficult to explain, given the language difficulties.

Gregor gave me all the photos he'd shown me the day before and I put them in the tin.

And that was it really, between Gregor and me, because his ship left that night. I stood on the beach, watching and waving until I couldn't see its lights any more. Oh, and I gave him my address and he wrote something that looked like hieroglyphics on the back of one of the photos. I wondered if I'd imagined it all, but I had my tin and my photos and the little warm spot in my heart as proof that I hadn't.

Shelley and Pamela called me a slag and put it about that I'd slept with all six sailors. Word got back to Mum and Dad and I was grounded for months. The rows between them got worse. And for a long time I really did think I was bad—I made a lot of bad choices after that anyway.

But in the darkest of times there has always been the memory of Gregor's kiss and his kindness and the way he made that weekend special. It was the best weekend of my life.

But life gets in the way of love sometimes. For me that's forty-five years, two marriages, and two divorces. And seven house moves, which means that Gregor and I have corresponded only sporadically; sometimes it was months or years before we were back in one another's lives again. But it's as though the thread of what we had that wonderful weekend could be frayed but not broken. I've kept every letter and card he sent because he paints beautifully with words and I've been there with him as he went to the theatre or the ballet. I've walked the banks of the river with him and seen the egrets and the pike. And I've sat down beside him while he painted the willows dipping their leaves into the water at sunrise. I rejoiced with him when Leningrad became his beloved St Petersburg again.

So, it's taken me a long time to get to where I am today… standing in the queue at Heathrow to get my passport checked. I'm flying to St Petersburg to visit all the wonderful museums and the baroque churches and the bridges and the river at long, long last.

A year ago I got a computer and I Googled Gregor's name. I almost stopped breathing when it came up first time. He'd been very modest about his achievements in his letters but it seems he's a well-known artist over there and his paintings are in lots of galleries. And I'm going to see them. He's got work in museums, too. Including one of me in the polka dot dress.

Gregor's widowed now. Me…well, let's just say that despite my two marriages and a handful of relationships no one ever came close to Gregor.

My passport has been examined and I move towards the departures lounge. Getting closer. It may work out for us or it may not—but the fact that Gregor has his painting of me in a museum must count for something. The tin he gave me is in the pocket of my jacket. I run my fingers over the decorated lid as though reading Braille—I know each stone, each shape, every pattern. They aren't sapphires, of course—just coloured glass. But they're precious to me…and I'm taking them back to Russia.

With something that still feels like love.

Christina Jones

Christina Jones has been writing all her life. Since having her first story published at fourteen she has had more than two thousand short stories published in magazines around the world. She also writes romantic comedy novels and has recently won the Pure Passion Award for *Love Potions* and the Melissa Nathan Comedy Romance Award for *Heaven Sent*.

She lives in rural Oxfordshire with her husband, daughter and a houseful of much-loved rescued cats, works as a part-time barmaid for the company—writing's a lonely business!—and the people-watching inspiration and never has her head out of a book—preferably a crime novel. Her favourite authors are Peter Robinson and MC Beaton (alive) and Dickens and Agatha Christie (dead).

Before becoming a Proper Writer, she had twenty-seven jobs—ranging from nightclub dancer to auxiliary nurse via band booker and doughnut maker—and was sacked from nineteen of them for writing when she should have been working. Christina's lifelong ambition is to own a model railway.

Find out more about Christina and her books at her website www.christinajones.co.uk

The Wrong Trousers

In the steamy, humid atmosphere of her small dry-cleaning shop, Brenda folded Simon's dark blue evening trousers along the knife-edge creases and arranged them carefully on a padded hanger. Grinning foolishly, she allowed herself to run indulgent fingers across the trousers' satin-smooth finish. Not a snag, Brenda thought, caressing the material. Not a loose thread. Not a rough edge. Not an unfinished seam. Matching the dark blue jacket waiting to be pressed, this suit—Simon's suit—was, like its owner, absolute perfection.

Brenda sighed. She loved being in love. She especially loved being in love with Simon.

Love had been something of a stranger in Brenda's life. Never having been the pretty one in her group, or the funny one, or the confident one, or the—dare she even think it—the sexy one, she'd had casual and rather unsatisfactory boyfriends when she was younger, but the elusive butterfly of love had somehow always fluttered past her.

Now, at almost forty-eight, love in all its rainbow glory had arrived at last, to brighten Brenda's grey existence in the gorgeous form of Simon.

Pressing the suit jacket, inhaling the fragrance, Brenda resisted the urge to kiss it. She loved all Simon's clothes but this dress suit was her favourite. It must have cost a fortune.

Some men had cheap and nasty suits with too tight jackets and badly fitting trousers—but not Simon. Simon had the best.

She liked Simon's lounge suits, too. And his pure cotton shirts. He always looked as if he'd just stepped out of one of those posh clothes catalogues. Brenda allowed herself another happy sigh—Simon knew what was what. Simon was a gentleman. A real gentleman.

Since they'd met he'd treated her so well and was always so polite, listening to her as she chattered about her day, smiling that heartbreaking smile. Simon made her feel as though she was the most important and interesting person in the world.

Of course, they hadn't known each other that long and there were still a lot of things she didn't know about Simon—but that was half the fun of meeting someone new, wasn't it? Finding out.

Brenda moved on slowly and tidied other hangers. Suits, shirts and ties arrayed at one end of the rail: dresses and skirts at the other, like two lives coming together. Like her life and Simon's. She chuckled girlishly.

She looked out at the powder-blue sky and the warm sun and was glad to be alive. Thinking of Simon made her feel like that… Giggly, like a teenager with her first crush. Simon, with his light brown hair, twinkling brown eyes and his low, expensive voice, had brought champagne bubbles into her lemonade world. And tonight—oh, tonight…

She glanced at her watch. Lunchtime. Surely there was just time to nip out and get her hair done? She had to look her best tonight.

Brenda reached for her coat. Tonight, Simon would be wearing the dark blue dress suit to the Chamber of Commerce Social Evening—which was why she'd already got it pressed and waiting—and she'd be wearing her green taffeta frock. Hopefully. The green taffeta, which had hung in her wardrobe for a decade, was a size fourteen. Brenda was a good size sixteen. However, buoyed by Trinny and Susannah, she'd invested in a pair of magic knickers to work their spell so she could slither into the green taffeta and dance the night away in Simon's arms.

They'd be like Scarlett O'Hara and Rhett Butler. A handsome couple just made for each other.

Ruby, the hairdresser who never turned a customer away, snipped and combed and snipped some more, and looked a bit put out that Brenda didn't want rollers.

Brenda insisted, 'Nothing too rigid. I want to look young and carefree.'

'What's the occasion, then?' Ruby frowned, rollers being her speciality. 'Going somewhere nice?'

'Chamber of Commerce,' Brenda smiled at her reflection. The hairstyle was coming along nicely. Her normal tight curls were now tousled and feathery. 'Social evening.'

'Oh, I'm going there, too.' Ruby raised her voice against the whine of the hairdryer. 'Is this what the new hairdo is for?'

Ruby upped the volume of the dryer, scalding Brenda's scalp. 'It's hardly exclusive! Everyone in the High Street is going to be there! Who are you going with?'

Brenda pretended that the question was lost in a particularly vicious roar from the dryer. She smiled happily at her almost-youthful reflection. She didn't want to discuss Simon with Ruby. Ruby was a terrible gossip—if she knew Simon and Brenda were an item, all her clients would know by teatime.

'There.' Ruby snapped the hairdryer into silence and surveyed her handiwork proudly. 'Quite nice, though I says it as shouldn't. Makes you look like a fat Lulu.'

Her hair had taken years off her, Brenda thought, glancing at herself in the High Street shop windows on the way home from Maison Ruby. Why, she might even stamp her feet tonight and cry, *Fiddle-de-dee!*

Giggling at the thought, Brenda unlocked her flat and almost leapt up the stairs. Simon would be here soon to collect his suit. She knew he'd need plenty of time to get ready. The thought of seeing him filled her with delight.

An hour later the shop door opened and Simon walked in, smiling. As always, Brenda's heart drummed a love song and her knees went weak. This, she thought happily, was what she'd waited all those years for. This was why poets eulogised and singers sang and romantic novelists wrote.

This was True Love.

'You've had your hair done.' Simon's whipped-chocolate voice was straight out of her dreams. 'Very nice. It suits you.'

Brenda blushed and fluffed at her new carefully dishevelled layers. Simon made her a bit tongue-tied. She hoped that he didn't think she was boring. She found it so difficult to know what to say sometimes. Still, he was smiling and admiring the spotless dark blue jacket and telling Brenda he didn't know what he'd done before he met her.

Brenda blushed some more and dreamed of later that evening when, dressed in the green taffeta, she'd be dancing in his arms, her hands resting lightly on his broad shoulders beneath the jacket's satin-smooth material.

'This is perfect.' He beamed, looking, she thought, exactly like Roger Moore when he was 007. 'You are a clever girl…'

Brenda now blushed from her toes to the roots of her newly

coiffed hairstyle. 'You're welcome,' she said softly. 'Nothing but the best for you.'

Simon smiled again, showing his perfectly capped teeth, and Brenda's heart gave a flutter of pure joy.

The joy started to dissipate just as Brenda was spraying on her scent. The green taffeta frock swirled and rustled around her as she danced a few tentative steps round the flat's bedroom. Yes, she could move. Eat your heart out, *Strictly Come Dancing,* she giggled to herself. The magic knickers had constricted her nicely into a svelte size fourteen.

The taxi would arrive in ten minutes. In less than half an hour she'd be at the Chamber of Commerce, and she and Simon…

Then the doorbell rang.

'Bother.' Brenda stopped spraying the scent, grabbed her handbag and trotted downstairs in her fifteen-deniered feet. 'The taxi's early—and I haven't quite finished my make-up. Well, he'll have to wait until I've got my last layer of mascara on and found my dancing sandals and—' She pulled the door open.

It wasn't the taxi driver. It was Mike from the corner shop. He gazed at Brenda in wonder. 'Blimey, Bren! You're a right bobby-dazzler!'

Brenda blushed at his outspoken comment. 'Er…thank you… I'm just off out—did you want something?'

'My trousers.'

'What?' Brenda peered at him. Mike was wearing a beige polyester jacket, a frilly evening shirt and jeans. He looked a bit like Jeremy Clarkson. 'What trousers? Have you been drinking?'

'Not yet.' Mike beamed. 'But I hope to, later. I'm going to the shindig at the Chamber of Commerce and I've got the wrong trousers. You gave me these when I came in earlier. Here…'

Brenda looked in horror. Her heart sank like a stone. Mike was clutching Simon's best dark blue evening trousers.

She dropped her handbag. 'Oh, no! That means that—'

'That I was expected to go to the most important social event of the year,' Simon growled, choosing that moment to march up to Brenda's door behind Mike, 'in these!' He flourished Mike's trousers under Brenda's nose. 'Cheap, tatty, nasty—'

'Hold up, mate!' Mike grabbed his beige polyester trousers from Simon. 'They're my best slacks. Brenda must've got them muddled.'

Brenda quailed. Simon was so angry. And somehow suddenly not quite so handsome.

He snatched his dark blue trousers from Mike's hand. 'And that surprises you, does it? The woman's as giddy as an inebriated squirrel—probably from spending all day inhaling dry-cleaning fluid!'

'Excuse me?' Mike suddenly puffed up much bigger. He jabbed a finger at Simon's increasingly pompous chest. 'You'll apologise for that remark! Brenda here is one of the most charming, helpful and sweet-natured ladies you'll ever meet.'

'And away with the fairies most of the time.' Simon still frowned heavily. 'Good Lord—how difficult is it to match the right trousers to the right jacket? A child of five could do it!'

Brenda, watching Simon's handsome face become hard and snarly, clamped her lips together really hard. She wouldn't cry. She wouldn't... How could she have made such a silly mistake? Daydreaming about Simon, she must have slid his jacket over Mike's trousers and vice versa.

Stupid, stupid, stupid!

Mike still glared at Simon. 'I'm waiting. Brenda's waiting. We want an apology.'

Through her misery, Brenda looked at Mike with new eyes. He was very brave—and so kind. Then she sighed. How wrong she'd been about Simon...

Mike took a step closer to Simon, his fists bunched.

'Er—' Simon huffed and puffed and seemed to shrink.

'Oh…whatever… Yes, yes, of course… I'm sorry, Brenda. You've always been wonderfully efficient in looking after me and my clothes—I apologise. I was just flustered—I need my suit—I need to be at the Chamber of Commerce—and my wife's waiting in the car… Again, I apologise…'

Wife? Simon was *married?* Brenda reeled again. And Simon thought she was—was—giddy—and silly? Her eyes hurt. She blinked. She'd been so stupid… So very, very stupid…

'Apology accepted,' she said stiffly, hoping Simon wouldn't notice her glittering eyes. 'And I'm sorry, too—you're right, I must have got them muddled. My mistake.'

Simon nodded curtly. Then looking warily at Mike, he clutched his trousers and slunk away.

'Bad tempered so-and-so,' Mike sniffed. 'And all hoity-toity about nothing. He only works at the travel agents, for heaven's sake. He doesn't even own his shop—not like us, eh, Bren?'

Brenda wasn't really listening. She swallowed, watching a diminished Simon scramble into his car and drive away beside his young, slim, blonde, pretty wife.

Brenda took a deep breath and smiled at Mike. Her voice wobbled a bit. 'Thank you, Mike. You were wonderful. My knight in shining armour.'

'My pleasure.'

Fortunately, Mike didn't seem to have noticed her distress at all and was now hopping around in her doorstep, trying to change into the right trousers.

'Close your eyes, Bren,' he muttered. 'This is going to be a bit tricky.'

Brenda closed her eyes. She supposed Simon was right—she was silly—silly enough to have had sad romantic fantasies about someone she knew nothing about. How stupid she'd been, knowing that both she and Simon would be at the Chamber of Commerce tonight and thinking that he felt the same as she did.

Foolishly imagining that he'd sweep her off her feet, be her partner for the evening—and for the rest of their lives…

She'd been building up silly dreams like some giddy girl— dreams that could only burst into teardrops.

And, the worst thing of all—she'd judged both Simon and Mike on their appearances, hadn't she? And got it terribly wrong…

'You can look now,' Mike continued cheerfully. 'I'm decent. Oh, and is this your taxi? Going somewhere nice?'

'I was going to the Chamber of Commerce Social Evening, too,' Brenda said miserably. 'But I don't think I'll bother now.'

'Why on earth not?' Mike grinned. 'You look a million dollars, Bren. Belle of the Ball and no mistake. Don't let old Simple Simon spoil things. Forget him. Can't waste an opportunity like this—we'll share the cab now I've got me trousers on. Grab your dancing shoes and your handbag and we'll go and trip the light fantastic.'

'I need another coat of mascara and I haven't got my sandals on and…'

'You don't need no more slap,' Mike said cheerfully, peering at her. 'You looks good enough to eat. Come along—choppy-chop! Just find them sandals and we'll be off, Bren, love.'

Oh, why not? Brenda thought, her heart still aching at the loss of her dreams, still horribly embarrassed at her stupidity, still horrified by her poor judgement.

She could always avoid Simon—and his wife—couldn't she?

'I've always had a soft spot for you,' Mike confided, holding the taxi door open for her. 'Always thought you looked a bit like Lulu. Older and fatter, of course, but just as pretty.'

Brenda felt her gloom lifting a little at Mike's brutally honest back-handed compliment. She smiled at Mike. Dear, dependable, down-to-earth, untidy Mike, with his nice down-to-earth clothes. As far removed from phoney, sartorially suave Simon as it was possible to get. A thoroughly decent man.

'Have you?' Brenda asked as the taxi purred away and Mike—nice, kind, gentle Mike—snuggled beside her. 'Really? I'm very flattered…'

'Good-oh.' Mike beamed at her like a big adoring puppy. 'Only I thought you'd never really noticed me.'

'Of course I've noticed you—and,' Brenda admitted with a little giggle, suddenly realising that love didn't necessarily have to arrive with fanfares of celestial trumpets and cascades of rainbow fireworks, 'I've always noticed your trousers…'

Geoffrey Harfield

A first prophetic feature on the coming IT revolution was published by Geoffrey Harfield in the early nineteen-sixties. During a career in photography and advertising in the seventies he wrote PR and sales copy and began writing historical fiction eighteen years ago. His preferred period is 1860 to 1945.

Geoffrey has reviewed plays and shows for local theatre and completed four or five historical saga romances with characters in the conflict of the Russian revolution, World War Two and the IRA troubles. He now writes fiction each day and reviews books for the Historical Novel Society.

As a visual thinker, his books, often set against a background of travel, photography, arts, landscape, cities, opera and music, feature his fascination with human relationships. Thinking deeply on philosophy, war and religion, he believes in the essential goodness of humanity.

The Splintered Mirror

'Come on, Lil. Get yer hat on, girl. The bioscope starts at seven.' Rosie straightened her stocking seams. At twenty, dark hair and a clear complexion made her the prettier of the two sisters.

'Keep your 'air on, our Rosie,' Lil whispered. The eighteen-year-old envied Rosie's glossy brown curls. 'Mam don't know I'm going.'

That second winter of the war, Rosie had a date with her boyfriend, Cyril, from the work's office. Lil would play gooseberry at the pictures again. She wondered if she would ever get a boyfriend because she hardly ever went out, except with Rosie.

'I suppose we'd better tell Mam,' said Lil. She plonked a widebrimmed hat over mousy hair, shrugged into her coat and wrapped a scarf round her neck.

'At least in the pictures it'll be warm,' Rosie said. 'The cold's as sharp as ever tonight. Harold's snug in bed and, with the two of us out, Mam'll be warm and cosy by the kitchen range.'

Lil thought how nice it would be to be warm and cosy with

a boy on the back row of the pictures, safe from bombs. 'What if we get—'

'We'll be safer in the pictures from them Zeppos.' Rosie pulled on her boots, buttoning them up her shapely calves. 'I wouldn't fancy driving one of them things in this cold. Them poor buggers up there.' She raised her eyes to the ceiling of the hallway in the terraced house. 'Enough to freeze the balls—'

'That's enough of that, Rose, my girl.' Mabel Hoskin appeared from the kitchen. A comfortable woman in a wrap-over pinafore, she tried to bring up her daughters respectably.

'Sorry, Mam.'

'Keep that language for your fancy bloke, if you're ever lucky enough to find one, that is.'

Lil let out a strangled giggle, then quickly clamped her mittened hand over her mouth. 'Her? A fancy man? Not our Rosie.'

Mabel wiped her hands on her apron, then looked Lil up and down. 'And where d'yer think you're going, Lillian Hoskin?'

'Going to the pictures with our Rosie, if that's all right, Mam.' She flipped her scarf over her shoulder.

'Go on then, both of you, before you wake Harold up. And be back by nine-thirty. D'yer hear? An' do as they tell yer if there's an air raid.'

The two sisters left quietly.

With their father in France, Lil knew their Mam's only con- solation was that their brother, Harold, was in a reserved occu- pation. He worked early mornings at the arsenal and slept evenings. Rosie and Lil, like many young women, worked days filling shells at the Woolwich factory so the men could enlist and go off to fight.

Nevertheless, Lil was beginning to have a conscience about making shells to kill young men. Sometimes in her dreams she would see the terrifying things her shells did and it worried her.

At the corner of Victoria Road the sisters turned into the

High Street. The shop windows looked dull and dreary with their lights off. The cinema was a block ahead.

Suddenly a blinding flash shone behind a warehouse. Half a second later they heard a shattering explosion and the tinkling of glass.

'Blimey! I didn't know there was a raid on. Did you 'ear the siren?' Lil looked up at the night sky.

A long silver Zeppelin hovered over the street, suspended in the indigo heavens. Pencils of light shone bright onto its silver flanks as the searchlights found it.

'Watch out!' Rosie pulled her sister into a lingerie shop doorway. 'At least if they get us here we'll 'ave clean undies.'

'I'll need clean undies if this gets much worse.' Lil cowered in the corner by the door with her hands over her ears. 'Can't we go back 'ome? I'm frightened.'

'No, you can't. You know Cyril's waiting and you're my chaperone in case anyone sees us. There'll be 'ell to pay if I was seen alone wiv 'im.'

Another bomb exploded. Lil stuck her fingers in her ears and wailed.

This time the explosion was just behind the shop. The plate glass window blew out onto the pavement with a loud crash. The merchandise followed in a whoosh of wind.

An oval cheval mirror toppled at the girls' feet. Rosie gasped as the reflected flames revealed cracks running the length of it.

'Oh! My Lord,' she cried. 'That's seven years' bad luck I'll get, our Lil. A splintered mirror!'

'That was the blast,' said Lil, recovering her composure. 'It always blows things out. An' don't believe that rubbish about bad luck to come. We're 'avin' it already.'

She glanced round at the debris. 'Here. Look at them.' She pointed at the array of lingerie lying on the pavement. 'Cyril'd like you in one of them.'

With a wicked grin she held up a pair of pink French knickers from the top of the pile, shaking out the chips of glass.

'Shut up you and follow me. I told Cyril five to seven and we're late, thanks to Fritz up there.'

'Perhaps the cinema's blown up. What if it's gone an' Cyril's waiting by a pile of rubble? Where will you do your courting then?'

'You mind yer own business, my girl. Just stay wiv me till I send you off. Right? If he gets too fresh I'll yell for yer.'

With glass crunching underfoot, the two girls hurried carefully along the street to the cinema. Luckily the picture house was undamaged. Daring the cold outside, Cyril was waiting.

Rosie smiled. 'Hello, this is Lil. You've seen 'er at the factory. She's me little sister but she knows what it's all about.'

Lil didn't mind so much being called little sister but she was not sure what else Rosie meant.

Cyril's mouth dropped. 'All this bombing? She knows about all that?'

'No! Not that, yer silly boy. She knows about this.' She grabbed Cyril by his coat collar and planted a deep kiss on his lips.

Grasping her meaning, Cyril rubbed his hands together. 'Right,' he said. 'Then let's go in. It's startin' in five minutes.'

Lil was happy being a gooseberry with them but she was not going to be taken for granted. She took out a shilling to pay for her own ticket.

At the ticket office the manager was on duty with his hat and coat on. 'Sorry, folks but they're all down the cellar. Buy your tickets and join them. This Zeppelin raid won't last long. Then we'll start the film.'

Lil stepped forward with her shilling. 'One for the stalls, please.' Rosie looked at Cyril.

'Well…we must do as the man says. Two stalls seats, please.' Cyril handed over a florin, took the tickets and pocketed the change.

With Lil leading, they followed the manager's directions to the shelter, a reinforced basement under the stalls. Lil held the door for the others. As Rosie stepped hand in hand with Cyril down the cold concrete stairway, Lil guessed she'd have regrets. There'd be no hanky-panky allowed in the cellar.

The stuffy air raid shelter was packed with couples of all ages. In a corner she spied a small cubicle with a sign on the door saying WC. She smiled. Some wag had added *inston* to the W and *urchill* to the C.

Finally she saw a small space on a bench in front of a pile of film boxes. 'Here, Rosie, you two can squeeze in there.'

Rosie waved her hand. 'Move along, luv. Cyril, you sit down there and I'll perch on yer knee. Thanks, luv.'

Still standing, Lil said, 'What about me?' All the benches seemed to be full. 'Anyone got a gap?' she called out.

'I've go' a gap, luv. Yer can 'ave this.' An old man bared his teeth in a gurning face to show her the gap in his mouth. His neighbours giggled with amusement. Lil just smiled at the joke.

'Here, luv,' a young soldier with black hair called out. 'There's a seat 'ere.' He shoved up and made a place.

'Thanks, ta!' She smiled and sat down. Through the cigarette smoke she could see Rosie and Cyril getting closer. Rosie had her arms around Cyril's neck and was stroking his face.

'You on yer own, then?' The soldier puffed at his cigarette.

'Yeah. I'm the gooseberry.' Lil grinned. 'It'll suit me sister and her boyfriend if I keep me distance.'

'Well…that's satisfaction all round, then. Here. Do you want a Woodie?' He offered her his packet of Woodbines.

'Yes. Ta. Might as well start now as later.' She took a cigarette in her left hand and lit it from the match he struck. She coughed as the tarry smoke hit her lungs.

The soldier paused, stroked his moustache and then turned to her. 'You got a boyfriend?'

Lil knew what the chap was getting at. She'd no desire to get involved with a soldier down in an air raid shelter. A little white lie would do no harm.

She nodded sadly. 'He had to go back off leave this morning. He's in the navy.' She took another tentative puff on her cigarette.

'Oh! I see.' The soldier straightened up boldly. 'Well, that's that, then.'

'What's what?'

'You spoken for. I'm not the sort of chap to muscle in on another bloke's girl.'

'That's very thoughtful of you.' She turned away and lowered her eyes. 'My name's Lil. What's yours, then?'

'Albert. I know it's old-fashioned but my friends call me Bert for short.'

Lil offered her right hand. 'How d'yer do, Bert?' They shook awkwardly in the tight row of people.

The possibility of him firing the shells she made in the armaments factory, at German boys just like him, set her thinking.

He's no worse than I am, she resolved. 'Are you…do you fire them shells? Are you in the artillery…Bert?'

'No,' he said meekly. 'I'm in the Ordnance. Just a humble pen pusher. But they're teachin' me to type,' he added proudly.

Lil stopped to think. This poor lad who wanted to fight the Germans was stuck in an office in Blighty being taught a woman's job? But what about the shells?

'So you send them shells we make over to France, do you?'

He nodded sadly. 'By the thousand.'

Before she could reply a man's voice from the other side of the basement boomed out. 'Listen everybody. Ain't that the All Clear?'

There was silence as they strained to hear. From outside and above came the long siren note. Conversation began again.

'It's over,' said Lil.

'Thank Gawd for that. Now Jerry's made his point, can we get on with the film?'

Bert and Lil stood up with the others waiting to go back to the cinema. 'I suppose you'll go and sit with your sister, then?' he said, looking into her eyes.

He was taller than she'd thought. 'No. She'll be all right with Cyril. I'll wait for 'er when it's over.'

But before they could file up the stairs into the cinema there was a shout. The crowd jostled and a furious Rosie pushed through.

'If that's the way you carry on when I'm with you,' she shouted, 'yer can see the ruddy film on your own.'

Rosie buffeted Bert and Lil without seeing them.

Then she turned to roar back again. 'Makin' up to that floozie like that when I was sittin' on yer knee. I've seen her 'anging about 'ere. She's nothin' but a tart.'

Lil watched, amazed and embarrassed, as her sister forced her way through the crowd and disappeared upstairs.

When Bert and Lil arrived in the foyer Rosie was nowhere to be seen. They took their seats in the back of the stalls. Lil turned to look round. 'She's not here, either. I can't see 'er.'

'Perhaps she gone 'ome. All in a huff like.'

'It's not like our Rosie at all. Cyril must 'ave fancied 'is chances better with some other girl.' She tucked her hair back under her hat brim. 'No accounting for taste.'

'A chap's got to know where to draw the line, I say.'

Lil, the plain younger sister, began to respect soldier Bert. She liked him. And the more he kept his hands to himself in the back row of the cinema, the more she felt happy and secure with him.

After the titles came up they stood for 'The King'. Bert touched her hand and said, 'Now you've lost your sister…would you like me to walk you home, Lil?'

She squeezed his hand and looked up into his shining eyes.

'Yes. That'd be nice. Thanks. I bet our Rosie's already 'ome by now.'

Hand in hand they trod carefully along the debris-strewn pavements, past the piles of rubble and turned into the street where the Hoskin family lived.

'Oh! That's good,' Lil said. 'No bombs 'ere, thank Gawd.'

But Bert's mind was on other things. 'Can I see you again?' he ventured. 'Like tomorrow, Lil?'

'Yes. That'd be nice.' Lil was beginning to walk on air.

'Same time at the cinema? The film's changing. An' it's my treat this time.'

'Okay. Thanks, Bert. See you then.' Curb your enthusiasm, my girl, she told herself.

They had arrived at the front gate. Lil turned and patted Bert's hand. 'Thanks, Bert. It's been a wonderful evening despite… everything. Till tomorrow, then?'

She watched as he turned. Under the blackout she could barely see his face but she was certain a tear glistened on his cheek. Her heart jumped.

As the lightness and joy of the first stirrings of love buoyed her up, she bounced up the short path to the front door.

A figure came out of the shadowy porch. 'Caught you, you little tart,' spat Rosie. 'I went out with my bloke and came back with nothing. You went out with nothing and came back with a feller. You cunning little madam,' she snapped. 'Life's not fair.'

'You can say that again, our Rosie. I don't believe in them daft superstitions. That splintered mirror brought me good luck. Not bad.'

Margaret Kaine

Born and educated in the Potteries in Staffordshire, Margaret Kaine now lives in Leicester. Her short stories have been published widely in women's magazines in the UK, Australia, Norway, South Africa and Ireland. _Ring of Clay,_ her debut novel, won both the RNA's New Writers' Award in 2002 and the Society of Authors' Sagittarius Prize in 2003. She has now published six romantic sagas about life in the Potteries between the fifties and seventies; her latest novel, _Ribbon of Moonlight,_ is also set partly in Paris. Translations include German and French and all details of her books can be found on her website www.margaretkaine.com

Streetwise Romance

'I could have come with you,' Cat complained, 'if I hadn't got this gig.'

Laura gazed at her daughter with exasperation as she saw yet another tattoo on that firm young shoulder. 'No problem, I'll be fine.' She stifled a twinge of guilt that she'd chosen the date deliberately.

'Well, just be careful!' Cat frowned. Her actual name was Catherine—but, as she complained, it was hardly the name of a budding rock star. 'You know what you're like—not at all street-wise!'

'I don't intend to walk the streets, Cat.'

'You know what I mean. You're such an innocent, Mum, always have been.'

Laura bit back a retort. What, she wondered, made young people think that they'd invented everything? Sex, drink, drugs… Not that Cat did drugs—Laura was sure about that, even if she had her suspicions about the others.

'A romantic, that's what you are!' Cat bit into another chocolate digestive.

Now that *was* true. Laura's husband had always said that she saw the world through rose-tinted glasses. 'It makes you expect too much of life—and of people,' he'd added with bitterness, when she'd refused to have him back after his second affair. Now he was living in Australia with a girl half his age.

'Is there anything wrong in being romantic?' This pretend hardbitten daughter of hers didn't fool her for a minute with her spiked hair and nose stud. Cat worked hard at her image, knowing that it earned her a place in the band.

'Don't forget your mobile,' were Cat's parting words.

But, as Laura drove towards the beauty spot in the Peak District, she reflected that it was worrying about her daughter's safety—not her own—that was making her feel so stressed.

It was on Saturday evening, bees humming lazily in clusters of flowers tumbling over dry stone walls, that Laura discovered the small restaurant and chose one of two tables facing a balcony. As a young waiter placed a crisp white napkin on her lap she thought, with pleasure, that this was exactly the ambience she needed. To feel pampered, relaxed, a world away from the anxieties of everyday life—which was, after all, why she'd come away on this weekend break.

Her bedroom was pretty and comfortable, with fluffy pillows and a cosy armchair. Her morning had been spent wandering around the small market town, then lingering over coffee and a delicious Danish pastry; the afternoon strolling along country lanes. And now, wearing an ivory silk blouse that suited her tanned skin and dark hair, she had found this perfect place. Pure hedonism— could hedonism be pure? she wondered. She didn't care; she could only wish she'd thought of it before.

She spent several minutes choosing from the menu, surprised

to see that she was still the sole occupant. 'You're very quiet,' she said when the young waiter came to take her order.

'This is our last night; I'm afraid we're closing.' He shrugged but didn't elaborate.

Although at first she was content to gaze down at the valley, it seemed odd to be the only guest and it was a relief when the waiter ushered someone else on to the terrace. The man, tall and grave, looked around and hesitated. She saw his expression of uncertainty as he saw the lone table next to her own, then he gave a slight shrug of apology and murmured to Laura, 'It's a pity to waste such a lovely view.'

They sat within a few feet of each other. Neither spoke, and yet strangely she was aware of him. Aware in a way she'd almost forgotten. She cast a furtive sideways glance. He was remarkably attractive and she guessed by the touch of silver in his hair that he was in his late forties. The service was slow; no other customers arrived and, eventually, as they waited for their main courses, he turned and remarked on it, adding, 'This does seem slightly ridiculous—just the two of us sitting here in silence. Do you think it might be a good idea to combine? Please—say if you'd rather not.' His smile was warm and friendly and, deciding he was unlikely to be an axe murderer, Laura smiled back. Seconds later he was seated opposite.

He told her his name was Julian and that he was staying a couple of days with friends who'd gone off to see a play. They began to talk, just pleasantries at first—about the area, the food they were eating, the fact that the restaurant was closing down. Julian ordered a bottle of wine which even Laura could recognise as an excellent vintage. He told her that he was widowed, having lost his wife six years previously. 'It's got better,' he said, 'as time has gone on. But life isn't the same.'

Laura said quietly that she had divorced her husband two years ago. 'He found a younger model.' She tried to keep the pain and humiliation out of her voice.

Julian reached out a hand and fleetingly covered hers. 'He must be a blind idiot.'

Later, over coffee and brandy, Laura could sense the electricity between them. Each time their eyes met, there was a message there. Was she imagining it? she wondered. Did he feel the same?

'Laura, I can't tell you how much I'm enjoying being with you,' he said. 'It's as though this evening is removed from everyday life—do you know what I mean?'

She nodded. 'I almost feel as if I'm in a dream.' She smiled at him. 'I don't even know what you do.'

'Nor I you,' he said. 'And I don't think we should tell each other—not yet. I love this slight air of mystery.' He leaned forward and lightly touched her hand. 'I am right—you feel the attraction, too?'

His voice, low and musical, held a note of appeal that made Laura's insides feel like melted chocolate. Smiling into his eyes, she said, 'Yes, I do.'

It was late when eventually they rose from the table and left the terrace. Walking through the empty and dimly lit restaurant, Julian paused by a baby grand piano. 'Would you mind—just a few minutes?' he said to the waiter. The young man smiled politely. What a boring evening for him, Laura thought, he's dying to close. But Julian was already lifting the lid of the piano and seating himself on the mahogany stool.

A few seconds later, the haunting melody of *Clair de Lune* filled the room. Laura rested her back against the wall and listened, her gaze lingering on broad shoulders, capable hands rippling along the keys. The young man coughed and, abruptly, Julian stopped. 'That was lovely,' Laura said. 'You play very well.'

He smiled and then they were outside, walking hand in hand

to where their cars were parked. Julian said anxiously, 'Tomorrow, Laura. You will see me tomorrow?'

'I'd love to!' She began, 'I'm staying ...' but Julian was holding up a hand. 'No, just for now I want to think of you as my woman of mystery. Don't let real life intrude. You know the stile opposite the church? Shall we meet there—say at eleven o'clock?'

She smiled. 'I think you're as romantic as I am.'

'I am tonight.' Slowly, he drew her into his arms. There, in the moonlight, they kissed and Laura wanted it never to end.

Later, she drifted into a blissful sleep, hugging the memory of the evening. And tomorrow, she thought drowsily—I wonder what tomorrow will bring?

It was three a.m. when her mobile rang.

When she reached the hospital she rushed frantically to the desk. When she entered the ward and saw Cat's frightened eyes, huge in her pale face beneath a head swathed in bandages, Laura could only just manage to whisper, 'I'm here now.' It had been a hit and run. And Cat had been too drunk to see the car coming.

It was four months before the facial scars faded. And one morning, as they sat drinking coffee at the kitchen table, Cat began once again to upbraid Laura for being so romantic. 'You do still think of him, don't you? I can tell. You get that soppy look on your face.'

'Okay, I admit it.' Laura shrugged. 'But we were ships that pass in the night, that's all.'

'You blame me, don't you?' Cat's tone was miserable.

Laura felt ashamed that sometimes she did. She pushed the unworthy thought from her mind. 'Don't be silly,' she said. 'You're better and that's all that matters. I wish now that I'd never told you about him.'

'Then,' Cat persisted, 'are you going to stop going to these orchestral concerts? You don't enjoy them.'

'Yes, I do! At least I'm beginning to. I just thought…'

'I know—that *he* might be there. It's fantasy-land, Mum.'

'Well, he must like classical music.'

Cat rolled her eyes. 'Everybody knows *Clair de Lune,* Mum—even me! In any case, he sounds a bit of a weirdo. I mean, you—a woman of mystery—I ask you!'

Laura turned her head away. How could anyone else possibly imagine the magic of those few hours?

And it was true, she *had* begun to enjoy the concerts; for their own sake, not just because she was hoping to see Julian again. One Friday evening, she even travelled as far as Manchester.

And there, in the large concert hall, she saw him. Laura could only stare in shock, her heart hammering against her ribs. Julian, incredibly handsome in white tie—was walking on to the platform. And later, as the strains of Chopin's *L'Etude* piano concerto faded away, she sat amidst tumultuous applause, scarlet with embarrassment as she recalled her trite comment about his ability. She watched Julian enthral the audience with his sensitive playing and knew that, for her, nothing had changed. The magic was still there. But now uncertainty swept her. Surely she was being naive, foolish even, to think that he would remember? It had been months ago—just a pleasant evening, an interlude in his busy and high profile life. Although her life too was busy—being a teacher these days was hardly a sinecure. But Laura was sure of one thing—she had no intention of leaving until she'd found out.

And so, later, she stood at a distance from the small group of autograph hunters waiting at the stage door and drew her red cashmere scarf closer against the chill. Members of the orchestra began to emerge, some talking, others looking weary as they headed towards their coach.

Then at last Julian appeared. He paused, smiling at his fans and, when the last one left, he turned up the collar of his coat and began to walk towards a limousine. Laura was in his direct line of vision, trying to look nonchalant as if she was waiting for someone, nerving herself for disillusionment.

But he came to a halt, his eyes widening with incredulity. For one long dazed moment they stared at each other—then Julian gave a curt nod and walked past. But there was no doubt that he remembered her—Laura had seen the shocked recognition in his eyes!

'Julian!' Her voice carried in the night air.

He turned. 'Yes, Laura?' His tone was cold. 'I waited, you know. For two hours!' He turned again and began to walk on.

She called after him but he didn't answer, merely climbing into the rear of the car as a chauffeur opened the door. Laura ran up and thrust her phone number at him. 'Please, take it,' she pleaded. 'I can explain…ring me…'

Julian simply leaned forward and spoke to his driver. Seconds later, he was gone.

In despair, she watched the tail lights disappear and then, stunned and disappointed, slowly made her way to the car park. As she drove home she had to fight the tears. Was there anything more pathetic than a woman of her age dreaming of romance? With an unsatisfactory marriage and divorce behind her, she should have known better than to expect a happy ending.

The next day Cat said loftily, 'He won't ring, you know. He's way out of your league. In any case, you've damaged his male ego.'

Laura was in no mood for Cat's teenage superiority and turned away, unaware of a sudden flash of concern in her daughter's eyes.

And so the weeks passed, with Laura pouring her energies into her students, wishing that her daughter would study harder for her A levels. At night, she waited anxiously for Cat to return in safety from one of her gigs.

It was one frosty morning just before Easter that Cat shouted down the stairs, 'Can you get that, Mum?'

With impatience, Laura put down her coffee. 'Are you in?' she called.

'Yes, but it may be for you!'

'Fat chance,' Laura muttered, her spirits low after a cold. She picked up the receiver.

At the sound of his voice, she could hardly breathe.

'I feel terrible. I'm so sorry—not to have given you a chance to explain. I'm afraid it's my worst fault—stupid pride. Of course you had to do what you did…'

'If only we'd agreed to meet at a bar or restaurant, rather than by that stile…'

'Yes, but it seemed romantic at the time.' Julian's tone was anxious, full of apology.

'But how…?'

'After last night's concert, I was accosted by a rather alarming young lady—called Cat? Is that really her name?'

'Catherine,' Laura murmured with delight and, glancing up, saw her so-cool daughter standing on the stairs with—as Laura said later—a soppy look on her face.

Theresa Howes

Theresa Howes started life as an actress, working in all aspects of theatre from washing showgirls' tights and selling ice creams to playing a variety of roles, including overgrown schoolgirls and nineteenth century tragic heroines. Those periods euphemistically known as 'resting' gave her the time to start on that first opening chapter and, since then, she has never looked back. Although yet to have a novel published, she has been joint runner up of The Harry Bowling Prize, shortlisted in a Write a Bestseller competition run by Channel 5 and Poolbeg, and was longlisted for Lit Idol.

She has won many short story competitions and had a number of stories published in a popular weekly magazine. Her ambition is to write novels and short stories that women will want to read, and to write them well.

To see more of Theresa's work, please visit her website at www.theresahowes.co.uk

Carved out of Love

Jen rubbed the polished wood between her fingers. The object, slim and ornately carved, sat in her young hand, elegant in its rustic simplicity. She was proud that her great-grandfather's pocket-knife had given shape to it. She ran her thumb along the cuts, smoothed over and worn with so much love. Now, they were nothing more than scars on the burnished sycamore, embedded deep as the grain that ran through the wood, once as life-giving as veins. She slipped it into her pocket as Winifred opened the door.

'Come in, my dear. It's nice of you to visit.' Jen's heart went out to the old lady, round-shouldered and stooped as a longbow, shuffling her way back into the cave-like darkness of the cottage that had been her home for almost a century. Jen followed, straining to hear the scratched out words that struggled to find form in the ancient voice.

'I was sorry to hear about your great-grandpa. Still, it was a big age.' Winifred nodded to Jen to take a seat as she lowered her thin frame into the rocking chair, her fingers claw-like and scuttling in their eagerness to find support for her antique body.

'There aren't that many of us left who remember the Spanish Civil War, those that took up the cause and never came back. Your great-grandpa was one of the lucky ones.'

Jen found it hard to imagine her great-grandfather as a young man, strong-limbed and courageous enough to take up arms in a war he wasn't obliged to fight. Yet she knew the heart of the man and loved him for the soul that, even at the end of his life, would have risked everything in the name of a just cause.

Jen ducked to avoid the age-darkened beams that ran above her head in sharp relief to the white distempered walls.

An irregular window cut out of the south-facing wall of the cottage, framed with a cheerful curtain, let in just enough light. Two hard chairs stood around a small table covered in the same red checked cloth that hung at the window, and a stove belted out the kind of dry heat that caught at the back of the throat. Everything was softened at the edges, rubbed away by so much use, and overshadowed by the Welsh dresser that took up the length of the back wall.

Each shelf of the dresser held a clutter of mismatched china, dusted and shamelessly chipped, proudly displaying spider webs of cracked glazing. The battle-scars of a lifetime of wear. Each cup and saucer, each dinner plate betraying a different origin through its pink rosebuds or bold red peonies, through its battered gold edging or delft blue patterning.

It wasn't the plates that held Jen's eye but the rows of decorative wooden spoons that hung from the edge of each shelf by a series of tiny nails. There must have been seventy or more, lined up like soldiers waiting for the signal. Each one different in its hand-carved intricate design. 'What a lot of spoons you have. However did you collect them? It must have taken a lifetime.'

Winifred failed to respond. She remained still as the grave, her ancient skin as crackled and fine as the glazing on the chipped brown teapot that stood on the table between them.

Small dabs of moisture formed in the corners of eyes the colour of the slate that covered the floor. It was the same slate that sat deep in the ground upon which the cottage was built.

Unable to contain her curiosity, Jen rose from the chair, remembering to dodge the low beams, and took a step towards the dresser. 'Do you mind if I...' She gestured towards one of the more elaborate spoons, as if to take it from the shelf. Winifred gave a nod of consent.

Jen lifted the spoon. It was much like the one in her pocket, the one her great-grandfather had given her only moments before he died. She cradled the delicate object in her palm, stroking it gently with the fingers of her other hand. Its polished smoothness was as warm as a living thing. She ran her fingers over the tiny heart shapes that had been cut into the handle and marvelled at the links of chain that extended from it. It was hard to believe it had been carved from a single piece of wood.

Jen placed it carefully back on its nail and picked up another. This one had a heart-shaped bowl and a handle carved into elaborate flowers, fine as embroidery.

Returning it to its rightful place, she ran her eyes along the rows of spoons, the older ones darkened with age, the more recent ones of a lighter hue. Some had keyholes cut in, others had two bowls, or three. Hearts and flowers appeared on most. One or two were made up of intertwined vines. Others displayed birds or complex knots. Jen could see the work of the same hand, the same heart in every one.

She thought of the spoon in her pocket. It was more elaborate than anything she could see before her. Her great-grandfather had carved a cage out of a single piece of wood. Within that cage, rattled two distinct hearts. It was his last and his greatest work. He had sat by the fire every evening during the final weeks of his life, carving the intricate pattern, smoothing and polishing until it was perfect. His only wish had been that Jen give it to Winifred after his death. It would be the last love spoon he would ever make for her.

Jen turned back to Winifred. 'They are all so lovely. Wherever did they come from?'

'That's the mystery.' Winifred began to rock her chair slowly as she spoke, absently smoothing her crisp cotton apron across her lap. 'Tradition says they are meant to be anonymous. If the admirer is shy, they hide behind the carvings. Sometimes giving clues, sometimes not. The message is in the symbols. Hearts. That's obvious. A symbol of love. The same with flowers. Keyholes, the key to the heart. Chains, being forever linked together. And so on.' Winifred's voice trickled away. Despite the meaning of the words, her tone implied there was no mystery to unravel.

'There are so many,' replied Jen. 'These spoons must have been sent over a lifetime. Are you saying you don't know who carved them?'

'Yes and no. They started appearing just after the war. The Civil War, that is. None of your World Wars. I found the first one on my doorstep only weeks after I heard that David had been killed somewhere in Spain. It was your great-grandpa that came to tell me. They'd gone off to fight the Fascists together. Side by side. Like brothers they were.'

'David was your sweetheart?'

Winifred nodded, unconsciously patting her neatly bobbed silver hair, now thinning and wiry, a faint shadow of the style she'd worn on the day she'd waved her young man off to war. In that single gesture, Jen saw a flash of the beautiful woman that had once inhabited the tired body that now sat beside her. And she knew exactly how she had inspired years of devotion.

'We were supposed to marry on his return. I still wear the ring he gave me as his promise.' Winifred held out her hand. Jen leaned forward to look at the simple gold band, displaying the two hearts and a crown, now loose on Winifred's shrunken finger. 'Welsh gold. So pure it's almost yellow. Mined from this very land you see about you.

'The spoons kept appearing. Over time. Always after a great storm. As soon as I heard the wind howl and the rain lashing, I knew…'

'What did you know, Winifred? That there'd be another spoon waiting for you as the weather calmed?'

'David. It was David. He was always there. In the hills. He swore he'd never leave me, you see. Whatever happened, he'd come back to me. And he kept his promise. Our hearts will always be entwined as closely as the hearts carved on those spoons you see hanging from the dresser.

'Even now, I hear his voice in the raging wind, singing the song we always loved. Or, on calmer nights, when it merely whistles and whips about the house, I hear him whisper the words of the poem we learned together in Sunday school.'

Jen watched as Winifred's faded lips struggled to form the silent words of a lyric, too sacred to voice in the company of another. It was a moment or two before she woke from her memories and joined Jen once again in the real world.

'Your mother said you had something for me.'

Jen's hand reached into her pocket. Her fingers ran over the polished wood of the spoon. She felt the cage carved out of a single piece of wood. Disturbed by her touch, the hearts forever trapped inside their wooden bond nudged against each other. She raised her head once more to the dresser and ran her eyes across the spoons. Each had been carved with love, with years of silent devotion.

Her fingers slipped from the hidden spoon, causing it to drop deeper into her pocket. 'It was nothing really. Great-grandfather, before he died. He asked me to give you…his love.'

Winifred's face creased to a paper frown. 'Ah. He was a deep one.'

Unable to fulfil her great-grandfather's last wish, Jen felt awkward. She was suddenly desperate to leave the cottage, to leave Winifred to her memories.

'I should go now. Please don't get up. I'll let myself out.' And, without another word passing between them, she turned to leave.

As Jen closed the cottage door behind her, she looked towards the disappearing sun and pulled at her collar to screen her neck from the biting wind. She'd forgotten how quickly the weather could change in the hills, how a pleasing sky could suddenly turn to anger. The clouds promised a storm; there was no innocent threat about it, but certainty.

She walked halfway down the path before stopping. She squared herself up to the first needles of rain and dug her hands deep into her pockets against the bullying wind as the rugged farmland shuddered around her.

She turned back to face the cottage, tucked low in the ground and snug against the elements. This time she crept quietly, so as not to disturb Winifred. She pulled the last love spoon from her pocket and placed it on the doorstep.

Then she ventured along the exposed road that led up the hill to where her great-grandfather lay freshly buried. At the top, she stood beside the grave, proud against the lashing rain.

She looked down on the tiny cottage that stood as more than just a white stone in the distance. A pearl embedded in the grey landscape. She pulled at the loose strands of hair that had blown across her face and stuck against her tears.

Taking a deep breath, she kissed the air for her great-grandfather and whispered her goodbye.

Gill Sanderson

Gill Sanderson is really Roger Sanderson, an ex-college lecturer who used to teach English Literature on weekdays and mountaineering at weekends. He was a Committee member of the RNA for many years and still helps with the organisation of the annual Conference. He wrote the scripts for over eighty Commando Comics before starting to write Medical Romance for Harlequin Mills & Boon. Background material comes from three of his children; Mark is a Consultant Oncologist, Helen a Midwife, Adam a Prescribing Nurse. He has just finished his latest novel—*Christmas at Rivercut Valley*—and has written over forty other books. On occasion he still teaches the odd seminar on how to write Romantic fiction. For more information, visit www.millsandboon.co.uk/authors/GillSanderson

An English Love Story

I'm Helen Bright. You've probably heard of me. Most people have.

In the age of the television celebrity, I am one. Even if you haven't seen me hosting quiz shows, you've probably read articles. Everything from tabloids to quality magazines has run features on me some time or another. Most of the stories are even true: the press have got a living to earn, so I make myself open to them. It gives them less reason to invent anything.

People like me. They like my dry Yorkshire down-to-earth wit. They like it that I'm friendly. They like it when I bend rules so the contestants we all love do well. They like me making fun of my producer having to fend off protests from the Independent Quiz Vetting Council. I'm popular. Me, Helen Bright, riding high.

Somewhere I read that when a Roman general won a victory he was allowed to lead a parade through Rome. Captives dragged along in chains behind him, the public cheering like mad, him regal in a super-polished breastplate and helmet. But standing behind him on the chariot was a fellow dressed more plainly. At intervals he'd lean forward and mutter in the general's ear. The words, roughly translated, were, 'You might be a long way up, but that means there's a long way to fall.'

Ma is the one who stands behind me on the chariot. She points out that my face and my figure were given—she usually adds, by her—everything else has to be earned. The Brights have always worked for every penny.

No glamorising the facts, either. A reporter once made the mistake of asking about my 'rags-to-riches' story. Ma sat him in our front room and costed each outfit in the photo album from Babygro upwards. No rags for *my* daughter. And that without a man in the house! Her eyes had dared him to ask why.

Me and Ma against the world and I wouldn't have it any other way. *'You're not clever,'* she'd said once, *'but you're a taking little thing, so that's what we need to develop.'* And we had. She worked all the hours God sent to find money for the singing and drama lessons that led to talent shows where I was spotted. In return, I bought the Old Rectory in Barham for us instead of our two-up-two-down terrace—not that we were bothered, but Barham expected it once I was taken famous. I pay her a handsome salary—*not* an allowance, Ma has her pride—to manage my local engagements.

My compact, comfortable London flat is fine for the days when I'm working, but home will always be Barham where I was born and raised. A small Yorkshire market town where people know me and where the television Helen Bright is ignored unless she's needed to open fetes or run charity auctions or make speeches.

Sounds too good to be true, doesn't it? And I do appreciate everything I've got, really I do. I'm also frightened by it. My agent is talking about the next stage in my career. All he can see is the pound signs. Ma, though, Ma can see the other signs.

'It's your body-clock, isn't it?' she said last weekend. 'You're thirty-two. You can hear it ticking.'

'Sort of,' I mumbled. But I'm too busy to do anything about it. And too scared. Say it in five words, Helen. Say what you've suddenly realised you want.

A husband and a family.

Sam Thwaite managed Thwaite Farm. It had been in the family for a hundred and fifty years and done well, but these days, it seemed to Sam, you had to be an accountant, not an agricul-turalist, to make money out of farming. A bent accountant would be even better. Sadly, the men of business used by the Thwaites for the past century had no idea how to bend.

Sam's father, John, owned the farm. A massive heart attack and a moderate amount of good sense meant that he could not now run it but, as he pointed out—often—there was nothing wrong with his brain. He could still observe, summon up his vast ex-perience, and advise. Sam wasn't always as appreciative of this as his father expected.

'In a few years,' John said at supper, 'the Government will take a much more realistic view of the problems farmers face. There'll be measures in place to help us earn an honest living again. *Then* you can have a go at this organic idea you're so keen on.'

Not for the first time, Sam reflected that his father having enough time to read *The Times, The Guardian* and *The Telegraph* from cover to cover each day wasn't necessarily a good thing. 'We need capital now, Dad. Even if we don't go for organic certification— which *would* make money in the long run because we could charge more—machinery needs replacing. If we sold the top field—'

'No! The land's been in the family for generations! Selling the old barn nearly broke my heart.'

Sam grinned. 'It nearly broke the heart of the builder we sold it to. Come off it, Dad, the woodworm had to link arms to hold it upright. We're well rid of it, he did a good job on the conversion and it paid for the new milking machinery. But we need more.'

John pushed his plate away and picked up his book. *'Pride and Prejudice,'* he murmured. 'Jane Austen knew a thing or two. It was all about marriage and money in those days. You need to get married, Sam. You'd like it. And it's time I had a grandson for the succession.'

'What?' Sam stared at his father in horror. This was not the kind of conversation they had. Detailed discussions of a cow's procreative endeavours, yes. Him, no. He really would have to start getting Dad out of the house more. It was all very well his father watching daytime television and discovering the library but it was giving him hopelessly unrealistic ideas. Almost as unrealistic as Sam's last short-lived girlfriend who, it turned out, had wanted to add his acres to Daddy's acres so Daddy could go into ostriches. Sam had retreated fast.

'Yes,' John was saying now. 'You need to marry a rich woman. It would solve all our problems. You'd be happy—'

'I'm already happy.'

'You'd get your breakfast cooked for you—'

'I've cooked my own breakfast for fifteen years.'

'There'd be…er…other things—'

Sam was momentarily silenced.

'And she could put some money in the farm—purely as a loan—and make a nice profit out of it in a few years time. She could look after the hens. Organic hens. Your mother used to enjoy hens. Made a tidy sum on the eggs.'

He would definitely have to get Dad out more. 'And where do I find this wonder-woman?' asked Sam, regaining the use of his tongue. 'An advert in the *Farmers Weekly?* Wanted, one wife. Must be rich and willing to work on the farm.'

'I'll have a scout round,' said his father.

'Don't overstrain yourself.'

All the same, Sam looked at the lit farmhouse windows as he did his late rounds, mulled over his fragmentary love life—the number of women prepared to go out with a chap who was up at five a.m. and knackered by eight at night being strictly limited—and had to admit that it would be rather nice if there was a wife there to come back to.

I'd had one of those days.

Woken very early, wrapped up two editions of the current quiz show by noon, then met my agent and a hot-shot producer for a lunch designed to advance my career to the Next Level.

Breakfast TV. The phrase made my agent go hushed and reverent. It made me go panic-struck. Once you're on breakfast TV there's no way out. Sofas stretched in front of me as far as my mind's eye could see. And all of them under the glare of studio lights, not comfy and cosy in the glow of a wood fire.

I'd be a natural, burbled the producer as he ordered, and he'd had *such* a clever idea. It was to be called the Bright and Early Show, co-hosted by me and a lovely actor called Timothy Early. Timothy was lounging next to him. He wore a beautiful blue shirt that matched his beautiful blue eyes. When he smiled, his teeth outshone the sun. He was irresistible, you just ask him. He was also as thick as a hundred-year-old oak tree. He didn't get the hint when I removed his hand twice from my thigh. I had to stab his fingers with my dessert fork.

'I'm bleeding,' he said, the blue eyes filling with tears and the rosy lips wobbling.

The producer looked shocked. My agent gabbled that I wasn't usually difficult.

'I don't think this is going to work,' I said, and left.

The train north was summer-crowded, hot and delayed. The taxi driver at York was convinced his daughter would go down well on telly and told me about her all the way home.

Ma was waiting, meal ready on the table as always. And, as always, she was ready with the news, too. She's that way. Good or bad, it has to be told at once. 'We're out tomorrow night. Been invited to Thwaite Farm.'

I looked at her in dismay. It was a ground rule that whenever I came home I had one clear day to do nothing and see nobody. I was happy to perform whatever services Barham required of me at other times. I liked it. But I needed that one clear day. 'You go, Ma,' I said. 'I'll stay here.'

'You've got to come. People would think you were getting above yourself if you were invited and didn't come.'

To be thought you were getting above yourself. One of Ma's pet terrors. One of Barham's cardinal sins.

'Oh, so I suppose that's settled. Who's invited us?'

It would take an eagle eye to detect that Ma was embarrassed. But I had that eagle eye and I could see the beginnings of a blush on her cheekbones.

'An old friend. Name of John Thwaite.'

'I know all your old friends and none of them is called John Thwaite.'

'Because he's been busy farming all his life, that's why. But now he's retired and I've had a coffee or two with him at St Wilfred's Friday Morning Club.'

'Ah,' I said. The Church of St Wilfred provided an invaluable social service in Barham. On Friday mornings it collected all the gossips in the town and gave them coffee and free rein. There was a theory that one of the reasons the local paper never sold too well in Barham was that the news was spread more efficiently by the Friday Morning Club.

'Anyway,' went on Ma with her usual casual aplomb, 'he showed me a photo of his son. Nice lad. About your age. Manages the farm. John thinks he should be married and raising a family by now, but he never seems to find anyone suitable.'

I shut my eyes, then opened them very slowly. 'Since when did you run a dating agency, Ma?'

'I'm looking out for you. It's what mothers do.'

'I can find my own men.'

'You've not done very well so far. Time's marching on, you know. And think what a fool I'll look if you don't turn up when I've said you will.'

'Oh, we can't have that, can we?'

'No, we can't.' Sarcasm just bounces off Ma.

I could get out of it. I could develop a cold and walk down the High Street coughing and everyone would sympathise. But the spectre of today's disastrous lunch rose before my eyes and changed my mind. It would be good to remind myself what normal men were like. A farm manager had to be better than Timothy bloody Early. Someone with honest dirt on his hands. Ma's agenda didn't have to be mine. All I would have to do was be pleasant for a couple of hours. I'd been doing that all my life.

Sam looked at his father's inscrutable face and then at the kitchen table. A tablecloth that only came out on Christmas Day. Silver cutlery from the great canteen. A vase of flowers. And boxes with the discreet emblem of Katie's Kitchen, the expensive delicatessen on the High Street.

'What's all this?' he said.

'We've guests for tea. Lady guests. So you'd better get yourself cleaned up.'

Sam blinked. 'Lady guests?'

'I've invited Marion Bright. I've known her for years and met up with her again at the Friday Morning Club.'

Sam stared. This was what came of getting Dad out of the house. 'You said guests.'

'She's bringing her daughter. Helen. The one that goes on television.'

'Helen Bright! Coming here!'

'Marion Bright and her daughter coming here. I've got nice food, the room's pretty as a picture, the only scruffy note is you.'

'Oh, Lord,' said Sam, and rushed upstairs.

He knew of Helen Bright, of course he did. He'd seen her on the telly in those dark days after Dad's heart attack, when the flickering box in the hospital waiting room was the only thing that kept him anchored to sanity. He'd seen her in Barham High Street now and again, too. Just last week on his way to an appointment at the bank, she'd been in front of him, walking tall, swinging her arms in the sunshine, breathing as if the air was a benediction and she loved it. Hardly knowing what he was doing, he strode past her and then stopped to look in the newsagent's window so he could watch her coming towards him. She was beautiful and, even when not on TV, gave out an aura of happiness. When she went into the shop, he followed, listening to her chat to the girl at the counter. She'd smiled at him when she finished and he'd smiled back, only realising when the sales assistant asked what he wanted that there was absolutely nothing he could think of to buy. Dad had been surprised to be presented with a bar of chocolate after a trip to the bank, but he'd eaten it anyway.

And now Helen Bright was coming here! What should he wear? Not work clothes. Not slipping down to the pub for a quick pint clothes. But not agricultural show clothes, either. Too posh. Sam looked at the limited smart side of his wardrobe in bewilderment and settled for a white shirt, agricultural college tie and his jacket on the back of the chair in case he'd got it wrong.

I recognised Sam Thwaite immediately. He'd been in the newsagent's last week. When you're on television a lot, people believe you're part of their life and that they, in some sense, own you. I don't usually get that in Barham but I'd got it from him. I didn't mind, though, because there had been an odd tingle between us. I was getting the tingle again now. Oh, it was going to be so *annoying* if the tingle was reliable and Sam and I ended up getting together.

'This is John Thwaite,' said Ma, wearing her best poker face.

I smiled and shook John's hand. He was in his sixties, still a good-looking man, still with a presence. I'd have bet good money on him not 'retiring' easily.

'And this is my son, Sam,' he said.

The expectation from him and Ma was palpable. I had to bite the insides of my cheeks to stop laughing. And then Sam took my hand. No ingrained dirt, a firm but not over-strong grip. A tentative, slightly worried smile.

'I'm very pleased to meet you, Miss Bright. Welcome to Thwaite Farm.'

I was completely, utterly, overwhelmingly charmed. Such manners. I stood there with my hand in his, like the rawest beginner on life's stage. It was only when Ma made a tiny satisfied sound in her throat that I came to. 'I'm pleased to be here,' I said. 'Do call me Helen. It's a lovely setting you've got. I hope you'll show us around the farm.'

His face lit up. 'I'd love to. It's been in the family a hundred and fifty years. Mixed, originally, but now it's mainly cattle. Holsteins and Jerseys for milk. Herefords for beef.'

I avoided Ma's eye and was glad when she started up a conversation of her own with John. I didn't want her to see that I loved Sam's enthusiasm. I didn't want her making anything of it.

When we sat down to tea the late sun came through the windows, warming the mellow stone walls of the old farmhouse kitchen. I had to stop myself laughing again, though, when I realised what we were eating. Amongst a spread of dishes was my favourite tomato and red pepper salad from Katie's Kitchen. My favourite spinach quiche, ditto. And the Katie's Kitchen to-die-for chocolate cream pots. Somebody had made sure I was being well fed. I doubted it was Sam, so thank you Ma and John.

'Show Marion and Helen the farm while I clear away, Sam,' said John when we'd finished.

'No, I'll help you wash up,' chipped in Ma smartly. 'I'd rather do that than look around.'

'Thank you,' said John, far too smoothly. 'You'd best see if any of the spare boots fit Helen, Sam. She'll need a pair of your thick socks in them, mind.'

'Of course,' said Sam. He looked at Ma doubtfully, obviously having trouble with the idea that someone would rather wash up than see over his beloved farm. He hadn't realised yet that Ma didn't do subtle.

It was odd, putting on a man's socks. Weirdly intimate. The wellingtons were a little large. I could probably have fitted both feet into one boot. 'Good thing there's no press photographer here,' I said. 'The sight of me in a silk dress and knee-high wellies would make his day.'

Sam looked worried. 'Do you mind? We could always—'

I put a hand on his arm. 'I want to look around your farm,' I reassured him. 'With you,' I added, because it was true.

He moistened his lips and then launched himself into farm-information mode. I didn't mind. I learnt more about the habits of cows than I'd ever dreamt existed. Did you know they're fitted with a tiny transmitter and you can tell when they're in season by checking their movements on a computer? They walk with a spring in their step when they're in love. Just like people.

But I wanted to know about Sam, too. Why hadn't we run across each other when we were growing up?

'Boarding school,' said Sam. 'Quite a good one. A cabinet minister and a couple of generals amongst the Old Boys. The Thwaite lads have always been sent there, and with my mother dying...' He shook himself. 'It was all right, I suppose, in spite of not being co-ed.' He sighed. 'But if I'd known at the time what it was costing, I'd have stuck my heels in and gone to Barham Comprehensive, like you.'

And that, I thought, explained the shyness. And possibly also the way he genuinely didn't seem to know how good-looking he was. No one to tell him.

'What's it like, being on television?' he asked.

'Hard work,' I said. 'Up early, home late. Whenever I'm not working, I'm sleeping.'

'Like me,' he said, looking astonished. 'I'd have thought it was all posh parties and socialising.'

'Not if I can help it. I network over lunch, not dinner. I cram as much as possible into my London days so that I can get back here as often and for as long as I can. Barham is where my proper friends are, where my home is.'

He helped me over a stile, holding my arm just the tiniest bit longer than was necessary. 'I…er…I don't suppose you'll be in Barham next Saturday, will you?' he said with a rather desperate casualness.

I speedily consigned an appointment with my personal shopper to the bin. 'I will be, as a matter of fact. Why?'

His mouth worked. 'Would you…would you like to come to the Young Farmers' Summer Ball with me? It's at Moreton Castle.'

No casual air now. This was important to him. 'I'd love to, Sam.'

Dusk was beginning to fall as we walked back to the farmhouse. Sam had to brace me as I slipped in the over-large boots. The second time he took his hand away, I replaced it on my arm. 'I need you to steady me.'

'Of course,' he said, but I didn't complain when after five minutes his fingers slid very gently down to lace with mine. My heart was beating the weirdest rhythm. It was almost like being courted.

★ ★ ★

Sam waved goodbye as the cab taking Helen and her mother home disappeared through the farm gates. They hadn't had that much to drink but Helen was evidently a woman who thought things out in advance and didn't take chances. Much like him, really. He still savoured the feeling of her hand inside his, hugging the burgeoning whisper to him that something might be happening.

His father stood in the doorway, smiling broadly. 'Well done, lad,' he said, slapping Sam on the back. 'I knew you could do it!'

'What are you talking about, Dad?'

'Helen Bright, of course. As nice a lass as I ever saw. Her money's just what Thwaite Farm needs. Good child-bearing hips, too. How far did you get with her?'

'How far did I—?' Sam stared at his father in horror, all his tentative hopes, all the thoughts that hadn't even got as far as being tentative yet, dissipating like particularly feeble mist. He swung round abruptly. 'I'll do the rounds of the buildings,' he said. 'Don't wait up.'

When he came back, the downstairs was dark. He felt his way to the office. Dad might decry computers as inventions of the devil but to Sam they were a useful tool. Useful in other ways, too, he thought, as he took Helen's card out of his wallet. *It was nice to meet you tonight,* he typed without giving himself time to think. *I'm worried I pressured you into the Ball. If you don't want to go, just say so.*

There, he'd done it. Scuppered Dad's interference. But, amazingly, an answering email came straight back. *Don't be silly. I'm looking forward to it. Forgot to say—I'm running a charity quiz at Barham Comp tomorrow night. Do you want to watch? I'll tell them at the door to let you in as my guest, if you like?*

If he liked? Was she mad? *Thnak yopu,* typed Sam, his fingers bumping into each other in his haste. *I'd likj ethat.*

The quiz was fun. Sam laughed at Helen's jokes, was impressed by her deft handling of a team that was Taking It All Too Seriously, and was smitten all over again by her charm. He walked her back to the Old Rectory where John had been spending the evening. 'I think he did too much yesterday,' he confided. 'It's not like him to be bothered about being left in the house alone. He doesn't ever mind when I slip out for a pint.'

Helen shrugged. She was holding his hand again, which felt—nice. 'Ma wasn't going out tonight anyway. She was in a right fret, though, making sure there wasn't a speck of dust anywhere in the living room. I worry about her sometimes. What's she going to do when I'm not—' She paused.

Sam looked down at her. 'Not what?'

'Not in the public eye any more. People can fall out of favour frighteningly fast in this game.'

Sam wondered what she'd really been going to say.

He and Helen were sharing their table at the Ball with two other farmers and their fiancées. People were constantly stopping and chatting, mostly to Helen. Sam couldn't get a word in edgeways and was beginning to feel irritated.

Still, it was a ball, so they could escape and dance. It was a mixed pleasure and penance to be on the floor with Helen. Pleasure, because he was holding her and she smelled wonderful, felt wonderful and smiled at him in a very beguiling way. Penance, because whatever his feet were doing, it wasn't the same as hers.

'I'm getting this all wrong,' he said apologetically.

'No problem. Slow down, hold me closer and just sway a bit.'

That felt gorgeous. 'Are you sure this is dancing?' he said.

She chuckled. 'Whatever it is, it's fun. Are you enjoying it?'

Words didn't come close. 'Oh, yes.'

The evening grew warmer. Couples were slipping outside to stroll in the fairy light strewn grounds. But, when Helen said she'd like a breath of fresh air, Sam knew the moment of truth had come. He liked her company and, now that he had her to himself, he was enjoying himself again. The last thing he wanted to do was to spoil the evening, but he still felt she was here under false pretences.

Still, he slipped an arm around her waist as they strolled across the night-scented terrace and continued down the steps to a secluded bench. And, when she turned her face up to his, it was more than he was capable of not to accept the unspoken invitation and kiss her.

Kissing Helen was the most wondrous thing in the world. It almost made him forget what he was going to say. But the image of his father standing in the doorway applauding him made him pull away.

'Sam?' said Helen.

'There's something I have to tell you,' he said in a dull tone. 'Something about me.'

'Whatever it is, it can't be as bad as that gloomy voice suggests. Come on, shock me.'

'The farm needs money. I need to spend more in order to recoup what we owe. I can do it, I know I can, but the bank isn't prepared to extend our loan any further. My father's suggestion was that I marry a rich woman. You're the rich woman he picked.'

He didn't know what reaction he'd get. He sat there, shoulders slumped, waiting for her to demand he take her home. She didn't. She gave a great warm peal of laughter.

'It isn't funny!' Sam was slightly nettled. Here he was, baring his soul, and she was laughing at him.

'Oh, Sam, it is. People have been after my money or my body since I was sixteen. So far, no one's been very successful at getting either, but it does mean I've learnt to spot a man on the make at a hundred yards. You aren't a man on the make.'

Sam thought about this. 'I do quite fancy your body,' he ventured.

She grinned at him in the near-darkness. 'I'm glad. What about my cash?'

'All Dad's plan. He set the whole thing up. I had no idea. But it *was* great when you came to tea.'

'And do you think your father managed to get my mother to bring me to tea without her knowing exactly what he was up to?'

Sam considered this convoluted sentence and considered what he had so far seen of Marion Bright. 'No,' he said eventually.

'Too true. He might think he's been working on her all these weeks at St Wilfred's but, if I know Ma, she's been working on him at the same time.'

'So where do we go from here?'

'Well, we could go back into the ballroom and tread on each other's feet some more. Or we could stay here and continue that kiss.'

'We'll stay here,' he decided.

But just as their lips were about to meet again, she said, 'Sam—thank you for telling me.'

'I couldn't not,' he mumbled. And thereafter the Young Farmers' Summer Ball got very magical indeed.

Sam hadn't drunk a lot, but he felt so intoxicated by the end of the ball that he was glad he'd borrowed Helen's forethought and booked a cab. Apart from anything else, it meant they didn't keep annoying the traffic by stopping several times on the way home.

At the Old Rectory, the living room lights were on.

'That's not like Ma,' said Helen, looking anxious. 'She usually sits up in the kitchen if she's waiting for me. And it's really late. Will you come in with me?'

'What sort of daft question is that?' said Sam. He took her hand in a reassuring grip.

They went into the living room. And there Sam's mouth fell open just as Helen's was doing. Marion Bright and John Thwaite were sitting side by side on the sofa, also holding hands.

'Ball finished already?' said his father. On his face was an expression Sam hadn't seen for years. 'I don't know what you youngsters are coming to. We used to dance until three in the morning.'

'It is three in the morning,' said Sam.

'Is it? Fancy that.' He looked down at his and Marion's linked hands. 'Er…well…the fact is that Marion and I have fallen in love and are going to get married. We thought you two ought to be the first to know.'

'That sounds reasonable,' said Helen faintly.

'Did you know that four couples from St Wilfred's Friday Morning Club have got married this past year?' I said to Sam as we strolled along one of his hedgerows two days later. I had wellingtons of my own now, and as it was one of those heady summer days when it felt good just to be alive I'd tempted him away from the farm office to christen them with a walk.

'I believe you,' he said. Poor Sam, he was still in shock. So was I, really.

'Their combined ages come to just under six hundred years.'

He looked as if he couldn't take many more astonishing facts. 'I still don't get it. I thought Dad's plan—and your Ma's, come to that—was for you and me to get friendly.'

'It was,' I said. 'Serves the interfering so-and-so's right, falling in love themselves. Do you mind?'

'No, I think it's great. But if she's going to take an interest in the farm, too, I hope she's got some more up-to-date ideas than Dad.'

I kissed his nose. 'I doubt she will. She's too busy with all the pies she's got fingers in in Barham.'

He looked sideways at me. 'It wasn't a *bad* plan, mind.'

I grinned at him. 'No, it wasn't. But I'm not about to tell them that. Are you?'

'Absolutely not.'

We stopped for a lengthy kiss. Considering his claimed lack

of experience, he was getting pretty good at this. *Practice makes perfect,* he said when I mentioned it. I got the hint that he'd like to practise quite a bit more.

We got back to the farmhouse to see Ma's little runabout in the yard. They'd set the date, she said, and she gave me the choice, right there and then. I could be bridesmaid or matron of honour. But I'd have to be quick because she wasn't going to hang around.

'I'll be Bride's Attendant,' I said. I can do forceful just as well as Ma. It was her I'd learnt it from.

She narrowed her eyes. 'And John's moving to the Old Rectory. It's nearer the library for him and I can't be doing with driving in and out of town all the time.'

Sam looked as though this was the best present he could have had. He wasn't being rushed though, any more than I was. 'That sounds grand,' he said. 'If you'll excuse us, I promised to show Helen the milk yield forecasts. She's considering investing in our organic programme. She agrees that's where the money's going to be in the future.'

We went out in a dignified fashion and collapsed in the office, giggling like kids. 'All the same,' said Sam, sliding his arms around me, 'I don't think we should wait too long, do you? Certainly not six hundred years.'

Not even six hundred minutes, the way I was feeling right now. But he was cautious and sensible and I thought I was falling in love with him so, 'Six hundred hours?' I said as a compromise.

I saw him work it out in his head. His face lit up. 'Perfect. Enough time for the banns and a few days to spare for emergencies.'

Banns. *Banns?* My heart pitter-pattered like a two-year-old's.

'When are we going to tell them?' he asked.

Good Lord, he meant it. I felt silly with delight. 'How about just after they hear the first banns announced in St Wilfred's?'

His eyes laughed down at me. He truly didn't seem to have any doubts about this working at all. 'They'd never forgive us,' he said.

I thought of Ma, mouthing *body-clock* at me as we'd left the room just now. 'Oh, yes, they will,' I said. Probably in about six hundred hours and nine months.

Debby Holt

Debby Holt lives with her husband in Bath. She started writing short stories when her five children were small. She wrote her first novel, *The Ex-Wife's Survival Guide* in 2006. Since then, she has written three more: *Annie May's Black Book, The Trouble with Marriage* and *Love Affairs for Grown-Ups.* Having been a spectacularly useless teacher in the past, she is fully aware of how lucky she is to be doing something she loves. She can be reached at her website www.debbyholt.co.uk

Wind of Change

It was perhaps no coincidence that Lily fell in love with her father-in-law five hours after her husband told her they had to move to East Grinstead.

Not that there was anything wrong with East Grinstead. For all she knew, it might be the most charming place in the world, adorned with leafy parks, well-stocked playgrounds, fantastic shops and brilliant schools. The point was, she might not know what East Grinstead *did* have but she knew what it did *not* have.

It did not have the small group of friends who had babies like her and understood the terrors of inexplicable puking and sleepless nights. It did not have a mother who lived just fifteen minutes away and was happy to babysit at the drop of a hat. It did not have the comfortable GP who had overseen her pregnancy and made her feel she was the most stoical patient since records began. In short, it was not and never would be home.

She had been looking forward to this evening. Robert's father was back in England for a holiday and was treating them to supper with him and Annette, his latest lady friend. Lily had never before met her father-in-law. He had walked out on his wife and three children when Robert, the youngest, was five, following a heart which had subsequently taken him up various blind alleys before finally settling on his present companion.

Lily had heard many stories about him. He had travelled round Argentina with a beautiful ballet dancer, lived for eight years with the daughter of a fascist colonel in Madrid and left her when he discovered she was too like her father for comfort. Now, he lived outside Avignon, where he was part-owner of a crumbling castle.

Lily *had* been looking forward to this evening. It was typical of Robert that he should break his news to her today and thus effectively sabotage her chance of enjoying a single moment of it.

In the car, she sat mutinously while Robert droned on and on. He had to go where the money was…it was too good an opportunity to turn down…good to have new challenges…who knew what the future would bring and so on and so on until Lily told him to shut up. 'If you could hear yourself!' she said furiously. 'You speak only in clichés and if you tell me that clichés are only clichés because they're true, then I will scream! I'll tell you what clichés are—clichés are meaningless statements that are used by people who haven't the brains to say anything original. I don't care about following the money or seeking pastures new or facing new challenges. All I know is, you want to take me away from my mother, my friends and the people I love and all you offer in return is a place called East Grinstead!'

'East Grinstead has a lot to offer…'

'I loathe East Grinstead! I hate East Grinstead and at the moment I hate you! Don't talk to me now! Just don't talk to me!'

So they drove the rest of the way in silence while Lily looked out of the car window and thought grimly about the ghastly evening ahead.

In fact, it was not ghastly. The restaurant was a place as well-known for its fabulous food as its even more fabulous prices. From the moment she followed Robert through the mirrored dining room to the table by the fireplace she knew she was going to have a good time.

Robert's father—'Please call me Hal'—was tall and slim with a thick mane of dark hair. Only his sideburns were flecked with silver. He had a pair of mesmerising grey eyes which focused on Lily and remained focused on Lily for most of the evening. 'But you're beautiful,' he said. 'Robert never told me you were beautiful.'

He ordered champagne. 'Robert told me this afternoon about the job promotion.' He insisted the waiter serve Lily first and watched her gravely as she took a sip before asking, 'What do you think? Is it all right?' just as if Lily had drunk champagne for more than the three previous occasions in her life—and the first time didn't count since it had turned out to be a dodgy sparkling wine on special offer from Somerfield.

Both before and during dinner, Lily received all his attention. Fortunately, Annette, small, blonde and pretty, seemed equally enraptured by Robert and chatted happily to him about France and dogs and French politics; only Lily could see that Robert was not only aware of his father's close interest in his wife but equally aware of his wife's delighted response. Lily didn't care. She didn't care at all. At least Hal didn't talk in bloody clichés. At least Hal wasn't the sort of man to expect a woman to receive life-changing decisions without any sort of discussion.

Hal asked Lily question after question. He wanted to know where she came from, whether she had siblings, how much she liked her parents, what she'd done before she had had the baby and whether she'd return to work sooner rather than later.

She protested. 'I'm talking about myself too much.'

'But I want to know about you,' he told her. 'I'm greedy for knowledge of you.'

Lily laughed. 'I can't think why!'

'Can you not?' He sounded amused and she looked up into his astonishing grey eyes, looking at her with naked desire, and she found herself staring back at him like her baby looked at the washing machine. The washing machine could entertain the baby for hours. Lily was pretty sure Hal could do the same for her.

It was crazy. He could have been her father. Come to think of it, of course, he *was* Robert's father. He was also making her feel more attractive than she had felt in what seemed like forever. She was no longer a sleep-deprived wife or a harassed mother who had still not recovered her pre-pregnancy figure. She was, for this evening at least, a fascinating, sexy woman of mystery. And if Robert and Hal's lady friend were to suddenly, miraculously, be called away at the same time and if the restaurant had a discreet bedroom going spare and if Hal asked her to slip between the sheets—admittedly there were rather a lot of ifs here but, hey, stranger things had happened—she would almost certainly say yes. Although she might undress in the dark so he couldn't see her stretch marks.

A little ashamed of her mental adultery, she tried to incorporate the other two into the conversation over pudding. Even then, she was aware of Hal's wonderful eyes fixed on her. He was a magician, she thought; he has woven a spell and now I am in thrall to him.

It was just after the waiter had brought the coffee that Hal insisted on pouring Lily a second glass of pudding wine. Until now, Lily had had no idea there was such a beverage as pudding wine and she realised she liked it very much. Hal smiled at her and then glanced with less enthusiasm at Annette, who was telling them all about the best pudding she had ever tasted, a chocolate steam pudding laced with gooseberry jam and brandy. Lily thought it sounded vile.

And then Hal farted.

For a moment Lily froze. She glanced at Annette, who continued to go on about the chocolate steam pudding as if nothing had happened. Lily cast a quick sideways glance at Hal, who was stirring sugar into his coffee.

Lily looked at Robert. Her husband returned her look with a face scrupulously devoid of expression, apart from a twitch at the left corner of his mouth. Lily bit her lip and looked again at her husband and this time he raised his eyebrows while continuing to blandly meet her eyes. Lily could feel a giggle threatening to surface and hastily downed half of her glass of water.

'Tell me, Lily,' Hal said, 'how do you feel about being dragged off by Robert to East Grinstead? It seems a bit rough on you now you have a small baby. I'm not sure I'd want you to make such a sacrifice.'

Lily was tempted to tell Hal that moving one's wife to East Grinstead was marginally less wicked than walking out on one's wife and family or indeed flirting with one's son's wife while ignoring said son who one hasn't seen for five years.

Instead, she glanced at Robert and then frowned thoughtfully at Hal. 'Well, I'm not so sure,' she told him. 'Until now, I couldn't see the wood for the trees, but now I'm rather looking forward to ploughing new furrows and going to pastures new.' Robert, she observed, was biting his lower lip. 'And at the end of the day,' Lily continued remorselessly, 'we all know there's light at the end of the tunnel and every cloud has a silver lining and I shall leave no stone unturned in my efforts to locate the silver lining in East Grinstead!'

She smiled sweetly at Hal and then at Robert, but Robert didn't notice. He was too busy draining his glass of water as if he'd just crossed a desert.

Really, Lily thought, it was extraordinary how powerful a fart could be.

Sophie Weston

When Sophie Weston was born, her father took one look and said, 'Good grief, she's cross-eyed and ginger.' He got away with it because he'd braved ice and snow to get there.

This family legend taught her three things: life is dramatic (Sophie has been a bank regulator and consultant to the IMF); nature is dangerous (birdwatchers, crocodiles); the world is unfair (clever clogs who deserve a poke in the eye won't get it if they're funny).

Her novels for Harlequin Mills & Boon, like _The Englishman's Bride_ and _In the Arms of the Sheikh,_ reflect these enduring truths, as well as her travels from Brisbane to Brazil, by way of the Arabian Gulf, and her long-term love affair with London.

Her love of language broke out in _Getting the Point,_ a panic-free guide to punctuation for adults, co-authored by her alter ego, Jenny Haddon. Find out more at www.sophieweston.net

Cinderella, Revised

Even as a child, I hated fairy stories. I have never been able to deal with the irrational. I mean, take Cinderella. There she was, dumped in the proverbial by her father's inadequate financial management and poor choice of successor spouse, and she sees *marriage* as a way out of her problems? Nah. Not a chance.

If you're a girl, kind people give you a lot of fairy books. Especially if your mother legged it, taking the family silver and some of your father's prize inventions with her, before you were four years old. My father hated reading aloud, so he taught me to read the stories to myself as soon as he decently could. By the time I hit play school, I already knew all the major ones—*Sleeping Beauty, Snow White, Puss in Boots* and, of course, *Cinderella*. They did not represent life as I knew it. In a word, they stank.

Oh, my father made half-hearted attempts to convince me in the matter of upholstered pumpkins, talking animals and fairy godmothers. But it wasn't long before I was heading up the revolt of the Brampton village five-year-olds. It ended up with a Little Talk from Teacher when Father came to pick me up from school. The first of many.

'Nicole is very strong-minded,' said Mrs Durham. She wore angora and hugged a lot. It was an unfortunate combination.

'That's my girl,' said my father, pleased.

'She certainly has decided views. Of course that's a good thing. But she has upset some of the younger ones.'

My father considered. 'Deliberately?'

'No, of course not. Nicole is not malicious.'

'That's all right, then.'

'Mr Blake.' Mrs Durham banged the register down on her old-fashioned desk. 'It is *not* all right. When our lovely parents want their little ones to know that there is no tooth fairy or Santa Claus, they will tell them. They don't expect to deal with the fallout from a guerrilla myth buster in class.'

I saw my father grin. 'My Nicole is a realist.'

'She's giving the reception class nightmares. It's got to stop.'

So he took me home and we talked. I had the feeling that he was on my side, though adult solidarity prevented him from saying so.

'You see, sausage, people can't bear much reality. It upsets them.'

'Harrumph.'

'If you *have* to tell people why you don't believe in fairies, make sure they're over eighteen, right?'

I promised. He knew that I would keep my promise. That was one valuable life lesson my mother taught me. If you walk out on a promise, you really mess people up. I didn't want to do that.

My father ruffled my hair. 'And you might want to keep an open mind on handsome princes.'

I was puzzled. 'Why?'

'For later,' he said vaguely.

I checked that out with my godmother when she came on a rescue mission. The bailiffs had taken our furniture and we were sitting on wooden wine boxes.

'Handsome princes?' she pondered. 'Fabulous beasts, like unicorns and talking bears. You can't rely on them.'

And then she fixed my father with a fishy eye. 'Harry, this has got to stop. I can let you have a cottage and you can do jobs on the estate until you sort yourself out.'

'If you say so, Barbara,' said my father, resigned.

My godmother is a fixer. My father says she was a fully paid up supportive wife and mother until her husband died. Then there was a puff of green smoke and she turned into a six-meetings-a-day businesswoman at the age of sixty. She started off managing a bunch of expatriate properties in southern France, more or less as a hobby, and ended up as a serious property developer. She's tiny, elegant and ruthless. I adored her. So did my father, though he used to tease her for being bossy. He said she was sound.

Barbara talked French to me all the time, so school became okay quite quickly. The French, I found, weren't as soppy as the English about rabbits in frock coats or princesses who didn't get up for a hundred years. Even so, I was not a popular babysitting assignment. From my point of view, babysitters were adult and therefore fair game. I usually started them on Cinderella's lost slipper.

'Shoes can't be made of glass. Where did they bend?' I would say, flexing my foot to illustrate. 'You couldn't walk. You'd break the shoes and cut an artery.'

They all argued. It's odd how people will do that, on principle. Their parents told them when they were kids that Cinderella left a glass slipper behind. It's a pretty idea with a lot of tradition, so they don't question it. And they get shirty with people who do.

Suzi Leclerq was still arguing the point when my father came home at midnight. The next week, Danielle Masson left in tears and didn't come back.

Only one person stood up to it: Charles Ferdinand de Cazalet from the chateau. But then, he was older than the others, nearly seventeen, and going to be a *vicomte* one day. Besides, I didn't think he believed in fairy stories any more than I did. When I expounded my theory about glass footwear being inimical to movement, he stopped reading and considered the issue seriously.

'You could walk if you picked your foot up without bending it.'

We clumped about the big downstairs room for a while, trying out his theory. I had to concede that it was possible. Just.

'But you couldn't dance,' I said triumphantly. 'And the story *says* she danced with Prince Charming all night.'

He looked at me over the top of his glasses. 'Galileo could have taken your correspondence course,' he muttered. 'Okay. We try. We dance. That will prove whether it is possible.'

But even holding hands and raising our knees to wonderful right angles—Charles Ferdinand was the first person to introduce me to the concept of right angles, along with fulcrums and, ultimately, cyberspace—we couldn't dance without falling over.

'You win,' he said. 'No more fairy stories.'

After that, he read me *The Count of Monte Cristo*. I might have trouble with glass slippers but I could believe in revenge. After my mother announced she wasn't coming back, ever, my father was hazy with drink and grief five nights out of seven. He thought I was asleep and didn't know. Barbara used to watch him worriedly and was always dropping in to check up on us. Oh, yes, revenge was a winner.

One of the major tenets of fairy stories is that mothers are always sainted and usually dead. Mine wasn't either. She popped back into our lives from time to time, alternately truculent pseudo-feminist and poor-little-victim. She shredded my father in the process. Even as a child, I knew that wasn't fair.

If you think I'm unnatural, take away the fairy-tale glamour and my mother was a pain in the butt. That was the bit of reality that my father couldn't bear. It made me feel protective and sad. I wanted to think he could do *anything* and he couldn't. Still, that was a useful life lesson, too.

Anyway, there you have it: my father and me living on frozen pizza and ice cream in a draughty, borrowed cottage; me bicycling to school in the nearest town; my godmother doing her best to find my father jobs and keep him off the crème de menthe—he didn't like most alcohol and was never really a natural drunk. And then he met Kim.

Your fairy-tale stepmother is officially poisonous. Kim was not. Kim saved our lives.

They got married when I was twelve and we moved into a big terrace house in London. I had to give up the bicycle—Kim said it was too dangerous and my father agreed—but apart from that we all blossomed. Her girls loved having a real inventor as a dad to help them with science homework. He turned up at their various performances, too. Kim had a man to cook for, entertain with and generally fuss over. My father was quite simply in heaven. He got slim—Kim didn't hold with pizza—and sleek and he started selling his inventions for the first time in his life.

No, there was absolutely nothing wrong with Kim. Except for her political stand on pizza, of course, but I could live with that. And she was a fantastic stepmother, apart from one thing. She was a real girly girl. More important, so were her daughters, Saffron—blonde, most popular girl at the pony club—and Lucinda—long golden curls, lead actress in every school play going. They laughed a lot—good—hugged a lot, like the suffocating Mrs Durham—not so good—had endless conversations about men and how to please them—bad, bad, bad.

I used to leave them on their own as much as I could. When my father asked why, I told him.

'Oh, dear,' he said. Then, 'Look, Nicole, women…well, women see life differently from people like us.' He thought about it. 'I mean…um…oh, *hell!* Just give them a chance, okay?'

I did my best. My father took us back to France for a holiday, which helped, and my godmother gave me Jane Austen, which was even better. Jane gave me an insight into those girlish confidences and she made me laugh. Apart from husband hunting, I liked the way she saw the world.

Kim and her girls flung themselves into village life. By the end of one week they knew more gossip than I had learned in my whole life. They came back with the news that the Vicomte had run out of money and was renting the chateau to a movie star. We all went to the *fête des vendanges,* the big piss-up at the end of the wine harvest. Kim insisted that we dressed up, which was a new experience. I was embarrassed but, actually, quite liked it. Saffron lent me a really pretty T-shirt and did my hair. Lucinda painted my nails—after she'd cleaned them. They danced. I didn't. My father put his arms round all of us and hugged hard.

I'm glad that he was so happy. Because only three months later he was dead.

Heart attack. Stress, the doctors said. It turned out that my mother had been suing him for the money he'd made from one of his inventions. He hadn't told us because he didn't want to worry Kim. But the work and the worry had eaten away at him. And there was no money; it had all been hived off into a special account to pay the lawyers.

Kim collapsed. That's the downside of being a girly girl. You only work as half of something.

Anyway, I was thirteen and pretty together. I rang my godmother, after the doctor had put Kim to bed with a sedative. 'You'd better have the cottage again,' said Barbara, practical as always. 'I'll find Kim a job and we'll work out how to keep you all at school.'

She got Kim into the chateau as some sort of housekeeper and me into the local *lycée.* Saffron and Lucinda were in the middle of exam courses, so they stayed in England during term time and came out for the holidays.

It worked quite well. Kim was lonely for the girls but she got used to it. She didn't get used to missing my father. Neither did I. It brought us together in an oddly comforting, unhuggy sort of way. Every so often she would say something like, 'I must teach you to cook. It's the way to a man's heart.' And then she would laugh, and sigh. 'No, you must do things your own way. That's what your father wanted.'

The girls tried to buff me up a bit when they came home but I stayed a tumbledown sort of person. I got things done, in my own time, in my own way. But I didn't win prizes and I liked to keep out of the spotlight.

Eventually I let them lend me dresses. I refused to highlight my English mouse to streaky blonde but did have it profession-ally cut. I didn't turn into a fairy princess but, on my sixteenth birthday, I did get asked to dance at *la fête des vendanges* junket by the lake. Result!

Saffron was in veterinary college by then, but she came back for a long weekend and caused a serious upset in the batting order of the local dating scene. Vet or not, she was blonde highlit, manicured and perfumed to baroque standards. By com-parison, Guy Leclerq's comment to me, 'When did you stop looking like a stonemason's mate?' was modest. But Kim took it as a personal tribute.

The de Cazelets were there, of course. They might have moved out of the chateau but they still owned most of the land. The old Vicomte, Gaspard, Charles Ferdinand's grandfather, was a notorious lecher of whom the village was perversely proud. He danced with the prettiest girls and took Saffron to see the sunset. But that year the real crowd puller was the movie star and his glamorous actress wife, half his age. She danced more with Charles Ferdinand than Gaspard—or anyone else, indeed—and was nowhere to be found at sunset time. Charles Ferdinand had ditched the glasses for contacts but otherwise looked the same to me, though not, apparently, to Saffron and Lucinda.

'Hunky,' said Saffron, moistening her lower lip. She was prowling in his direction when Vicomte Gaspard cornered her.

'Fit. Who would have thought it?' Lucinda sounded as worldly as you would expect from an aspiring actress. She headed towards him like a heat-seeking missile but the movie star's wife got her strike in first.

I came across him in the baker's on Sunday morning. Kim was reading the papers; Saffron and Lucinda were nursing hangovers, so I was buying the croissants. It was a nice walk and I liked the smell of the *boulangerie.*

'Hi,' I said to Charles Ferdinand.

For a moment he looked all the way down his considerable nose and I thought: he doesn't recognise me. Anyone else, I would have thought, suit yourself, and pushed off. But he had read me *The Count of Monte Cristo* instead of stupid kids' stuff, after all. I decided to be generous. He was wearing big sunglasses, so maybe he had a hangover, too. 'Nicole. Nicole Blake.'

'*Nicole?*' He whipped off the shades and stared at me incredulously. 'The fairy tale hater?'

'Yup. That's the one.'

He looked enormously relieved for some reason. 'Great to see you. Er…did you see anybody with a camera as you came down the hill?'

'No.'

'Great,' he said again. 'You're a star.' And gave me a surprisingly enthusiastic hug.

I was gratified but puzzled. It was the Saffron, the best gossip collector of the family, who explained later.

Charles Ferdinand, briefly home from the States, had flirted too much with Madame Not Quite Movie Star. Someone had told the papers and a couple of paparazzi were lurking, looking for a photo of him. Hence the shades, I suppose. I mean he wasn't rich and famous. Not then.

He became so later. He whizzed through Harvard Business School and was all over the computer press. I knew because I visited the specialist websites regularly. In spite of my interrupted education, I was following in my father's footsteps. Only I didn't invent machines. I did computer games. I started as a teenager. I was good, too.

In fact, I was all set to turn into an attic-dwelling geek when Kim threw me out. Literally.

'Okay, no college if you don't want to go. I think it's time you went travelling.'

I was horrified. Geeks don't like to be disturbed. 'What? Why?'

She gave me an old-fashioned look. 'It's about time you got out into the world and made a few mistakes. And you need to do it in decent privacy.'

I argued but she was adamant. The movie star's wife had left and the housekeeper retired, so Kim was moving into the chateau to run it and handing the keys of the cottage back to my godmother.

'You want to get rid of me!'

'It will be good for you. Barbara,' she added, 'agrees with me.'

So I went. Well, I had a laptop and I could work on the games in the evening. There aren't many places without Internet connection these days. I waitressed and couriered in Europe and Australia and the States. And yes, I made plenty of mistakes and learned from all of them. Particularly, as my father had foreseen, in the handsome prince department.

He was called Julian. He was tall and rail thin, with shoulder-length wavy red-gold hair, always slightly dishevelled, as if some departing love had not been able to resist rumpling it. He usually looked as if he were listening to angelic music. Actually, the curvature of his eyeball was such that he couldn't wear contacts and Julian was too vain for glasses, so the misty look was really because he was blind as a bat. But, by the time I found that out, I was fathoms deep in love.

We had a long summer of unmutual passion, with Julian being deep and non-committal and never staying the whole night, and me making the dates and trying to forecast his every whim. Not good.

There's a bit in *Persuasion* where poor over-the-hill Anne Elliot argues with friendly Captain Harville about the relative faithfulness of men and women. She ends by declaring: 'All the privilege I claim for my own sex (it is not a very enviable one; you need not covet it), is that of loving longest, when existence or when hope is gone.' The reader is supposed to sigh and sympathise and agree. I should have been more alert to that instead of beaming over the book's happy ending. It's insidious.

It took me over a year to work out that tenacity to a failing relationship isn't heroic; it's suicide. And another couple of years to recognise that the trouble with women is that when we fancy the pants off some guy we have to convince ourselves we like him as well, that he's a Good Thing. I can't tell you the number of times I've seen perfectly sensible women talk themselves into pretending that some jerk is a kind, decent, funny human being. Some of them can keep it up for a lifetime. At least I didn't go that far.

I took my broken heart off to a luxury Mexican resort on the Pacific coast, where I learned to serve drinks upside down—there was a rail and you needed to concentrate—and to do a mean samba on the bar. Oddly enough, I ran into Charles Ferdinand there.

The chief barista and I were discussing whether we needed to raise the tempo one evening when a voice behind me said, 'Of all the gin joints in all the world, I have to walk into hers.'

He'd given up the contacts and gone back to glasses. After Julian, I thought it was a good sign. He'd acquired a sort of beach front chic that would have made him look the last word in surfer dude if it hadn't been for the white gold Rolex Air King on his tanned wrist. Baristas can tell a Rolex at twenty paces. But then, I already knew Charles Ferdinand had hit rich since the last time we'd met.

'What are you doing in Mexico?'

'They call it team bonding.' He grimaced, very French. 'My HR person insists. They call me Chuck and get to beat me at beach volleyball.'

I said it was great to see him and swung the tray up above my head to worm my way through the increasing crowd. The noise was coming up to party level, so with a bit of luck I wouldn't have to shake my tail feather tonight. I really didn't fancy doing it in front of a guy who had read me Dumas.

Charles Ferdinand was still there when I got back to the bar.

'When do you punch out?'

'We party on till morning.'

'Then let me buy you breakfast.'

I didn't think he'd stay the course, but he did. So we walked through the morning-grey streets to the beach and ate scrambled eggs and refried beans at the shack where the dive guys hung out. We watched the sea shimmer and the sky turn lemony-pink as we caught up.

'The company runs itself now. Time to go back to France and grow up. I've got a chateau to save.' He sounded regretful. 'Have you been back?'

I shook my head.

'Will you?'

'Probably not. Kim and I…er…fell out.'

'Want to spend the weekend with me?'

I was over the handsome prince delusion. Besides, nobody you've known since you were eight is a sex object.

He came back to the club again, every night for a week. Every night he asked the same question and I said no. It was only on the last night that he asked why.

'Because life doesn't have to imitate art.'

That startled him. 'What?'

'Bloody fairy stories. Bloody Jane Austen. They're all the same. Yet more proof that the human race doesn't learn.'

He blinked. 'You feel strongly?'

'I don't want a fantasy. Or a night of passion with a Rolex, for that matter. Go home and get on with your chateau.'

He went, looking thoughtful.

I didn't regret it. Not for a moment.

And then I got an SOS from Barbara. Kim had lost her job and was acting seriously weird.

'I've put her in the cottage but she needs someone with her. She's very withdrawn.'

'Why?'

I could hear her shrug. 'My guess is she fell for the boss.'

'The movie star?'

'Exactly.'

More of the human race on its self-destructive course again. 'Bugger.'

'Too right,' agreed my godmother cordially. 'If ever there was a woman who believed in fabulous beasts, it's Kim. She needs to get out more. But she won't. Won't even go to the Ball, they tell me.'

I was suspicious. 'What Ball?'

'The Welcome Home Charles Ferdinand, Thank You for the Paint Job Ball.'

I didn't blame Kim. The chateau must be a desert now that the guy she was in love with had left. It wasn't just gratitude for all that nurturing that brought me home in the end. It was fellow feeling.

What I hadn't bargained for was that I would then get an invitation myself. It came on a stiff bit of card, engraved like a royal proclamation. Vicomte Gaspard requested the pleasure of my company, promising supper, dancing and fireworks. I sent a polite refusal. A ball meant dancing and the only dancing I knew how to do required a long bar and minimal clothing. Not the chateau's style at all.

But the only interest that Kim showed in life was talking about what I might wear for the Ball. So I cut her a deal: if she'd go, I'd go and she could choose the party dresses. My *Elfinventor* computer game had turned into a nice little earner so I could afford the best.

The project got her out of the house. Heck, it even got her to Paris for a couple of days, though she did get away from me at one point and only turned up several hours later, soaked to the skin. I deduced she'd done one of those weepy walks along the Seine. But at least she wasn't crying in corners any more.

As the Ball approached, Kim ordered us a limousine. I thought we could walk up to the chateau through the woods as we usually did, but Kim said it was muddy and she wasn't arriving at a ball in wellington boots. So we did the full Cinderella Entrance. I was wearing a greeny, gauzy thing but Kim was defiant in scarlet lace. I could have cheered.

For a man who had sacked her, Vicomte Gaspard was surprisingly confident. I'd have spat in his eye. But Kim went off with him to drink champagne, just as if he wasn't a foul exploiter. I made my way to the conservatory and kicked a couple of tree ferns. They're big. They can take it.

Of course, I was wearing flimsy shoes, all spiky heel and tiny straps. I sat on the edge of the stone fountain and took the right one off so I could massage my painful foot.

Then the lights went out.

I jumped, gave a small and deeply shameful scream and dropped my shoe in the water.

Out of the darkness, Charles Ferdinand said in deep amusement, 'You're supposed to run away first.'

'What?'

'Before you lose the shoe.'

'Don't,' I said dangerously, 'call me Cinderella.'

'I wouldn't dare. I remember your views on fairy stories. I've got the scars to remind me.'

He strolled forward. It was quite difficult to make out the conventional dark dinner jacket in the gloom. A flicker of pale something was presumably his shirt. Some residual light glinted off his glasses. I thought: I must put something like this in the next *Elfinventor*. It feels quite alarming.

I swallowed. It was loud. 'Why have you turned out the lights?'

'So everyone can see the fireworks,' he said, surprised. 'They'll all be in here in a minute.'

I felt a fool. 'Oh.'

'So we'd better be quick.'

It is quite easy for a man with a grasp of strategy and a good deal of local knowledge to sweep you up into his arms if you've only got one shoe on. Especially if it has a high and narrow heel and you can't see what you're doing. You kind of have to hang on to anything you can grab.

I did. I'm not proud of it.

Being kissed against the clock is not ideal. You have one eye over your shoulder all the time, metaphorically speaking. Besides…well, Charles Ferdinand! He wasn't a guy, he was a babysitter!

Then everyone else came in for the fireworks and I ran. Okay, I had to leave one of my shoes in the fountain but I hobbled along until I found a corner to tear off the other one. Then I headed for the kitchen, where I guessed I would find the chauffeurs wheedling food out of the caterers.

I was right. Only there was another surprise—our limousine wasn't hired. It belonged to the movie star. And the driver couldn't take me home because the boss was somewhere in the house trying to make his peace with Kim. Everybody beamed.

Human nature, I thought. Dumps you in it every time.

So I pinched some wellingtons and marched home through the wood. It was not pleasant. I was furious and the boots were three sizes too big. The stars were fogged over by Charles Ferdinand's fireworks and the dark air smelt of cordite. Typical!

Kim did not come home that night. Presumably she was with her guy. I wondered if that was why she had been back so late in Paris, too. I decided not to worry.

I slept badly and put it down to my bruised foot. Or, possibly, being alone in the cottage for the first time ever. Well, I'd better get used to that, until I decided what I was going to do next.

I was pretty sure that everyone at the chateau would be recovering from last night. So, if I got in early, I could leave the beastly wellingtons, retrieve my party shoes and be away before anyone got a whiff of me. By anyone, of course, I meant Charles Ferdinand. Mind you, I didn't think even he would go into full Handsome Prince mode in the sober light of morning.

So I put on my own walking boots and got there before eight. It was one of those bright winter mornings. The lawn was as powdery white as Marie Antoinette's wig. When I ran across the grass to the conservatory door, it crunched underfoot like frosted sugar.

Maybe that's what gave me away, that crunching. Because the moment I slipped in and pressed the door closed very softly, a curtain of floor-to-roof jasmine parted and Charles Ferdinand was among those present again.

He couldn't have been to bed. He'd lost the jacket and the bow tie and was hollow-eyed. The morning-after shadow along his jaw was sexy, though.

Charles Ferdinand? *Sexy?*

'Looking for this?'

He threw the shoe down on a mosaic table.

I backed up against the door. 'Um…yes.'

'I knew you'd come sneaking back when everyone was asleep.'

'I didn't want to disturb—'

'All that nonsense about being a rationalist. You're not rational, you're a coward.'

At first I thought he was teasing but then I could see he wasn't. Charles Ferdinand had had a strategy and it hadn't worked. Now he was not joking any more.

It was disconcerting. I went all hot and cold and didn't know how to deal with it. Quite exhilarating in a high velocity sort of way.

'You don't like fairy tales because you're a control freak. You call it logic but basically you just have to be in charge all the time. And fairy tales are full of chance and sex and weirdness that nobody planned.'

He pushed a hand through his hair and I saw that it was shaking. He was *shaking?* Yes. Only a little but it was unmistakable when you looked closely.

Adrenaline.

Well, okay, adrenaline plus chance and sex and weirdness.

I drew a long breath and that sounded shaky, too. I had a right to shake. I'd come through the icy morning and—

Okay, who am I kidding? I was as high as if I'd had an intravenous shot of last night's champagne. High and a bit scared and horribly vulnerable, yet hopeful, all at the same time.

He didn't see any of that, of course. 'Oh, God, Nicole, what will it take to get you?'

There was a pause. I floundered.

Then I said, in a voice I didn't recognise, 'You could try giving me my shoe back.'

'What?'

I'll say this for fairy tales. They give you an alibi for behaving like a total twerp. I felt myself going pink around the ears. But I swallowed hard and sat down on the wrought iron loveseat. And stuck out my foot, in its sensible rambler's boot. Anyone but a man seriously in love would have laughed like a drain.

Charles Ferdinand didn't laugh. He gave that little shake of his head that people do when they're trying to clear their vision. And then he pushed past the plants and went down on one knee—and we slipped right into the Happy Ever After.

Well, if I'm honest, he made a complete pig's ear of taking off my boot. Couldn't get the hang of the laces at all. He was better at taking off the other stuff, though.

So, contrary to expectation, I didn't spend the next night in the cottage alone. And I have to admit that, if Charles Ferdinand isn't *quite* a prince, he is certainly fabulous. Even my godmother agrees with me. Though I wouldn't give two hoots if she didn't. When it comes to choosing a handsome prince, godmothers don't get a vote.

As for what happens next, I haven't a clue. It will probably be irrational. I'm looking forward to it.

Katie Flynn

Katie Flynn was born in Norwich and attended Norwich High School, where she was extremely happy and extremely undistinguished. Published at the tender age of eight, in Enid Blyton's _Sunny Stories,_ she joined a Writers' Circle as an adult, publishing short stories, articles, etc, only turning to novels in 1971 because the postal strike cut off her main source of income!

At first she wrote under several different names—Saxton, Turner, Balmain—but her Katie Flynn books were a delight to write and proved far more popular than she had dreamed. She has now published nearly ninety novels, twenty-seven of which are Flynns. Her most recent titles are _A Mother's Hope_ and _In Time for Christmas._ Find out more at www.katieflynn.com

Click!

Mary sat at the table in the kitchen of her daughter's tall London house, the evening newspaper spread open at the TV listings. In fact, she scarcely saw the words in front of her because she was listening. Listening for two pairs of footsteps descending the stairs—her daughter, Laura, ready to go and play bridge, and her grandson, Matthew, in his football kit. Once more Mary would have to hear poor Laura apologising all over again because she and Matthew would be out all evening—and because there had been a coolness between them after what Mary thought of as 'the affair of the gingerbread'.

Mary's famous sticky gingerbread was a great favourite with eleven-year-old Matthew. The previous evening Laura had come into the kitchen just as Mary poured the rich, delicious mixture into a tin. 'Mother, it's awfully kind of you, slaving away at the cooker but *do* think of Matthew's figure.' Laura had clearly tried not to sound impatient. 'Gingerbread is delicious but they're always talking about obese children on the telly and I'm sure that's the last thing you'd want.'

Mary had been tempted to remind her daughter that, at Matthew's age, Laura had eaten large quantities of gingerbread and yet retained her slender figure. Instead, she had promised not to cook fattening food again, though Matthew's wistful expression had gone to her heart.

However, the small incident had made her think. Her father had always said, 'Two women into one kitchen won't go', and how true that was. She and Laura had got on well when each had her own home but Mary suspected that good relations would not last if she remained in her daughter's house indefinitely.

Then she heard the thunder of feet and Laura and Matthew burst breathlessly into the room. Laura gave Mary an impulsive hug. 'Mum, I hate to leave you alone again,' she said remorsefully. 'If only you knew people here! And don't tell me you have lots of friends in your village because it's at least a mile from your cottage and Dr Ellis said after your last bout of bronchitis that you simply mustn't live alone. If only Father hadn't left…'

Geoffrey, Laura's father, had been a self-satisfied, arrogant man, who had left Mary for a younger woman when Laura was only a few months old. Mary had been relieved she had not had Geoffrey's interference when bringing her daughter up but it did not do to say so. Geoffrey and his second wife had lived in the States for many years and Laura was intrigued by them, so Mary never said a word against her ex-husband.

Laura was still speaking. '…so when summer comes we'll all go down to your cottage and see if we can find someone to live in because I know you'd be far happier back in your own place.'

Mary considered her daughter's suggestion. Living with a stranger had no appeal for her. She had her garden, her WI meetings and her work in the village charity shop. Once at home, her life would be full. However, it was pointless to say so.

Laura glanced at the newspaper. 'Going to watch TV? There's an old film on later; you'll enjoy that.'

Mary, who had no intention of watching television, bent her thoughts to escaping back to her cottage, at the far end of a narrow tree-hung lane in Norfolk. If only she could find a friend to share it with her, then Laura and Dr Ellis would agree to her returning. But people had their own homes, their own lives.

Then she had an enormous piece of luck. She had been sitting in Matthew's room whilst he tried to teach her how to use his PC. He had called up a program called *Friends Revisited* and explained how it worked. 'You type your name in that box and the name of the friend you want to contact in the box below and, in the box below that, the dates you were last in touch...or you can just enter your own name and see if anyone responds.'

Mary had nodded, feeling excitement begin to bubble. 'That's very interesting,' she had said mildly. 'You called me a technophobe the other day, young man, but I'm beginning to think I might yet surprise you. Tell me how to reach this program again.'

Matthew had done so before Laura called from downstairs that supper was ready.

As Mary's daughter and grandson struggled into their coats and headed for the door, Laura called over her shoulder, 'Bye, Mum! When Matthew arrives home, you might make him his bedtime drink. He'll be back before I am.'

'I can make my own...' Matthew began indignantly, but his mother cut across him.

'Gran won't make a mess in the kitchen, like you would.' She turned to Mary. 'Enjoy the film, darling, and don't wait up!'

Mary went to the window; she must make sure she was not going to be interrupted before she made her next move. But it was all right; the road was empty. Mary's evening was her own.

Immediately she set off for the stairs. She bypassed her own room and climbed increasingly slowly up the next flight. Her chest squeaked and her knees creaked and she clutched the banister with a thin hand, but she made it to the upper landing and gazed anxiously into Matthew's small room. If the PC was switched off…

It was all right, however—he had left it switched on. Thank God, Mary thought devoutly, slipping into the room and closing the door gently. Smiling, she slid into the chair and touched the mouse and the screen immediately flashed into life. Mary leaned forward, telling herself that, since this computer had been her present to Matthew, she had every right to have a little play on it. Nevertheless, she did feel a pang of guilt as she made her selection. She touched a few keys and there it was, *Friends Revisited*. Breathlessly, she scrolled down the screen to the spot where it commanded her to fill in her own name and that of a person she wished to meet once more. Her fingers hovered over the keys and, even as she typed, her mind went back to the war, and Stonebridge Farm and the evacuees.

Her best friend had been Johnny Brown. She typed in his name, 1939–45, which was when they had last seen each other, and was astonished when the screen, which had had black letters on a white background, suddenly turned to a deep celestial blue with a sort of sparkle to it, and words began to form themselves into sentences.

Mary? Well, it's a blooming miracle! I've been trying to contact you for…oh, for ages. When you think we've not met for the best part of a lifetime, it really is a miracle. How are you? Where are you? And how did we come to lose touch all them years ago? I suppose it were my fault because I kept moving on and I lived in France for several years and in Spain for even longer. What about you?

The cursor was flashing, waiting for her to reply. She began to type, the words appearing on the screen so fast that it was all she could do to read them.

Of course it was your fault, Johnny! I wrote to every address you sent, but your letters just stopped coming. Then I got married and moved away from Norfolk, though I moved back five years ago. What about you?

I'm back in England and I can't believe I've found you again. Gee, Mary, we had some fun at Stonebridge Farm, didn't we? I often think back to the war because I reckon they were the best years of my life. Remember that first day? I'd been there a full eight hours when I saw this odd little figure coming through the wicket gate into the orchard…

Click!

She was seven again and completely out of her depth. She had been labelled, given a bag containing her night things, a change of clothing and her packed lunch. She had travelled by train and bus and pony cart to this place, Stonebridge Farm, where Mrs Ray had taken her up to a small attic bedroom which, she was told, she would share with another evacuee. 'I'm to have four of you, two girls and two boys, and I'm now cookin' your suppers, so you run off and play outside, dear, while I get on,' Mrs Ray said. 'Go into the orchard—Johnny's out there, he'll show you around.'

Mary went cautiously out of the back door and into the farmyard where hens pecked busily and a large cockerel looked at her out of his hard little eyes. Mary read malice in his glance and, as he ran towards her, headed for a small wicket gate, beyond which she saw grass and fruit trees. She slid through, closing it firmly behind her.

Ahead, beneath the nearest tree, lay a large rosy apple. Mary's mouth watered. Her packed lunch had been eaten long ago and now she was hungry. She bent and picked up the apple. Mrs Ray—call me Aunt Mabel—had said she was getting supper, but

Mary was hungry *now*. Might she eat the apple or would that be stealing?

She was pondering the point when she heard a rustling in the boughs above her head. Immediately she thought of danger; a leopard might be up there, planning to make her his next meal, or a large ape might object to her picking up the fallen apple. Hastily, she backed away and was about to throw the apple down when a voice addressed her. 'Who's you? Bet you can't see me!'

Mary saw an extremely dirty face looking down at her. Not a leopard then, nor an ape, but a boy. Even as she took in his appearance, he slid through the branches and dropped at her feet. He was skinny with nondescript brown hair cut cruelly short, a grey shirt too small for him and trousers both dirty and ragged. They stared at one another in silence for a moment. 'Who's you?' the boy demanded again.

'I'm Mary Scott. And you're Johnny…oh, I know, Johnny Brown. The lady at the farm said you were in the orchard, only I forgot.'

The boy held out a grimy hand. 'Hello, Mary,' he said. 'Were you goin' to eat that apple?'

'Are we allowed?' Mary said rather doubtfully. He looked the sort of boy who would take what he wanted, what her mother would call a rough sort, but at her words he bent and picked up an apple, saying with a touch of scorn, *'Course* we're allowed! The old gal told me I could do what I liked. What did she tell you?'

'She said you'd show me round,' Mary remembered, brightening. 'Have you been here long?'

'Yeah, ages,' Johnny said vaguely. 'I'll show you everythink.' He bit into his apple, then jerked his head towards the wicket gate. 'C'mon, there's all sorts to see.'

But as they approached the gate Mary hung back. 'That hen— only I think it's a cockerel, the one with the red thing on its head—came after me,' she said. 'It hates me and it's got ever such a sharp beak.'

Johnny grabbed her hand and towed her into the farmyard. 'Wait till you see the geese,' he remarked. 'You want to show 'em you're not afraid, then they'll leave you alone.' The cockerel rushed at them and Mary shrank back, but Johnny kicked out at the bird and it retreated. 'See? Show 'em you ain't afraid and they'll back off. Which d'you want to see first, hosses or pigs?'

Click!

Abruptly, Mary found herself back in Matthew's bedroom, staring at the screen. Yet Johnny's words had conjured up a picture so lively and real that she had been seven again and back at Stonebridge Farm.

Mary? I don't reckon they were the best years of your life, but they were pretty good, weren't they? D'you know what? While I were waiting for you to reply I were back in that orchard. Ain't memory a funny thing though? That happened gettin' on for sixty years ago, yet I remember it as clear as though it were yesterday.

The cursor blinked. Mary began to type.

It was the same for me; though I can't always remember things which happened a few days ago. My memories of Stonebridge Farm are still clear as clear.

She stopped typing to think and was not surprised when letters began to dance across the screen once more.

Remember that cockerel? And the geese which lived by the pond? Remember the day the gander cornered us…?

Click!

They had been having a picnic on the banks of the river and there it was, the river gurgling along, the willow trees that over-hung it and the four evacuees—herself, Johnny, Sarah and Bert. She and Johnny were nine now and had spent the morning helping in the hayfield. It was a glorious June day and Mr Ray had hurried the work through, starting very early so that the children were free to please themselves by four o'clock.

Aunt Mabel had packed them sandwiches and bottles of her homemade raspberry cordial. 'We'll eat later tonight, 'cos of working in the hayfield,' she said. 'Now, don't go gettin' into mischief. Bert and Sarah, you're the oldest, so make sure young Johnny behaves himself. And Mary, of course.'

Bert and Sarah had promised, but as soon as the picnic was finished the older two wandered off along the bank. Bert was a keen fisherman and about a quarter of a mile further up the river lay a deep pool in which lurked a large trout. Sarah was not in-terested in trout but she was interested in Bert and would go wherever he went.

Sitting on the bank with their feet overhanging the gurgling brown water, Mary and Johnny kept very quiet until the older couple were out of sight, then they looked at one another and grinned. In this particular spot the water ran fast and deep, gouging out pools that could not be seen from the surface. Johnny could swim but Mary could not, so this stretch of the river was forbidden to them. Further downstream the banks sloped gently away, the river widened and the children were allowed to paddle and play in the shallow water.

But Sarah and Bert were gone and Mary was sure that Johnny could teach her to swim in five minutes, as he had claimed, and after two years of living in one another's pockets, their inten-tions did not need to be put into words. Mary undressed and kicked off her sandals. Then she waited whilst Johnny stripped down to his underpants.

Presently, he turned to look down at the water swirling past the bank. 'It looks awright,' he said. 'Best let me go in first, though, in case…'

Too late. Mary pinched her nose with her fingers and jumped. She did not intend to let Johnny call her a scaredy-cat, but the water…it closed over her head. Desperately, her feet searched for the bottom, but failed to find it. She gulped water but had enough sense to know she must fight clear of the river before she tried to breathe again. Then—oh, bliss—a hand seized one of her plaits and jerked her painfully to the surface. She had time to fill her lungs just as Johnny let go of her plait and grasped her wrists. 'You're agin the bank,' he wheezed. 'Hold on and we'll have you on dry land afore you know it.'

Mary felt grass beneath her fingers and grabbed, seeing that the bank at this point was an overhang and was giving way. Johnny must have realised, too, for he began to propel her further along, clearly hoping to find a spot where they could both get out.

And indeed, after ten minutes more of struggling, they reached a firm section of bank from whence they should have been able to scramble ashore. It was a warm day, but Mary was beginning to feel both cold and tired, so it was with relief that she heard Johnny exclaim, 'Ah, we'll get ashore here awright, kiddo! I'll give you a punt up…'

Mary's top half was safely on the bank when she heard the hiss. Looking up, she saw a pair of huge webbed feet, then a broad feathered breast, a long neck, a dangerous-looking orange bill and a pair of hard little blue eyes. And behind the gander came his wives, hissing, all looking capable of death-dealing blows. Behind her, Johnny's voice said urgently, 'Remember what I told you, if they think you're afeared…but you ain't.

Here, you cling on and I'll come past you and give old Gabriel a punch on the snout.'

'What about our clothes?' Mary wailed. She was hovering between letting Johnny go past her and trying to outface the flock herself when Johnny pushed her fully onto dry land. He began to scramble past but suddenly Mary was filled with righteous fury. How dared the geese try to drown her? They were not supposed to be here. They lived in the broad meadow where they had a big pond to swim in. Gabriel bent his head on its long neck, menace in every movement, but righteous fury was a warming emotion and Mary faced up to him. 'Get back to your pond, you nasty bullying beast!' she shrieked and followed it by snatching up a little branch that lay at her feet and bringing it down on Gabriel's head with all her might. Gabriel hissed again, opening his bill and snapping it closed, but now there were two of them, standing shoulder to shoulder, Mary with her little branch and Johnny… Johnny didn't need a weapon—he often boasted that his feet were tough as boots from treading the London pavements—and now he lashed out, kicking at Gabriel so that the gander actually reeled whilst his wives gathered round him, no longer aggressive, seeming to have forgotten the children altogether.

'C'mon!' Johnny shouted, grabbing her hand. 'I hope I've killed the bugger but I reckon he's only stunned. Not a word to Aunt Mabel, mind, else we'll never get another chance for me to teach you to swim.'

Click!

Back in Matthew's room, Mary opened her eyes and stared at the screen. Once more, she had been transported into the past and knew that it must have been the same for Johnny when letters began to flicker across the screen.

Them geese! Gabriel were downright evil, though he never quite got over being beaten up and druv back to his pasture by a couple of kids. And I did teach you to swim. Ain't that so, kiddo?

She chuckled to herself.

Oh, yes you did. Remember the time you took me scrumping for custard apples? You were going to sell them...

Click!

It was early, very early, when Mary awoke to find Johnny shaking her shoulder. 'Gerrup, kiddo,' he hissed. 'Don't forget, we're goin' scrumpin' for apples today.' Mary dressed hastily and they sneaked out of the back door and across the yard to where a pearly mist hung over the meadows, filling the little lane like milk in a cup and blurring outlines so the familiar became strange, the mundane exciting. The sky was palest blue with a touch of rose to the east, which presently grew and grew until the rim of the sun, huge and golden, appeared, dazzling their eyes with its brightness. 'I've never been out so early before,' Mary breathed, her whole body tingling at the beauty that surrounded them. 'Everything looks so different. What is so magical about sunrise, Johnny?'

'Nothin'; it ain't magical, it's just that the shadows are the wrong way round,' Johnny said prosaically. 'Got your collectin' bag? I hopes as Mr Charley never gets up afore the sun. But he's old, even older 'n Mr and Mrs Ray.' He grabbed Mary's hand and began to pull her towards the lane. 'If we don't hurry the old feller'll be in the milkin' parlour and it's only a step from there to his orchard. Remember what Frankie said. Tuppence for every apple we takes him.'

'I know what he said and I know you said it wasn't stealing because Mr Charley doesn't harvest his apples but leaves them on the ground for his pigs,' Mary said uneasily. 'I'm sure if we offered to pay Mr Charley, say a penny a fruit…'

Johnny, however, gave a derisive snort. 'You'll never be rich,' he said dismissively. 'Custard apples is big. Tuppence isn't enough to charge really, but I reckon when Frankie's pals have had a taste of 'em, we can up the price.'

'Aunt Mabel's custard apples are the same as Mr Charley's,' Mary said, 'but you didn't suggest that we might take any of hers.'

'Of course not. That would be wrong,' Johnny said righteously. 'I ain't no thief. Besides, everyone knows scrumpin' ain't stealin'. You wouldn't call a blackbird a thief, would you?'

Mary giggled. Johnny's logic was about as straight as a corkscrew. She liked Mr Charley. He was a rosy-cheeked, bow-legged little man, who had once been a jockey. He was at least sixty, Aunt Mabel said, but he rode around his farm on a capricious slender-legged ex-racehorse called Dancing Daylight, and the children admired both his skill as a rider and his courage in farming without the help of a wife or some land girls.

Now, they stole into Mr Charley's orchard and began to pick, taking the best and ripest fruit and ignoring the windfalls in the long wet grass. In the strengthening sunlight they could see Mr Charley's farmhouse through the trees. It was small, more like a cottage really, but Mr Charley had taken on a couple of sturdy fourteen-year-old evacuees and the three of them somehow managed all the farm work. Mary could not stop herself, however, from glancing apprehensively towards the house. Boys, she thought, were unpredictable; for all she knew, Roy and Stuey might be early risers, might suddenly appear… Her blood ran cold. She opened her mouth to share her fears with Johnny, just as he turned to her. 'I've been thinkin',' he said gruffly. 'I reckon we'll leave these bags of fruit on old Charley's doorstep. Then we'll ask Aunt Mabel if we can take the windfalls from her custard apple trees 'cos there's kids at school what scarce ever gets to taste an apple; what d'you say?'

Mary felt warmth and gratitude flood through her. She might have known Johnny would have second thoughts; he so often did. She beamed at him, picking up the heavy bag of fruit, feeling it lighter because it was no longer stolen. 'You're right, Johnny,' she breathed, as they began to make their way towards the little farmhouse. 'Oh, I do love you!'

Click!

Once more the screen flickered, once more letters formed into words that chased across the screen.

Scrumping for custard apples—as if I could possibly forget! Good job you were with me because, as I recall it, it were your expression which made me think that perhaps what we were doing was a bit mean like. Then Aunt Mabel said we could take as many windfalls as we wanted. She were a kind woman. And if Mr Charley guessed we'd meant to steal his apples he never let on. But I say, kiddo, where are you now?

Mary explained:

Right now I'm staying with my daughter Laura, in London. I was pretty ill last winter so they said I shouldn't live alone but I'm not happy away from my cottage. Where did you say you were?

Where d'you think? I'm in the Smoke, of course, same as you. Well, that's a coincidence, if you like! We could meet up, see each other in the flesh. What part of London, Mary?

Mary was suddenly excited.

Bloomsbury, Enderby Gardens. Are you anywhere near us? Oh, Johnny, it would be wonderful to see you again! Do let's meet!

Johnny typed, his excitement, she was sure, as great as hers:

Near? Why, I could be on your doorstep in ten minutes. But what will your daughter say? Reunions are only fun for the people involved.

Mary assured him:

She's out, and so's my grandson, the one who owns this computer. Ten minutes! Gosh, I'll be on the doorstep, see if I'm not. It's number 20. Will you come in or shall I come out to you? I'll put the kettle on...

But the screen was no longer celestial blue and Mary guessed that Johnny had closed down. Too excited to care what her grandson would think when he returned to his room and found the program had mysteriously changed, Mary abandoned her perch and almost ran to the door. Down the stairs she fled, surprised to find that the flight up which she had crawled so painfully now presented no problem. It must be excitement, she decided, reaching the front door, snatching it open and staring down the road, feeling elated when a black taxi came round the corner and stopped at their gate. The vehicle was empty, save for the driver, who got out of his cab and walked around to open the passenger door.

She hurried down the path, thinking that it was no surprise that Johnny was a taxi driver; he had always liked cars. She had last seen him when he was fourteen or so but there was something about the man on the pavement which was instantly recognisable. It *was* Johnny, she knew it! He no longer looked fourteen, of course, but neither did he resemble a man in his late sixties, and when she hesitated on the pavement he gave her his old familiar grin before ushering her into his cab and walking round to slide behind the wheel. Only then did he turn to her and she saw a flash of mischief in his dark eyes. 'Hello, kiddo, it's grand to see you,' he said. 'Where would you like to go? To your Norfolk cottage? Or Stonebridge Farm, down in Devon? Or just up to the stars?'

And suddenly Mary knew why he looked neither young nor old. And why he had come for her. She even understood why she had skimmed so effortlessly down the flight of stairs up which she had toiled earlier. She touched her window and it disappeared beneath her fingers, letting in a breeze as sweet and gentle as any she had ever known. 'Oh, Johnny, you choose; I do love you,' she said, as she had said once before, and felt the wind float her hair away from her neck, felt her body young and supple once more.

'We always did click, didn't we?' Johnny said jauntily. He pulled back on the steering wheel as though it were a joystick and the black cab and its occupants rose slowly into the air. 'Then, if you're agreeable, we'll head for the stars!'

Margaret James

Margaret James has been a member of the RNA for twenty-two years. She has written thirteen published novels, many short stories and she also teaches creative writing for the London School of Journalism. Margaret's first novel was *A Touch of Earth,* a family saga set in Herefordshire, where she was born and grew up, and her most recent is *The Penny Bangle,* set in Dorset and published by Robert Hale. But her personal favourite among her novels is *Elegy for a Queen,* published by Solidus, a small independent that has a varied and fascinating list. Margaret now lives in Devon, which she loves, and has a website at www.margaretjames.com

The Service of my Lady

She's been crying again. Even though she's got a load of make-up on, I can always tell.

'Where do you want it, Mrs Atherton?' I ask as she signs for it.

'Oh—just here, in the hall.'

'Okay.' I lug the boxes in, help her unpack the cereals and tins and bags of frozen chips. As she carts stuff into the kitchen, the sleeves of her top ride up. I can see all the bruises and I want to say something else. Like—he isn't worth it. Like—he's got no right. Like—why don't you leave him?

But, once I've put the stuff down on the table in her hall, a hall as big as my mum's kitchen, lounge and hall combined, all I say is, 'Have a nice evening, won't you?'

She only sort of smiles. It breaks my heart. When she's happy, she's got this really gorgeous smile and that's what made me love her in the first place. When she smiles, it lights her up. It makes me glad inside.

Now, as I turn to leave, this gleaming black Mercedes comes

thundering down the drive and screeches to a halt outside their mansion. The master's home and Mrs Atherton is shaking, looking like she's going to faint, and I feel sick myself. It's just that he's so bloody big, her husband. All neck and great broad shoulders, thick dark hair slicked down, blue eyes like bits of glass.

'Something you want?' he asks me, looking mean. I shake my head. I don't get smart with blokes like him; he'd wipe his shoes on me. I just pick up my boxes, get back in my van, drive off and, I can tell you now, I'm almost crying, too.

Gavin, the other driver on my route, he reckons Mrs Atherton's well fit. 'Yeah, I'd give her one,' he says, and grins his stupid grin. I want to thump him. Let him dare say anything about her face or body. Just let him bloody dare. I'll smack him, hard.

So, yeah, right, life goes on, the days go by, my boring life's still shit, and I'm still dreaming about lovely Mrs Atherton, her lovely, lovely mouth, her lovely smile. She has her stuff delivered once a fortnight so she'll be on my rota in a day or two, if bloody Gavin doesn't get her road.

She usually wants her shopping about five o'clock on Friday, so I make damned sure I'm on that shift. But Gavin knows I'm keen and he winds me up about it, gets the other lads to join in, too.

'I reckon it's your lucky night tonight,' he's always saying, grinning his disgusting gappy grin. Didn't his mother take him to the dentist when he was a kid? Didn't he ever learn to clean his teeth? 'Evening's drawing in—lonely housewife, hubby still at work—only shopping channels on the telly. So, how old, d'you reckon? Twenty-seven, twenty-eight? Bra size—what d'you think? Thirty-six, I'd say, a C or D cup, tell us when you manage to get it off? Look, lads, he's blushing!'

But, as it happens, I see her before Friday. On Wednesday morning, half past ten, coming out of Barclays as I'm going to get some fags and she's got her head down and she walks right into me.

'Sorry,' she mumbles.

'It's okay, don't worry.' God, she looks a mess—hair all any-how, no make-up, but she's still bloody lovely. 'Look, can I do anything to help?'

'I beg your pardon? Do I know you?'

Does she know me? I've only been going to her house as reg-ular as clockwork for the past three years. And does she know me? 'I bring your groceries,' I say.

'Oh, yes—of course.' She pulls her hankie out, dabs her face a bit, sniffs. There are tears in her eyes.

'Er…Mrs Atherton, you don't look very well. D'you want to go and have a coffee somewhere?' I can't believe I'm saying this. I'm terrified her husband'll turn up, rise up out of a manhole cover like a genie in a pantomime and thump me good and proper. 'You look like you could do with one.'

'I'm sort of in a hurry. I had to come to town to get some lens solution; I'd run out. But now—'

'But now?' I prompt.

'My car won't start. It's in the shoppers' car park and when I put the key in the ignition nothing happens. I thought I'd leave it there and get a taxi. But there isn't any money in my account. I don't know what to do.'

'Where were you going?'

'Oh, God.' She starts to cry, she's standing there and sobbing and people are gawping as they shuffle past, old age pensioners tutting and girls with buggies bashing into us.

It's against the rules. I'll get the sack. I need the job—I've got an overdraft, I owe my dad a grand and I've got the payments on my Honda. 'I'm on my break,' I say. 'My van's parked down the High Street. Wherever you're going, I'll take you there.'

'All right,' she says. 'Come on.'

I can't believe I'm doing this. Mrs Atherton's in my van, I'm on the motorway with tons of bloody groceries in the back, people are waiting for their stuff and here I am, halfway to bloody Ascot.

She knows the way; she's good at giving directions. 'It's just down here,' she says, and points to where there's gates and signs— they all say private road, piss off, you peasants, and she says, stop here, you can't go through the gates unless you have a permit.

'I'm going to stay with Mummy for a while,' she adds. 'Till Mark comes to his senses.'

'You want to do your face?' I ask. 'I mean, before you see your mother?'

'Yes, perhaps I should.' She rummages in her handbag, gets out pots of stuff. It's lovely, watching Mrs Atherton do her face, and soon she looks much better. 'Okay,' she says. 'Thank you for the lift. You've been my knight in shining armour.'

She starts to get out of the van but then she glances back and clocks my face, which even I can feel is glum, because I don't want her to go.

'I'm so sorry—what was I thinking?' She looks at me, her eyes are soft, her mouth is beautiful and, yeah, I'm close enough to kiss her—if I dare. 'You must have used an awful lot of petrol.' Opening her bag, she finds a tenner and sticks it on the dash- board. 'I'm afraid it's all I've got.'

'You—you don't have to pay me!' I'm mumbling, muttering, and I feel my ears glow red. 'I didn't do this for money. Mrs Atherton, if you ever need—'

'I know.' She smiles, but it's a sad and lonely smile. 'I've seen the way you look at me. You're a nice man. I'm grateful for your kindness. But—'

'It doesn't matter.' I force myself to smile. 'You take care now, eh?'

'I'd like to meet again,' she says. 'I mean it.' She's going to touch my sleeve and I think, please don't, Mrs Atherton, don't spoil it, please don't think I'd want—

But now she scrabbles in her handbag. 'Here's my business card,' she says. 'Ring me on my mobile, any time. We'll have a drink.'

Ginny Atherton MA—it's printed on the card in swirly writing. *Interior Design*.

'Ginny,' I say, and roll the sound around my mouth and it tastes nice, as good as she would taste.

'Actually, my real name's Guinevere but I never use it.' Mrs Atherton giggles, and it sounds like water falling over mossy rocks in summertime. 'My mother is a bit of a romantic. Do you have a name?'

'Yeah, it's Lance. Lance Taylor.' I manage a sort of grin. 'I dunno why my mother called me Lance—it's like calling someone gun or hammer.'

'Lance. My goodness, how appropriate.' She laughs, and it's almost like her usual laugh, light and bubbly like a bar of Aero. 'Do *you* have a business card?' she asks.

Me? A card? She's kidding, yeah? I rip a bit of paper off an invoice on my clipboard. I scribble down my name and mobile number. 'Here,' I say. 'If you get stuck, if you're in any trouble…'

'Thank you, Lance. You're sweet.' She smiles, and then she pats my arm, and it's like a million volts go through me, like angels start to sing. She gets out of the van, then she walks off down the street, out of my life.

I watch until she goes into the house. But now, before I drive away, I look at her business card again. I stroke her lovely name. Ginny. Ginny Atherton, short for—what did she say her name was, Guinevere?

I stroke her name again, and then I tear her card into a dozen little pieces and shove it in the ashtray with all the orange peel and chewing gum and other rubbish.

Why would I need her card? So I can torment myself, wondering if I should ring, wondering what she'd say, if she would tell me to get lost, that if I carried on harassing her she'd be reporting me to the police?

Why spoil everything?

If she ever needs me, she knows how to find me.

I've never felt so happy as I start the engine, as I drive away.

Eileen Ramsay

Eileen Ramsay shares a birthday with Jane Austen and with Beethoven but had heard of neither when she wrote her first stories. She was seven. Educated in Scotland and the United States, she taught in both countries—often about Austen or Beethoven. Her writing for children and adults has won several awards, including the Constable and Pitlochry trophies from the Scottish Association of Writers and the RNA's Elizabeth Goudge Award. In 2004 she was shortlisted for the Romantic Novel of the Year award.

She is currently writing her—she thinks—twentieth novel. For more information about Eileen and her writing, visit www.eileenramsay.co.uk

The Adventures of Kitty Langlands

The Honourable Katherine Langlands started up from the depth of the armchair in which she had been curled. It could not be true. It was intolerable, indefensible—and probably illegal. This new book, fetched only an hour ago from the bookshop on Milsom Street, announced to the world that it had been penned by none other than Miss Kitty Langlands, who was, according to the publisher, A Lady.

'Indeed you are,' Miss Langlands addressed her delightful image in the glass above the fireplace, 'but you did not write this book.'

Before she could say more, the door opened and her companion and erstwhile guardian, Aunt Barnett, entered. 'I've sent for tea, Kitty, and, nasty day that it is, I thought we might sit by the fire together, you with your new book and me with mine. Ridiculous to need a fire in August, don't you agree?' She looked at her great-niece, who was still staring into the mirror. 'Excessive examination of one's image is not at all becoming, Katherine.'

Kitty flopped down in her chair, her pale lilac overdress lifting delightfully to reveal petticoats that fluttered like disturbed butterflies. 'I didn't even see my face, Aunt. It's this book that Moffatt fetched for me, *Lady Abigail's Dilemma,* by one Miss Kitty Langlands, Lady of this parish.'

'Never say so.' Miss Barnett held out a thin blue-veined hand—heavily adorned with rings of inferior quality but definite artistic merit—and Kitty passed her the offending book.

'Looks delightful,' pronounced Miss Barnett just as Moffatt brought in the tea tray. 'Who is Kitty Langlands?'

'Why, I am, Aunt.' She turned to the maid. 'Moffatt, did you not see my name upon this cover?'

'No, Miss.' Moffatt examined the cover as if she had never seen it before—which was indeed the case. 'I asked Mr Abernethy for the latest publication and he had it already wrapped for you; you would be sure to love it, was what he said.'

Kitty fumed silently while she waited for Moffatt to make her exit. Moffatt did everything in great style and always slowly.

'I'm sure he did,' she said as the door closed behind her maid. 'He must have seen the name and—oh, my dear Aunt Barnett, he can't have thought I penned it.'

Miss Barnett sipped her tea and reached for a Bath teacake, quite delightful and surprisingly inexpensive.

'I doubt it, my dear, else you would scarcely be purchasing a copy. Is it poorly written?'

Kitty frowned. The merits of the book had not occurred to her. 'I haven't read it.'

'Then do so, my dear, but after tea. Moffatt has warmed the teacakes.'

Of no use to expect Aunt Barnett to think clearly while her mind was fully focused on her stomach. Kitty gave little credence to her late papa's oft-repeated, 'Hard to believe she used to ride to hounds like a cavalryman.' She bit into a teacake. Indeed they were good. Resolutely she put it on her plate and picked up the novel. Kitty Langlands, not Katherine, but everyone who was anyone knew that her late papa had always addressed her by the diminutive.

She put her hand on that part of her anatomy which concealed her heart, now beating slightly faster than the norm. It had been written by one of her own select circle. How dreadful. No. No one she knew would do such a thing. She opened the book and began to read. It was in the first person and purported to be the adventures of one Miss Kitty Langlands, new come to Bath. Well, that was false. Why, they had lived here always.

There was almost total silence in the room for some time. Kitty read, absent-mindedly sipping tea and finishing her buttered teacake as she turned pages, while Aunt Barnett devoted herself conscientiously first to the afternoon tea and then to the improving book of sermons that was her chosen cross for the week. She intended to take Canon Hartley to task upon its contents when he lunched with them on Sunday.

Had she been less involved with either the quality of the china tea or the sermons she might have seen agitation make its way across her great-niece's countenance, followed by incomprehension and finally anger.

'This is an outrage.' Kitty stood up, stamped her little foot and raised her voice more than was becoming in a lady of gentle birth. Aunt Barnett was so startled that she spilled her tea and choked on her teacake. Kitty tried at one and the same time to summon Moffatt, wipe up the spill—before it quite ruined the carpet— and pat her guardian fairly forcefully between her shoulder blades.

'Good heavens, Kitty, I'm like to die from the battering before I choke on the crumbs,' wheezed Miss Barnett when Moffatt had succeeded in rescuing her. 'What is the matter with you today?'

'It's this book, Aunt. It's me, Kitty Langlands. My entire life is here laid out for everyone to read.'

'Never say so,' said Miss Barnett again, while again reaching for the book.

Kitty sank gracefully to her knees beside Miss Barnett's chair and took the book back. 'You may read it later, Aunt, for indeed it is quite amusing and Kitty, the heroine…in truth she quite charms, and one can understand immediately why the Marquis fell in love with her and carried her away from her wicked stepmother into a life of unparalleled grandeur.'

Miss Barnett looked at her niece and laid a hand gently on her forehead, expecting to find it burning up with some fever that would necessitate the summoning of Dr Mildew—excellent medical practitioner, and really, blame for his name could scarcely be laid at his door. Miss Langlands' brow, however, was perfectly cool. 'Kitty, my very dear, we do not live a life of unparalleled grandeur.' She looked round the room, comfortably and fashionably furnished, but noted that the antique printed velvet on the occasional chairs should really be replaced. She sighed. Kitty could afford it but to be without those chairs at this moment in time would be a veritable nuisance. 'Neither, Kitty, have you been carried away by a dashing Marquis from a wicked stepmother. You do not have a stepmother, wicked or otherwise.'

'Why that's you, dear Aunt,' stated Kitty in a tone that welcomed no rebuke. 'Naturally it cannot be quite truthful. You are a companion and not a wicked stepmother.' Noting the expression of dismay on Miss Barnett's lined face, she hugged her impulsively. 'Indeed you have spoiled me most dreadfully since the day dear Papa asked you to come to live with us. But look here—' she rifled through the pages '—here is Kitty Langlands at the subscription library and in a dress of pale green silk under a coat of brown velvet, and with frogging on the front.' She looked at her companion, as if daring her to say that this was not proof positive. 'And here—' again she flicked through the book '—Miss Kitty Langlands is dancing and enjoying other entertainments in Sydney Gardens in a gown of white muslin bedecked with pale pink rosebuds in silk. Do I not possess the very one?'

One frail hand on her heart, the other covering her mouth lest she utter something regrettable, Miss Barnett looked from her niece to the book. 'But dearest,' she ventured after a few moments of near panic, 'every young girl wears white muslin and most of them adorned in some way or another with rosebuds. They are—this year—*le dernier cri.*'

With a cry of triumph Miss Langlands turned to page one hundred and forty-three, quite three-quarters of the way through the book. 'And who, pray, rides a chestnut mare with one white foot and in a riding dress of dark blue with silver epaulettes and a hat with not one but two silver feathers?'

Miss Barnett stared. Could it be the truth? Miss Langlands was the heroine of the tale but, unless she not only walked in her sleep but wrote romances in a like state, some person unknown had appropriated her name, her position in society, her very life and, probably, was making a great deal of money by so doing.

Upon more sober reflection, Miss Langlands did indeed find many similarities in the book's heroine to several other young ladies in a like position. They walked, they rode, they danced, they drank tea, they shopped, they dined and, yes, it had to be said, they looked and hoped for a perfect husband. If he were not discovered in the first season, their mamas—had they any sense—lowered the sights of their guns a little.

No other young lady, however, had been singled out in this way. Bath, delightful in many ways, was more gossip-ridden than even the tiniest country village and in no time at all *everyone* would be reading this vile tale and she, Kitty Langlands, would be the subject of the gossip. She would be forced to hide behind the pillars of the Concert Room at this evening's concert. No, she would be unable to attend because—if she had read the offending book today, so, too, had half of Bath.

'And I do so enjoy Mr Mozart's music,' she said and, after explaining her remark, had perforce to reassure her companion. 'Indeed, Aunt, we shall take refuge in the truth. I did not pen this novel. Thousands of dead Langlands must be turning in their respective graves at the idea: a Langlands—a Romantic Novelist. The very thought revolts.'

Langlands, long gone to their just rewards, made no comment at all but several of Kitty's young friends did, most of them with wonder and appreciation.

'How brave of you to use your own name, Kitty. Tell me, am I Priscilla, for have I not a pale lemon muslin with a double scallop around the hem?'

None of the young ladies saw themselves as the spoiled though beautiful anti-heroine and, no matter what they professed, none believed that Kitty was not the author—one bluestocking was even heard to misquote Shakespeare, a few lines from Hamlet. Their mamas proclaimed that they were deeply shocked and one engendered extreme anger in the Honourable Kitty by avowing that she knew exactly what Kitty's late papa would have had to say upon the subject. 'He left you well provided for, Katherine, and so there is no need to stoop to this.'

Kitty fumed but she was not a milksop and decided to do something constructive. She would see Mr Abernethy.

Mr Abernethy, however, had no idea of the identity of the author and obviously cared less. 'Copies, my dear Miss Langlands, fairly fly from the shelves, and I have taken orders for—would you believe it—two dozen more.'

Kitty turned swiftly from the bookseller's imposing desk and dashed straight into the arms of an—she was not so upset that she did not notice—extremely handsome young man. 'I beg your pardon, sir.' She bobbed a half curtsey and made to leave but he had her arms to steady her.

'The fault was mine, Miss…?' he began, but Kitty disengaged herself and hurried from the shop. She had loved Milsom's but would never darken its doors again. Why, she had spent a fortune in there since she had left school—at least five guineas in the past few years—and what help had the manager been? None. She slowed down because she was remembering the man into whom she had cannoned. If Abernethy had been more helpful, she would have been calmer and could have introduced herself. So easy and perfectly acceptable to have said *Langlands* when the gentleman had hesitated. For he was definitely a gentleman—but who? She had not seen him about town, in the Baths or at the Assembly Rooms. Should she take the air on the morrow, she might see him, and she could smile hesitantly, apologetically.

But she did not see the stranger and, having other things to consider, pushed him to the back of her mind. Less than a week after the distribution of the book, because they could no longer bear the constant calls upon them—Fotheringham, their rather grand butler, swore that he had quite worn a pathway on the hall carpets—Kitty began to make plans to withdraw from Society. She could not remove, unfortunately, to her beloved home now inhabited by her papa's heir and his young family, but instead gave instructions to her man of business to look for a small house in Wiltshire where they might hope to live quietly until such time as the furore over the book—surely a matter of days—should die down.

But it did not die down. So pleased was Kitty Langlands by the success of her first adventures that she dared to pen another, in which she, now married to her dashing Marquis, saved England from that upstart Napoleon by methods and plot lines which survived better without too much examination. The Prince Regent was quite *bouleversé* and asked, indeed demanded, that the next adventure be dedicated to him. Nor was he averse to a small—albeit important—role in the adventures.

That was one step too far for Miss Kitty, now languishing in the depths of Wiltshire.

'Enough, Aunt Barnett. I will sue the writer and, if I cannot find her, I will sue the publisher.'

The first step was to pen a letter to 'Miss Kitty Langlands'— in quotes to show that the real Miss Kitty Langlands was well aware that there was an impostor using her name.

The publisher did not deign to reply. Miss Langlands was informed that that is often the way with publishers but she wrote again, more strongly this time, invoking the names of not only most of her quite illustrious ancestors but also all her living friends and relatives. The list was formidable, mere Honourables quickly giving way to several Lords, who backed off in the way of a real live Marquis, doddery and somewhat gout-ridden, but the publisher was not to know that.

Reading the books for the third time—one must be sure of one's facts—Kitty waited, sighing now and again for the oft-derided pleasures of Bath; at least one might dance in Bath. The wilds of Wiltshire had delivered one elderly vicar and too many anxious would-be novelists.

'Might we not form a circle?' one had had the audacity to say to Aunt Barnett, who quelled the upstart with a piercing look.

One day, when an early winter frost had turned the branches of the trees to silver and Kitty was beginning to face the fact that she might indeed be spending the Christmas season miles from all she knew and loved, a lone horseman was seen trotting up to the front door. Aunt Barnett saw him from Kitty's bedroom, Kitty saw him from the library, her favourite room, and several servants from any room where they were sure that they might gaze unobserved.

Aunt Barnett, in her salad days a not insignificant judge of horseflesh, looked at the horse and was impressed by what she saw. Kitty, being romantic and scarcely nineteen years old, noted the rider. He was tall and well made and he sat the horse as if they had been fashioned together to make one glorious whole. Who could he be? A neighbour? Surely not, for all they had met thus far were well into their dotage.

A grandson or great-nephew, perhaps, mused Miss Kitty as she waited. She was seated primly perusing a slightly out-of-date periodical when Fotheringham opened the door and announced, 'My Lord Longdale, Miss Kitty.'

Kitty looked up; Lord Longdale looked down; their eyes met. A spark of recognition flickered.

'My Lord,' whispered Kitty.

'Miss Langlands,' breathed His Lordship.

They might still be frozen thus had Aunt Barnett not coughed delicately and asked Fotheringham to send Moffatt in with a tea tray and perhaps a glass of the late Lord Langlands' excellent Spanish sherry.

Lord Longdale bowed and took the seat selected for him by his hostess.

'How good of you to call, my Lord,' began Miss Langlands, who was almost, but not quite sure that she had met Lord Longdale before. 'I do not recognise your title as one mentioned by our landlord.'

'Indeed, Miss Langlands, my home is in Norfolk.' He looked into lovely brown eyes and was almost, but not quite sure that he had glimpsed those eyes before. Memory stirred.

'Norfolk?' Both ladies were astounded. 'You have not rid from Norfolk today?'

His Lordship laughed. Miss Kitty noted that it was a particularly pleasant laugh. 'Indeed, no. I'm putting up for a day or two at a delightful hostelry in Marlborough.' He stopped talking and looked down at his rather rain-spattered riding boots. 'I apologise for coming in all my dirt, Miss Langlands, ladies, but...' he reached into a pocket of his riding coat and produced a letter '...I received this.'

Kitty, who recognised her own hand, sprang up from her chair. 'How came you by…' she began and then a flush rose from the bosom of her gown, covered her very pretty face and hid itself in her hairline. She looked down, an action which rather annoyed her guest since he was trying desperately to see her eyes. 'I see it all. You are acquainted with…her,' she finished dramatically.

'No, indeed, ma'am,' said his Lordship, now towering over her. 'You see, I am her.' He remembered that he was both an author and the product of a classical education. 'That is, I am she.'

'Never say so,' said Miss Barnett, who had been unusually quiet—but quite fascinated—throughout.

Kitty, who was overwhelmed both by his size and his statement, looked down and, catching sight of the fringe of her very fine Paisley shawl, twisted it furiously between her fingers in an attempt to recover her composure. Remembering that she was a Langlands, she took a deep breath and turned again to face him. 'You jest, sir. You are Kitty Langlands?'

'Indeed I am. I thought you had it quite worked out. Longdale—Langlands. I should have checked more thoroughly but, in full flush of creativity I thought myself vastly clever. Indeed, I never meant to embarrass you.'

'Embarrass me?' Only extreme good breeding prevented the Honourable Kitty from yelling at him. She spoke quietly. 'You have not only embarrassed me, sir, but you have…ruined my life.'

His Lordship was quite aghast. 'Never say so. Most people who write to the publisher are great admirers of Miss Langlands. Several have even sent interesting plot-lines for further adventures.'

Miss Barnett sniffed. 'Many from Wiltshire, I'll be bound. Miss Langlands has been held up to ridicule and scorn, sir. No young lady of decent family writes silly romances, at least not under her own name. It's just not done, sir.'

'Of no use to say I had not the slightest intention of causing…' began the author but he was cut short.

'I beg you will excuse me,' said Miss Langlands, standing up before sweeping, head held high, bosom heaving and a spine a guardsman would have envied, from the room.

Miss Barnett followed her and was replaced by Fotheringham, who handed His Lordship his hat and gloves. There was nothing for His Lordship to do but take his leave.

'Longdale,' pronounced Aunt Barnett, who had dispensed with the sermons and was seeking greater understanding in a book cataloguing the history, titles and lands of even minor members of the aristocracy, 'Good bloodlines, old title… Charles Augustus Henry, he's the eleventh earl. Mother, Lady Letitia… Oh, I remember them now. Two delightful children and not a brain between them. They married too young… Had three children, according to this. I remember only two, this Charles and a sister, Charlotte Eugenia, but—' and she thumped the heavy tome '—there's another boy still at school and, school fees being what they are… The sister—good heavens, she should have come out a year since and have we seen her, heard of her? No. And His Lordship was never in Bath, else we would have met him there.'

'We did,' began Kitty. 'At least I did; I bumped into him in the bookshop.' She stopped, remembering clearly strong hands holding her, blue eyes smiling down into hers. Her heart lurched uncomfortably. 'I thought him handsome, and all the time he was merely engaged in research.'

Miss Barnett was still considering the Longdales and tapped her forehead with her spectacles as an aid to deeper thought. 'She could be an antidote, but most unlikely in that family. You were right to dismiss him, Kitty. Not only has he quite disgraced himself by sinking to the depths in which he's wallowing but he's poor as a church mouse and must therefore be on the lookout for a rich wife, which is what his parents should have done.' Even to her that sentence sounded odd and she tried to explain. 'That is, he should have found himself a rich wife and she a rich husband.'

Kitty was attempting to picture the handsome young Earl wallowing but could not. 'He's scarcely wallowing, Aunt Barnett. Indeed I wish I had given him more time to explain himself. It has just occurred to me that he came to apologise, even to make restitution.' She sighed. Such a pity to have shown him the door so precipitously. Langlands, Longdale. The similarity between the names might well have afforded some amusing, yet harmless, discussion.

'Longdale Priory, Norfolk,' read Miss Barnett, but Miss Langlands pretended not to hear.

Lord Longdale had ridden away from the house in a mood to continue straight to Norfolk but remembered in time that he had left not only his second best suit but also his carriage at the inn and turned off the London Road before he had gone too far out of his way. He had been busy reflecting that his sister Eugenia was a dashed pretty girl, even without all the little elegances that women of substance could afford, but The Honourable Kitty Langlands quite put her in the shade. What was it? Her stylish dress, her hair, her eyes—such lovely brown eyes. There had been the hint of a tear in them and Lord Longdale cursed himself for causing that tear.

'Dash it,' he told his horse, who obligingly pricked up his ears to show that he was listening. 'Have I not spent my life trying only to pay Father's debts and support the family? I had no thought of hurting anyone, especially someone as lovely as Miss Kitty. You fool, Charles. How came you not to know of the Langlands family? I'll never write another word.' Harry put down his ears, snorted and danced in the road to show that he was not at all in sympathy with this last.

'You're right, of course. Have I not promised that dashed publisher three volumes? Edmund's school fees come round with maddening regularity.' He slowed Harry to a walk and, deep in thought, returned to his lodging.

The next morning found him returned to Miss Langlands' rented home. He had judged his timing so that the ladies would be finished breaking their fast but not yet seeing the necessity for any luncheon. Therefore, he would not gain their opprobrium by forcing them into involuntary hospitality, should they even allow him across the threshold.

The Honourable Miss Langlands was, according to the very frosty Fotheringham, riding around the policies, properly accompanied.

Perfect, decided His Lordship. On horseback and watched by a sturdy groom, Miss Langlands need fear no intimacy. He took the path pointed out, somewhat reluctantly, by the butler and discovered Miss Langlands only a few minutes later.

He swept off his hat and bowed low, and his bow gave Kitty—who had spent the night tossing and turning—time to calm her racing heart.

'You, sir?'

'Am come humbly to beg your pardon, madam, and to attempt an explanation, and perhaps, with your help, to devise a plan of action.'

'Trilby,' began Miss Langlands, but the groom merely looked at her, stony-faced. Staff who had known one for ever were the very devil. She turned to Lord Longdale. 'We shall return to the house and talk there.'

In the library, with Miss Barnett sitting near the open window—for the weather had unexpectedly changed—and Moffatt noisily hovering outside, Miss Langlands faced the Earl. 'Well, sir, I do believe that I may have been unfair yesterday and would hear what you have to say.' She looked at him expectantly. 'Sit, sir.'

Longdale, who was quite accustomed to saying, 'Sit, sir,' to his favourite dog, smiled somewhat wryly and sat in the proffered chair. 'Miss Langlands, again I offer my humblest apologies.'

Kitty was looking, not at him, but at the fabric of her riding habit, noting the mud on the hem.

Lord Longdale tried to gather his thoughts which, despite his having tabulated them several times, seemed to be skittering around in his head like leaves caught in an autumn wind. Unused to silence, Kitty looked up and the one wayward thought he had captured went flying away again.

'You have such beautiful eyes,' he blurted out before he could stop himself.

'Sir, you are too bold.' It was not Miss Langlands but Miss Barnett who spoke.

The Earl blushed.

Charming in a young man, thought Miss Barnett.

When Lord Longdale met Kitty's eyes again they were smiling. 'You were saying, sir.'

'I am a very new novelist, Miss Langlands, and had no notion on the pitfalls that await the unwary. I should have checked but saw only the similarity... Deuce take it, I have said this already.' He looked around, perhaps for inspiration. 'This is not your home, Miss Langlands. The embarrassment caused by my little novels...'

'Oh, never call them little, sir. You do them and yourself an injustice. They are quite delightful. I could only wish that you had elected to use your own name.'

'I could not use my own name, madam. My family is re-spectable.'

'Exactly.' Miss Langlands frowned and her eyes flashed. 'You said it right, sir. This is not my home. My aunt and I have been forced from it because of the buzz of—' she could not think of a word strong enough and took refuge in '—gossip, unpleasant, malicious gossip engendered by the publication of your novels. I have no father, sir, no brother. I am alone.'

Miss Barnett coughed discreetly.

'Alone,' said Kitty firmly.

'I have racked my brains, Miss Langlands, but can think of no way to undo the harm and indeed I cannot even promise not to cause more. You see, I am contracted to write three more adventures and, ghastly subject, but needs must, I have received payment.'

'Can you not return it?'

'I would, dear Miss Langlands, indeed I would but… I have paid Edmund's school fees for the next two years. One never knows in publishing, you see, today's favourite is tomorrow's has-been and it would be unconscionable that he not receive the education befitting a boy of his class.'

Kitty nodded sympathetically. 'Quite. Edmund is your brother?'

'Yes. Nice chap. Prepared to rusticate just with the library, you know, but Eugenia insisted, too. At first I had thought to finance a debut since she intends to marry for love and there is no one in Norfolk. First Edmund, then Eugenia…she knows everything about fashion, you know, but only from the pages of magazines, and some of them sadly out of date, but—' he brightened '—she's terribly helpful, for my young ladies are correctly dressed, are they not?'

'Yes,' said Kitty, frowning, but with thought rather than anger. 'Your Kitty wears at least three gowns that I have worn myself. Very clever in Eugenia.' She spoke of the absent Eugenia somewhat absentmindedly, for the thought had occurred to wonder whether or not His Lordship wished to marry for love, as she did herself. 'There is no help for it, sir. You must be bold.'

'And admit to the world that a Longdale writes novels?'

'Indeed, there is no help for it, sir, for I cannot have it that the world thinks a Langlands guilty of writing them.'

He bowed his head. 'True.' Regardless of etiquette, he got to his feet and strode up and down the rather fine carpet. 'Deuce take it. What am I to do?'

'Was there no other way than…writing?'

'Last three earls…were not businessmen and there is nothing. I did think of becoming a highwayman, Miss Langlands, but I forced myself to think sensibly instead of romantically. Highway-men do usually get caught, y'know.'

'Surely, sir, marriage to an heiress would cure all your ills?'

'Have you seen any of the heiresses on the go this past few years? Antidotes every one. No, madam, I intend to marry for love.' He smiled down into her eyes. 'You're not an heiress, I suppose?'

Aunt Barnett's ears seemed to prick and there was an expression on her face that told Kitty clearly that her companion was not at all happy with the conversation. She ignored both look and ears. Did a reasonable competence make one an heiress? She would have to ask her man of business. She shook her head dolefully.

'Pity.'

Kitty blushed delightfully. Surely he had just complimented her. How dared he? He had no business to do so. 'I regret that I am quite poor, sir.'

'Katherine?' Miss Barnett was seriously overwrought. From whence had this delicately bred girl found this ability to lie like a trooper?

Kitty ignored her. 'Indeed, I shall have to accept the first offer that comes my way, should one ever do so.'

Lord Longdale fell to his knees before her—no mean feat in riding boots—and possessed himself of her hands. 'Marry me, Miss Langlands, for I fell deeply in love with you the moment I saw you in Milsom's. I looked for you everywhere but you had gone. I don't care that you have no money. I'll pen another story, oh, never fear, not about Kitty Langlands. I'm sure I can invent a perfectly acceptable substitute, especially with you by my side to inspire me.' He stopped, for the object of his adoration had said nothing, and, to Miss Barnett's horror, pressed a kiss upon Miss Langlands' lips.

Suffice to say that the adventures of Kitty Langlands lasted through the three contracted volumes. Then, alas, the readers of England tired of gentle tales of domesticity. Kitty Langlands and Kitty Langlands sat down and created a dashing highwayman, one Rupert Devereaux, who galloped across England stealing hearts—and purses—on his merry way. He died nobly on the penultimate page of the sixth volume of his adventures and was much missed by the ladies of Wiltshire—and several in Norfolk.

Lord and Lady Longdale, however, having paid all bills and restored depleted coffers, and being extremely busy with their estates and with Charles, Sophia and Sebastian, Marcus and later Elizabeth, lived happily ever after.

Diane Pearson

Diane Pearson has been both editor and author for most of her working life. Her first novel was published in 1967 while she was working as a full-time book editor at Transworld Publishers—a post she held for thirty-eight years. Two of her major novels, *Csardas* and *The Summer of the Barshinskeys,* became bestsellers, both in the UK and in America. She has had many short stories published, both science fiction and romantic, and her latest novel was *Voices of Summer,* set in the world of opera and operetta, of which she is an ardent fan.

At the 1993 British Book Awards she was voted Editor of the Year.

Diane has been the president of the RNA for many years and has given time and commitment above and beyond the call of duty. The Association thanks her.

The Censor

It was when he was transferred to the English/Hungarian section that he first came across the lovers. He said the word to himself with an inward curling of his lip—lovers were part of the culture of the typical bourgeois, capitalistic West, a media filled with romantic rubbish to divert people from the truth of real political needs.

However, he was interested in the lovers because, in the English section, you didn't get much correspondence between people who thought they were in love. Mostly the letters were from sons and daughters who had defected to the West. When he had been in the German section—he was fluent in both languages—there was the occasional sentimental letter but inevitably they petered out. He was very good at spotting when correspondence was becoming dangerous and had once prevented a high ranking party member from defecting to West Germany, for which he had received a commendation and a rise to Censor, status two.

But these lovers interested him, partly because—he gathered from delving into the back files—that it had been going on for some time, but more than that because the English woman was a classical singer and he had been to one of her concerts about three years before when she had come over on a British Council visit. Music was his one indulgence. In the evenings or at the weekends he often took work home; he enjoyed it, and he read a lot, mostly histories and political volumes and he listened to Radio Budapest. But he did permit himself to go to concerts—not the opera, he hated all vulgar emotional rubbish, but pure music, well performed. He had enjoyed the singer's concert—Mozart, Handel, Bach and some early English music that he hadn't heard before. She had been good and he would like to hear her again.

The Hungarian lover was a chemical engineer with a teaching post at the university. Not a grade one risk but, nevertheless, a distinguished scientist who, if he defected, would bring bad attention to the government. So he reported to the Director, pointing out that this had been going on for some time and that his predecessor hadn't seen fit to treat it as a special case.

The Director had looked at the file and said that they would monitor the professor's apartment and treat the case as priority two. And so every time a new letter arrived the Censor would push all his other work aside and read the letters from the lovers. He remembered her well—she was a striking woman and the voice was pure and accurate. He could recall her looks, tall and slender with very long fair hair. She had worn a plain black dress which, he had thought at the time, was correct. He didn't know what the man looked like, although he did research the file, but it was obvious that, although he was a professor of chemical engineering, he also knew a lot about music. Their letters were mostly in English—the professor was fluent—but she had learnt a little Hungarian, a difficult language that she'd mastered rather well. A lot of their correspondence was about what concerts she was preparing for, what recitals he had attended. The Censor got very interested and often found himself taking part in their 'discussions', sometimes angrily because he didn't agree and sometimes nodding at their descriptions of certain passages of music. The letters were not really sentimental at all. They told each other that they loved, but not too often, and their more intimate passages were intelligent and—it was not a word he liked to use very often—sincere. She had never been married, he had married young and divorced in his late twenties. She was in her late thirties and he was forty-three. He had been to London twice to attend conferences and that was obviously where they had met, but it was impossible to find out how—again the fault of the predecessor.

Then the correspondence changed. She was coming to Budapest again, part of another British Council tour, and there was much agitated liaising because he wanted her to stay in his apartment in Pest and the Cultural Attaché at the Embassy was trying to control her residency at an approved hotel. The Censor got very involved with this and found himself getting irritated with the Cultural Attaché. Did he think Hungarians were so barbaric that they didn't know how to treat a distinguished artiste? Eventually the lovers won out and it was settled—she would remain with him for the ten days of her visit. That was all right with top security. The professor's apartment was already monitored. She gave the time of her arrival, she was coming on from Vienna by train and as the time for her visit drew near the Censor became more and more restless.

She would be arriving at nine-thirty in the evening and he couldn't settle that night, switching the radio on and off, pushing his meagre meal away untasted. Eventually, he put his coat and hat on and walked all the way to the Western Railway Station, arriving at nine-twenty. There were crowds of people there so he couldn't begin to guess which one was the professor. Sometimes the emerging passengers exited from the side entrance but he guessed she would be in one of the first class carriages so he waited at the end of the platform. The train came in and heaving crowds surged to the barrier. He couldn't spot her anywhere and began to grow anxious—perhaps she had exited from the side entrance, after all. And then, when the crowds had thinned, he saw her, walking up the platform with a smallish suitcase. She didn't hurry. She stopped just inside the barrier and a slow radiant smile spread over her face. The Censor turned and there was the professor, a tall rangy man, thinning hair and deep set brown eyes. He knew it was him because he wasn't moving, either, and her smile was reflected in his face. They just stood and looked at each other for several moments, then he beckoned and she came forward.

The Censor had imagined they would rush into each other's arms, the kind of thing you saw in vulgar Western films. But they just stood smiling at each other and then, very slowly, he took her hand and raised it to his lips, his eyes still locked onto hers. Then he put her hand under his arm, picked up her suitcase and led her away. There was some confusion because two representatives from the British Embassy had come to greet her and the Censor found himself getting annoyed with them. Why didn't they just leave the professor to look after her and get her home? He followed them through the station and finally they got into a car together and drove away and the Censor went home, feeling curiously deflated and cross. He had never liked the British Embassy anyway, especially the Cultural Attaché who represented the British Council. He was sure some of their members in Budapest were subversives, spying for the West.

He went to two of her concerts; he couldn't manage all of them because some were during the day and one was in Miskolc, too far for him to go. There was also a performance in the Matthias Church and he went to that, although he didn't approve of religious performances. But it was the last concert that she sang in Dowland. The accompanist moved away from the piano and picked up what the programme said was a lute. And she began to sing. The Censor felt a strange pain swelling inside him—a pain that made him close his eyes and clench his fists together. *In Darkness Let Me Dwell*—sadly the voice rose and fell and died away and the Censor felt all the things he wanted to forget stirring in his heart. He recalled his mother, whom he had deliberately pushed out of his mind for many years and for many reasons. She was dead now but he could recall her quite clearly and he wished…oh, he wished so many things. As silence fell over the hall he opened his eyes and the pain receded a little. The audience began to applaud but he couldn't. He stared at her on the platform and wondered why her voice had hurt him this way. He could see the back of the professor sitting in the front row and she looked directly at him again, that radiant smile spread over her face.

He knew when she was leaving; it had been in the letters. This time she was flying out, directly back to London, and he got there in plenty of time to wait for them at the airport. Again they didn't embrace; the professor just held her hand again and kissed it and then she put her other hand up and touched his face. He watched her through the control gates and, as she went up the steps to the plane, she looked back once, smiled and raised her hand.

When the Censor got home he realised that, although she had come in with one suitcase, he had seen her put three into the luggage check-in. He felt a twinge of unease but then dismissed it. It was very possible that she had sent luggage ahead when she came from Vienna and it was more than likely she had been given gifts during her stay. The thought wouldn't quite go away and he wondered if he should report it to the Director. No. The Director had said it wasn't a priority case. He would just keep a watchful eye on the letters from now on.

The correspondence began again, musical, interesting, sincere, just as it had been before. Sometimes she wrote little bars of music to illustrate a point she was making and the Censor, who could read music, would hum the bars to himself. Once she sent a poem by an English poet called Elizabeth Barrett Browning, *How Do I Love Thee?* and she had it set to music, a melody of her own devising, which the Censor found he could not get out of his head. Then there was an exchange which was different—it was sad and stemmed from her.

> *Although the world for me is a happy place because you are in it, sometimes I am filled with despair because there is no hope that we can ever be together. We see each other once a year, twice if we are lucky, and when you leave my life is empty. We write, we speak on the telephone and these contacts warm my heart, but still I am sad.*

The Censor read that passage several times. It disturbed him, though he couldn't think why, and he waited impatiently for the professor's reply.

> *Beloved, sometimes I, too, am consumed by despair about our impossible future. But then I try to tell myself that what we have is more than many have. I know you, the most important person in my life, are there. I can reach out to you in some way or other and feel blessed. I have a vivid memory of you which I can recall whenever I wish. It is not you standing on the concert platform, so remote, so lovely, creating a world of beauty with your incredible voice, but you in the rain, in the Bukk mountains five years ago, your hair wet, your body drenched and your eyes filled with tears of anger because the hunter had shot the deer. I loved you so much then and I love you still. I know one day we will be together, I don't know how but we will and I hold fast to this as you must, too.*

Five years ago in the Bukk mountains! He went back to the file but there was nothing about how this had come about, just letters over four or five years, and he felt again an impotent fury that he was unable to chart their contact from the beginning.

Then there came hints in the letters that the Censor found disturbing. She was selling her apartment in London and buying a bigger one. She sent greetings from a colleague who was a chemical engineer and whom he had met when he was attending the London conferences. She was arranging her future engagements to be centred in London for the next two years. There was one indiscreet line from him in a letter. '*I cannot wait to be with you again*'. But how could he be with her again? She wasn't coming to Budapest and he wasn't listed as going abroad. The Censor's sixth sense—the one that had alerted him to the party member defecting to Western Germany—was aroused. He felt the professor should go to security alert and every night he determined to report to the Director the next morning, but then he decided he would just wait for the next letter.

The professor now began to write little bars of music of his own. They weren't good, not like hers, not melodic and after a while the Censor didn't bother to interpret them. Nothing happened, and then he learned, quite accidentally from a colleague who cleared category two subjects for foreign travel that the professor had been invited to Vienna, to give a lecture at a symposium. It wasn't London, of course, and there was no mention of it in his letters but the mood of the writing changed; there was an excitement, carefully concealed, but it was there. The Censor was alerted and he was able to find out quite easily the date of the symposium. He would marshal all his facts before passing them on to the Director. The one thing that was strange was that the professor made no mention to her in his letters that he was going to Vienna for two days. Why wasn't he telling her this so she could come to Vienna and be with him? He got the transcripts of their telephone calls but there was no mention of Vienna. He decided that now he must report to the Director.

His instincts were very good about incidents that could become dangerous and so he prepared his report, sent it upstairs and waited to be called. The Director seemed pleased with him.

'Of course he will be monitored by the security officer from the Hungarian Embassy in Vienna,' he said, looking at the Censor through his pebbled glasses. 'But, in view of your suspicions, I think we had better send two security officers to accompany him on the train.'

'I should like to accompany the guards, Director.'

'Why?'

'I know these people. I have studied them. I'm sure when we get to Vienna the woman will be there. I can be extra vigilant.'

The director whirled a pen in his fingers.

'I think I could be of assistance, Director. And I speak fluent German.'

The pen whirled a bit more. 'It is most unorthodox but your record is very good. Very well. We shall arrange for you to travel with the security officers and stay in the same hotel.'

'Thank you, Director.' He felt elated. He had never been to Vienna and now he was going on an official assignment. He would be senior to the security officers and if anything happened he would be credited with the success of the operation. He would most probably be promoted again to Censor category one and possibly become a more influential member of the party.

They all sat together on the train. The professor knew at once what was happening when he saw them. His face became strained and angry and he took papers from his briefcase and buried himself in them.

When they arrived in Vienna, she was waiting for him at the station. The Censor suddenly realised how it had happened—it flashed into his brain and he cursed himself for not picking it up sooner. It was the music—the bad music from him. It was a code they had arranged and he had told her when he was coming to

Vienna. That was why neither of them had mentioned it in their normal letters.

The professor went straight to her and tried to take her hand but the security guards bustled him away, through the station and into the car from the Hungarian Embassy. She was following behind and the Censor had never been so close to her before. She was taller than he was and there was a point, when he was waiting for the others to get into the car, when he could have touched her. He looked back out of the car window as they drove away and saw her standing there. She seemed very alone and sad.

They monitored him carefully at the hotel. That evening the professor had to attend a reception with the other members of the symposium but they never left his side. He telephoned her when he got back to his room and they listened carefully, but nothing alarming was said. Just, 'I wish I could see you' and 'I love you' and then the professor put the phone down, knowing, of course, that they were listening in.

The following morning they sat in the lecture hall beside him, listening to the delegates droning on about things they didn't understand. The professor's lecture was the last of the day. The Censor sat in the front row; he had been quick to place himself there but the guards had been too late and the front row was filled. In Hungary, of course, they could have turned out two delegates from their seats but here they were powerless so they were two rows behind, one at each end.

The professor began to talk and the Censor allowed his thoughts to drift away, wondering what she was doing and if she would be at the station when they left. He glanced out of the window and saw that snowflakes were whirling past the glass. He was sure she would be at that station.

The professor finished his lecture and began to answer questions. Then, as the chairman stood up, the professor suddenly turned and ran, not down the platform steps where people were waiting to congratulate him but to a small door at the side of the platform. The Censor was instantly on his feet, climbing the steps and running towards the side door. He looked back and saw that the delegates from the front two rows were surging to the platform and the security guards, in spite of pushing, couldn't get through. The Censor ran through the door and down a passage to where he could see swing doors leading outside into the snow. He was right behind the professor when he saw the car waiting outside— a large black car with the British diplomatic flag flying from the bonnet and the engine running. And she was standing by the open rear door, standing with snowflakes whirling around her fair hair piled high on her head. She wasn't smiling. She beckoned to the professor and he saw her mouth the word 'quickly'.

He was level with the professor. He could put his foot out and trip him, he could grab his jacket and pull him back. He knew the guards were not far behind. Instead, he placed himself squarely in front of the swing doors so the guards would be delayed. He watched the professor run, throw himself into the car and she slipped in beside him. As the swing doors slammed into his back and pushed him to the ground the car pulled away and he caught one last glimpse of them through the car window. She was in his arms, her head buried on his shoulder.

Afterwards, when he had been demoted to Censor status four and received an official reprimand—and he knew he was lucky that nothing else was going to happen to him—he thought of her often, standing by the car in the snow. He knew it was unlikely she would ever come to sing in Budapest again but they had made a recording of her last concert and he frequently played the record, especially *In Darkness Let Me Dwell,* as he looked at her photograph on the old programme.

AFTERWORD by Jill Mansell

Oh, no, and now we've come to the end! Wasn't that fantastic? I loved every story, I'm sure you did, too, and we'll all have our own particular favourites—that's what's so delicious about an anthology. There's something for everyone. And the great thing about these short stories is that if your attention has been caught by an author whose name might not be familiar, they're highly likely to have had novels published that you'll enjoy, too.

Echoing what Katie said in the Foreword, I'm so very happy I discovered and became a member of the Romantic Novelists' Association. A more welcoming, friendly and genuinely supportive organisation would be hard to find; their help and advice is priceless and the social events always a joy. I've made so many good friends as a result of belonging to the RNA, and being in regular contact with fellow writers makes all the difference when it comes to the day-to-day process of inventing characters, keeping them interesting and keeping control of them. Because other writers are the only ones who can truly understand!

So to each of you who has enjoyed this book, please carry on reading and revelling in romantic fiction in its many and varied forms, and let's all celebrate love and happy endings!

26k
23

47.

28k